THE
BOTANISTS
TRACKS

MICHAEL REIT

ISBN (eBook): 978-3-903476-09-7
ISBN (Paperback): 978-3-903476-10-3
ISBN (Hardcover): 978-3-903476-11-0

Title Production by The BookWhisperer

PART I

KRAKÓW, POLAND
APRIL 1943

CHAPTER ONE

S ix students sat scattered across mismatched tables and chairs. Felcia Hodak looked on as they furiously scribbled and allowed herself a wry smile. It had been over three years since she taught at Kraków's prestigious Jagiellonian University. In August 1939 her boss had called her into his office and announced she would be promoted to associate professor, taking over several classes. It had been Felcia's proudest moment, and she had taken to the preparations with zeal. How much her life had changed since.

"I don't think this is quite right."

She looked up to see the confused face of Julian, the youngest—and brightest—of the group. "What's that?" Felcia stood and crossed the short distance to his little table, leaning to follow where his finger was pointing at the textbook.

"I can't make this formula work, however hard I try."

"Let me see what you've got so far." She patiently listened to his reasoning and quickly identified where his train of thought veered off the rails. It took her five minutes to convince him the formula in the book was correct after all, and he reluctantly returned to the assignment.

Felcia returned to her small desk and enjoyed the quietness of the surroundings, the soft scribbling of pencils on paper the only sound. The clock on the wall ticked over to half past five. They had half an hour left, another ten minutes to finish the assignment. It gave her some time to consider her position. A botanist by trade, she'd discovered she enjoyed teaching a wider array of subjects in her clandestine classes. When Professor Sobczynski approached her to teach high school students a year ago, she hadn't expected she would enjoy it quite as much as she did. Now she couldn't imagine spending her afternoons anywhere else but in the small apartment in the nondescript building just outside Kraków's city center. She checked the textbook, but it was hardly necessary. She could solve these equations without even thinking about them, and she was curious to see how the students had fared.

"Okay, everybody, that's it." Her voice was soft, but she spoke with authority. "I know Julian had a creative interpretation of the formula, so I can't wait to see what the rest of you came up with." The other students chuckled while Julian looked up bashfully, and Felcia gave him a quick, reassuring smile. "Kasia, why don't you start?"

Before the tall girl could speak, the screech of tires and roar of engines sounded from the street two stories down. Felcia raised her hand to signal silence, but it was unnecessary. The entire class sat frozen, six pairs of eyes focused on the window. Felcia could feel her heart beating in her ears as the vehicles halted in front of their building, brakes grinding. Doors opened, boots landed on the pavement, and a booming voice shouted commands in a language Felcia had become accustomed to hearing everywhere for the past three and a half years. Fear gripped her throat, and she swallowed hard. *I'm in charge, I need to be strong.* Her hands were shaking and she gripped the sides of her desk. The young students in her care looked oddly calm, with the exception of Kasia, who was shaking in her seat.

"Everybody stay quiet," Felcia whispered just loudly enough to get the students' attention. "We don't know they're here for us." She had trouble believing her own words, and she hoped her voice didn't betray her. Two of the students nodded; the others turned their gazes to their desks while they listened to what was happening outside.

Car doors slammed, and for a moment all was quiet outside, but

Felcia could feel their presence, even from two stories up. A gruff new voice barked a short command that spurred the men back into action, their boots pounding on the pavement. Felcia held her breath. Seconds later the unmistakable cracking of wood confirmed a door was broken down. The building's front door. Felcia closed her eyes and tried not to despair. *Keep it together. These kids can't see you break down.* The sound of boots reverberated through the open staircase of the building.

She opened her eyes; there was nothing she could do but wait. There was only one way out of the building, and it was no longer an option. If they were coming for her, she was leaving with her head held high. She'd seen enough of the men in green uniforms to know they fed on the fear of those they hauled off. Listening closely, she estimated there must be at least a dozen of them, if not more. She would not fight or cower; she would deny them that pleasure.

Slowly rising from her chair, Felcia placed her hands flat on the desk. Her students looked up wide-eyed, and she made it a point to meet each and every one of their gazes. The first of the intruders had reached their floor, heavy footsteps audible at the far end of the hallway. She took a deep breath and glanced at the rickety wooden door that was their only protection. They would be here any moment now.

"We will not show fear. We will stand tall and proud. This is our country, not theirs." Felcia's voice trembled while she whispered the words loud enough for the students to hear. "Say nothing."

The stomping reached their door, and Felcia took two steps toward it, placing herself between her students and their assailants. She could feel the eyes of the six young people burning into her, and she threw her shoulders back. *No fear.*

Time appeared to stand still as Felcia braced for the inevitable.

When the crash came, she shut her eyes but caught the shriek welling up from her throat before it could escape her lips. Floorboards creaked as boots thundered inside, a host of voices screaming a confusing number of commands in German. High-pitched voices of children mixing with the baritones of grown men jerked Felcia back to the present. She opened her eyes to find their front door intact. She shook her head in confusion as the sounds of the raid flooded her senses.

She turned around to find her students gaping back at her. They looked horrified, surprised, and relieved as their heads were turned to the wall to their right. The adrenaline coursing through Felcia's veins subsided and she took a deep breath. *They're not here for us.*

The family of four kept to themselves. Felcia estimated the two girls were five and seven, both cute as buttons with their blond curls. The brutes in green hauled them down the stairs, their little wails for their mama echoing. Felcia could hear the woman's voice begging to follow her daughters, but her pleas fell on deaf ears. Felcia's heart froze with fear. Had she been teaching her underground class next to a hiding place all this time?

The woman didn't respond, repeating in a stupor her pleas to join her daughters. Felcia couldn't imagine what she was going through. The little girls had reached the street below, their cries filtering in through the open window.

"Let her go, and I will lead you to the Jews." A strong male voice spoke defiantly, and Felcia gasped in horror. "You can do what you want with me, but please spare my wife and children. They have nothing to do with this."

Felcia returned her attention to her students—Kasia had gone pale as a sheet, while Julian looked like he might throw up any moment. The other four sat motionless, captivated by the horror unfolding on the other side of the thin wall. *They have probably only heard of these things happening.*

"Fine, we'll let her join your daughters." Felcia recognized the voice of the man who had issued the order to storm the building earlier. "I'm a father myself, and I understand you need to think of your family. You're making the right decision."

It was silent for a moment, then soft footsteps sounded. A number of heavier footsteps followed, and Felcia heard the jingling of keys. Felcia let out a breath she didn't know she was holding as she pictured the man walking toward the hiding place. *It must destroy him to betray those people.* Even though Felcia didn't have a family, she understood his choice. A door creaked open, and Felcia closed her eyes.

A loud crash shook the floor, and animal-like roars resounded from the other apartment. The sound of something wooden splintering against the wall was unmistakable, and it was followed by a roar of pain. One of the Germans swore loudly as he called for his colleagues. It took a while for the men in green waiting in the hallway to make it to the room, and the struggle continued. *They're fighting back!* Her pulse was racing, but she also knew the efforts of those brave souls on the other side of the wall would be in vain once the other troopers arrived. More cries in Polish and German. Felcia could almost see the people from the hiding space hacking away with whatever crude weapons they possessed.

The fight ended as abruptly as it started. The backup from the hallway arrived and opened fire without warning. The guns in the confined space sounded like explosions, and Felcia's hearing went in an instant, a high-pitched ringing in her ears blocking out all other sound. Unable to follow what was happening in the apartment next door, she felt disoriented as she shook her head, trying to regain hearing. The ringing only intensified as she heard distant, muffled gunshots. Despite that, she could still feel the reverberation of the guns fired on the other side of the wall.

She held her hands over her ears and forced herself to focus. *I need to keep these kids safe.* Looking up, she saw the students in her little classroom were in various states of disarray. Julian and Kasia sat shaking, while the other four had covered their ears, their heads down on their tables, withdrawn into their own refuges. Felcia stood and waved at them, drawing Kasia's eyes, who tapped the girl sitting next to her. Within seconds, she had the attention of all six students. They looked up at her wide-eyed, but with clarity. Felcia put one finger to her lips, while she motioned with her other hand up and down slowly. The students nodded and remained at their tables while they waited for the violence to subside.

The sound of her surroundings rushed back to Felcia. The shooting had stopped, but the effects of the massacre could be heard through the wall. People were groaning, one man wailing incoherently and incessantly.

"Take the live ones outside and line them up in the middle of the street. Leave the bodies." It was the same voice she'd heard before, no doubt the commanding officer. Felcia looked to her students and was relieved none of them had moved. They sat motionless as they listened

7

to the events unfolding next door. More cries seeped through the wall as the German soldiers dragged people outside.

It took but a few minutes for the apartment to be cleared as the wailing faded down the stairway. Felcia stood and walked to the window, peeking through the blinds and into the wet street below. She caught the first soldiers exiting the building, unceremoniously dragging their prisoners down the building's small steps and into the street. Even from the third floor Felcia could see that the men forced to kneel in the middle of the dark street were in a sorry state. Blood was forming puddles around them, and one was unable to stay upright. One of the troopers grabbed him by the hair and jerked his head backward. It drew no response from the apathetic man as his shoulders slumped forward, his entire upper body held in place by the German's iron grip on his hair.

Felcia wanted to look away, but something forced her to keep watching. *These people deserve to have witnesses.* Four men were lined up when a woman stumbled out of the building, almost losing her balance as the soldiers pushed her down the steps. Her panicked cries filled the empty street as she collapsed to her knees in front of one of the soldiers, holding up her hands in a pleading gesture.

"Please don't kill me! My children need me. What will happen to my darlings?" Her voice was shrill and filled with emotion. Felcia felt her eyes burning, her heart aching for the woman. The soldiers paused and looked back. A large man in a different uniform appeared from the building. He stopped and looked down at the woman on the wet pavement. When he opened his mouth, Felcia recognized the voice of the commander.

"Get up, woman, and face your death with some dignity. Your children will be taken care of. You forfeited your life when you hid those filthy Jews in your house."

An ear-piercing shriek filled the night sky as the woman collapsed on the ground, tremors taking over her body.

In a move that surprised Felcia, the German commander unbuckled his sidearm and aimed it at the woman's head. She was still banging her hands on the pavement with the same relentless energy. With what appeared like a shake of the head the man pulled the trigger, silencing the woman as her lifeless body slumped onto the cold, wet street. He calmly replaced his gun and stepped over her body, toward the men lined up in the middle of the street.

A flick of the wrist was enough for four rifles to go off simultaneously, bringing silence to the street once again.

CHAPTER TWO

Sabina Krupka stepped into the kitchen to find her parents halfway through their breakfast. She gratefully accepted the boiled egg her mother handed her.

"Eat, eat. You've got a long day ahead, don't you?"

"Full day at school." She cracked the egg, pleased to find it soft-boiled—just how she liked it. "It's a nice break from spending my afternoons in that stuffy filing room." She scooped her egg onto a small piece of dark rye bread and took a bite.

Her father frowned from across the table. "You should be pleased with that job, Sabina. It's difficult to get a job these days, never mind a cushy one in an office."

"You've seen the girls working the fields and factories, right?" her mother chimed in.

Sabina sighed. They had this conversation at least once a week, and it was exhausting. "I know, I know. I'm thankful, but I love going to school. It makes me feel at least a little normal."

Her father's face softened, and he put his fork down. "I'm sorry, sometimes I forget you're only seventeen years old. You've grown up so quickly these past two years. Your mother and I are proud of you for juggling school and your job."

Sabina took another bite. Her parents meant well; it wasn't easy for them, either. It was hard to believe it had been three years since the Nazis evicted them from their home in Rajsko. And they had been among the fortunate ones, as her father worked a job as an overseer in a nearby mine. It meant they were assigned a new house a few kilometers up the road in the city of Oświęcim. Most of their neighbors were less fortunate, deemed less essential by the Nazis, and moved to the new General Government area a few hundred kilometers to the east. Sabina hadn't heard from her friends who had moved there, and she often worried about them. Especially knowing what horrors were unfolding only a few kilometers down the road.

Her father finished his plate and stood. "Speaking of work, I should be heading out. No doubt the Germans will be bringing plenty of new workers into the mines today, and we need to get all of them up to speed." He placed his plate in the sink and let out a heavy sigh. "For what it's worth, anyway."

"That bad, still?" Her mother stood and put a hand on his arm.

"It's only getting worse, I'm afraid. They upped the quotas last week. I've worked in this mine for twenty years, and what they're expecting from these people is impossible." He leaned on the table and met Sabina's eyes. "Even if they sent us strong, well-fed men used to working in the mines, we would struggle to reach half of the quota. But these people, well, you've seem them on their marches to work every morning, right? Every day, they drop like flies. Yesterday, we had four carts loaded with bodies before midday." His voice trembled, and Sabina felt sorry for her father. It wasn't the first time he shared the miserable conditions in the mines. At first, he'd tried reasoning with the SS officers, but they had quickly told him to shut up and just do as he was told. When he insisted the workers they sent from the camp were in no way capable of doing the backbreaking work required, they had told him it wasn't his problem, nor theirs. He'd also received a visit from one of the senior SS men, informing him they expected him to carry out his job without complaints, or they would find someone more agreeable. The threat had been clear, and her father now exclusively voiced his concerns within the confines of their home. He grabbed his coat and kissed her mother before heading for the door.

"Try to stay away from the SS, love. There's no reasoning with them," she said. "We just want to see you back home safely."

He smiled and nodded as he stepped outside, closing the door. Sabina quickly finished her plate, scooping up the remains of her egg with a piece of bread. She cleared her plate and looked at her mother.

"He'll be okay, Mama. Papa understands there's no sense in trying to change their minds by now." She hugged her mother, who put on a brave face.

"I know, dear, but you know your father. He has trouble ignoring injustice, even when there's nothing he can do about it. He always tries to find a way."

"He'll bite his tongue, Mama. Don't worry." Her mother shrugged, and Sabina stood and made for the front door. "Papa will be fine, he always is."

The walk to school was about twenty minutes. On a good day, she took a trail around the city, doubling her commute but surrounding her in greenery and views of the Soła River running below. Today, she was running late and took the short route cutting through town.

Elena Glowa was waiting as she crossed the central square, and Sabina smiled on seeing her. Both born and raised in Rajsko, the girls had grown up together and had been inseparable since their first meeting in kindergarten, now almost a dozen years ago. Elena's father worked as a signalman for the railway, and they had also been exempt from moving to the General Government.

"You're late!" Her friend stood with her arms crossed, tapping her right foot. "You know we can't be tardy for school, or they won't let us in before the break. And we've got that exam we need to prep for, remember? I need Mr. Pach to explain it to me one more time before I feel ready." Elena's words came at her rapid-fire, and Sabina couldn't help but smile as her friend spun on her heel and started crossing the square at a breakneck pace. Sabina hurried to catch up with her.

"Sorry, breakfast took a little longer than usual." She glanced up at the church's bell tower, which indicated it was half past eight. "We've still got plenty of time. Don't be so fussy!"

"Well, I don't like to take any chances, Sabcia. Keep moving." Elena always used Sabina's childhood nickname.

They reached the other side of the square and quickly traversed the narrow side streets. It wasn't until they exited onto a larger street that Elena slowed her pace, turning to her friend. "One other thing. Have you heard about what's happening back in Rajsko?" Sabina frowned and shook her head, and Elena tutted. "You do work at the municipality, don't you? Shouldn't you be the first to hear about new developments in the area?"

"I work in the archives. The only thing I'd be able to tell you is how many new people arrive in the camp every day, if I cared to pay attention." Sabina blew raspberries. "But besides that, they don't really tell me anything."

"Fair enough. Well, then let me tell you what I've heard. Apparently, there's a big construction area around our old school."

Sabina tilted her head. "When they moved us they just demolished all the houses to make room for their farm buildings and set up those huge fields. Are they expanding the farms?"

"My father passes by every day on his way to work, and he said there's hundreds of men erecting buildings around our old school. The area is littered with building materials. He even spotted large rolls of barbed wire."

"Barbed wire?" Sabina arched her eyebrow. Prisoners from the nearby Birkenau camp tilled the fields of Rajsko, commuting from their barracks in the main camp to the farming outpost. The presence of guards was enough to deter anyone from making a run for it. Besides, few of the prisoners were in any shape to attempt an escape even if they wanted to.

"Sounds like they have big plans. Maybe it won't be just a farming outpost anymore," Elena said casually. They walked in silence for a few minutes, but Sabina needed to know what was going on.

"Let's go there after class."

Elena stopped and turned, shock on her face. "You're kidding, right? We're not allowed anywhere near there."

"Aren't you curious? I want to see what they're building." Sabina felt a jolt of adrenaline at the thought of returning to the place she'd grown up. "I haven't been back to Rajsko for over a year. We'll keep a safe distance. If we see any Germans, we'll get out of there quickly."

"I really don't want to get into trouble. Maybe it's better if you see if anyone at work knows more about it?"

"Come on, we'll be very careful!" Sabina said, a little louder than she intended. Thankfully, there was no one else around. "I promise it'll be fine."

They turned off the main street and into another narrow alley. The girls stopped in front of an unassuming two-story house. Its once-white-turned-gray paint, like that on the surrounding buildings, was chipped. Sabina tugged on her friend's arm. "Come on, it'll be an adventure."

Elena looked at her and let out a deep sigh. "Fine. We'll go right after school. But we'll observe from the trail running above the road and stay out of sight."

"Yes, promised." Sabina held out her hand and Elena reluctantly shook it.

"Let's go inside, or we'll be late after all." Elena rapped her knuckles on the old wooden door, and they only had to wait for a few seconds before the door creaked open. A man wearing large glasses appeared and smiled when he recognized them.

"Girls, so glad you're here. Quick, come inside before anyone sees you."

"Good morning, Mr. Pach," the girls said in unison as they entered the old building. Their teacher led the way and Sabina was pleased to be at school. Even though education beyond primary school level was strictly forbidden, Sabina and Elena attended underground classes three times a week. Sabina was one of the top students, but as she sat down at her small desk that morning, she could hardly concentrate on the day's material. She was too distracted by what was happening at her old school in Rajsko.

The sun was already creeping toward the horizon by the time the girls made it to Rajsko. Their classes had gone on longer than expected, as it wasn't just Elena who had a lot of questions to prepare for their exam. It had frustrated Sabina, as they now had less time to investigate Rajsko. They couldn't be caught wandering between Oświęcim and Rajsko after dark. Elena had proposed going another day, but Sabina wouldn't hear of it; she wanted to see what was going on today.

They found an elevated spot between the bushes across the road from their old school building. Sabina squinted as she marveled at the hive of activity around the farming camp. Elena's father hadn't exaggerated.

"There have to be at least a hundred men working on those buildings behind the school alone," Sabina whispered, her eyes focused on a group of men pushing a large cart loaded with wooden beams. "They all look alike."

"The buildings or the men?"

Sabina chuckled, realizing her mistake. The men did all look alike, sporting the shaved heads and faded blue-and-white striped uniforms of the Auschwitz-Birkenau concentration camp. She pointed at the identical-looking buildings a bit farther away. "That set of buildings there, they look much like the barracks in Birkenau, don't they?" Elena nodded, and Sabina continued. "And there's the barbed-wire your father mentioned. That's not enough to block off the entire camp, though."

"Perhaps they're just using it for a part of the camp?" Elena suggested. "But why?"

Sabina scanned the scene in front of them. The construction site was surrounded by lush fields dotted with women wearing identical prisoner uniforms. It was April, and Sabina knew enough about crops to see they were tending to cabbages. On the far right side of the camp about fifty women were making their way back in the direction of Oświęcim. "What if they're preparing to house those women working the fields in the camp?"

Elena frowned. "Why would they do that? They can just have them make the walk from Birkenau every day. Seems like a lot of work."

Sabina was discouraged. "I suppose you're right. But why else would they expand the camp like this?"

There was movement on the road as a large truck approached. The girls ducked, keeping their heads low as it passed. The truck stopped in front of their old school building, and a burly SS officer jumped out. He scanned the area and stalked toward a group of prisoners, lifting heavy beams onto a cart. The man barked commands at the dozen men, who dropped a beam and followed him. The SS man opened the tarp and pointed inside the truck, then at the school building. Soon, the men were carrying large boxes—marked "Fragile"—into the building. The officer watched over the prisoners like a hawk, shouting at them to be careful.

"Whatever's in there must be valuable," Sabina mumbled, more to herself than Elena. When her friend didn't respond, she turned her head. Her heart dropped. Towering over them were two men wearing the distinctive uniforms of the SS. Sabina was used to dealing with the German soldiers in the municipal registry, and her eyes instinctively went to their jacket collars. They were marked with only the double lightning bolt *SS*'s, identifying them as *Schütze* or *Oberschütze*—the lowest-ranking members of the SS guard corps.

"Don't you realize this is a restricted area? What are you doing here?" The tallest, sporting a thick bundle of blond hair, addressed them in German. Sabina had enough grasp of the language to understand, and she took a deep breath to compose herself. From experience, she knew the best way to handle these lower-ranking soldiers was to make them feel important.

"I'm sorry. We were just on a hike around the city when we realized we were close to our old home. We grew up here." She pointed in the direction of Rajsko, and forced a smile. "Then we saw the activity around our old school and we just wanted to see what was going on."

The soldier looked at her suspiciously, tutting before he responded. "That's all well and good, but you can't be here. Especially now that there's so much going on. You wouldn't want to be mistaken for escaped prisoners."

Sabina felt a chill run down her spine. She had her papers on her, but she was hesitant to produce them without being asked. It would be better if they could get away without a fuss. She held up her hands and spoke in her most innocent, sweet tone.

"We understand. Apologies. We'll continue on our way and I promise we'll steer well clear in the future."

The blond soldier looked her up and down again and appeared to weigh his options. The other soldier then made the decision for him.

"Why don't we just let them go? They're just girls. What's the harm? They got lost." He turned to Sabina. "Right?" His face wasn't unfriendly, and she nodded.

"I suppose so. But we'll need to report this." The blond soldier looked uncertain.

"Nonsense, two girls lost on their stroll through the woods is hardly something we'd want to bother the commander with." The other soldier waved his hands at the construction across the road. "He's got enough on his plate. Let's just send them on their way."

The tall soldier's eyes bored into Sabina's, and she felt nervous as she held his stare, not wanting to seem weak or suspicious. *I have nothing to hide.* After what felt like minutes, he slowly nodded. "Fine. But if I see you around here again, it will be a different matter." He waved his arms impatiently in the direction of the road. "Just stay on the road as you go home. It will be dark soon, and you don't want to get lost in the woods."

Sabina nodded and motioned for Elena to follow her. Her friend didn't need to be told twice. "Thank you, sir. This won't happen again."

When they were out of earshot, Sabina glanced over her shoulder. The soldiers were still watching them. She picked up her pace, suddenly anxious as the adrenaline faded. She wanted to get as much space between the soldiers and them, before they changed their minds.

"That was close," Elena said when the road turned, obscuring them from the soldiers' view. "I told you we shouldn't have gone. I'm never going back."

"You're right, I'm sorry. We shouldn't get this close to the camp again."

Chapter Three

Felcia sat across from the man who'd been a mentor to her over the past five years. Professor Sobczynski leaned forward and reached for the bottle of vodka. He refilled his glass and held it out to Felcia, who shook her head.

"Thank you. I have a class to teach later."

He smiled. "Might help with the jitters, you know?"

"I'll be okay, professor. I'm glad you took some time out of your busy schedule for me."

Sobczynski took a sip and smacked his lips, set the glass down, and made a dismissive gesture with his hands. "My days aren't as full as I would like, if I'm totally honest. The most challenging part of my new job is to make sure all the classes have enough textbooks and writing material. Meeting with you is a delightful break from that grind." There was a fatherly affection in his eyes. "It feels a lifetime ago when we would sit in my office at Jagiellonian and you would suggest improvements to my lectures. Do you remember?"

Felcia felt her cheeks blush at the memory. "I was perhaps a little too brash after you promoted me. I wanted to impress you."

"Nonsense!" He slapped his hand on the table before downing the last of the vodka in his glass. "I didn't promote you to be docile. You were a welcome change from many of the others, who simply did as they were told. I was proud of you; you proved me right in promoting you." A sad look crossed his face. "It's a shame you never got the chance to teach those classes."

She remembered the day the Nazis came for the professor. It was November 6, 1939, only a few months after her promotion. Felcia and Professor Sobczynski made an early start, eager to finish planning the curriculum. All senior staff were summoned to a presentation on the future of education in Poland by Kraków's Gestapo chief Bruno Müller, now that they were under German rule. Sobczynski instructed Felcia to continue working on the curriculum. To this day, Felcia wondered if the professor sensed something wasn't quite right when he asked her to stay in his office. Less than half an hour after the professor crossed the street for the meeting in the Collegium Novum building, the campus was in turmoil. Trucks pulled up in front of the building, and when she looked out the window, the armed policemen jumping out told her everything she needed to know.

It took less than thirty minutes for the Gestapo—assisted by the police—to herd some of the country's brightest minds into the backs of the trucks, kicking those who didn't move quickly enough for the German brutes' liking. Professor Sobczynski was one of the last to be escorted from the building. As he made his way down the steps, he looked up and their eyes met. He gave her an almost imperceptible shake of the head while mouthing, "Hide." Felcia had hurried from campus, and she hadn't returned to the university after that, terrified she would be next.

"Tell me what happened the other night." Professor Sobczynski had refilled his glass and looked at her keenly. "Your message sounded urgent. Are you all right?"

Felcia recalled the raid in the apartment next to her class, her hands shaking as she described what happened to the woman in the street. "It was all so senseless. There was no need to kill that woman."

"They were hiding Jews in their home. If they hadn't fought back, she may have ended up in one of the camps, but as soon as those men attacked the Gestapo, they forfeited their lives." Sobczynski's voice sounded oddly detached, used to the rule of terror inflicted on their country. Felcia nodded: this wasn't her first encounter with Nazi violence, having seen the bodies of resistance fighters and other alleged criminals swinging on lampposts across town as she made her way to work in the morning. Yet, the other night was the first time she had witnessed an actual execution. She looked at Professor Sobczynski as he took another sip and reminded herself he had survived Sachsenhausen for three months. *What horrors he must've witnessed in a German concentration camp.* It had changed him—somehow he had hidden depths, enough to insulate himself from the terror. But there was also a fury burning underneath his calm, detached exterior. A mere three months after returning to Kraków, Professor Sobczynski reached out to Felcia to ask if she would be part of his underground teaching program. She didn't need to think about it, agreeing on the spot to become one of his first recruits.

"You're worried about getting caught, aren't you?" The professor crossed his legs, his bright green eyes piercing hers.

"When the trucks arrived in the street, I was certain they were there for me."

"How did that make you feel?"

"Terrified."

Sobczynski filled his glass and then another, sliding it across the table to Felcia. He raised his vodka in salute, and they clinked glasses. Felcia took a sip and enjoyed the warmth of the vodka sliding down her throat, instantly relaxing her.

"You can always quit, Felcia. I realize teaching these classes is nerve-racking on the best days. There's always the threat of getting caught, of someone talking to the wrong person. Hell, the bounties offered for ratting out fellow Poles have gone up recently, so it might even be your suspicious and greedy neighbor that reports you."

Felcia took another sip of her vodka to calm her nerves. *This isn't helping.*

He caught her look and raised his hand. "I know this isn't what you want to hear, but I think it's important to repeat. Higher education for Poles is prohibited. It's illegal. That's why we went underground. But never forget why we're doing this." His eyes were sparkling, his cheeks a little puffy from the alcohol. *This is the man I remember from Jagiel-*

lonian. "We're doing this because we can't sit by while the Nazis destroy Polish culture and science. This war won't last forever, and there will be a day when they are swept from our lands, and we're an independent state again. We *will* survive this and come out stronger. And when the time comes, we need those young minds, the future generations, ready to rebuild Poland. And that's why we do what we do, Felcia."

Listening to the professor, a fire ignited inside her. She'd spent the past two nights questioning her commitment, the thought of quitting so tempting, so easy. But now she realized it was never an option. She was part of something much bigger than herself. She cast her mind back to the night of the raid. The couple that hid those Jewish people had risked so much, and paid the ultimate price. In a sense, Felcia felt strangely connected to them; they were all part of the resistance. They had a common goal, albeit with different means. The promise of a free, independent Poland. She turned back to the professor, who studied her intently.

"I'm not going to quit." She stood, the vodka making her feel light-headed for an instant. She composed herself and looked Professor Sobczynski straight in the eye. "If you'd excuse me, I have a class to teach."

The afternoon class went by quickly, despite a few testy moments when cars passed by in the street below. They'd started by talking about what had happened the other day, and Felcia had been impressed by her students' willingness to share their feelings. They had been nervous about coming to class, but they felt showing up was essential to who they were, and who they would be in the future. Felcia had shared some of Professor Sobczynski's inspirational thoughts, and they soon returned to their textbooks.

Felcia was tidying up when Kasia approached her. The other students had already left, and the girl had evidently waited to get a word alone with her.

"What can I do for you?" Felcia gave her a warm smile. She had a lot of time for Kasia, who was always punctual and often one of the first to ask questions during class.

"I was thinking about what you said earlier, about Poland being a free country again." Kasia spoke in a soft but determined voice. "Do you really believe that will happen?"

"Yes. It's why I do what I do. And it's not just me. There are good people everywhere."

"Like those people who were murdered the other night?"

"They died for what they believed in. Others fight back, sabotage German operations, or teach." She felt pride well up in her heart.

Kasia looked uncertain as she shifted her weight from one foot to the other. "Now I feel like I'm not doing anything meaningful."

Felcia instinctively put her hand on the girl's arm. "You shouldn't think like that. You continuing your education is one of the best forms of resistance. We'll need bright women like you once the war is over."

A weak smile played on Kasia's lips as she blushed. "I don't think I'm that smart."

"Most smart people don't." Felcia smiled as she picked up her backpack. "Now go home. I'll be right behind you. I just need to check a few things in the back. I'll see you on Thursday."

"Good night, Felcia." Kasia disappeared into the hallway and Felcia leaned on her desk for a moment. It had been an intense class as they shared their emotions around the earlier raid, and now Kasia requiring some more assurances. Felcia felt she'd handled it well while she folded the chairs and hid them in one of the closets. Satisfied the living room no longer resembled a classroom, she turned and left the apartment.

In the hallway, the evidence of the raid was still visible. The remnants of the door hung loosely on its hinges. Felcia considered peeking inside but thought better of it. She made her way down and stepped into the street. It was a chilly night, and she pulled the collar of her coat a little higher. There were few people out, and she enjoyed the relative peacefulness of her walk. She treasured walking the streets of her hometown by herself. The early mornings and evenings were especially pleasant, when the sunlight hit the tops of the buildings, but the streets were shrouded in semidarkness. Felcia liked to look up and admire the contrast between the buildings' brightly-lit facades and shadow-filled storefronts at ground level.

The solitude also gave her an opportunity to process the day's events.

She opened the door to her building and stepped inside, crossing the small courtyard to the stairs leading to her second-floor apartment. The lights of the elderly couple's apartment next door were on. She slowed down as she passed their kitchen window, where she spotted Mrs. Adamski peeling potatoes. She waved and the woman returned a wide, toothy grin. Even though Felcia enjoyed living alone, she had to admit it was nice to have some interaction with the people around her. Felcia unlocked her door and stepped inside. It was cold and she kept her coat on as she shivered. *Better get the heat going first.* She crossed the small hallway and stepped into the living room, where she opened her wood-fired heater and tossed a few logs inside. She was about to light it when there was a knock at the door. Felcia wasn't expecting anyone.

She crossed to the front door and opened it. Two men wearing black coats stood on the other side. One of them frowned, then produced a smile that sent a shiver down Felcia's spine.

"Miss Hodak?" He spoke with such conviction that his words were phrased more as a statement than a question, and all she could do was nod. His smile widened as he took a step toward her. "Would you mind coming with us?" Again, it wasn't a question, but it was the heavily accented Polish that made Felcia's heart skip a beat.

"What's this about?" Felcia managed to stammer.

The man's face hardened as he spoke the next words. "We've been informed you are involved in illegal activities. Matters that threaten *the Reich.*" There was no accent when he pronounced the last two words. The other man also stepped forward and they each grabbed an arm, firmly pulling her into the hallway. Felcia wasn't sure the tears welling up in her eyes were from their iron grip or the realization of what was about to happen.

She didn't remember much of the ride or her arrival at the prison. The only thing she recalled was getting tossed into a cell with at least a dozen other women, and space for only half of them. All bunks were occupied; Felcia found a spot in the corner. In various states of shock, some of the women had withdrawn into themselves, oblivious to their surroundings. Others looked around with shifty eyes shooting between their cellmates and the occasional guard passing by in the hallway.

Felcia sat with her back to the wall and closed her eyes. The men who had picked her up hadn't spoken on the way over, nor had anyone in the prison told her anything. The uncertainty was gnawing at her, and she felt her temples throbbing, a headache imminent. She tried to block out the sobbing of the women around her, the constant screaming in the cells farther down the hallway, but it was impossible. Covering her ears with her hands, she pulled up her knees and placed her bone-tired head against them.

Felcia almost jumped out of her skin as she awoke with a start. A gruff voice was barking into her ear.

"Get up. Don't you think the rules apply to you? Get moving before I beat your sorry ass outside!" The large man wearing a guard's uniform prodded the tip of his baton between her shoulder blades, and Felcia shot to her feet. The cell was almost empty, the door open. A stream of women ahead were shuffling single file in the hallway. Her brain was still foggy after getting yanked from her sleep.

A sharp blow to her cheek had her seeing stars, and she struggled to stay on her feet.

"I told you to get moving!" The voice of the guard sounded slightly distorted as a burning sensation spread across the right side of her face. A violent shove in the small of her back forced her toward the open cell door. "Single file, and keep moving!" the guard yelled into her now painful ear. Without another thought, Felcia squeezed into a small space between two other prisoners. She was relieved to see the guard move in the other direction, entering the next cell.

Felcia moved with the crowd as guards harried them out of the hallway and into the central courtyard. The brightly lit red brick buildings—each with barred windows—towered above them, contrasting with the dark sky. She breathed in the cool night air, clearing the fog from her mind, but not the pain. Her cheekbone was throbbing, and when she rubbed it, she felt a bump forming.

She was given no time to consider her injury as men in green uniforms shoved them toward open trucks. The woman in front of Felcia was grabbed by her hair as she hesitated when one man barked a command in German. He was at least twice her size and tossed her into the back of a truck like a rag doll. She slammed face-first into one of the wooden benches, almost knocking her unconscious, and lay dazed on the floor. Some of the other women helped her up onto a bench. Blood was pouring from the woman's nose, but the man in green had already moved on.

Felcia made sure the same fate didn't befall her, hastily boarding the truck she was sent to. It filled quickly, and as soon as the tailgate was closed, the truck's engine fired up, and they hobbled out the gate, into the dark streets. Felcia shivered, as the wind had free rein in their truck. She sensed wherever they were headed would be worse than the prison.

CHAPTER FOUR

It was a little past midday when Sabina and Elena stepped out of the school building. Sabina took a deep breath and savored the taste of fresh spring air after spending most of the morning in the stuffy room upstairs.

"So, what do you make of what's going on at our old school?"

Elena shook her head. "You're still thinking about that? Can't really say I'm surprised. You can't leave well enough alone, can you?" Her tone was somewhat mocking, although Sabina knew Elena was just as curious. "Maybe you can ask your boss at work?"

"I wanted to ask him about it yesterday, but he was out. I haven't seen him around for a while. But you're right, he would probably know what's happening." She kicked a pebble down the street. "I'll see if I can corner him tomorrow."

"I'm sure you'll find out soon enough. You always find a way." Elena sounded distracted, her gaze on the clear blue sky above.

Sabina stopped and turned to her friend. "Something on your mind?"

Elena returned her attention to Sabina and shook her head.

"You sure?"

"Well, maybe just one thing." Elena sighed and motioned to a bench overlooking the city's square. Both girls sat down. "It's my father. He's been a bit off these last few days."

"Off how?"

"He's been very quiet, hardly talking when he's at home."

"That's hardly unlike your father. I've never heard him speak more than necessary."

"True." Elena gave a wry smile. "But it feels different. I think something's going on at work."

"Did you talk to him about it?"

"I couldn't. He would just say everything's fine."

"Your mother?"

"She would probably tell me to mind my own business, and say my father has enough to worry about without having me on his back." Elena's voice cracked a little, and Sabina felt sorry for her friend.

"Maybe your father is just going through a rough patch at work. He certainly doesn't have the easiest job with all those trains arriving at all hours."

"He's often called to work in the middle of the night. He's told me the Germans mess up the signals, blocking some of the main lines. Then they need him to fix it." She sighed and stood from the bench. "Maybe I'm imagining things or making too much out of this."

Sabina rose as well, putting an arm around her friend's shoulders. "I'm sure your father will be just fine in a few days. And if he isn't, you should talk to him. He might surprise you."

They crossed the square and hugged before heading in opposite directions. It could hardly be a coincidence that Elena's father was going through a difficult time as well. Were the Germans running into problems? She looked in the direction of the monstrous Birkenau camp, its sky darkened as always by the heavy plumes of smoke rising from the numerous chimneys. She shivered: when the Germans at the camp ran into problems, they usually solved them by stoking the fires even hotter, blackening the skies over Oświęcim and beyond for days.

Sabina found her mother in the kitchen as she entered through the back door.

"You're home early. I didn't expect you for a few hours," her mother said as she lifted the lid of a large pot and stirred the thick liquid with a wooden spoon.

"Mr. Pach let us go early. He said we could use the extra time to study for our exams." She peered over her mother's shoulder. "What are you cooking? Smells delicious."

"Cabbage soup. I snagged some from Piotr at the market. He says it's been a wonderful winter and these should be nice and tasty."

Sabina remembered the abundance of crops in the fields at Rajsko and hoped some of it would go to the prisoners, although she knew better. Whenever she encountered any of the men or women from the camp, they looked severely malnourished. She'd seen some ripping grass from the side of the road and stuffing it in their mouths. Putting the thought from her mind, and made her way toward the living room. As she entered, she froze in place at the sight before her: her father engaged in conversation with a tall, scruffy man standing by the front door. The air between them was tense and thick, as if words were being left unsaid. When they caught sight of her, their voices trailed off into an uncomfortable silence.

"Sorry, Papa, I didn't know you were home already. I'll just head upstairs to my room." She knew when to make herself scarce. Her father nodded, silently observing her as she made her way up the stairs.

Sabina closed the door and leaned against it. She strained her ears, but it was impossible to make sense out of the distorted tones filtering through her door. The only thing she could make out was the urgency in both her father's and the stranger's voices. The front door opened and closed a minute or two later, and she moved from her door and fell onto the bed with a sigh. She sat up. Something was off. Her father was hiding something. And she didn't like it one bit.

The awkwardness continued at dinner. Her mother's cabbage soup was as delicious as it smelled, and her father had complimented her twice in the first two minutes. Apart from that, he sat quietly, shoving spoonfuls into his mouth to avoid having to speak. Sabina glanced at him and couldn't fail to notice the shifty eyes, tense shoulders, and nervous tapping of his foot. Her mother appeared content to eat in silence, and after making it halfway through her bowl, Sabina could take it no longer.

"Papa, are you all right?"

He looked up and appeared surprised. "Of course, dear. Why?"

"Who was that man this afternoon?"

"Just someone from the mines. We needed to catch up on operations. He's new, assisting me with the new influx of workers from the camp." He grabbed a hunk of bread and took a large bite, returning his attention to his soup. Sabina cocked her head as he purposefully avoided meeting her eyes, then picked up her own spoon and continued eating. *Fine, you don't want to tell me what's really going on? I'll find out.*

Sabina entered the municipal registry a little before eight the next morning. As always, she was one of the first clerks to arrive, and she walked through the long hallway with open doors to empty offices. It would be teeming with clerks within an hour, all working on processing the new arrivals in their district. Ever since the Germans converted the military base in town into a prisoner camp and renamed it Auschwitz, they required more and more assistance from the city's registry. It meant the people working in the municipal building were some of the best informed in the area.

As a lowly clerk in the archives, Sabina wasn't privy to this information, but she'd made plenty of friends higher up. Among them her boss, Mr. Piotrowski. She made sure she stayed on his good side by always taking extra shifts when asked. In return, he was normally patient enough to answer her questions. It was Piotrowski who had warned her when the Gestapo planned to raid a number of the underground schools. Mr. Pach had suspended his classes for a month, and the Gestapo found little of value: a number of deserted houses with outdated textbooks and literature. It appeared to have placated them, for Mr. Piotrowski informed Sabina that he'd heard reports of a positive outcome sent to Berlin from the local Gestapo branch. After that, Mr. Pach had resumed his classes at different locations. As a result, Sabina had a strong ally in her teacher.

She entered the large archiving room in the basement and wasn't surprised to find Tosia standing next to a table with a large cardboard box filled to the brim with brown files. Next to her stood a cart with more boxes piled atop each other. A quick count showed at least twelve boxes this morning. Sabina suppressed a sigh and forced a smile as Tosia turned to greet her.

"Morning. They dumped these here before I had a chance to take off my coat." Her expression was neutral, but her voice betrayed her annoyance. "I'm sure they'll have more files for us later, but this will keep us busy for most of the morning. If we hurry, that is."

Sabina hung her coat on the small rack in the corner and walked toward her colleague and friend. Tosia and she had started in the archives a few weeks apart, and they had seen a few other clerks come and go in the two years they'd been here. She playfully squeezed Tosia's shoulder.

"We'll just take 'em one at a time, and we'll have these files stacked away before you know it." A hint of a smile appeared on Tosia's face, and Sabina continued. "It's dreadful weather outside anyway, so we might as well make the best of it in here." She turned toward the cart and grabbed one of the boxes. It was heavier than she expected and she gripped it tighter before placing it on a table next to Tosia. Scanning the first few files, she recognized some of the names. These were Dutch prisoners assigned to the mines. Felcia started sorting the files alphabetically without much effort, her mind conjuring images of the trains passing by. These people came from cities all over the Netherlands, but there was only one place the trains departed from for Auschwitz —Westerbork.

"You've got the Dutch arrivals, don't you?" Tosia's voice was surprisingly loud and startled Sabina.

"Yes, quite a lot of them assigned to the mines." She thought of what her father had said about the new arrivals and wondered how long these men would last.

"I think I've got the same shipment. Seems like this was a good batch. Lots of them assigned to work." Tosia's voice trailed off, both of them aware of the alternative to being assigned to the backbreaking work in the mines, factories, and other German industries surrounding the camp. They continued without speaking for a few minutes, the silence only interrupted by the soft rustling of paper. Tosia then pushed her stack of files away and turned to Sabina, lowering her voice.

"I told you some of my friends work in Birkenau, right?"

"Sure. Didn't you say they help out with some of the wiring in the buildings, electrical repairs and such?"

"Yeah, and as such they're in contact with the prisoners almost every day. They recently told me something interesting."

Sabina peeked up from sorting her files. "What's that?"

"The prisoners have been asking them to smuggle in extra food and medicine."

"That's nothing new, though, is it?" Sabina returned her focus to the job at hand, underwhelmed by Tosia's supposed news. According to her father, this had been going on for months.

Tosia appeared undeterred by Sabina's lukewarm response. "Perhaps not. But what is new is that more guards are in on it."

Sabina stopped sorting for a moment. "They are?" Her father hadn't mentioned this.

"For a cut of the payment, they're willing to look the other way. Some of the workers are cleaning up, apparently. They're going into the camp in the morning with a few extra potatoes and carrots, and coming back with nuggets of gold."

Sabina had an idea where the gold came from, and grabbed her stomach as it churned. "Are your friends in on this scheme?"

Tosia shook her head, not catching Sabina's tone. "Not yet, they think it might be too dangerous. But they're considering it."

"They will end up in the camp themselves if they are caught." Sabina grabbed a large stack. "I'm going to file these." She hurried off, glad to be away from Tosia for a few minutes. The idea of outsiders enriching themselves off the prisoners didn't sit well with her. If they were going to bring in extra supplies, they shouldn't profit from it. Had they actually seen the state these prisoners were in? She yanked open one of the large cabinets and furiously dropped a number of files in the first compartment. Her father's words came back to her—he stood up for the workers at his mine, and he hadn't asked for anything in return. She was certain he'd help them out with extra rations if given a chance.

She felt her heart swell, and then drop when she remembered the stranger in their home. Her mother had avoided discussing the subject, and Sabina had left for work none the wiser. She closed the filing cabinet and walked back to Tosia, who had just opened a second box, the table littered with fresh files. Sabina checked the clock and saw it was almost ten. Mr. Piotrowski would be in by now.

"I'll be right back. I just need to check something upstairs."

Tosia grunted in acknowledgment, and Sabina rushed from the room. It frustrated Sabina that she didn't know what was going on with her father, but she would find out what was happening in Rajsko. Mr. Piotrowski would surely be able to tell her. She greeted a few people in the hallway, then reached her boss's office. His door was closed, and she knocked.

No answer, and she knocked again.

"Looking for Mr. Piotrowski?" A voice behind her startled Sabina. It was her boss's assistant, Mrs. Formella. Sabina pulled the documents she was holding closer to her chest.

"Is he in? I haven't seen him all week."

Mrs. Formella wrinkled her nose. "He's out on official business. He'll be back on Monday. Can I help you with something?" She peered over her small, round spectacles with a look that suggested she would rather do anything than help Sabina.

Sabina masked her disappointment and shook her head. "There's no rush. It's not that important. I'll ask him when he's back." She turned to leave, but Mrs. Formella grabbed her elbow.

"Next time, check with me first. I wouldn't think you have time to come up here from the archives, do you? Last I heard, they're keeping you pretty busy down there."

Sabina shook off the woman's hand and considered a retort, but she bit her lip at the last moment. Instead, she gave a polite smile. "I'll keep that in mind, thank you." She turned, ran, and slammed the door of the archiving room. Tosia looked up wide-eyed, but quickly returned to her work when she saw Sabina's face. Sabina would have to wait until after the weekend to find out what was happening in Rajsko. She gritted her teeth and vowed she would at least find out why her father was acting so strange before the end of the week. Sabina grabbed a new box and dropped it onto the table.

CHAPTER FIVE

The journey had been uncomfortable. The cattle car hardly had enough space for forty unfortunate passengers, never mind the sixty that were crammed in alongside Felcia. Their train slowly rolled to a stop. Bright light filtering through the cracks in the walls showed this would differ from the earlier interruptions since leaving Kraków two days prior. After that departure, the train had simply come to a stop in a field or train depot without further explanation.

The single bucket of tepid water ran out within hours, and the empty bucket alongside it overflowed with excrement a few hours later. When the train moved, the wind blowing through the cracks in the walls provided some relief from the stench. Unfortunately, the train stood still most of the time, and their requests to open the doors were ignored. After the first night, people had stopped asking.

Felcia heard movement outside. Her mouth felt lined with cotton, her tongue sticking to her palate. Yet she resisted the urge to cry out. *Are those barking dogs?* Her exhausted mind could be playing tricks on her. Farther down the train, she heard the first doors slide open with a loud clang. *We're here.* Her eyes shot to the small pile of bodies in the back of the car. The relief of knowing she would soon be able to step from the death trap that was the boxcar was short-lived.

The door of her car slid open, and she was blinded by bright lights obliterating the darkness. She shielded her eyes with a hand as she tried to get her bearings.

"Raus! Raus! Schnell! Get out! Move, move! Onto the platform!" The people near the door could not respond to the commands before they were pulled out by scowling men in dark green uniforms. Two of the women lost their balance and landed face-first on the platform. The men in uniforms didn't seem to notice or care as they continued to bark commands while indiscriminately yanking more people from the boxcar. As a result, those disembarking trampled the women on the ground. More uniformed men appeared, this time with dogs. Alsatians bared their fangs while barking manically, some snapping at prisoners who tripped and didn't get up quickly enough. Felcia jumped from the boxcar, careful to make sure she stayed on her feet upon landing. She looked up and down the platform. Men, women, and children disembarked the train in a flurry of panic, eager to avoid the guards strutting up and down the platform, dishing out random blows with their batons. The coppery scent of blood hung in the air, along with something else—fear. Children held onto their mothers' skirts, while women tried to comfort crying babies wrapped around their chests. Men desperately shielded their wives as they were harried and beaten into rows of five.

Felcia rode the wave of confusion as she allowed herself to be pushed into her own lineup. A woman in her mid-thirties stood in front of her, holding onto her trembling son. Felcia looked back into the boxcar and noticed men in striped uniforms had climbed aboard, unceremoniously loading the deceased onto a cart placed alongside the boxcar. She cringed at their hollow faces—prisoners.

She didn't get a chance to dwell on what was happening as a voice only a few meters in front of her demanded her attention.

"To the left!" A man wearing a doctor's coat barked at the elderly lady at the front of their line of five. When the woman greeted him with a confused look, the SS trooper next to him grabbed her roughly by the arm and pushed her in the intended direction. Felcia looked at the stream of people heading left and noticed they were mostly young children and elderly people. A few women hobbled alongside the group, some carrying babies, others holding their children's hands. Some boarded waiting trucks, but most were told to keep moving along the tree-lined road and out of sight.

"How old is he? Surely he's older than twelve?" The doctor spoke to the woman in front of Felcia, his hard eyes inspecting her son. The woman shook her head, and Felcia heard the panic in her voice.

"No, he's only ten. Please, let me stay with him!"

"Mama, mama, what's happening?" the boy cried in Polish, unable to understand the man's words, but realizing something was very wrong. "Mama!"

The doctor looked the woman up and down, then shook his head. "You look strong enough to work. You're going right. The boy will go left." He jerked his thumb sharply in both directions, and when the boy turned around and looked up at his mother in confusion, the SS trooper took a step forward.

"Where is he going? When will I see him again?"

A flash of sympathy crossed the doctor's face. "You'll see each other again in a few weeks, I promise you that."

The woman knelt in front of her son and cupped his face. "Be strong, Arvad. You just do as you're told, okay? This man promised we will be together again very soon." She pointed at the SS doctor, who now appeared impatient, but didn't press the trooper.

"But Mama, I want to stay with you!" The boy wrapped his hands around her neck, tears streaming down his face." Felcia couldn't bear to look at them any longer and looked away. Seconds later, the SS trooper tore the boy from his mother's grasp and carried him toward the trucks to the left. His mother was already lost in the crowd heading right when Felcia stepped forward to face the doctor. He looked her up and down, nodded approvingly, then jerked his thumb to the right.

She wasn't sure how long she'd been walking when the people in front of Felcia slowed down. From the train, the procession appeared to go on forever. With hawkeyed guards at regular intervals, they'd walked on until reaching the barbed wire fence. At first, Felcia thought her eyes must be deceiving her. The fence hummed, and beyond it the darkened horizon was filled by the outlines of barracks.

They walked down a road lined with more barbed wire on either side. It was quiet, and Felcia imagined the barracks' occupants would be fast asleep. She had no sense of time, but there wasn't a hint of the sun. In the cold, quiet night, she considered her future. She had sensed being sent to the right was somehow a good thing. The doctor had said as much when he told the woman ahead of her she was strong enough to work. Felcia did wonder where the older, weaker people and children were taken. Perhaps to a different camp? She put the thoughts out of her mind; there was no sense in speculating. She tried to swallow and couldn't. Her thirst tortured her without mercy; she didn't have energy to worry about what happened to those sent left.

They were marched to the back of the camp, passing two buildings with long chimneys belching out heavy plumes of dark smoke where the barracks ended. After fifteen minutes a large, coarsely constructed building rose up in front of them.

"Keep moving, come on! We don't have all night!" The SS troopers became restless as they opened two large doors. Felcia was close enough to the front to be swept inside with the masses. She entered a spacious room the size of an Olympic swimming pool. The room soon felt cramped as more women were pushed inside, up until the point where Felcia could feel the elbows of those next to her jabbing into her ribs. She shuddered, struggling to breathe, and closed her eyes, trying to block out what was happening.

The large doors closed. As if on cue, the guards lining the walls started yelling at the women to undress. Felcia looked around in shock and saw the other women looked just as horrified and confused about the command.

"Get moving, you filthy pigs! Take off your clothes! You're all prisoners, and you will do as you're told!" a burly guard barked, while he lashed out at the nearest group of women. His baton hit one of the women in the back of the head, and she collapsed to the ground with a sickening thud. It had the desired effect as panic filled the room and the women started undressing.

"Just leave your clothes on the floor. You won't need those dirty rags anymore!" the same guard yelled. Reluctantly, Felcia undressed to her underwear while keeping an eye on the guards lining the walls. All were men, and they were grinning and whooping at the women. Without warning, one guard walked over to a young woman and ripped off her bra. The woman shrieked, covering herself with her arms—with no way to defend herself, he tore down her panties. He leered at her, then returned triumphantly to the guards. They roared with laughter while the poor woman collapsed to her knees and sobbed.

"What are you all standing around like that for?" the large guard in charge yelled. "Take off *all* your clothes, and line up against that wall!"

A few moments later, the women stood naked as the day they were born, shivering in fear and embarrassment. Felcia didn't even feel the cold, but she felt the eyes of the guards all over her. Next to her, a woman clutched a piece of paper and a few photographs.

"Drop those papers! You won't need any identification papers or photos inside the camp!" A guard tapped his baton against the woman's wrists, prompting her to pull the papers closer to her chest. From the corner of her eye, Felcia could see the guard's face twist in rage. She drew a sharp breath as the guard swung his arm back with lightning speed and landed a vicious blow to the woman's elbow. The woman yelped in pain and opened her hands. Photos and papers—memories of a lifetime—gently drifted onto the cold concrete floor as the woman reached for her painful elbow.

The guard wasn't finished yet. He drew back his baton and landed another blow, this time to the side of the woman's head. Felcia heard a sickening crack as the woman next to her collapsed onto the floor like a sack of potatoes. The thud with which her body landed on the floor made Felcia's mouth fill with acid, and she barely managed to suppress the urge to throw up. Without another look, the guard stalked off to find his next victim.

Felcia looked down to the woman on the ground. She wasn't moving, and blood was pouring from her ears and nose. Panic rose in Felcia's chest as she looked around. She caught the eyes of one of the soldiers sitting a few meters away—studying her with a curious expression, waiting to see how she would respond.

Her body was still shaking, her mouth dry and her heart

hammering in her chest. Her mind, however, found a way to take over. She remembered the raid in the apartment a few nights ago. *I can't show them my fear.* With a clarity she didn't know she still possessed, she blinked hard as she held the soldier's gaze for another moment, then averted her eyes to the floor. She balled her hands into fists and clenched her jaw as the blood of the downed woman seeped into the jumble of clothing. *I won't let them beat me to death in this godforsaken place.* Felcia closed her eyes for a moment, mouthing a silent prayer.

"To the showers, all of you!" The same voice boomed through the room, jolting Felcia back to the present. The mass of naked women shuffled toward another open door, each responding to her surreal situation in her own way. While Felcia was quiet, the surrounding women wept while they tried to cover their nakedness. Passing through the door, the first thing Felcia noticed was the change in temperature—it was freezing. It soon became clear why: the windows and doors were wide open.

"Get in line for your haircut!"

Felcia had barely recovered from the shock of the cold when she was roughly grabbed by her hair and manhandled to a stool in the back of the room. A young woman wearing a prisoner uniform stood waiting with a pair of scissors. Felcia sat on the stool in a daze and looked up at the woman. The first thing she noticed were the eyes. Bright green, but carrying an immense sadness as she took a handful of hair and lifted the scissors.

"I'm sorry," she whispered in Polish before she started cutting Felcia's hair with surprising speed. Felcia didn't move as long strands of her dark, curly hair rained down onto the floor. She felt detached from her own body, as if this were happening to someone else.

When the woman stepped away, Felcia looked down at the floor. Her hair had formed a dark brown carpet of curls. Instinctively Felcia's hands went to her head and felt nothing but a few tufts of hair spread irregularly across her scalp. When she looked up to meet the young woman's eyes, there was sorrow. Felcia opened her mouth to speak, but the young woman quickly shook her head, her eyes shooting to something happening behind Felcia.

Before Felcia could turn around, strong hands grabbed her by the elbow. A sharp pain shot through her arm as she was dragged away.

"We don't have all day. Keep moving." A man's voice, his foul breath close to her ear as he pushed her toward a door marked "Showers."

Felcia stumbled through the narrow door and into a room filled with women sporting haircuts similar to hers. Some were completely bald, and Felcia felt a pang of jealousy. *At least their haircuts had been done evenly.* She caught the ridiculousness of her thoughts and admonished herself. *Is this really the time to worry about looks?*

She shivered while she waited in line. Women were harried through the showers in a matter of moments, with guards yelling at them to keep moving. When her turn came, she tried to sneak a bit of extra time under the scalding water. It was an odd sensation to feel the water directly on her scalp; her thick, curly hair no longer soaking up the first blasts from the showerheads. She closed her eyes, the water burning her freezing limbs. She didn't care; for a moment, the water entering her ears blocked out the wailing, screaming reality of the shower room.

Her relief was short-lived. A sharp blow to her kidney had her gasping for breath as she doubled over in pain. Another blow to her wet buttocks brought her to the ground, and she was only just in time to catch herself with her hands.

"Get up, you piece of filth!" A guard was standing over her, his baton raised menacingly. He didn't seem to care that he was getting wet while he barked at her. "Or the next blow will end you."

Despite the pain radiating from her back and hips, Felcia jumped up and followed the stream of shivering women exiting the shower room, expecting another blow at any minute.

Exiting the shower room, they entered another room where all the doors and windows were open. The wind had free rein and more women in prisoner uniforms appeared. Without a word, one of them smeared a lotion with the distinct smell of disinfectant on her head, under her armpits, and between her legs. Felcia was only vaguely aware of the hands touching her, her mind and body numb from the abuse she'd endured in the past hour. Her head was pounding as a woman's distant voice instructed her to keep moving. *Keep moving. That's all we need to do. Don't stop.* Felcia did as she was told. Any resistance she may have had was foiled. *Don't give the guards a reason to notice you.*

In the next room she was handed a pile of clothes. She dressed without thinking, slipping on the undergarments and oversized striped prisoner uniform. She joined another queue and, once she reached the man behind the typewriter, stated her name and home address. The man then handed her two pieces of fabric.

"Get this stitched onto your uniform over there." He pointed to the far side of the room, where a host of women worked their thread and needles at a furious pace.

It took less than a minute for the older Polish woman to stitch Felcia's red triangle with its series of numerals into the left breast pocket of her uniform. The woman averted her eyes while she worked, which was fine with Felcia, who had no energy left to say anything.

Light streamed in from the door to the next room, raising her spirits. *Surely it's almost over. Maybe they'll let me rest for a moment. At the very least, they need to give us some water.*

The next room was small compared to the previous ones, and on the far side she could see the door leading outside. However, as she entered, it was clear the SS had saved the most horrifying experience for last. Constant buzzing mixed with cries of anguish from the men and women sitting on small stools made for an otherworldly spectacle. Felcia could hardly believe her eyes as she observed a dozen prisoners wielding needles and ink.

She involuntarily took a step back, but before she knew what was happening, she was placed on one of the stools. A man with soft features inspected the numerals on her chest, then gently took her arm.

"This will only hurt for a bit. Please try not to move," he said in Polish. Felcia wanted to say something but was shocked into silence by an intense, burning pain on the outside of her arm. It felt as if it were on fire, and she suppressed a cry. Tears formed in her eyes as she looked down at her arm. The man was methodically tattooing the numerals from the piece of fabric on her chest onto her arm.

It took less than a minute, and when she stood, her legs felt wobbly. Her vision was still obscured by tears, but she didn't care to wipe them away. She stumbled out of the building alongside another woman. The sun was rising steadily, giving Felcia her first glimpse of the vast camp ahead of her. She gasped as she attempted to count the barracks stretching to the horizon.

Felcia looked down at the raw tattoo on her arm. The numerals meant nothing to her, but she was certain of one thing. What happened in the building behind her was only the beginning. She was a number now.

CHAPTER SIX

Sabina sat at her small desk in her room. It was Sunday afternoon, the only day of the week she didn't have to go to school or work. The regular clerks were off on Saturday, but Sabina liked to go in and work in the morning. Mr. Piotrowski had at first protested, but when the files of new arrivals kept piling in during the weekend, he'd soon relented. It was a good way for Sabina to earn a bit of extra money and to stay on her boss's good side.

On Sundays Sabina preferred to get most of her homework done in the morning, and when the weather permitted, she enjoyed going on hikes in the nearby forests. That wasn't always easy, as the Germans would often change the rules about where she was allowed to go. Her venture to Rajsko the other day was a perfect example. *Well, that wasn't really an accident.* She grinned at the memory; those young SS soldiers had been easily fooled.

She turned the page of her book and read a few lines before her mind drifted. She put her book away, stood, and walked to the window. It overlooked the front yard and the road passing their home. They lived in a quiet area on the outskirts of the city, and there was hardly any traffic, especially on Sunday. She sighed, feeling restless and considered calling on Elena. Perhaps they could do something together. The front door opened and she heard her father's voice below.

"I'll be back in about an hour. It's just a quick errand in town."

Her mother's voice answered from inside, but her response was muffled. Sabina raised an eyebrow. Her father hardly ever went into town, and certainly not on a Sunday. He preferred to spend his day off at home, either tending to the many plants and trees in their yard, or smoking his pipe in the living room when the weather wasn't good enough to sit outside. *What is this errand in town?* Sabina's interest was piqued, and she turned on her heel, crossed the room, and stepped into the upstairs hallway, just in time to hear her father close the front door. She stalked down the stairs, careful not to make too much noise, considered telling her mother she was leaving, but decided against it. Her mother would have too many questions.

She carefully opened the front door and held her breath as she closed it. Crossing through the small front yard, she braced herself for her mother calling her back, but all remained quiet. Sabina looked up and down the road and saw her father hurrying in the direction of the city center. Sabina followed him at a safe distance, hoping he wouldn't turn around.

It was only a short distance to the town square, and Sabina's stomach fluttered in anticipation. She was certain wherever her father was going had something to do with his odd behavior of the past few days. The stranger hadn't reappeared in their home, but her father had been unusually quiet and curt with her. It had been torture not to ask him again, but when her father didn't want to talk, it was better to leave him be.

He crossed the square and headed straight for the small tavern on the far side. Sabina waited until he'd entered before emerging from the cover of her side street. There was no reason why she couldn't be in the center either, but if her father spotted her, she'd have to admit it was a bit odd for her to be wandering around here on her own. However, she couldn't just enter the tavern—there were only ten tables inside, and her father would spot her the moment she walked in. Before she could decide on what to do next, she saw another familiar figure emerge from one of the streets on the other side of the square—the man who'd visited their home a few nights ago. Sabina felt a surge of triumph. *I knew it.* She watched him hastily cross the distance to the tavern, confidently stepping inside.

Despite every fiber in her body screaming for her to go into the tavern and ask what was going on, Sabina controlled herself. She didn't want to make a scene; if her father didn't want to tell her what was going on in their home, he certainly wouldn't respond very well to her confronting him in such a public place. *No, I need to be smarter about this.*

She scanned the square, which was almost deserted. Most people were likely enjoying their day off at home. Most of the shops were closed, but the door to *Joanna's pierogi shop* was open. Sabina checked her pockets and smiled when she felt a few coins. She hurried to the small store, the smell of warm pierogis hitting her nostrils as she stepped inside.

"Sabina, what a pleasant surprise! Not often that you grace me with your presence on the weekends!" Joanna herself rose from her small chair behind the counter with a big smile. She'd run the pierogi shop for as long as Sabina could remember. Even when Sabina still lived in Rajsko, she would make the detour to the shop after school.

"I just had a craving for pierogi, and I was bored at home," Sabina said, returning the smile while she casually eyed the menu next to the counter. It was hardly necessary; Joanna knew exactly which of the dumplings were her favorite.

"The regular, then?" Joanna was already reaching for a couple of onion and spinach pierogis from the display counter.

"Two, please." She took a few coins and placed them on the counter.

Joanna took three and smiled. "One on the house." She transferred them to a large pot of boiling water on the stove behind her before scooping up the coins.

"You're too sweet."

"So, what's new with you, young lady?" Joanna leaned on the counter, her dark brown eyes sparkling as she lowered her voice. "Still going to school when you're not working at the municipality?"

Sabina nodded. "Mr. Pach keeps us busy, and I enjoy being there."

"I think most of you attending his classes do." Joanna turned around and took the pierogis from the pot, transferring them to a small plate before setting it on the counter. "From what I hear, he's a good teacher."

"He's taking a big risk doing what he does." Sabina leaned against the counter and took a steaming dumpling, blowing on it before putting it in her mouth. She closed her eyes and savored the taste of the caramelized onions as she bit through the soft outer layer of the pierogi.

"You all are, just by being there."

Sabina swallowed and opened her eyes. "Not as much as Mr. Pach, though. If he gets caught, I wouldn't be surprised if the Nazis took him to the camp."

The mention of the camp down the road caused a silence, as Joanna didn't immediately respond. Sabina quickly took another pierogi and half turned toward the window, giving her a good view of the square. It was deserted, and she was certain she hadn't missed her father leaving. She was keen to change the subject.

"How's business for you, Joanna? I'm surprised you're open today. Shouldn't you have a day off as well?"

The woman behind the counter smiled. "And what would I do? Sit at home?" She shook her head and pointed out the window. "It might be quiet on the square now, but there'll be more people coming and going later. And they'll be hungry and stop in for a quick snack. And while they wait or eat, they love to talk."

Sabina understood, and a thought struck. "Heard anything interesting lately?" She attempted to sound casual as she popped the last pierogi into her mouth.

"Other than news of more trains coming in every day, not really. If you didn't know any better, you'd almost think the Germans are running out of people to put to work." Her voice trailed off, as both women understood the ominous meaning of her words.

"Anything about the work going on in Rajsko?"

"Rajsko?" Joanna looked puzzled, and Sabina felt a pang of disappointment. "What's going on there?"

"I was hoping you'd heard more about it. It looks like they're expanding the farming outpost into a camp." Sabina detailed the findings from her recent hike with Elena. Joanna listened without interrupting her, her eyebrows raised when Sabina told her about the SS soldiers discovering them.

"You should be more careful, Sabina. I know you think you're just a girl, but you're almost an adult. Besides, if they're really building something important there, they won't take kindly to you snooping around." There was concern in Joanna's voice, but Sabina also detected some disappointment. Despite her friendly exterior, Joanna was one of the best informed people in the city. If she thought exploring around Rajsko was dangerous, Sabina had better take notice.

"You're right. I should be more careful."

Joanna had turned around and was fiddling with the stove, and Sabina decided talking to Mr. Piotrowski would be best. If anyone knew what was going on near her old home, it would be him. *I hope he's back tomorrow.*

She returned her gaze to the square, where the tavern door opened and the now-familiar stranger stepped out. Sabina's pulse increased as she followed him with her eyes. He kept his gaze on the cobblestones as he hurried away toward one of the side streets. Sabina quickly turned to Joanna, who still had her back to her.

"Joanna, any chance you know who that man is over there?" Her voice had a bit of a stammer in it, and she hoped the shopkeeper didn't detect her excitement.

"Which man?"

Sabina turned back and was surprised to see the man had disappeared. She rapidly scanned the empty square and thought she detected some movement in one of the narrow side streets. *Damn it. Too late.* Joanna knew everyone in town, and if the man was from around here, she was almost certain the shopkeeper would've recognized him.

"You don't mean your father, do you?"

Sabina's father had exited the tavern, looking a bit shifty as he shielded his eyes from the bright daylight. Adjusting his cap, he started crossing the square, and he would soon pass the pierogi shop. Sabina didn't want to risk him entering the shop, making for an awkward encounter. "I didn't know he was here as well. It'll make for a nice walk back home. Thanks for the pierogi!" She was already out the door before Joanna could respond.

Her father was halfway across the square and spotted her as soon as she exited the shop. He looked surprised at first, then his face betrayed a hint of resignation.

"Are you following me, daughter? Didn't you have homework to finish?" His voice was gruff, but it was impossible to miss the twinge of acceptance. *He knows.*

Sabina couldn't help but smile. "Papa, I saw the stranger who visited you at home."

He started walking from the square, with a small shake of the head as Sabina fell in line. "I suppose you followed me from the moment I left the house?" When she nodded, he continued. "Then you know I met with him just now."

"Who is he, Papa? And why are you so mysterious about it? You're never this secretive. Does Mama know?"

He didn't immediately answer as they made a turn away from town. It was the route Sabina liked to take when she wasn't in a hurry. Evidently, her father felt the same. Only a few clouds lined the sky, and the trees lining the road cast long shadows. The smell of pines felt comforting, almost as if they were on a hike. They walked in silence for a few more minutes before her father sat down on a weathered wooden bench along the path. He patted the space next to him and she also sat.

"Sabinka," he started, using the nickname he hadn't used since she was a little girl. "I'm proud of you for holding down your job in the municipality and continuing your studies with Mr. Pach." His voice sounded a little off. Sabina wanted to say something, but she sensed she should stay quiet. Her father cleared his throat before continuing. "I know the move away from Rajsko hasn't been easy on you. God knows, with everything happening around us, you would be forgiven for strug-gling at school or work." He looked up at the blue sky directly over their heads, then looked into the distance, where the camp crematoria's chim-neys darkened the sky.

"I try my best, Papa," Sabina said softly, and he nodded, keeping his eyes on the horizon. "Besides, I like my job, and I love Mr. Pach's classes. They keep me sane and give me a sense of normality."

A smile crept onto her father's face. "It makes me happy to hear that, Sabinka. Because we need that attitude. I'm worried about our country, and about what the future may hold. I see so much evil at the mines every day that it's hard to imagine there are still good things happening in Oświęcim."

Sabina was surprised by her father's words and turned to him. "You're never this downbeat, Papa. What's wrong?" Elena's earlier words about her father's troubles at the railroad flooded back into her mind.

"The SS don't care about whom they send to the mines. The men that arrived the other day aren't anywhere near fit enough to do what we ask of them. These new arrivals are scholars. They don't know how to wield a pickax. Even if they did, they wouldn't be able to swing it more than five times before needing a break." He shook his head, dismay in his eyes. "We tried to teach them, and they really did try, but they don't stand a chance. More than half of the men that arrived on Friday collapsed before the end of the day. The journey from Holland exhausted them, and the SS finished them off in the mines the next day." He looked at the mossy ground in front of them, a few birds chirping in the trees the only sound breaking the silence.

Sabina wasn't sure how to respond. He hadn't explained the appearance of the stranger in their home, but this didn't feel like the moment to force the issue. Before she could say anything, he recovered his composure. He straightened his shoulders, raised his chin and looked at her with those strong, determined blue eyes.

"The man you saw in our home and in the square earlier is someone who has the same concerns about where our country is headed. Who wants to do something about what's happening in our town, in the mines, and in the camp."

"Do something?" Sabina gasped. Despite her father's modest description of the man's ambitions, it was clear what he was. "He's part of the resistance."

Her father nodded, his jaw set a bit tighter. "He's asked if I would help them."

"How?" Sabina was taken aback, her heart beating faster as she struggled to process the revelation. Her father, a man of the resistance?

He must've noticed her concern, for he held up his hands. "It's nothing big, I promise. They just want me to keep them informed of what's happening in the mines. It's nothing I wouldn't do anyway." He took her hand, a sad smile on his face. "I can't stand by and watch these men drop like flies every day."

"Just be careful, Papa. If this man is part of the resistance, I'm sure they'll use your information to sabotage the Nazis one day."

"I hope they do. I'm counting on it."

He sounded determined, and Sabina looked at her father in a new light. She felt a surge of affection and pride. Her father was a cautious man, and if he'd decided to help the resistance, he must've thought long and hard before agreeing to do so.

"Shall we head back?" Her father rose and held out his hand. She let him help her to her feet, her knees feeling a little wobbly at the news as they continued down the path. On a whim, she decided she wanted to share her most recent discovery as well. Her father listened silently as she told him about the Nazi expansions near their old home.

"And you're worried about me." He chuckled, a mischievous look on his face as she concluded her story with the run-in with the SS soldiers. "Sounds like you need to follow your own advice." Sabina looked away, feeling abashed. "Seriously, though, Sabinka, you really need to watch out. Especially if they're expanding the camp."

"I know. I won't go back. I'm going to ask Mr. Piotrowski instead."

"Sounds like a better approach. He should know."

The trees thinned as they neared the main road. They would be back home in a few minutes, and Sabina was disappointed that this rare bit of time alone with her father was about to end. Evidently, he felt the same, for he stopped and looked at her with a serious expression.

"Sabinka, let's keep everything we talked about between us, okay? Don't tell your mother about your trip to Rajsko, for she would only worry."

"What about your new friend? How much does Mama know?"

His eyes narrowed slightly, then he caught himself and his face softened. "I'll tell her when the time is right." Without waiting for her response, he continued toward the road. Sabina remained in place, her eyes on his broad shoulders and strong legs as he stomped forward. When she left home an hour ago, she had been upset with her father.

Now he had let her in on his biggest secret, and she had never felt closer to him. He turned around, an inquiring look on his face.

"Are you coming? Don't want to keep your mother waiting!"

Sabina smiled and hurried to catch up. She would keep his secret, and not tell a soul. And if he ever asked, she would help him with whatever he needed.

CHAPTER SEVEN

After her harrowing arrival in Birkenau, now over a week ago, Felcia was assigned to a barracks in the vast women's camp. She had miraculously found a spot between two other women in a bunk in the back and had passed out the moment she lay down. It mattered not that her bed was composed of nothing but cold, hard wooden planks, and that she had nothing to cover herself with. She was too exhausted to notice.

When the barracks came to life in the evening, Felcia had followed the other women outside for roll call. It had passed in a daze, and the only thing she remembered was the watery portion of soup she inhaled afterward. When she woke to the screams of the block elder the next morning, she felt like she'd only closed her eyes for a few seconds. Despite her exhaustion, she followed her bunkmates' lead and stood at attention.

Her first full day was, mercifully, a Sunday. She didn't realize this at the time, but as the only day off for prisoners, it gave her invaluable time to recover from the trauma of her journey and arrival. She spent the morning cleaning the barracks with some of the other women. In the afternoon, she got some rest in the sun.

When she lined up for roll call the next morning, she was assigned to assist in the *Zentralsauna*, the very place she'd arrived at two nights prior. She was part of the prisoner *kommando*, work detail, handing out clothing to new arrivals. Well, what had to pass for clothing.

"But these are men's pants! I can't walk around in those. And these undergarments are at least two sizes too big!" The woman across the table stood with an exasperated expression, blood trickling down from the small wounds on her poorly shaven head. Felcia looked back apologetically and remembered how she'd felt only two weeks ago. The woman's eyes were pleading, confusion lining her face.

"I'm sorry, this is all we've got." Felcia's eyes shot to the SS guard a few meters away. He was looking in the other direction. She took pity on the woman, who looked to be in her late forties. *How did she make it past selection on the ramp?* Felcia lowered her voice and blurted. "Look, once you get to your block, you might find people to trade with. For now, you need to keep moving before one of the soldiers sees you holding up the line."

The women opened her mouth, then thought better of it. She nodded and moved on. The next poor woman approached, and Felcia handed her a similarly mismatched pile of rags. This woman must've overheard the previous conversation, for she simply nodded and walked on without complaint.

The morning passed quickly, with Felcia sorting the baskets of clothing while she waited for the overseer to call for them. It wouldn't take long for the last of the new arrivals to report outside after getting their tattoos. Felcia rubbed her arm. The wound had healed remarkably quickly, but she hadn't gotten used to the unsightly, crudely tattooed number on her forearm. She was grateful for the long-sleeved shirt that covered it up. Still, she had to roll up the sleeve at every roll call and inspection.

"Hey, how did it go this morning?"

She turned around to find her friend Marzena, who quickly knelt down next to her to rummage through the basket of clothes. They had met on Felcia's first day in the clothing kommando. Marzena had shown her around, having arrived a month before Felcia. They were of the same age, and had quickly bonded—Marzena stressed the importance of always looking busy to Felcia. It had been invaluable advice, for she had seen women nearly beaten to death for appearing idle for the briefest moment.

"About as well as it can get in here." Felcia took some extraordinarily large underpants from her basket. "I suppose it's a good thing I didn't try handing these out to anyone this morning. Not sure they would be of use to anyone in here."

"You could pitch a tent with these." Marzena took the garments from Felcia and tossed them in a basket in the back. Felcia let out a soft laugh. She appreciated her friend's dark humor: it was the only way to survive the corner of hell they'd arrived in. Marzena smiled, then her face turned serious. "Did you not notice the women passing by today all looked odd?"

"Odd?" Then the face of the older woman complaining about her clothes flashed into her mind. "You mean older?"

Marzena nodded. "Older, frailer, you name it. Most of these women wouldn't last a day working in the camp's conditions. I would've expected them to have been sent left on arrival." Her voice was strained, but she spoke with authority, not a trace of doubt in her words.

"It does seem odd."

"And there was something else I heard. They weren't tattooed."

Felcia stopped in her tracks, holding onto a piece of clothing. "I thought I heard the needles whirring next door."

"Yes, the younger, fitter women went through the normal process. But many were simply waved through after collecting their uniforms." Marzena looked as confused as Felcia felt. Felcia was about to say something when her friend's attention was drawn to something happening behind her. Marzena's eyebrows shot up, concern immediately clear on her face. "Oh shit. This can't be good."

Felcia turned around and felt her heart drop. The entourage entering from the tattoo room struck fear into the hearts of even the bravest prisoners. At first sight, the handsome man wearing an impeccably tailored doctor's uniform looked out of place in this factory of death. But prisoners who had had the misfortune of looking into the cold, calculating eyes of Dr. Josef Mengele knew their hours on this earth were numbered. Few lived to tell about their encounter with the Angel of Death. Walking alongside him was Maria Mandl, the *SS-Lager-*

führerin of the women's camp, the most powerful woman in Auschwitz-Birkenau. Felcia had heard of her brutality but had been fortunate never to witness it. She dared glance only at Mandl's face for a moment, but it was enough to send a shiver down her spine.

"Don't make eye contact." Marzena's voice sounded oddly distant as she turned back to find her friend sorting clothing again. She followed her friend's lead, hoping Mengele and Mandl would pass through their section without incident. It was not to be.

"Drop what you're doing and follow us, now." The screeching, grating voice of Maria Mandl rang out like nails being scratched on a chalkboard. With her teeth on edge, she rose from the basket and rushed toward Mandl and Mengele, who had moved to the door leading to the showers.

The women of the clothing kommando hurried to line up before Mengele and Mandl. The doctor observed them with a relaxed—even disinterested—look on his face, but Mandl tapped her foot impatiently, her eyes fixed on a woman approaching from the far side of the room. Mandl's eyes looked murderous, and Felcia braved a quick peek at the woman unfortunate enough to have caused the Lager-führerin's ire. Her breath caught in her throat when she saw the woman limping toward them, her face tense and red from exertion. The room went quiet, only the woman's rushed steps and labored breathing audible.

Felcia turned her attention back to Mandl—who looked ready to murder the limping woman—and Mengele, who, much to her horror, was looking straight at her. Not sure what to do, Felcia held his gaze, mesmerized by his piercing brown eyes. She even thought she saw a faint smile on his face. She shuddered, her heartbeat returning to normal when he turned to Mandl, interrupting their moment.

"Shall we? We've got a lot of work to do." He spoke calmly, his every word articulated to perfection. It reminded Felcia of the German educators visiting her university after the invasion. It already felt like a lifetime ago, and she suppressed a sigh.

A look of annoyance flashed on Mandl's face, but she recovered quickly enough, turning to Mengele with a curt nod, her face a passive mask of deference. The limping woman had caught up just as they started moving, and Felcia was pleased to see another woman supporting her.

As they walked through the shower room, Mandl addressed them in a loud voice. "I want you girls to make sure the women in the next room remain calm. Most of them are Polish swine like you, only even more useless. I'm quite sure they won't understand most of what I tell them, so you'll be there to help them."

Help them with what? Felcia glanced at Marzena, who shrugged her shoulders.

"Once we're done, you'll escort them through these rooms to the exit, where guards will be waiting. They won't need to go through the usual process." She stopped and turned to look at the women following her, and Felcia did her best to avoid making eye contact. "No showers, no new clothes, no tattoos. Just get them outside and to the guards. Once they're all outside, wait at your normal posts. Understood?"

None of the women spoke up. Felcia felt herself shaking a little, and the fear in the room was tangible. What had they gotten caught up in?

The large doors to the main room were still closed, and Mengele and Mandl produced gloves from their pockets. It was then that the Lager-führerin unstrapped a large baton from her belt. They nodded at each other and opened the door.

The scene was overwhelming. The room where Felcia had entered with a couple of hundred women two weeks ago was now filled with at least a thousand women, lined up in neat rows of twenty. They stood silently waiting in mismatched clothing. It appeared some had just arrived, still wearing their own clothes, while others wore the camp uniform.

The sorry group of women was surrounded by dozens of SS guards wielding pistols and rifles. Felcia had never seen such a show of force. As she followed Mengele and Mandl, she noticed many of the women had one thing in common. Their faces and exposed arms were covered in boils and ulcers. Barely hiding her shock and disgust, Felcia scanned the sea of faces. Many had scratched at the no doubt itchy patches, only making it worse. Others looked like they had survived whatever disease they carried and were on the mend, only a few spots blotting their faces. *What happened here? Who are these women?*

Without warning, Mandl stepped toward the nearest row of women. Careful not to get too close, she inspected the first woman. Within a second or two, she appeared to make her judgment, using the tip of her baton to push the woman from the line. Mengele stood at a distance, looking on with an amused expression. Mandl processed the first row in less than a minute, separating all but two women from the row, essentially creating a new row. As she moved to the next row, Mengele slowly walked past those unfortunate enough to have been selected by Mandl. Mengele took slightly longer, but his inspections consisted of no more than a quick glance at the women's faces. With two, he requested they lift their shirts to inspect their upper bodies.

When Mengele finished his inspection, he signaled to the guards standing by. "Escort them to the assembly point." He turned and picked out Felcia and Marzena from the group of prisoners standing awkwardly near the door. "Assist them. Tell them to follow you and that all will be well. Once they're outside, return here."

Felcia's hands trembled as she neared the terrified women. She translated Mengele's message while her eyes drifted to where Mandl was selecting even more women. It appeared only those with hardly any signs of illness were spared her wrath. She was already up to her fifth row as Mengele worked through the second row.

Felcia and Marzena had little to do as the women fell in line between four SS troopers. Outside, another cordon of soldiers stood waiting, barking orders at the women to move to the front. Felcia was never so relieved to return to the walls of the Zentralsauna. The guards hardly paid them any attention as they walked back, the next group of selected already making its way through the room.

"Where are they taking these women?" Felcia kept her voice low, staying close to Marzena.

"I don't know, but judging by the way they look, it won't be good. It can only be one place, really."

"The gas chambers."

Marzena only nodded as they returned to the main room, where the selection continued without delay. Mandl was in the back, and only a handful of women still stood where she had gone through.

Felcia and Marzena made the walk another four times. Felcia now counted only thirty in the room, which less than an hour ago was filled with more than a thousand women.

"You'll process these women after they've had their showers," Mandl said as she casually put her baton away. "I trust you'll be able to carry out your normal tasks, even with such a small number." She scanned the group while Dr. Mengele took off his gloves. Felcia avoided her gaze but felt the Lagerführerin's gaze pass over her. "You."

Dread filled Felcia as she slowly lifted her face. Much to her relief, Mandl wasn't looking at her. Instead, her eyes were fixed on the woman with the limp. Felcia felt sick with apprehension.

"You're in no state to work here. You can't keep up with the demands of this job."

"I can, Frau Lagerführerin, I promise you I can." The woman's voice was filled with terror. Felcia kept her gaze on the floor ahead of her. "Please, let me show you I can."

"No," came the icy response from Mandl. "You'll join the women outside."

A wail cut through the large room, followed by loud sobbing. The woman pleaded incoherently as the guards dragged her away.

Mandl turned to Dr. Mengele, looking pleased. "I think we handled that rather well. These women deserve no better. Disgusting specimens, a threat to camp hygiene."

"The guards will take them to Block 25, yes?" Mengele spoke evenly. "In quarantine?"

Mandl nodded. "As you instructed."

"Very well. We'll monitor them and see what we do with them in a few days. If anything is necessary, of course."

Felcia felt her stomach turn at the revolting words spoken so casually. She looked at the blank faces of the women around her; not all had understood the Germans. Marzena had, though, and her face had also gone pale. They both realized what the quarantine in Block 25 meant.

Mandl turned back to them, her face twisting into a snarl. "Well, what are you still standing around for? Get these women processed. We've got a new group coming through in an hour!"

Felcia felt like she had been punched in the gut. Another group? As she followed the other women of her kommando, she suddenly felt very tired. There would be no rest this afternoon. Only more death.

Three days after the selection, Felcia was sorting clothes with Marzena while she waited for the next group of arrivals to come through the Zentralsauna when a guard approached her.

"You two. You don't look like you're too busy. Come with me. And bring an empty basket."

Felcia stood and controlled her apprehension. *What does he want from me?* It was never good to be singled out. The memory of the limping woman selected by Mandl was still fresh in her mind. She glanced at Marzena, who gave her a quick nod of encouragement. It did little to settle her nerves.

The guard picked another four women, seemingly at random. It made Felcia feel slightly better. They stepped outside into the bright May sunshine, and she savored the warmth of the rays on her face. It was around noon, and she was hardly ever allowed outside the Zentralsauna at this hour. Her days began when she entered the building right after roll call, and she didn't emerge until evening. Often, with the growing number of arrivals, that meant the sun had already set. No matter what happened next, she decided she was going to enjoy this rare luxury.

The walk from the Zentralsauna to the front of the women's camp took almost fifteen minutes. Following the uneven path, they reached the most southeastern corner of the camp. The guard stopped in front of two buildings connected with red-brick walls some two meters high. Marzena gasped, and Felcia turned around.

"Block 25." Marzena's face had lost all color. Were they somehow being placed in the quarantine block as well? Panic gripped her throat—she hadn't done anything to deserve this. She worked hard. She then looked at the basket she was carrying. Why would they make her take the basket to the quarantine block?

The gate opened and the women followed the guard. The sight in the courtyard between the two buildings was as gruesome as Felcia had ever seen. Bodies were piled up against the walls, with rats scurrying by, gnawing at limbs. The stench of death was overpowering, and Felcia breathed through her mouth to suppress the gagging feeling in the back of her throat. The hollow eyes of the dead followed them as they crossed the courtyard toward an open door to the left.

The guard stopped and turned next to the door. His eyes went to the piles of corpses outside, and he seemed to consider something before speaking. "Inside you'll find more dead and dying women. You're to strip the clothing from the dead. Each of you will fill your basket before coming back outside. Only take clothing you think can be used again. You have one hour. If your basket isn't full by then, you'll stay here."

Despite the threat of disease looming inside, the alternative of a permanent stay in the quarantine block was enough to see the first women move through the dark doorway. Felcia looked at Marzena, whose face had regained some color, and took a deep breath.

"Don't touch your face or mouth."

Felcia stepped inside to find Block 25 set up much like her own. Simple wooden bunks stacked three high lined walls and the middle of the room, creating two narrow corridors. What made the block different from her own was the heavy air. The incessant coughing of the women in the bunks made the air feel heavier. She glanced to her left, inspecting the women in the bottom bunk—the same poor creatures selected in the Zentralsauna a few days ago. They seemed even worse now, their lifeless eyes looking up at her without any expression. The boils on their faces had grown to such an extent that they were covering most of their noses or mouths. Some were more conscious than others but didn't manage to produce more than a gargling sound in the back of their throats. With an apologetic nod of the head Felcia continued on. There was nothing she could do for these women. And if there was, she had no time to waste. Her basket was still precariously empty.

It didn't take long for her to find the first corpse. A young woman not much older than Felcia lay on the side of a bunk. Her eyes and mouth were wide open, almost as if surprised when death came for her. Her body was still warm, and Felcia started the gruesome task of undressing her. As she did, tears burned in her eyes. Whatever had killed this young woman was somehow allowed to fester in the camp. As a final death sentence, the woman was brought to this block, where she was deprived of even the meager supply of food and water the regular prisoners received. It took Felcia a few minutes to undress the woman, and when she finished, she apologized to her, and said a small prayer. Then she stood—there was no time to linger.

Fifty minutes later Felcia reported to the guard at the gate. She gripped her basket tightly, overflowing with clothes from the dead. She wasn't going to take any chances. Satisfied, the guard signaled for her to exit the yard. There was movement in the corner of her eye and she turned to see a woman crouching near one of the piles of corpses. Pausing to see if her eyes weren't deceiving her, she looked more carefully. A wave of nausea overwhelmed her as her brain processed what she saw. The woman was nibbling at the buttocks of one of the corpses.

The contents of Felcia's stomach spilled onto the ground as her chest heaved, her shoulders shaking. Her eyes were watery, the overpowering bitter taste of bile in her nose and mouth. Panic almost overpowered her when she felt a hand on her shoulder. Relief flooded her senses when she recognized Marzena, who took her friend's hand, lifting her back to her feet.

"Come, let's not linger here. We need to get back to the Zentralsauna."

Picking up her basket, Felcia stumbled through the gate. She wasn't completely sure, but it almost seemed like the guard threw her a sympathetic look as she passed. As the group left Block 25 behind, Felcia was relieved to find that everyone who had entered the courtyard an hour earlier had emerged again. But most importantly, Marzena and she had survived.

CHAPTER EIGHT

S abina looked at the clock above the door and sighed. It was only eleven—the morning was creeping by. Tosia caught her look and smiled.

"Tough morning?"

"It's okay, I'm a little restless, that's all." Sabina placed a box overflowing with files on the small cart and pushed it along the row of filing cabinets. It had taken her the whole morning to sort the files—the Belgian and French arrivals' names were so similar.

Tosia got up from the small stool and moved around her desk. "I'll help you with those. I need to stretch my legs." She pushed the cart, and Sabina was grateful for the assistance. "Any reason in particular you're restless?" There was surprise and curiosity in Tosia's voice.

Sabina shook her head. The week had passed in a blur as she attended her underground classes in the mornings and showed up for work in the afternoons. She still found it hard to believe her father was involved with the resistance. When they returned home, her father had acted as if everything was normal, and from what Sabina could tell, her mother didn't suspect a thing. Or perhaps she suspected something was going on but decided, unlike Sabina, not to act on it? Sabina had observed her parents during mealtimes that week, but there was nothing unusual about their behavior. It was now Friday, and Sabina was convinced her father's small part in the resistance was their little secret. It excited her, and she'd spent most of the week thinking about ways to help him. She worked in the municipal registry, after all!

When she came in on Monday, she had been eager to find her boss. Even before her father's revelations, it had been hard not knowing what was happening in Rajsko, but now it felt like her responsibility to find out. She'd controlled herself until noon, but then made her way toward his office. The door was closed, and she'd been disappointed—and a little annoyed—to find his assistant, Mrs. Formella, particularly pleased to inform her Mr. Piotrowski would continue to be away for most of the week. And no, she didn't know when he'd be back. Sabina was certain his assistant knew exactly when Mr. Piotrowski was to return, but enjoyed keeping Sabina in the dark.

They reached the filing cabinets in the back and Sabina opened one drawer, mechanically sorting the files into the right alphabetical order. She hardly saw the names.

"Remember when I told you about people from town smuggling in extra food for the prisoners?" Tosia spoke softly while she picked up a handful of files.

Sabina didn't look up, keeping her eyes on the files. She tried to keep her contempt out of her voice. "And exchange it for the gold the prisoners loot off the corpses? You said your friends were interested in joining this scheme as well."

"Some were caught the other day."

"Really?" Sabina paused, looking up this time. Sadness lined Tosia's face, and she instantly regretted sounding so judgmental a moment ago. "Were your friends part of those caught?"

Tosia shook her head. "No, they tried to get in touch with the people running the operation, but they kept turning them down."

"Turns out it was a good thing they weren't involved." Sabina's mind went to her father, and worry clutched her stomach. "What happened to those caught?"

"My friends said they were betrayed from the inside. Some Kapo finding out about what was going on turned them in to the SS guards. They stopped them at the gate on the way out, and they were caught with gold and silver on them. The SS took them away, and nobody has heard anything from them since." Tosia's face hardened. "But I think we all know what will happen to them."

Sabina picked up some of the files and the women worked in silence for a few minutes. It wasn't hard to picture what would happen to the smugglers. They had essentially stolen from the Reich, and there was only one punishment. She shivered as she thought of the torture these men would have to endure. Her father's face flashed in front of her. He said he also provided extra rations to some of the workers in the mines. Was he tempting fate?

"Sabina?" A low voice jolted her from her thoughts. When she turned, she was pleased to see a tall man wearing a faded brown corduroy suit near the door.

"Mr. Piotrowski, you're back!" She failed to contain her excitement at the appearance of her boss. She toned down her enthusiasm a little. "How was your trip?"

"As good as a trip to the administration can be." A modest smile spread on his face as he traversed the narrow space between the filing cabinets. "There's too much talk, too little action for my liking. I'm glad to be back home."

It was easy to read between the lines. Sabina suspected her boss had as little to say about how his office was run as her father did the mines. For a man like Mr. Piotrowski, who had been running the municipality for as long as Sabina could remember, she imagined it must be hard to take orders from the occupiers. He was, however, a skilled politician with invaluable knowledge of the area. That, combined with the importance of Oświęcim and surrounding area, was probably why the Germans had allowed him to remain in his position. "What brings you down here?" It wasn't common for him to visit the archives.

"I'm sorry to ask this of you, because I know you've got enough work as it is." He held up a thick envelope while his eyes scanned the boxes on the cart in front of her. "But I couldn't think of anyone better than you to deliver this to the camp in Rajsko."

Camp? Sabina managed to keep her face composed as she took a few steps away from the filing cabinet and toward Mr. Piotrowski. "You mean the agricultural unit near my old home?"

"Exactly. I thought you might enjoy the walk, and it will give you a chance to return to your old school." He handed her the envelope. "The Germans are expanding the camp, and they requested some extra information. Make sure you hand this to one of the officers in your old school building. They've made it their headquarters for now, or so I'm told."

With trembling hands, Sabina took the thick envelope. It was heavier than she'd expected, and she was instantly curious about the extra information the Germans considered important enough to request from the municipality.

The walk to Rajsko was very different from her previous visit. She walked alongside the main road without having to worry about patrols stopping her. German military vehicles of all sizes passed her going in both directions. Kübelwagens carried SS officers, easily recognizable as sole passengers in the backs, while trucks transported goods and soldiers in equal measure. She averted her eyes most of the time, but felt the gaze of young soldiers and guards as they passed by.

She reached Rajsko half an hour after setting off from the municipal building. Entering her old hometown by way of the main road felt odd —houses that used to line the road had been flattened, replaced by endless fields of prisoners in identical uniforms toiling away. The constant sounds of construction filled the air, intensifying as she reached the school.

The yard in front of the school building where she'd spent most of her childhood was filled with trucks. Men in striped uniforms were unloading large boxes as SS guards looked on from a distance, chatting and joking, occasionally barking abuse at the prisoners. Behind the school, in the clearing that used to be their sports field, stood five identical-looking buildings. Prisoners carried wooden planks from a stack in the middle of the field, with the incessant sound of hammers indicating they were hard at work inside the buildings. What took away doubt about the purpose of these buildings was the barbed wire fencing set up on the far side. These were prisoner barracks.

Sabina's hands felt clammy as she approached the school building. The memories of her youth flooded back, when she took the days spent in the classrooms for granted. It was hard to believe it had been more than three years since she'd stepped foot inside this building. There was a shout behind her, and she jumped out of the way as four men in striped prisoner uniforms rushed into the building. They carried one of the large boxes, the looks on their faces and their heavy breathing betraying the heavy weight of the box's contents. Sabina was about to step into the building when another voice called out.

"Halt! Where do you think you're going?"

She turned around to find a soldier wearing the familiar uniform of the SS approaching her. He walked at a solid pace, crossing the short distance between them remarkably quickly. Sabina opened her mouth, but he shook his head, pointing at the road she came from. "Did you not see the signs? This is a restricted area."

For a second, Sabina's mouth went dry. She looked at the guard, who appeared only a few years older than her, whose hand moved toward his belt, where a pistol was visible. *Is he going to shoot me?* Then she felt the large envelope in her hand, which grounded her, reminding her why she was here. *I'm allowed to be here. I was sent here.*

The guard neared and held out his arms, indicating for Sabina to follow him. *At least his hand is away from the pistol.* Sabina held up the envelope and swallowed hard before speaking.

"I was sent by Mr. Piotrowski in the municipal registry in town." She nodded at the road leading to Oświęcim, hoping the guard would understand. "He told me to deliver this to whoever is in charge of the camp."

The guard's eyes went to the envelope, the expression in them changing from annoyance and hostility to suspicion. "Is that so?" He wasn't quite convinced, but he didn't seem so sure of himself anymore either. Sabina decided to push forward.

"Could you tell me where I could find him? My boss said it was important these documents were delivered as soon as possible, and I don't want to disappoint him." In an effort to ease the tension, she smiled. "Perhaps you could take me to him? It might look good for you as well. I have no idea where to go." In truth, Sabina knew what the inside of the school looked like, and she suspected the new Nazi commander would've set up in the former headmaster's office.

The guard's eyes went between the envelope and Sabina's face. After a few agonizingly long seconds, he nodded. "Very well. I can't imagine why you'd walk in here like this otherwise. Follow me. I don't think the commander is in, but I'll take you to his assistant."

Sabina hid her relief as the guard brushed by her and into the building. She followed him, and walking into the hallway brought back memories. It was odd, because apart from the prisoners rushing around, very little had changed. The doors to the classrooms were open, the sound of construction was ever-present. The guard set a quick pace, and Sabina hurried to keep up with him.

They passed the open doors to what used to be classrooms, and it was clear the rooms of her former school would serve a very different purpose. Instead of desks and chairs filling the rooms, there were large tables with equipment Sabina didn't recognize. It looked scientific, and her interest was piqued, but she didn't get a chance to linger, with the guard glancing over his shoulder. "Come on, keep moving! I thought you said you were in a hurry to deliver your paperwork."

They reached the end of the hallway, where the headmaster's office used to be. The door was closed, and the guard knocked on the door next to it. A grunt came from inside, before the guard opened the door.

"Someone from town with papers for you, sir."

"Perfect. I've been waiting for those all morning. Send them in!" a deep baritone voice answered.

The guard looked disappointed as he waved Sabina in. She entered and was surprised to find the man with the low voice only a few years her senior. He wore an SS officer's uniform of the *Hauptsturmführer* rank.

The officer behind the desk stood up, and he appeared equally surprised to see Sabina. "I expected Mr. Piotrowski to deliver the papers himself, but I must say, I'm not disappointed to see you instead." He moved from behind the desk and held out his hand, a twinkle in his eyes. "I'm Paskal Sternhell."

Sabina didn't immediately respond as her eyes went to his outstretched hand. She was torn; what should she say? She was confused by his seemingly casual manner. She'd never met a Nazi who introduced himself, and by his first name, even. Realizing the encounter was getting more awkward with every second she left him standing there, she carefully shook his hand. "I'm Sabina."

"It's nice to meet you, Sabina. Please, take a seat while I check those papers." He waved her to the seat across from him while he held out his other hand. Sabina handed him the papers before sitting down. He opened the envelope and leaned against the desk. For a few minutes, he said nothing, nodding and making small notes. Sabina looked around the room, which was sparsely decorated. She remembered this used to be the room of the secretary to the headmaster, and it didn't look like Hauptsturmführer Sternhell had made many changes.

The officer sat down when he reached the final page. He tutted, then signed at the bottom and pushed the papers to the side of his desk. "Very well. It all looks in order. Please tell your boss I expect him to send me a report like this every week. If anything changes, I'll let him know." Sabina nodded, moving to get up, relieved to be on her way. Sternhell had different plans as he leaned forward in his chair, his hands on the desk. "So, Sabina, are you from around here?"

She sat back in her chair. "I am. I live in the city."

"You live in Oświęcim?" His pronunciation was off, but at least he used the original Polish name of the town instead of the new German version: Auschwitz.

She shuffled in her seat, considering her next answer. The man across the desk looked at her with interest, his blue eyes sparkling, his face relaxed. It didn't feel like an interrogation, and she hadn't felt uncomfortable since entering his office. Before she could help herself, she answered. "I do, we were moved to the city when the expansions to the camp began."

He raised an eyebrow, and Sabina worried she may have spoken out of turn. Then a thin, almost cautious smile appeared on his face. "Where did you live before?"

"Well, this used to be my school, actually."

"You're from Rajsko, even!" He stood and walked to the window facing the fields. "You can't be happy with what we've done to your town, then."

He stood with his back to her, and Sabina was thankful for the moment to compose herself as she processed his words. *Is he baiting me?* The Nazi's behavior thoroughly confused her. On the surface, he appeared completely different from the SS men she'd interacted with these past years. She struggled to come up with the right answer, and settled on "I was disappointed about having to move, but I'm glad we were only moved up the road. Many of my friends were relocated to the General Government."

"Yes, an unfortunate effect of the war." Sternhell turned around, his face serious. "But necessary, I'm afraid. Your father must have an important job if you were allowed to stay here."

"He works in the mines."

Sternhell nodded. "Crucial work, certainly."

Sabina didn't know how to respond, so she said nothing. Sternhell sat back down and observed her. For the first time, she felt conscious of herself, and she averted her eyes, focusing on the floor instead.

"You must be curious about what's going on here."

She looked up and was relieved to see the sparkle in his eyes had returned. "Well, there seems to be some construction going on."

He grinned at her understated observation. "I'm sure you noticed the equipment in your former classrooms as well." When Sabina nodded, he continued. "And those barracks behind the school."

"You're bringing prisoners into the camp?"

"We have some specialized work that needs to be done, and Rajsko is the perfect location. I'll help run the new camp, and I'm sure you and I will see more of each other."

"I don't know. I'm just a clerk in the archives."

He stood. "Does that mean you spend most of your time in a stuffy office?"

"Pretty much."

"Wouldn't you much prefer a walk to Rajsko every now and again?" He moved from behind his desk and walked toward the door. Sabina got up and followed him.

"If I could choose, yes."

He opened the door and held out his hand. "Well, then I'll have a

69

word with your boss. It was nice meeting you, Sabina. I look forward to seeing you soon."

She walked through the hallway, where the prisoners were still hard at work in the classrooms. As she descended the steps in front of the school, she wondered what had just happened. She'd never met a Nazi officer as open about what was going on as Sternhell. Whatever his intentions, he could be a valuable source of information—perhaps she'd found a way to help her father?

CHAPTER NINE

Felcia opened her eyes with a start. The women to either side of her didn't stir; light streamed in from the windows, indicating it was morning, although she had no sense of the exact time. They would be roused for roll call by the block elder and her henchwomen soon enough. She felt groggy, her senses still dulled from sleep. Then the sounds from outside filtered through. The revving of engines, voices of men calling out orders. The tailgate of a truck slammed open and her blood turned cold as dogs barked menacingly in the clearing in front of their block. She could almost hear dogs pacing the sandy ground, pulling on their leashes. More trucks arrived, the drivers shutting down the engines as they parked near her block.

Felcia was now wide awake. More women woke up to the commotion outside. Whispers went through the block as the voices outside grew louder. Felcia sat up, trying to make out the words of the men gathering outside. This wouldn't be a regular roll call. She looked across the aisle to meet Marzena's eyes. Her friend looked worried but composed as she sat in her bunk and gave an encouraging smile. Felcia was impressed by her friend's ability to stay calm as she gripped her shaking hands together.

The whispers had turned into a humming of voices, making it difficult to make out the words of the soldiers outside. Then a female voice thundered above all others. Felcia instantly recognized it, a sickening feeling of dread building in the pit of her stomach—Maria Mandl. Voices of the soldiers outside, and the women's whispers inside the block, died instantly.

"I want this done quickly and efficiently. We have a roll call to get to in less than two hours."

There was a slight delay between the tramping of boots outside and the door to their sleeping quarters bursting open.

"Everybody out, now! Get your clothes on and leave everything else behind!" Commands were barked in rapid succession by the SS guards streaming into the block. They banged the bunks with their batons, causing the few women who'd slept through the earlier events to wake up in a state of shock. Within seconds, the block had turned into a beehive. Women climbed from their bunks, those who hadn't slept fully clothed quickly dressing in their uniforms. Those not moving quickly enough were pulled from their bunks by guards keen to exert their authority.

"Hurry up! We don't have all morning, get moving!" One guard with a particularly raspy and loud voice passed by Felcia's bunk, pointing in the direction of the only door, on the other side of the block. Felcia grabbed Marzena's hand as she followed the slow moving procession of women shuffling through the aisle. With their bunks in the back of the block, they had to wait as the women closer to the door dressed. It gave them a moment to assess the situation.

"What do you think's going on?" Marzena spoke in a low voice, her eyes scanning the mass of panicked women, a number of them wailing from blows dished out by the guards as they looked to hurry them along. It made no sense—there wasn't enough room between the bunks for the women to move any quicker. It didn't matter to the guards as their batons indiscriminately rained down on the women passing by.

"It's too much force for roll call." It was all Felcia managed to mutter as she lowered her eyes to avoid attracting the attention of the guards. She braced herself for one of the blows but passed the next guard without incident. She kept her eyes on the heels of the woman ahead of her and slowly moved forward.

"Whatever it is, we need to stay together." Marzena's voice was determined, her grip tightening around Felcia's fingers.

They reached the door and stepped into the weak morning light from a sun still making its way up the sky, casting a long shadow over the clearing in front of the block. It made the situation even eerier as Felcia processed what she saw. The sandy area normally reserved for roll call was filled with the women of their block. Instead of lining up in their usual rows of twenty, they stood haphazardly between the numerous trucks parked across the sand. Guards surrounded them, some shouting at the women to enter the trucks while others appeared to wait for orders. The sound of eight hundred confused, scared women harshly lifted from their beds minutes ago was overwhelming, and Felcia felt the fear of the group rising in her throat. It was then that she felt a sharp squeeze of her hand. She looked up to find Marzena looking at her, her jaw clenched, eyes burning.

"We're not getting into those trucks." Her eyes shot to the empty doorway behind them; they had been the last to exit their block. "Come, quickly." She pulled on Felcia's hand.

"What are you doing?" Felcia's feet felt leaden, her fear paralyzing.

Marzena's tone harshened, her eyes spewing fire as she gibbered. "That's Mandl carrying out a selection. Look at the number of trucks. That's enough for our entire block. Get inside if you want to live." Another sharp tug. "Now!"

Her friend's words shook her from her stupor, and she allowed herself to be pulled back into the building. She glanced over her shoulder to see Mandl stepping forward and putting something to her mouth. As Felcia disappeared into the relative safety of the block's dim lighting, she heard a sharp whistle silence the hum of voices behind her.

Her heart pounded in her chest as they hurried past the empty bunks. Felcia was certain there were still guards inside, however it was completely silent but for the sound of their footsteps. Marzena didn't hesitate as she guided them to the back of the block and lifted a plank from the bottom bunk that served as a mattress.

"Get under there. The guards may come back for a final inspection."

Felcia did as she was told, a shudder coursing through her body as she lowered herself into the sticky mud. This was the collection point for all bodily fluids from the bunk's occupants, but she suppressed her disgust. Marzena was right; this was their only chance at survival. Her friend crawled into the tight space next to her and pulled the wooden plank back into place, shrouding them in darkness.

Mandl's grating voice carried in through the open door. Judging by the tone of the most powerful woman in the camp, it was impossible to miss the threat of her words, even if Felcia couldn't understand everything from her semi-submerged position. Mandl spoke for only a few seconds, but when she finished, the sound of barking dogs, screaming guards, and distraught women took away any doubt that something horrible was happening outside.

Felcia felt Marzena's breathing on her neck, and she took comfort from her friend's presence. Whatever happened next, at least they would be together. She didn't dare speak as she listened to the horrors unfolding outside. The guards' commands became harsher and shorter, the sound of batons striking, coupled with cries of agony, intensifying. Her heart bled for the women outside, some of whom she'd spoken to in the past few days, but there was nothing she could do.

After a few minutes in her uncomfortable position, Felcia's legs tingled. She tried stretching them, but there was hardly any space. She wriggled, suddenly feeling boxed in. Marzena must've sensed her discomfort, for she whispered almost inaudibly, "Slow and deep breaths. We can do this."

Felcia was about to answer when boots pounded up the short steps leading into their block. A moment later, voices broke the silence. This time, she could understand their words perfectly.

"All right, let's get this over with. I'm certain we didn't leave anyone behind." There was annoyance in the man's deep voice.

"Mandl's so paranoid. What does she think, that we can't empty a block full of Polish bitches?" The other guard, one with a distinctly higher-pitched voice, evidently shared his colleague's view. He grumbled some more as they continued down the block.

Felcia's throat went dry, yet she didn't dare swallow for fear of making a sound. The guards were quiet, but their heavy footsteps neared. Felcia could almost feel them reverberating through the sandy ground. She closed her eyes and slowed her breathing. All she heard were the approaching footsteps; Marzena's shallow breathing appeared to have stopped. *Is she holding her breath?* She could feel the presence of the guards passing by their bunk, and she instinctively stopped breathing. The guards stopped and one of them placed a boot on their bunk. Felcia almost jumped out of her skin, but she somehow managed to stay quiet. Her heartbeat was pounding in her ears, muffling the voices of the guards standing less than a meter away. She wished for her heart to slow down, fearful the SS men might hear it.

After what felt like an eternity, the guards walked away, the sound of their boots fading. The door closed with a loud clang, and Felcia let out a deep breath. She opened her eyes and heard Marzena exhale deeply. Surrounded by darkness, she suddenly felt as if the space was constricting, the walls closing in on her. She took a deep breath and almost gagged as the heavy, putrid air filled her nostrils. Felcia wanted nothing more than to escape her narrow confines.

"Marzena?"

"Yes."

"I feel like I can't breathe."

"I know." It was quiet for a moment, as if Marzena wasn't sure what her next words would be. Then, the gentle creaking of wood, and a sliver of light filtered into their hiding place. "Help me out a bit, would you? It's heavier than I thought."

They pushed the plank up and to the side, and both women crawled from the floor. Felcia's muscles ached, and she stood and stretched. Even though it felt good, she also realized they hadn't been in their uncomfortable position for that long. *I'm getting weaker.*

"Come, sit down." Marzena indicated for her to sit on the bunk. "Someone might come back; we don't want to make it too easy for them."

Felcia sat on the bunk opposite her friend. It was the first time the sounds from outside filtered back into her consciousness. Somehow, she had managed to filter out the unfolding mayhem. The sound of crying, desperate women was now mixed with the roaring of engines as they pulled away from the clearing.

"What do you think is happening?" Felcia asked, her eyes on the window above their head.

"Let's find out." To her surprise, Marzena stood and moved toward the dirty, stained windows. Felcia stayed where she was, closely watching her friend. Marzena squinted against the bright light, then a look of sorrow appeared on her face. "The yard is almost completely empty." She grimaced and sat back down. "They're loading up some bodies onto the last truck." Both women were quiet as the grim meaning of Marzena's words sunk in—some guards were too enthusiastic in their beatings, keen to impress their superiors. Many of the women in their block were only a beating away from death.

"What about the trucks?" Felcia dreaded the answer.

"They went up the road."

Marzena didn't need to say anything more. Felcia looked around the block, the silence of the empty bunks deafening. Her eyes stung at the memory of the eight hundred young women crowding the room less than an hour ago. They would be reduced to ashes darkening the skies before morning roll call had finished. She dropped her chin. Hot tears rolled down her cheeks as she surrendered to the overwhelming grief. She hardly knew them, yet they shared a bond, like everyone who passed through the gates of Birkenau. Felcia felt a hand on her knee. Marzena's face was shrouded in tears, and Felcia wiped her cheeks. Her friend's expression was soft, but her eyes were lined with determination.

"We had a lucky escape, Felcia. Let's not waste our good fortune." Felcia's mouth was dry, and all she could do was nod. Marzena's eyes went to the windows, then back to Felcia. "It can't be long until roll call. Let's wait for the other blocks to report outside and try to blend in."

Felcia eyed the door on the other side of the room with trepidation. All she wanted to do was return to her hiding space under the bunk, if it meant avoiding stepping outside into the danger. But Marzena was right; they would need to find a way back among the other women.

It took longer than expected for the first sounds of the waking camp to filter through the drafty walls. Felcia and Marzena had waited in silence; they were supposed to be dead. Surely they couldn't very well walk up to a different block and report with their prisoner numbers as if nothing had happened? Sooner or later, someone would find out.

The sounds of women's voices outside increased. Marzena stood up resolutely and held out her hand. "Shall we?"

Felcia took her hand. Her knees felt a little shaky, and she was grateful for Marzena's assistance as she helped her to her feet. They slowly walked toward the door, Felcia's nerves becoming more frayed with every step. Halfway through the block, she couldn't take it any longer. "How are we going to explain we're still alive? Do you intend to just join one of the other blocks and hope no one finds out?"

Marzena smiled weakly. "I don't know yet. But we can't stay in here. It won't take long until they start filling it with new arrivals. And we sure as hell won't survive if we're found in here when they do. I've been thinking about it just now, and while we're taking a massive chance by walking through that door, it sure beats the alternative. We don't have a choice." She continued toward the door without waiting for Felcia's response.

Frustration bubbled up inside Felcia. A flash of pain shot through her head, and she wanted to tell her friend she was wrong. That they could hide inside the block until nightfall at least. Take some more time to think things through. She was terrified of what she would find when they stepped outside. While it seemed safer to stay inside, Felcia realized the opposite was true. They needed to find a way to become useful again. She balled her fists and hurried after Marzena, who waited at the door.

Marzena looked at her when she reached the door, and Felcia nodded. They both took a deep breath before Marzena opened the door without hesitation. Bright sunlight momentarily blinded her, and for a second Felcia feared SS guards would be waiting for them outside. Instead, they were faced with the usual bustle of women moving from their blocks to the latrines as they prepared for the day. It felt like any other day, and the women hurried past without as much as a second look.

Encouraged, Felcia and Marzena stepped away from their block and merged into the stream of women. Felcia felt an odd sense of freedom, which was ridiculous considering the circumstances. Yet, she couldn't help but feel exhilarated with their escape from the block. "Where to next?" She spoke softly, her eyes scanning the women around them.

"Bathroom first. Then we should see if we can find some of the women working in the Sauna with us. Maybe they can arrange something."

Felcia was impressed. Marzena had worked in the Sauna for over a month and had made many friends with the women working there. It was as good a place to start as any. She walked on with an odd spring in her step.

Her optimism didn't last long. They were less than a hundred meters from their block when someone fell in line with them, walking much to close for a casual encounter.

"I thought my eyes were deceiving me for a moment." A woman's voice spoke airily, and Felcia turned. As soon as she did, it felt as if a brick were dropped in her stomach. It was their *Blockova*, the block elder in charge of their barracks. "But then I really saw you exit the block just now." Marzena let out a curse, and the woman flashed a toothy smile. "Why don't you come with me." It wasn't a question, and Felcia and Marzena followed the woman to the side of the thoroughfare, where she indicated for them to sit down on a crude wooden bench. She remained standing while they sat, forcing them to look up at her.

"Show me your left arm, both of you." Felcia felt sick as she held out her left arm, exposing the tattoo for inspection. Marzena did the same, and the woman smiled and nodded. "I don't know how you did this, but you survived Mandl's selection."

Felcia and Marzena remained quiet.

The woman waved dismissively. "You know, I don't even care how you did it. All I know is you've got a problem now, for they're bound to find you missing from their records once they've processed the women headed to the bakery now." Felcia flinched at the use of the crematoria's nickname, normally reserved for newcomers who didn't know what was happening in the buildings with the ever-billowing chimneys. "But you know, I can help you with that." The toothy smile again, more sinister than earlier.

Felcia chanced a glance at Marzena, who sat with her back defiantly straight, her face stern. Felcia clenched her jaw and forced herself to meet the Blockova's eyes.

"Very well, then. Here's my offer, and it's only valid for the next minute. I've got connections in the camp administration, and I can make your names disappear from the list of original prisoners of our block." She paused, her eyes shooting between Marzena and Felcia. "In return, you'll provide me with half of your daily food rations for the rest of your days at the camp." Felcia felt as if she'd been winded. She was about to open her mouth when the woman continued. "And you'll be assigned my assistants, forfeiting whatever jobs you're holding now."

Shock overwhelmed Felcia, and it must've shown, for the woman grinned. "I'll give you a minute to consider. Keep in mind that if you reject my proposal, you probably won't last until sunset. The camp administration can be very efficient. Especially when they're given some direction." She turned and took a few steps from them, casually whistling as she watched the stream of women making for the latrines.

Felcia turned to Marzena, who remained still as a statue.

"You seem unconcerned. She basically handed us a slow death sentence."

Marzena looked at her and slowly nodded. "Yes. But she didn't. And she's right; we have no choice but to accept her terrible terms." She put her hand on Felcia's shoulder and gave her a warm smile. "At the very least, this is a chance to survive. We don't know what tomorrow brings, but at least we've now got a chance to make it another day. And another."

Despite Felcia's misgivings about the Blockova, she couldn't deny she had offered them a solution to their most pressing problem. Even if it came with strings attached. The Blockova returned and gave them a questioning look. "I take it we have an agreement?"

Felcia and Marzena stole a quick glance at each other, then both turned to the woman and nodded. *Somewhere along the way, I'll have to cut those strings.*

Chapter Ten

I t had been three days since Felcia and Marzena had accepted the
Blockova's offer. Once they did, the woman's demeanor had drasti-
cally changed. She introduced herself as Tanya, and she was Polish, just
like them. Felcia wondered what Tanya had done to work her way up to
the coveted position of block elder as a Pole, never mind survive the
recent purge, but kept her questions to herself.

Tanya explained she was pleased to find them alive but hadn't asked
them how they had survived the block clearing. Felcia was certain it
wouldn't take long for the woman to probe them about it. For now, all
that mattered was that Tanya had been true to her word. When they
reported for morning roll call, the three had lined up where only the
evening before, eight hundred women had stood. The guard inspecting
the numbers hadn't as much as batted an eye when Tanya reported it
was just the three of them.

When they returned to the block, Tanya informed them they would
be part of the block's *Stubendienst*—responsible for the block's cleanli-
ness and handing out assignments to new inhabitants. Additionally, and
perhaps more intimidating a task, they would need to make sure all
women in the block reported promptly for roll call every morning and
evening. Felcia had seen the efforts some of the prisoners went through

to avoid having to attend roll call and work, witnessing the women of the Stubendienst drag the poor women from the block. More often than not, those protesting in the morning wouldn't return in the evening. Felcia dreaded having to convince these poor wretches to rise and go to work.

"It'll be hard at first, but I'm sure we'll get the hang of it." Marzena stood next to their bunk, which was located in a room separated from the main quarters. It was odd not to sleep in the crowded room anymore, but the block elder and her assistants had their own dwellings in the front of the block. Although the bunks were as uncomfortable as the ones in the main room, they had a semblance of privacy here. Felcia knew it was a luxury that came with obvious strings, as it added to the feeling of distance between them and the regular population. The new women had arrived the day prior, and she had already felt their envious glances. She couldn't blame them—she had felt the same when she was in their position.

"We'll stick together. Make sure we're never alone. We need to watch each other's back." Felcia heard the tremble in her voice but didn't care.

Marzena gave her a comforting look. "We're not going to be like the others. We'll help the women in our block. As long as they follow the rules, we'll look out for them, okay?"

"And if they don't?"

Her friend's face hardened. "Then we'll make it clear what happens to those who fall out of line. But we'll warn them first, with words. And if they won't listen, they'll find out soon enough."

Marzena's words did little to calm Felcia's anxiety, but she forced a smile. She would've been dead if she hadn't accepted her new role.

Tanya entered the room without knocking. "Ready to start the day? I need you to make sure the new arrivals understand they need to hurry and get to roll call in time. Yesterday afternoon was a disaster."

Newcomers didn't understand just how poorly the SS responded to tardiness. It wasn't until a number of the women were pulled from the crowd and beaten to death that they started paying attention. "I'd like to think they got the message yesterday."

The sound of voices and women moving about in the main room

was loud: she had become used to sharing her small room with the six women of the Stubendienst. The main room, housing some eight hundred women, had always been unruly. She just hadn't noticed when she lived in the middle of it. She took a deep breath and stepped inside.

"Listen up!" Tanya banged her baton against a metal pipe between the wooden bunks. That, combined with her loud voice, got the attention of the women, and a hush fell over the room. Felcia felt very conscious of her position as she stood next to Tanya, feeling hundreds of eyes turned in her direction. Tanya appeared unmoved as she spoke confidently. "For those of you who didn't get the message yesterday, being late to roll call is not an option. For any of us, but especially for me as the block elder. I want everybody out of the block within ten minutes. If you stay behind, it's at your own risk." She paused, her eyes roaming the women. "You can only stay behind if you're unable to move, and with permission from one of the Stubendienst." Tanya casually indicated the women standing by her side. "Now, move!"

There was only a slight delay as the women processed Tanya's words. Then they continued getting dressed, some hurrying to the front of the block in search of water; there was no running water today. There hardly ever was.

Soon, the first women left the block. Felcia stood near the door, pleased to see the room emptying quickly. At this pace, they should make it to roll call in time. She scanned the room, and she was dismayed to find a figure lying motionless in a bunk about halfway down the aisle. She sighed and moved against the stream, feeling a little annoyed at the woman. *Wasn't Tanya clear enough?*

She reached the bunk and looked down. The woman lay with her back to her and didn't move. "Get up. You need to get to roll call." There was no response, and Felcia poked the woman in the back. "What's wrong with you?"

This time, the woman stirred and turned to face Felcia. "Everything hurts. And I'm so thirsty," she croaked—her face ashen, eyes red. Felcia recognized the look—many of the women who arrived in the camp struggled to accept their new reality, falling into a stupor. Even though she felt sympathy, she couldn't allow the woman to stay in her bunk like this. She clenched her jaw and hardened her voice.

"If you don't get out of bed, you'll be dead before noon."

The woman's eyes went wide. "I can't. I can't move. My legs hurt. My head is pounding."

"Where do you think you are? We're all hurting. Look at the women around you. How do you think they're feeling?"

"I haven't eaten since I arrived."

"None of us have!" Felcia's raised her voice, drawing the attention of a few women passing, but didn't care. "But if you want to eat, you need to go to roll call. And then you need to work. Only prisoners considered *useful* get to eat." She thought of the sorry excuse for food they received each day, her paltry portion of watery soup now halved. She focused her attention back on the woman in the bunk—she had no idea what real hunger was. Not yet, anyway. Felcia wasn't going to let this woman give up so easily.

"Let me tell you what happens if you stay in your bunk." Felcia crouched down, their faces level. "The guards will come in and inspect the block once we've reported the numbers out at roll call. Anyone still in their bunk without a valid excuse will be taken by the guards."

"But I have a valid excuse." The woman's voice was weak, her determination wavering.

Felcia shook her head. "There's never a valid excuse."

"But they'll take me to the infirmary, at least."

"Maybe. But I doubt it. You don't look sick to me. Tired and scared, yes. But not sick." Felcia's voice softened. "The guards will take you to the back of the camp. You've seen the buildings with the ever-smoking chimneys, haven't you?" The woman nodded, her face blank. *She really hasn't come to terms with her situation yet.* "You don't want to be sent there." She held out her hand. "Come with me."

There was indecision in the woman's eyes and Felcia took her hand, gently forcing her from her bunk. To her relief, the woman got up. The rest of the block was almost empty, but for a few of the Stubendienst. Felcia supported the woman as they slowly moved toward the door.

"You need to appear strong, okay?" Felcia said as they stepped into the morning air, the rest of the women already lined up in front of the block. To their left and right the last women of the other blocks moved into their positions for roll call. She found a spot in the back of one of the lines. "Stay in this line, and don't move. Keep your head down." As she let go of the woman, she heard her grunt, and the woman collapsed onto the ground. Felcia cursed silently as she crouched down to help the woman up.

It was already too late. As she tried to convince the woman to get up, she heard the crunching of sand and gravel.

"What's going on here?" The voice was terse and authoritative. Felcia looked up to find a guard standing next to her. With effort, she pulled the woman to her feet.

"She was feeling a little lightheaded, but she's okay now." Felcia spoke with more confidence than she felt. "Right?" She looked into the woman's glassy eyes, trying to channel to her the strength she so desperately needed. She couldn't appear weak before the guard. To her relief, the woman nodded.

"Yes, I'm ... I'm all right."

The guard looked at the woman suspiciously and eyed her for a few seconds. Then he shrugged and returned to the front of the group. Felcia let out a sigh of relief and looked at the woman. "I'm going to let go of you. Promise me you won't fall down again."

The woman looked more determined, her eyes slightly more focused. "I won't."

Felcia let go and stepped away, holding her breath. The woman remained where she was, albeit on shaky legs. That was enough for now. Felcia turned around to find her place in line behind the woman. As she looked to the front of the group of women, her heart froze.

At the front, leading roll call, stood Maria Mandl. And she was looking right at Felcia. Even from a distance, Felcia could feel the Lagerführerin's cold, calculating eyes boring into her.

Mandl's eyes narrowed further, then she looked away, her attention focused on one of the guards near the front. Felcia's body relaxed as she exhaled deeply. Soon, guards moved up and down the ranks, counting the women and calling out their numbers. As the odd normality of roll call took over, Felcia's trepidation slowly faded. She couldn't help but glance toward Mandl a few times. Had she attracted the Lagerführerin's attention because she helped the woman in her block, or was there more to it?

The answer came an hour later. Roll call had passed without any notable incidents. About a dozen women had collapsed and had been dragged away by guards. As horrible as that was, Felcia had become used to it. The prisoner count had only been repeated twice before Mandl was satisfied, which was better than average. Most importantly, Mandl had been content to have the women stand at attention. More often than not, the sadistic commander of the women's camp would come up with creative ways to torture them while they were counted. Felcia vividly remembered one of the first roll calls she attended, where she sat on her knees while holding arms above her head for two hours straight. More than fifty women had collapsed or had been beaten to death by Mandl and her assistants when their arms failed them.

The first rows of women of the surrounding blocks started to move away from roll call as guards started barking orders. The women moved quickly, anxious to collect their mugs of watery coffee and a slice of toast before heading out for work. Felcia's eyes went to the woman in front of her, who had somehow managed to stay on her feet for the entire time. *She found strength somewhere, after all.* Felcia would have a quick word with Tanya about the woman's assignment. It would be best if she could regain her strength indoors. *The sewing workshop, perhaps?* Felcia allowed herself a modest smile: Marzena had been right. They could use their positions to do good after all.

The last women of the adjoining blocks moved away, and Felcia felt restless as no one in the rows around her moved.

A familiar voice sounded from the front. "I was very disappointed with your timekeeping yesterday. This block was a disgrace." Felcia's skin crawled, and she looked up to confirm what she already knew. Maria Mandl stood in front of the group, casually twirling her whip while her eyes roamed the rows of women. Felcia glanced at the faces of the women around her. Most looked on with neutral expressions, some curiously, and one or two hiding signs of fear.

"And to make things worse, I noticed a number of you appeared a little distant during this morning's roll call as well. This won't do." Mandl uncurled her whip, gently stroking the handle. Felcia averted her eyes, focusing on the ground in front of her. "So, I think it's only appropriate we partake in a bit of sport this morning, yes?"

Without waiting for a reply, Mandl snapped her fingers, and the guards that had idly surrounded the women sprang into action and dragged women from the lines. At first glance, it appeared to be at random, but as the women were hauled toward the front—where Mandl stood waiting—it was clear they had picked the frailest of the group.

As one of the guards came stomping down the lines toward her, Felcia held her breath. She was in decent shape, but there were no guarantees. Anything could trigger the guards: a wrong glance, a trembling hand, or simple bad luck. Keeping her eyes firmly focused on the ground, she prayed she wouldn't be picked.

"You. Come with me." The command was harsh, the guard's voice like ice. Felcia's heart skipped a beat as the woman in front of her moved out of the line. She felt a stab of sympathy but kept her head down. There was nothing she could do for the woman.

Then she felt a tap on her shoulder.

"You too. Let's go."

Aghast and struggling to believe what was happening, Felcia looked up. The guard stood with the woman she had helped, impatience in his eyes.

"Are you deaf?" He patted the baton on his belt, and Felcia took two steps toward the guard. He roughly grabbed her by the arm and pulled her along. As in a daze, Felcia let herself be escorted to the front, the SS woman's gaze on her. Tears welled up in her eyes as she was placed among some of the weakest women in her block. About a hundred women stood around her. She searched for Marzena, but was unable to make out her face in the crowd.

Felcia didn't get any more time to think about her situation as Mandl cracked her whip on the ground, the sound shocking her back to the present.

"This will do." Murder in the three simple words. "Since you're all new to the camp, it'll be good to see how useful you are. We have no use for weaklings here." She pointed at a cordon of guards standing about the length of two tennis courts away. "You'll run there and once you reach them, you'll return back here. Simple, no?" Before any of the women could respond, Mandl cracked her whip over the back of one of the women standing closest to her. As the woman collapsed with an ear-piercing shriek, Mandl yelled, "Go!" She raised her whip again, but Felcia only heard the crack as she sprinted off toward the guards in the distance. She vaguely heard another wail as Mandl no doubt struck a straggler, but then she only heard her own labored breathing, her heart pounding in her ears, the wind in her face. She was among the first to reach the guards, and as she turned around, she saw more than three-quarters of the women were barely jogging across the course. With gritted teeth, the muscles in her legs burning, somehow she found strength in sheer determination. Felcia was among the first ten women to return to where Mandl was waiting. The two women who had been struck by the whip lay motionless on the ground, soft grunts of pain escaping their lips. Their shirts were torn, their backs bloody from the beating Mandl had inflicted in the short time it had taken Felcia to cover the distance to the guards and back. Nausea built in the back of her throat; emptying the meager contents of her stomach in front of Mandl was a death sentence. Felcia bent forward and rested her hands on her knees as she struggled to regain her breath.

Mandl ignored Felcia and the women standing alongside her. Her eyes were focused on the women struggling back from the other side. Another twenty women crossed the finish line and were allowed to join Felcia's group. Then, Mandl stepped forward as the remainder walked and limped back. Some supported each other, their faces red from exertion. Mandl stood with her whip, and as the women approached, she pointed at every single one of them.

"To the right. Over there. To the wall, come on, hurry."

The exhausted women did what they were told, most collapsing on the ground next to the block Mandl pointed them to. A few brave women remained standing, even if it meant using their final bit of strength to do so.

When the last women returned, the initial group of a hundred was split unevenly. Standing near the block were seventy women in all states of exhaustion. A few had even passed out on the ground. Opposite them stood Felcia's group, a few meters from the fortunate women who weren't picked but stood watching in horror.

"Well, well. I didn't have high expectations, but this is pathetic." Mandl spoke to the group of seventy, scorn dripping from her voice. "I'll give you one more chance to prove you're worthy of living and working in the camp."

Felcia picked up on the threat, but judging from the blank, exhausted looks of the women, very few of them did. A shiver ran down her spine as she took a few deep breaths. *Am I getting away this easily?*

It was as if Mandl had heard her thoughts, for the Lagerführerin spun around in her direction. "And you'll show them how it's done, one more time!" Her voice was almost giddy, and Felcia suppressed a look of disdain.

Without warning, Mandl stepped toward the woman closest to her, roaring, "Run!"

The poor woman almost tripped over her own feet as she bolted from the Lagerführerin. Without another thought, Felcia joined her. This time, her lungs were burning halfway down the first lap. A sharp pain in her chest almost knocked her from her feet, but she took a deep breath and continued on. The guards appeared farther away than on her first run, and as she reached them and turned around, she felt her left calf cramp up. The sharp pain almost immobilized her, but she stretched her leg as she fought the blinding pain. She hopped forward, praying her right leg would hold. Sweat poured down her face, and her heart beat against her ribs so hard she thought it would burst from her chest any minute. Women passed her on both sides, and she felt herself falling further behind with every step. Nevertheless, she couldn't give up. The cramp was spreading to her hamstring, but she was still thirty meters from Mandl. More women crossed the finish line separating life and death.

Fifteen meters to go, and Felcia felt her strength waning, her vision clouded by tears as the pain became unbearable. She considered letting go, collapsing onto the ground and accepting her fate. She looked in the direction of the women lined up in front of their block. She was still hobbling forward when she saw a familiar face—Marzena. Her face was lined with determination, her eyes burning. She raised her fist, silently mouthing, "Come on!"

All thoughts of surrendering to her pain vanished. Felcia bit her lip hard and pushed her aching legs forward for the final meters. She didn't look up as she passed Mandl, expecting to hear the dreaded words any moment.

As she turned her head back, she saw Mandl move forward, her arm outstretched. This time, only ten women had made it—bodies were strewn across the makeshift track. At least twenty women had collapsed on the second try. Some still moved, their arms and legs twitching, but most lay motionless on the ground.

Was Mandl going to make them run until they all collapsed? Felcia wasn't sure how many more laps she could survive. Her legs were burning, the pressure in her chest constricting her breathing. She heard herself wheezing, and she realized she was having trouble breathing. *Is this what a heart attack feels like?*

She was vaguely aware of Mandl's voice in the background and forced herself to focus.

"We have no use for you in the women's camp. We have a truck coming in a few minutes."

When the truck arrived, Felcia watched the woman from earlier board it, sorrow flooding her heart. As Mandl's voice boomed for them to report to their work details, Felcia's eyes remained on the truck rolling away. It would turn left as it exited the women's camp—a short drive to the red-brick buildings with chimneys that never stopped billowing smoke.

CHAPTER ELEVEN

The next weeks of life in the camp passed with no big incidents. Felcia settled into her role as part of Tanya's Stubendienst. After Mandl's murderous example, the newcomers received the message loud and clear. It wasn't lost on many of the women that Felcia had been selected by the Lagerführerin as well. While Felcia was certain she had attracted Mandl's attention somehow, it meant the women of the block treated her with a newfound, and unexpected, level of respect. Mandl's trial had inadvertently made Felcia's job easier. Of course, in a block of eight hundred women, there were always problems, and Felcia spent most of the early mornings convincing a number of women to attend roll call. Only occasionally did she budge and allow someone to report to the infirmary, but not without warning them of the dangers of doing so. It was common knowledge that most women who reported to the camp hospital were sent to Block 25 instead of being treated. Felcia no longer censored her words, which was usually enough for even the most determined women to back down.

She made a quick final round through the block, checking the bunks to make sure all the women had made their way outside to roll call. When she was satisfied, she turned to the exit, where the bright

June sunlight streamed in. It had taken longer than usual, but summer had finally arrived.

Felcia's mood darkened the moment she stepped outside. Most of the women already stood lined up in the open space between the barracks. The sight at the front of the roll call area froze the blood in her veins. A crude wooden gallows had been erected. Five ropes swung almost innocently in the gentle summer breeze.

Taking her place in line, she looked up to find Marzena glancing over from a spot to her right. Her friend's face reflected the same fear gripping Felcia's heart, but Marzena still managed an encouraging, somewhat comforting smile. Felcia returned the gesture before turning her face to the ground, avoiding the terrible view.

Felcia had never witnessed a planned execution.

A shrill whistle silenced the few murmurs in the roll call area. Felcia raised her chin and focused her eyes on the back of the head in front of her. She did her best to avoid looking farther, but when the familiar voice of Lagerführerin Mandl boomed across the square, her attention was drawn back to the morbid structure.

"We'll carry out the roll call count as usual, and then I have a few announcements." Mandl stood atop the gallows, elevated a few meters above the prisoners. Felcia shuddered at the sight. The Lagerführerin's eyes drifted over the crowd as the guards started moving between the rows of women, counting every soul present. Felcia shifted her weight from one leg to the other. A trickle of sweat ran down her spine. She hardly noticed the guards passing by as she kept her focus on the woman ahead of her.

There hadn't been any reports of dissent recently. As part of the Stubendienst, Felcia was normally one of the first to hear about any problems in the camp. But things could change overnight. At the front, Mandl was inspecting the nooses, her back to the terrified prisoners.

Most of the guards had returned to the front, where they reported their counts to Margot Dreschel, Maria Mandl's second-in-command. The tall woman jotted down the numbers on a clipboard. When the last guard turned back toward the group, Dreschel addressed Mandl, who nodded. The roll call area had never been this silent, the prospect of multiple hangings paralyzing the women. Mandl inspected the last noose, making a point of firmly tugging it before turning back to the prisoners.

"I'm pleased we got the count done so quickly, so we can move on to more important matters." Mandl rubbed her hands together. For someone whose voice normally teetered on the edge of anger, the calmness of her tone was disconcerting. She was clearly looking forward to the proceedings as she casually waved toward the nooses to her right. "I wish I could say everything was going as well as this roll call, but unfortunately, I've received reports of a plan to escape."

A tremor of shock went through the crowd as Mandl paused to let the words sink in. Felcia's eyes were drawn to the nooses.

"As you can imagine, any such attempt would reflect badly on me." Mandl paused as she stroked the whip curled on her belt. "Now, I'm going to give the women involved in this escape sixty seconds to turn themselves in. Come forward now, and we won't have to use these." She pointed at the nooses, and a collective gasp went through the crowd. Felcia was as puzzled by the Lagerführerin's words as any of the other women. "Not today, anyway. If you come forward, you'll be moved to the penal colony." She placed her hands on her hips and signaled toward one of the female guards standing on the ground. The woman started counting out loud.

"One ... Two ... Three."

There was no movement in the crowd. Stepping forward was a death sentence.

"Fifteen ... Sixteen."

Felcia's eyes shot through the crowd.

"Thirty-six ...Thirty-seven." As the guard continued her steady count, her colleagues started moving between the ranks of prisoners, casting stern glances at the few women daring to meet their gaze. Felcia averted her eyes to the ground, studying her feet. From the corners of her eyes she could see the guards approaching, walking purposefully.

"Fifty-eight ... Fifty-nine ... Sixty."

Silence returned to the roll call area, but for the muffled sounds of the guards' boots moving between the prisoners' ranks. Felcia's heart pounded in her ears, every breath amplified as she clasped her shaking hands behind her back.

Maria Mandl let out a deep sigh. "This is disappointing, but not unexpected. I suppose my generous offer wasn't the right approach to deal with this." Felcia sucked in a breath as Mandl turned toward Margot Dreschel. "Do it."

Dreschel sprang into action and moved into the crowd, followed by two other guards. She didn't make it as far as the second row before pulling a girl no older than fourteen from the crowd. Terrified, the young woman collapsed to the ground. A nearby woman wailed and broke from the lineup, clasping onto the girl. Dreschel stepped back and smiled, her buck teeth sticking out. She signaled at the guards, who grabbed both women, hauling them toward the gallows.

Felcia felt sick and swallowed down the urge to throw up. Dreschel moved farther down the line as the two women were forced up the steps toward the nooses. Mandl stood by passively with her arms crossed in front of her chest. It was unlike the Lagerführerin not to get involved.

Meanwhile, Dreschel had selected another woman. This time, the woman came in silence, almost apathetically.

On the gallows, the guards had tightened the nooses around the first two women's necks. To prevent them from moving, each was held firmly in place by a guard. The women stood on small stools, shaking and crying. The younger reached for the other woman's hand, but it was brutally swatted away by a guard. At that point, Mandl moved toward them and said something Felcia couldn't make out. With a look of disbelief, the older woman cautiously reached for the girl's hand. This time, their hands were allowed to intertwine.

Dreschel was now only a few paces away. Felcia's ears were burning, the back of her shirt soaked. Dreschel pointed at a woman a few meters ahead of her. The woman's howl of terror pierced Felcia's bones and she closed her eyes. *Please, not me. Let her move past me, dear God.* She bowed her head as if to make herself invisible, silently praying.

"You." Dreschel's voice was right next to her ear, and Felcia let out a deep sigh. She opened her eyes in resignation, ready to step from the line. As she did, she was relieved to face Dreschel's back, as the guard was talking to someone in the opposite row. Her relief instantly turned to horror when she identified the woman Dreschel had picked. Marzena.

Time slowed down as Felcia watched her friend step gracefully from her row. She glanced beyond Dreschel, her eyes connecting with Felcia's. Despite her situation, she found the strength to give Felcia an almost imperceptible nod. Tears welled up in Felcia's eyes, but she blinked hard and tried to match her friend's courage.

Then Marzena was roughly pulled toward the gallows. The silent tears streaming down Felcia's face blurred her vision. She didn't care if anyone noticed. The only thing that mattered now was that she was with her best friend as she was led up the stairs at the front of the roll call area.

As Marzena reached the top of the structure, she walked slowly, her body rigidly straight, her head held high. She ignored Mandl as she stepped onto the small stool, holding out her neck. The guard roughly pulled her head back while he tightened the noose. Marzena didn't flinch, retaining her defiance. The four other women on the platform handled their situations in very different ways. The two women holding hands had stopped crying, silently facing each other. Next to them, the third woman was threshing about, fighting the guard. The prisoner next to Marzena looked resigned to her fate.

Felcia clenched her jaw as Marzena met her eyes. Despite the distance between them, it was as if Marzena was transferring her strength to her. Their eyes locked, and Felcia knew they wouldn't let go until the very last moment.

Mandl's voice boomed across the yard, but the words didn't register. Felcia could see the Lagerführerin kicking the stools from underneath the first two women's feet. Her attention was momentarily drawn to the macabre spectacle playing out only a few meters from Marzena. Even as the life was squeezed from them, the women held onto each other's hands.

Mandl kicked the next stool, silencing the fighting woman. Felcia quickly returned her gaze to her best friend. Despite the horrors unfolding next to her, she somehow managed to retain her calm composure. Felcia's throat constricted as she saw the woman next to Marzena drop. It wouldn't be much longer now.

Mandl moved in front of Marzena and, without delay, kicked the stool from underneath her. Felcia didn't look away, and when the Lagerführerin stepped aside, her friend's eyes remained locked on her. Her body remained rigid, not giving her executioners the satisfaction of seeing her struggle. Despite her brave fight, the life quickly faded from her bright eyes. Her face turned red, then a darker shade of blue. Finally, her body convulsed as she surrendered to the inevitable, the fire in her eyes forever extinguished.

Felcia stood in a daze, feeling as if she were hovering above her own body. Her heart felt as if the life had been squeezed from her instead, a part of her dying with Marzena. Her head spun as she struggled to accept what she had just witnessed. But her friend's lifeless body on the end of a rope confirmed her fate. All she wanted to do was curl up in a corner. There would be no such reprieve, as Mandl turned back to them.

"I trust this serves as ample warning for anyone thinking of escaping." The Lagerführerin's voice had returned to normal. Business as usual. "There's one small matter before you can be on your way to your regular work details." One of the guards handed her a piece of paper. "If your number is called out, step forward and report to the front."

Mandl started reading out the numbers in quick succession. Despite the empty, numbing feeling spreading through her body, Felcia listened. There was no time to feel sorry for herself. There would be time to grieve for her friend tonight, in her bunk. She needed to focus on her own survival now.

A familiar combination of numbers struck Felcia as a hammer blow. Slowly, she stepped out of the line, her legs heavy as she passed the rows of women on her way forward.

Mandl didn't look up as Felcia passed her and joined the group of about two dozen women to her right. The guard checked the tattoo on her arm, which was almost comical. No prisoner in their right mind would step forward if they weren't absolutely certain their number was called out.

Once again, Felcia found herself singled out. Hundreds of women from her block stood opposite her, most keeping their gazes on the sandy ground. A few scanned the faces of those gathered alongside Felcia.

When Mandl finished, some thirty women had been picked from

the main population. Mandl looked at the guard, who nodded. "They're all here."

"Perfect," she offered before she turned to the rows of women facing them. "You will report to your work details as usual now." She dismissed them with a casual wave of the hand. Then she turned to Felcia's group.

"Listen up." Mandl's voice demanded her attention, and she reluctantly looked up to the Lagerführerin's position on the gallows. "You will return to your block and collect any belongings you may have. I want you back here in fifteen minutes." Mandl spoke quickly, her tone as if the women were a terrible inconvenience. "Quickly now."

Twenty minutes later, Felcia sat in the open bed of a truck. It slowly pulled away from their block, bouncing down the unpaved road. They passed the other blocks as they drove toward the exit of the women's camp.

Felcia clasped a small bag containing some rudimentary toiletries. She treasured her well-worn toothbrush above everything else. She looked at the women on the wooden benches across from her—each as scared as she felt. *Where are they taking us?*

When Mandl sent them to pack their things, Felcia racked her brain thinking of what she might have done to be sent away from her block. It had come up blank.

The truck slowed down and reached the main gate of the women's camp. Felcia held her breath as the guards opened the barrier. Would they turn left, toward the crematoria? She swallowed hard. Her eyes stung at the thought of her life ending in the next few hours.

The truck's engine roared and they slowly started moving. An instant later she felt them turning. She closed her eyes and let out a deep breath. They had turned right, away from the black clouds in the back of the camp.

Rolling along the camp's main thoroughfare that split the women's and men's camps, Felcia was even more confused. The camp's main gatehouse loomed ahead of them. They were headed out of the camp. *Where are we going?*

PART II

Rajsko, Poland
July 1943

Chapter Twelve

Sabina approached the camp and felt her palms dampen. She clutched the folder in her left hand a bit tighter. It had been two weeks since her first visit and the construction chaos had vanished. An air of calm greeted her as she approached the two guards idling by the road turning into the camp. Their eyes were focused on her, and she made a conscious effort to keep her pace steady, doing her best to hide her raging nerves. *Relax, you're allowed to be here. The papers in your hands are proof of that.*

She reached the guards, and one took a step toward her, the hint of a smile on his face.

"It's not often we have visitors here. What's your business?" His tone was relaxed, his eyes scanning her face before focusing on the large folder in her hand. "Delivering something?"

"These are from the municipal registry in town. I was told to deliver them to Hauptsturmführer Sternhell without delay." The words came out easier than she'd expected. The guard's face showed recognition at her mention of Sternhell, which further emboldened her. She held out the folder. "Do you need to inspect the contents, or am I allowed to pass through?"

The man shook his head and stepped aside. "Do you know where to find Herr Hauptsturmführer?"

"His office is still in the old school building?"

The guard turned around and pointed at the building closest to them. "Yes, through the front door and to the left, all the way at the end of the hallway."

Sabina thanked him and walked on, briefly acknowledging the other guard, who gave her a curt nod. After a few seconds, she wiped her clammy hands on her skirt. That was easier than expected.

The school building was only ten meters from the entrance, at the front of the camp. Directly opposite the school building, across a gravel road, were a collection of greenhouses, with what appeared to be a large collection of beehives next to them. There was something *odd* about the buildings. Farther into the camp she noticed five prisoner barracks surrounded by a three-meter-high barbed wire fence. Instantly, Sabina realized what had been odd about the rest of the camp: the barracks were the only buildings fenced off by barbed wire.

She approached the entrance to the school building, where she had to wait for a group of women wearing prisoner uniforms to exit. The women looked in decent shape, their uniforms clean and new. One of them made eye contact and offered a weak smile, which Sabina returned. The woman didn't resemble anything like the malnourished walking skeletons she sometimes saw pass through town on their way to the mines or factories surrounding the camp. This woman looked well kept and well fed. It was an odd sight, and the woman's smile remained on Sabina's mind as she entered the hallway.

It was quiet, with only a couple of women wearing white coats passing her as she headed toward Hauptsturmführer Sternhell's office. The doors lining the hallway were closed, but women in lab coats were working behind the windows. She was keen to know what was happening in the former classrooms, but suppressed her curiosity as she neared the open door to Sternhell's office. The Hauptsturmführer was sitting behind his desk, his head down in paperwork. Sabina softly rapped her knuckles on the open door as she took a step into the office.

"Ah, Sabina, wasn't it?" Sternhell had looked up from his papers, a twinkle in his eyes. "Come in, come in. I was expecting someone from town, but I could only hope it would be you." He stood and pointed toward the chair opposite him, sitting down only after she did. Despite the awkwardness of the situation, Sabina couldn't help but appreciate the German officer's manners. She placed the large folder on his desk and folded her hands on her lap.

"Would you like me to wait while you go through the papers? I'm afraid my boss didn't give me any instructions."

He opened the folder and took out the papers, humming and nodding. Sabina waited patiently as he rapidly tore through the folder's contents, frowning, and occasionally signing something. Then he looked up as if sensing her eyes on him. He held up a hand.

"I'm sorry, what was that?"

She smiled. "Would you like me to wait?"

"Ah yes, please." He put the papers aside. "It all looks in order. I apologize, I'm a little busy today. Lots of things happening at the camp. Lots of new prisoners coming in these days."

Sabina remembered the women leaving the building earlier. They had to be part of the new arrivals. "I couldn't help but notice there are a lot of women in the camp." The words tumbled from her mouth before she could stop herself.

He faced her with an odd expression, and for a moment Sabina feared she had misunderstood his good manners and friendly tone. He was still a Nazi, after all. Then his expression changed, a smile forming. "Didn't I tell you last time you were here?"

"Just that this would be some sort of specialized camp."

He looked surprised, but recovered quickly enough. "That's right. We had prisoners come in from Birkenau to work the fields every day. Someone higher up decided that wasn't the best use of labor, and that's why those barracks behind the school were built. I'm sure you've seen those, yes?" When Sabina nodded, he continued. "And then someone, probably the same person, thought it would be a good idea to expand the farming operations a bit more, while we're at it."

"The greenhouses and apiary."

He smiled. "Exactly. And to make sure there would be as few problems as possible, we decided Rajsko would be a women's camp." He stretched up a little taller and puffed his chest out. "Along with Dr.

Caesar, I intend to make it one of the most productive camps in the Reich—we've got big plans."

It was clear something far more interesting than beekeeping or crop tilling was going on in the classrooms. Sabina had opened her mouth to ask when there was a knock at the door. A guard stood in the door opening, his face flushed.

"Sir, I apologize for interrupting you, but Dr. Caesar requests your immediate presence near the prisoner barracks." His eyes flashed to Sabina, quickly inspecting her before returning his attention to Sternhell. "If you would follow me, sir."

"Care to tell me what it's about?" Sternhell responded calmly, not making any moves for the door.

"Dr. Caesar didn't share, just that I needed to fetch you immediately." The guard sounded uncertain, not sure how hard he could press the Hauptsturmführer.

"Very well." Sternhell stood and pushed his chair under his desk. "Let me just finish up this paperwork." Sensing the guards discomfort, he added, "You can wait in the hallway. I'll be with you in a minute." The guard reluctantly stepped outside, leaving the door open.

Sternhell scanned the papers one more time, put them back into the folder and handed them to Sabina. "I suppose we'll need to continue our conversation at a later stage. It was nice to see you again, Sabina." He accompanied her out of his office, locking the door behind them.

Sensing an opportunity, Sabina gathered her nerves. "Could I use the bathroom before heading back to Oświęcim?"

The guard looked annoyed, but Sternhell seemed unperturbed. "Of course. I suppose you'll be able to find your own way out?"

"If you haven't changed the location of the bathrooms, I should be okay." *It worked!*

"Go ahead. I'm sure I'll see you soon." He pointed at the familiar door of the girls bathroom a few doors down. With that, the Hauptsturmführer and guard hurried on toward the exit.

Sabina watched them leave before opening the door to the bathroom. Nothing had changed since she had last visited the room almost five years ago. Memories of her careless youth flooded back as she opened a faucet, letting the water run for a moment before splashing her face. *Now what?* Maybe she should just leave and see if she could get more information from Sternhell the next time she was here? Then she thought of her father —how disappointed he would be if she came back without any useful information. Something was going on in her old classrooms. She took a deep breath, opened the door, and stepped back into the deserted hallway.

Her steps echoed in the hallway as she stayed close to the wall. She was still torn, she kept moving toward one of the doors lining the hallway. The simple sign marked it "Classroom 14." *This is where I used to take my math classes.* Sabina looked up and down the hallway once more. She was alone. The faint sound of women's voices filtered through the closed door, and while the glass in this window was frosted, Sabina could see movement behind it. She recognized some of the words, raising her spirits. The women on the other side of the door were speaking Polish. Her hand went to the doorknob, her fingers closing around the cold brass. She hesitated before her father's face appeared again. She took a deep breath and turned the doorknob.

"Where do you think you're going?"

A loud voice behind her nearly made her jump. Sabina quickly let go of the doorknob and spun around. Her heart dropped at the sight of the tall female guard staring at her.

"Are you deaf? I asked what you were doing there." The words came at her in rapid German. At the same time, the guard was inspecting her, her eyes shooting from her head down to her toes multiple times. "And where is your uniform?"

The last question shocked Sabina into action. "I'm not a prisoner. I'm a messenger from the municipal registry." Her voice sounded oddly high, her hands were shaking, but there was nothing she could do about it. She was caught red-handed.

"Is that so? Then why are you here on your own? The labs are off limits to anyone but the prisoner scientists." The woman spoke with authority, her eyes still boring into Sabina. "Who were you meeting with?"

Panic filled Sabina at the thought of the guard hauling her through the camp to find Sternhell. If he decided she was snooping around, they would lock her up inside the main camp. Dread almost consumed her at the terrible prospect.

"Did you lose your tongue again?" A sharp tug at her shoulder. "Who were you meeting with?"

Sabina looked at the guard and decided there was only one way out of this. No matter what happened, she could not have Sternhell know about this. Mustering all her courage, she held out the folder. "I had these papers signed just now, and I was looking for the bathroom." Her voice sounded somewhat more normal again. "I heard voices behind this door and wanted to ask if they could point me in the right direction."

The woman glanced at the folder, then fixed her gaze back on Sabina, locking her dark eyes onto hers. "Did you say you came from the town? What's your name?"

She stated her name.

"Well, Sabina. Here's what's going to happen. I'll show you out of the camp, and you'll go back to your job in the city." Sabina could hardly believe the guard's words. Was she letting her go just like that? "And then I'll verify your story with the camp administration. If I find out you've been lying to me, I'll come and find you in town. And trust me, I have enough resources at my disposal to find you."

A knot formed in Sabina's stomach. She replayed the earlier part of the conversation in her head, searching for anything that would incriminate her to the guard. Apart from the lie about searching for the bathroom, she should be safe.

"Do we understand each other?" The guard raised an eyebrow, ice in her voice.

She quickly nodded. "Yes, absolutely."

The guard took a step closer, uncomfortably in Sabina's space. "Nothing you want to add at this point? I will find you."

Controlling the urge to take a step back, Sabina met the woman's eyes. "I'm speaking the truth."

The guard held her gaze a few seconds longer, then turned around. "Follow me."

The walk out of the camp was done in silence. Mercifully, they didn't run into Sternhell, and Sabina said a silent prayer when they reached the road, where the same two guards who allowed her in stood.

They nodded at the woman escorting her, while the man she'd spoken to earlier gave Sabina a curious look.

"Did you find the Hauptsturmführer Sternhell all right?"

"I did, thank you." Sabina tried to sound as casual as possible, but the female guard's ears perked up at the mention of Sternhell.

"You were meeting Sternhell?"

"Yes." There was no point in denying it.

Her eyes lit up. "Perfect. I'll check in with him later." She signaled toward the road leading to Oświęcim. "Off you go. Perhaps I will see you later in town."

Without another word, Sabina turned and started walking. As she did, she couldn't help overhear one of the men addressing the female guard.

"What was all that about, Frau Dreschel?"

Dreschel.

CHAPTER THIRTEEN

Felcia woke up as light streamed in through the window near her face. When the truck pulled away from the Birkenau main gatehouse two weeks ago, Felcia had been convinced it was the end of the line. It had taken less than fifteen minutes to arrive at Rajsko. There, the women were assigned to their blocks, and Felcia had felt a sparkle of hope. That evening, she was questioned, and they confirmed she was indeed who she said she was. When the SS man processing her told her she was to report to the *Pflanzenzucht kommando*—the Plant Experimental Station—in the morning, she thought he was playing some cruel joke on her. But when she made it to her barracks, she discovered she had arrived in some odd agricultural research camp.

There was a very thin piece of fabric that served as a window curtain, but it did little to stop the bright July sunlight filtering in. The other women were climbing down from their bunks and moving about the small room. Even though the setup was much like her previous block in Birkenau, with three-level bunk beds lining the walls, these had mattresses and bed linen. Felcia had a bunk to herself, an unheard-of luxury in Birkenau, where the same space had to be shared by at least three women.

She climbed down, took her white coat from the hanger next to the bunk, and then stepped outside and hurried to the latrines in the nearby block. After washing herself with warm water, a true luxury, Felcia hurried to report for roll call. She was one of the last women to line up in the open space between the blocks that served as kitchen, washroom, and living quarters. Standing with her back straight and her eyes facing forward, she was passed by the guards taking the morning count. Despite the smaller numbers in the new camp—there were only about two hundred women lining up this morning—the brutality of the guards at any infraction of the rules was as bad as in the main camp. Felcia was relieved to see Maria Mandl wasn't overseeing roll call this morning. As it was a satellite camp of Auschwitz-Birkenau and populated exclusively with women, the prisoners of Rajsko fell under the jurisdiction of Birkenau's Lagerführerin. Thankfully, Mandl prioritized the morning roll calls there.

Roll call passed mercifully quickly, and Felcia joined the line of women near the kitchen. The wait was short, and Felcia soon held a steaming mug of very watery ersatz and a piece of very dark toast. She tried to take a bite but her teeth hurt as she did. Instead of trying again, she dunked the bread in the liquid, letting it soak for a few seconds. This time, she managed to break off a piece, letting it soften further in her mouth. By now, she was used to receiving bread that was a few days old. She looked forward to the end of the day, when the kitchen staff were allowed to cook some of the vegetables they grew in the surrounding fields—one of the reasons why the women in the camp were relatively healthy. That, and the absence of hard physical labor for most of them.

Felcia finished her breakfast and cleared her mug and plate. She joined the stream of prisoners passing through the open gate where three male SS guards observed them. Their living quarters made up only a very small part of the Rajsko camp, and it was the only part surrounded by barbed wire. Once outside the fence, the women were able to move freely between the different buildings and areas of the camp. Of course, if they were found in an area where they weren't supposed to be, they faced severe consequences. There was no real freedom in Rajsko, not even in the absence of physical barriers. Felcia joined a group of some thirty women heading into the largest building, at the front of the camp. She navigated the hallway to one of the doors in the back.

"Morning, Felcia!" The bright voice of her lab partner, Bianka, greeted her as she entered the small laboratory. "I missed you at breakfast."

In their two weeks working together, Felcia had appreciated the biologist from Warsaw's optimistic nature. They had arrived at Rajsko at the same time, and Bianka was one of the few women Felcia trusted. She still greatly missed Marzena, who still visited her dreams, and Felcia drew strength from the memory of her friend.

Felcia moved toward a small glass terrarium in the back of their narrow room, where two small plants were placed under a blue light. She checked the temperature and measured the leaves. "Looks like it's growing steadily," she said while noting the numbers down on a large sheet on the wall. "How are yours doing?"

Bianka moved between their workbenches and looked at Felcia's numbers. "About the same, although it looks like yours are growing a bit quicker. Makes sense, considering the higher temperature." Her tone was analytical, eyes shooting between the plants and charts.

There was movement in the lab next to them, separated only by a couple of large windows. Felcia gave the two women dressed in the same white lab coats a quick wave before returning to her workbench. Their workspace was a little cramped, but she was thankful for her new assignment.

She spent the next hour checking the growth of the small plants under the numerous glass domes in the laboratory. It was pleasing to see most of them were growing as expected.

"Felcia, are you all right?" Bianka tapped a pencil on her workbench, then her attention was drawn to the door. "Something's happening in the hallway. Better look busy."

"Thanks." She turned her face toward the closed door and heard voices and footsteps. Felcia lifted the glass lid from one of the terrariums and carefully set it aside. The heat radiating from the lamp onto her cheek was comforting as she leaned in closer to inspect the small plants with a pair of tweezers. A tiny yellow flower was starting to bloom from one of the stalks. "I was just thinking of what would happen if we succeed with this experiment. Do you think the whole camp will be filled with greenhouses to grow these little plants?" She looked up to find Bianka with a thoughtful expression on her face.

"I doubt they'll have the entire production here. More likely, I can see them setting up places to grow these little dandelions all over the Reich. If they can ramp up production faster than the Russians, it could mean the difference in winning the war."

Felcia looked up in shock. "You really believe that?" She hadn't thought of her work that way before.

"Well, think about it. The German army needs a lot of rubber; without rubber, no tires. Without tires, their whole operation slows down everywhere."

Felcia was just opening her mouth to respond when the door from the hallway opened. Both women turned to find Dr. Joachim Caesar, the *Obersturmbannführer* in charge of the Rajsko camp. Outside, two guards stood in the hallway. Felcia was surprised to see Margot Dreschel, one of Maria Mandl's henchwomen, among them. What possible interest could the brutish woman have in the work carried out in the laboratories? As if sensing Felcia's gaze, Dreschel turned around. Her gray eyes showed no emotion, her buck teeth protruding even though her mouth was closed. Felcia quickly focused her gaze on Dr. Caesar.

"Ladies, I hope you have good news for me." The tall officer spoke in clear *Hochdeutsch*, the accent of the German upper class, articulating every vowel, making him appear to speak slower than most of his counterparts. He approached the open terrarium Felcia was standing next to, a look of approval on his face. "This looks promising. Is it blooming already?"

"It is, Herr Obersturmbannführer," Felcia responded. "This specimen has been under direct light for a full two weeks now. It appears to have responded well."

"What about soil moisture?" Dr. Caesar stuck his index finger in the soil. "Seems a bit too dry to me."

Felcia nodded and pointed at similarly sized plants in the two adjacent terraria. "We've been testing different soil moisture levels across these samples. I haven't found the optimal mix of light and humidity, but I'm making good progress. So far, all of the plants are showing promising growth."

"Very good. When do you expect to have the results of those tests?" Caesar looked impressed, even if his voice betrayed little excitement.

"About a week or two, Herr Obersturmbannführer."

"Two weeks?" Dr. Caesar looked disappointed. "See if you can speed up the research somehow. I've got Himmler breathing down my neck about this."

Felcia felt flushed but remained calm as she responded. "I'll see what I can do, sir."

"If anything changes in the meantime, keep me updated. You can call on my office at any time, okay?"

"Of course, sir."

Dr. Caesar turned to Bianka and listened to her reporting very similar findings. They were making remarkable progress in the two weeks she'd been here. If her research continued in the same vein, they would soon be able to launch larger scale research on the production of rubber from the little Kazakh dandelions. Professionally, she was thrilled to work on the project, despite her ethical concerns about assisting the German war effort.

"Good work overall, ladies. Keep it up. I expect to see results shortly." With those words, Dr. Caesar left the room. As he stepped outside, Felcia felt Margot Dreschel eyeing her. She couldn't quite place the look in the guard's eyes, but it was enough to chill her blood. The door closed and a sharp feeling of foreboding took root in Felcia's stomach. Why did Dreschel look at her like that?

"Dr. Caesar seemed happy enough." Bianka leaned against Felcia's workbench. "And quite involved, too. That was his second visit this week."

"You thought he was happy?"

Bianka chuckled. "Have you ever had a boss who thought things were going fast enough? If he's got the attention of Himmler, this project is important."

Felcia nodded and returned to her plants. Dr. Caesar had treated Bianka and her with respect so far, so he wasn't the worst Nazi around.

It took her another half an hour to finish documenting the progress of her plants. Her experiment was progressing as expected, meaning she would be able to present results to Dr. Caesar within two weeks. Bianka sat hunched over her workbench, furiously writing on a large notepad.

"I need to check on the specimens in the greenhouse as well. I'll be back in thirty minutes."

Bianka grunted without looking up, and Felcia hurried outside and breathed in the warm summer air. The short walk down the main path lifted her spirits somewhat, and she opened the door to the greenhouse. The air inside was warm and humid and smelled like wet earth. It felt like home to Felcia, reminding her of the large greenhouses at Jagiellonian University.

Felcia passed a few other women as she headed to her section. It took her less than fifteen minutes to measure the size of the Kazakh dandelions in this environment. As expected, these were lagging behind the ones in her terraria. She noted this with interest and strolled back to the greenhouse's entrance. She savored the last moments in the balmy air before stepping outside.

In the distance, fields stretched far beyond the horizon. Men and women in prisoner clothing were toiling away in the sun. Felcia felt sorry for them: the poor wretches had to trek the almost four kilometers from Birkenau twice a day.

Felcia turned to go back to the main laboratory building and almost bumped into another woman. "I'm sorry," Felcia mumbled as she moved out of the way and looked up. Her heart froze when the face looking back at her was that of Margot Dreschel. *This isn't a coincidence.* "Frau *Aufseherin*," she quickly added while bowing her head.

"Imbecile Pole." The words came quickly, and Felcia braced herself for the inevitable beating that would follow. She clenched her jaw.

Nothing happened for a few long seconds, only heightening Felcia's trepidation. She was vaguely aware of a group of women passing them on the gravel road. Felcia could feel their eyes on her, and she couldn't help but glance at them. The fear was palpable as the women shuffled by without a word, averting their faces.

Finally, Dreschel spoke, her voice dripping with contempt. "Look at me when I address you, Polish pig."

With an effort, Felcia looked up. The overseer's eyes studied her with feigned indifference.

"You may think you're safe, working for Dr. Caesar. He's a nice man, isn't he?" Felcia didn't know how to respond, and it must've shown, for an ugly smile appeared on Dreschel's face, exposing her teeth in full glory. Felcia had to control the urge to wince at the sight. "You think you're safe in your lab, don't you? With your fancy little coat, pretending to be scientists." Dreschel spat on the ground in front of Felcia's feet, pieces of spittle landing on her exposed ankles. A shudder shot through her body.

"Frau Aufseherin, I apologize for whatever I've done."

Felcia had barely finished her sentence when Dreschel's open hand came at her from nowhere. A sharp pain exploded in her left cheek a second later.

"Shut up! You don't say a word unless I tell you to!" Dreschel's voice came through with a slight delay as stars danced in front of Felcia's eyes. She managed a weak nod, then Dreschel continued as if nothing had happened. "I've seen the way you look at me. You've got ideas above your station. You're nothing in this camp. You're filth." It was impossible to miss the agitation in Dreschel's voice, and Felcia kept her head down. "Just know I'm watching you. You may be safe when working on Dr. Caesar's project, but outside the laboratory, you answer to me like the filthy Polish vermin you are. You understand that?"

Felcia's eyes were burning, but she fought back the tears. "Yes, Frau Aufseherin," she said in a weak voice.

Another vicious blow to the side of her head.

"I can't hear you! Do you understand?"

Felcia's head was spinning, the dizziness making her nauseous. She knew if she threw up now, Dreschel would not stop, and she might finish her off. Conjuring her last bit of strength, ignoring the overpowering urge to give in to the sickness building up in her throat, she answered in a clear voice: "Yes, Frau Aufseherin!" After that, she collapsed onto her knees on the ground, her head hanging. She'd never felt so humiliated. A part of her didn't care if the torture continued—she felt numb. As she braced for another blow to her body, Felcia instead heard Dreschel step away from her.

"Good. I'm glad we've got everything cleared up, then." Dreschel's voice sounded almost cheerful, and Felcia looked up in surprise. The guard looked at her curiously, much like a cat would eye a cornered mouse, deciding what to do next. "One last thing before I let you return to your station. If you ever tell a soul about what we discussed, I will have you back in Birkenau before you can blink. And I promise you there won't be a Dr. Caesar looking after you there."

The very mention of Birkenau was enough to send tremors down Felcia's spine. If Dreschel sent her back, she wouldn't last a week. She looked at Dreschel and nodded her silent surrender. Dreschel held her stare a few seconds longer, then turned and casually walked off.

"Oh, one more thing. The next time there's a block selection, I'll make sure you don't get lost in the chaos somehow. You won't be so lucky a second time."

The words felt like a punch to the gut, and Felcia struggled for breath. *How does she know about that? Had Tanya sold her out?* Her eyes went wide. She then caught the face of the Aufseherin, who had turned back toward her. She looked especially pleased with herself. Felcia felt the blood drain from her cheeks—she had just confirmed whatever Dreschel had heard about her. This was never about her position at Rajsko, or any supposed favoritism by Dr. Caesar. This was about an unfinished job. And if Dreschel knew about Felcia's lucky escape, it was only a matter of time before Maria Mandl would hear about it.

CHAPTER FOURTEEN

Sabina opened her eyes, blinking hard. Her room was dark but for a sliver of moonlight in the window crack. *Why am I awake?* A series of rattling sounds in the distance pulled her from her trance. She reached for the small clock on her bedside table. The faint moonlight illuminated enough to show it was only one in the morning.

She sat up in her bed; she was now fully awake as she focused on the sounds in the distance. It sounded like fireworks, but Sabina knew these were guns going off somewhere nearby. It was unusual for gunfire to sound at nighttime, despite the proximity to the camp. The killings were mostly done in silence, and the rare executions carried out with rifles were done during the day. This was different. *An escape?* Excitement bubbled in her stomach, and she said a quick prayer for the possible escapees.

There was more nearby scattered gunfire, and even though she couldn't tell for certain, it appeared to come from the city, not the camp. *Have the escapees made it to the city?*

Then she froze as she heard the familiar sound of the house's front door creaking.

Sabina lay perfectly still, her breathing slow and shallow as her senses focused on the sounds of the intruder downstairs. Her mind was flooded with possibilities. Had one of the escapees entered their home in search of shelter? She listened hard, but the sounds died away.

Soft footsteps on the stairs, then labored breathing sounded through her door as the person reached the top of the stairs, directly opposite her room. She held her breath, praying for the person not to enter. She mentally went through the objects in her dark room—she had nothing to defend herself with. The best she could do was jump the person the moment they opened the door. She sat up in her bed, her eyes on the darkened shape of the door, the quilt still over her feet.

To her relief, the footsteps shuffled past her door. The feeling was only temporary as she considered where they were going next. Her parents' bedroom. Should she warn them? Scream for help?

The door to the master bedroom opened and closed softly. Sabina found herself frozen in place. Whoever was stalking around their home appeared to know exactly where they were going. They had gone straight from the front door to the second floor, not bothering to inspect the ground level.

Sabina decided if anything happened in the next room she would storm in and fight, no matter the consequences. *I'm no coward.* She pushed the comfortable protection of the duvet away and stood up, tiptoeing to the door.

Her ear against the door, Sabina stood in the darkness, waiting for the sound of struggle to spring into action. A crash, a shriek, or a muffled yell.

Everything remained quiet, and Sabina started to doubt herself. Had she imagined it all? Was her sleepy brain playing tricks on her? Maybe the earlier gunfire had triggered her imagination a little too much. She shook her head and returned to her bed. As she lay down, she was full of doubt. The sounds of the creaking door and footsteps on the stairs had seemed so real. But why had nothing happened after? *I really must be imagining things.* With that last thought, she drifted back to sleep.

The clinking of cutlery sounded as Sabina made her way down the stairs. Stepping into the kitchen, she saw that both her parents were already up and about. Her father sat sipping a large cup of ersatz at the kitchen table, while her mother was busy at the stove.

"Morning, Sabina! Eggs?" Her mother held a large frying pan in one hand, while the other hovered over a small box of eggs on the counter. When Sabina nodded, she took two and cracked them into the pan. There was a satisfying sizzling sound as her mother turned up the heat. "Did you sleep well?"

"Not too bad, I awoke a few times." Sabina sat down opposite her father. "What about you?"

Her father grunted something unintelligible while he set his mug down and scooped up the last of the egg yolk on his plate. Her mother was more cheerful.

"Slept like a baby. When I woke up this morning, I decided I was going to cook these eggs I bought from Mrs. Baranowski down the road. Somehow, she's keeping her chickens alive and they're still laying enough eggs for her to sell them. She told me she'll only trade with people she likes, and I suppose I've done enough to be on her good side." Her mother sounded triumphant; even in these bleak times she found ways to be optimistic or happy.

Her mother placed a plate with two fried eggs and a piece of bread in front of her. "Eat up. You'll need your energy today. You've got a full day at the registry today, don't you?"

"Yes, although I'm hopeful I might be sent to the Rajsko camp again." Sabina paused and glanced at her father, who was chewing his last piece of bread without responding. "There's a lot going on there, and I think we're helping them run the administration of new recruits."

Her father washed away the last bite with a large swig of his ersatz and stood. He winced as he pushed his chair under the table.

"Are you okay, Papa?"

He turned to her and nodded. "I'm fine. Just lay in the wrong position last night. My leg is a bit stiff. It'll pass as soon as I've done a few rounds at work."

Sabina's eyes narrowed. Her father's voice sounded strained, and as she watched him make for the front door, she noticed he walked with a slight limp.

Before Sabina could ask him anything else, he was out the door, mumbling something about having to prepare the morning shift before the Nazis arrived with new prisoners. It left Sabina sitting bemused at the table. *I'll find out what's going on tonight.* Perhaps she hadn't imagined the sounds of someone sneaking through their home that night after all.

After breakfast, Sabina left for work early, but she discovered a blockade on the road leading to the main square. A voice called for her to stop, and as she turned two Kübelwagens and the same number of SS guards were barring her way.

"Papers." The command was curt, the man's stern eyes boring into her.

Sabina reached into her jacket and pulled out her papers. He inspected them, giving Sabina a chance to peek beyond him. The square was swarming with SS troopers moving between the shops. Most congregated on the corner next to the pierogi shop, and fear gripped Sabina's heart. *I hope nothing bad happened to Joanna.*

"Can you tell me what happened?" She put on her sweetest voice as she smiled at the officer.

"No. This is an ongoing investigation." He handed back her papers and pointed at the street leading away from the square. "Square's closed."

Sabina cut through the side streets surrounding the square, passing a similar blockade on the other side. She considered asking these troopers for more information but decided it wasn't worth the hassle. The rumor mill would start up soon enough, and she was headed toward the place with the most reliable sources on what was happening in the area.

Twenty minutes later, Sabina walked into the town hall and headed for the municipal registry. It was teeming with colleagues moving about the hallways and chatting in offices, which was unusual for this time in the morning. There was a buzz in the air—something had happened. Sabina had the uncomfortable feeling that it had something to do with what had awoken her that night.

As soon as she stepped into the archiving room, Tosia approached her. "Did you hear about what happened last night?"

"Not yet, but I suppose you're about to tell me." Sabina did her best to hide the mix of anxiety and excitement building up in her stomach.

Tosia closed the door and gave her a conspiratorial look. "I'm sure you overheard the clerks upstairs talking about what they think happened."

"I didn't really hear what they were talking about. They just seemed very excited."

"Look, I spoke to one of my friends who's got a connection with one of the resistance cells." Tosia looked a bit nervous, a slight tremor in her voice.

"The same ones that work in the camp?"

Tosia hesitated for a second, then nodded. "Maybe. Yes. He told me their cell obtained weapons from the Home Army and ambushed a German transport near the bridge last night. They received a tip about the Germans transporting more weapons for the guards at Auschwitz."

"And?"

"Well, when they stopped the truck, the driver got out without protest. When they boarded the truck, a host of Kübelwagens approached from the other side of the bridge. The SS soldiers opened fire on them. Some of the men jumped into the river, but most on the bridge were killed." There was sadness in Tosia's voice.

Sabina's mouth went dry. It had been gunfire after all.

"What happened next?"

"Some of the men fought back from the side of the bridge, and put up a good fight, but they had to withdraw when more SS arrived from the camp."

"Why did they cordon off the square?"

"They're combing the area looking for those responsible. I think the Germans think they're hiding in the square. Apparently, a number were wounded as they fled."

Sabina's heart stopped at Tosia's last words. It all made sense—her father wasn't just an informant anymore. He had been part of the ambush.

CHAPTER FIFTEEN

F elcia joined the line in front of the kitchen. She counted at least fifty women ahead of her, but the line moved quickly as their tin bowls were filled with the evening's soup. It would be nothing special, but it would at least be better than what the prisoners in Birkenau would receive. Earlier that day, a stream of Birkenau prisoners working Rajsko's fields had been marched through the camp when Felcia was collecting samples from the greenhouses. For a brief moment, she thought she spotted Marzena among the pale faces, but then reality hit. Marzena was gone. Forever.

The scent of cooked vegetables penetrated Felcia's nostrils as she neared the large cauldron. She recognized the women scooping ladles of soup, one of them catching her eye, giving her a quick wink. Making friends with the kitchen crew was one of the best ways to receive better portions. Her stomach grumbled at the thought of dinner, and she licked her dry lips. A woman cut into the line directly behind her. Felcia barely acknowledged the move; it happened all the time as friends helped each other secure good spots. Those at the back of the line would find their portions watery and with very few vegetables—one needed to show up early to secure a satisfactory bowl of soup. Or make friends with the kitchen staff.

Felcia felt a tap on her shoulder and turned to find a tall woman about five years her senior looking at her with her eyes narrowed. "You're from Kraków, aren't you?"

Felcia immediately recognized the Krakovian accent. Feelings of home rushed back, and she found herself instinctively answering in the same accent. "I am." Then she caught herself. *Who is this woman, and how does she know where I'm from?* She crossed her arms and tilted her head ever so slightly. "Why are you asking?" Felcia instantly regretted the defensive tone in her voice.

"Let's keep the line moving, shall we?" The woman indicated the space forming between the women in front of them, ignoring Felcia's defensiveness. "Don't want to draw the guards' attention to ourselves."

Felcia took a few quick steps as she closed the line. She turned back to the woman but kept an eye on the movement of the line as well. "Well?"

The woman gave her a disarming smile. "You're doing a decent job hiding your accent, but I picked up on it immediately." Her eyes studied Felcia, who did her best to keep her face neutral. "But don't worry, I'm sure most people wouldn't. I know for certain because I remember you."

Felcia studied the woman's face, trying to decipher if and where they'd met before. Her mind was drawing a blank. Was she bluffing, trying to get a rise from her?

"You don't remember me, do you?" The woman's voice remained calm, although the corners of her mouth rose ever so slightly. She appeared confident, unbothered by Felcia's almost hostile response as they neared the front of the queue. "Why don't you get something to eat, and if you don't mind, I'd ask for a few minutes of your time over dinner."

What does this woman want? And why isn't she answering my questions?

"Why would I want to do that?"

The woman's confidence didn't waver. "Because we both worked with Professor Sobczynski."

They found a quiet spot next to one of the blocks, overlooking the fields. Felcia sat on a large tree stump, and the woman sat on the ground across from her. She didn't seem bothered that Felcia was looking down on her as she placed her bowl on her lap and took a first gulp of soup. The woman had also received a generous portion with plenty of cabbage, potato, and carrot. *Must be friends with someone in the kitchen.*

Felcia brought her spoon to her mouth, savoring the warmth of the broth. When the woman sprang the name of her old mentor on her, she had been unable to mask her shock. Despite her curiosity, she kept her composure. Inside, her mind was racing, excited at a part of her old life returning in the shape of this woman. The woman made little haste to start talking, focusing on her soup instead. Hiding her impatience, Felcia did the same, feigning indifference as she scanned the area around them. After a minute or two, the woman put her empty bowl aside and looked up at Felcia.

"You may not remember me, but I remember you, Felcia." She leaned forward and held out her hand. "My name is Klaudia. I worked in the administration of the biology group."

Felcia shook the woman's hand, forcing her brain to match the woman's name and face to a memory from her previous life. "I'm sorry, it's not ringing a bell. Have we met before?"

"You were quite the rising star. And I'm not surprised you don't remember me. My work was mostly in the background. Taking care of student registrations, making sure the classrooms were reserved, following up on any of the professor's requests." A sad smile crossed her face. "At least, that was my job—everything changed when the professor was taken away." Klaudia's voice cracked and she looked away for a second. When she looked back up, Felcia recognized the hurt in her eyes. It was the same pain she'd felt when she witnessed the professor thrown into the back of a truck by Nazi thugs. Klaudia was speaking the truth. Before Felcia could say anything, Klaudia regained her composure, her eyes clear and determined as she waved her hand in dismissal. "It's all right, Felcia. You don't need to feel bad about it. So many people worked at the university, it's hard to keep track of everyone. Hell, I doubt I would've recognized you if it wasn't for the many times the professor spoke about you."

"How so?" A pang of emotion shot through Felcia's body.

"I spent many hours working with Professor Sobczynski." She smiled. "He was a busy man, but that was partly his own fault. He was always too approachable to everyone working with him. And everything had to be done his way."

Felcia couldn't help but smile at the apt description of her former mentor. She could picture the professor as Klaudia spoke, bossing her around and telling her how things should be organized.

"That sounds like Professor Sobczynski all right." Felcia placed her half-finished bowl on the stump behind her and leaned forward. "But you're describing him when all was well. That means you must've worked at the university for quite some time."

"Ten years. I flunked my doctorate." A shadow crossed her face, but it disappeared just as quickly. "After that, I was offered a job in the administration."

"Let me guess, by Professor Sobczynski."

Klaudia nodded. "I ran into some difficulties when I was trying to finish the post-doc, and he was my supervisor."

It sounded exactly like something Professor Sobczynski would do. It also explained why Klaudia was so fond of the man. But she still hadn't explained why she'd approached Felcia.

"I'm sorry—as much as I like talking about Professor Sobczynski, I'm not sure why you approached me."

"The professor made sure the brightest students were assigned to your classes. We all knew the professor was preparing you for great things." She fell abruptly silent, looking for the first time as if regretting her words.

Felcia felt her hands trembling. It had been his idea for her to take the step toward the tenure track at the university, despite very few women succeeding in climbing the ladder all the way to a professorship.

"I'm sorry, Felcia. This must be a lot to take in." Klaudia's voice was soft. "But when I first noticed you in Rajsko, I could hardly believe what I saw. In fact, I wasn't certain it was you until I finally mustered the courage to approach you in line just now."

"That's quite all right. I'm glad you did. When did you arrive?"

"I was taken to Birkenau almost five months ago. I survived only because my best friend was assigned to the kitchen, and she slipped me extra food while I worked the fields." She chuckled as she pointed at herself. "A big, strong woman like myself would always be assigned to tough work like that. I'm sure without my friend's help, I wouldn't have survived. God knows I've seen enough women collapse around me."

"And then you were assigned to Rajsko?"

"Just like you. They needed someone with experience to serve as an overseer of sorts for the women brought in to work the fields every day. New faces coming in every day, needing to be told what to do. The guards weren't keen on doing that, so they must've figured I would make a good choice."

Felcia's interest was piqued. "These women come in from Birkenau?"

"Almost all of them, yes. I see some women from the main camp at times, but those are few and far between. I guess they only bring them in when they need someone with more specialized knowledge. Quite a few scientists and doctors in Auschwitz, from what I've heard."

Felcia looked at Klaudia. Could she trust her?

"Felcia, I need to confess something. There's another reason I sought you out, apart from our mutual connection in Kraków."

"Okay, what is it?" Felcia kept her face neutral, but a sense of foreboding rose in her stomach.

"Do you miss teaching?"

The question caught her off guard. "Yes," she stammered. "Of course. I loved it."

"What about the underground classes? Professor Sobczynski told me about those."

"It was different, more basic, but there was no alternative. It was the best means to the end we had at the time."

"So you enjoyed it?"

The faces of Julian and Kasia, her favorite students, came to mind. For a second, she wondered how they were doing, then she met Klaudia's intense gaze and nodded. "I loved it. Teaching those kids ... I've never felt anything more fulfilling."

"Did the fact that it was illegal, an act of resistance, make it even more important to you?"

"Yes." Felcia answered without hesitation, surprising herself. Her mind went back to the night the apartment next to her class was raided. She could still hear the children's heartrending cries from the backs of the trucks as their parents' lifeless bodies were left in the cold, deserted street.

"If I'm not mistaken, you're in one of the labs these days, right?"

Her focus switched back to the camp. "In the main building, yes."

Klaudia looked pleased. "Would you agree you're given a lot of freedom to do your work?"

"I guess so."

"From what I gather, Dr. Caesar is quite fond of his scientists, no? You're given free rein around the camp?"

Felcia didn't immediately answer as she assessed the reality of their different situations. Klaudia, despite her relatively privileged position as overseer, still needed to toil away in the fields all day under the watchful eye of the guards. By comparison, Felcia was free to move between the laboratory, the greenhouses, and the other buildings. She never needed a guard escort, unless she wanted to leave the camp. She chuckled at the thought; there was no reason why she would ever be allowed outside the perimeter. The memory of Dreschel ambushing her outside the greenhouse returned, but that had been an anomaly.

"Yes. We can move between the buildings within reason. And only in the daytime, of course." Felcia gestured at the fence separating them from freedom, only a few meters from where they were sitting.

"Within limitations, of course," Klaudia confirmed. "But still, your ability to move around the camp is unique. For Rajsko, but even more so for the other camps. Can you imagine this in Birkenau?"

Felcia shook her head. "Of course not. But what are you getting at?"

Klaudia stood and looked around conspiratorially before sitting on the tree stump next to Felcia. Their knees almost touched. "How would you like to save more women like yourself from the gas chambers?"

Excitement and fear constricted Felcia's throat. "How?"

Felcia lay in her bunk a few hours later. Most of the women around her were snoring, some muttering unintelligible words in their sleep. Despite her own exhausted state, sleep wouldn't take her. Her mind was tormenting her as conflicting thoughts raged indiscriminatingly.

At first, Klaudia's proposal had seemed so outrageous that Felcia had almost dismissed it out of hand. Thankfully, the woman had held up her hands before Felcia could do so, and she'd explained how everything would work. As Felcia listened, she had slowly warmed to the idea. Klaudia made it clear that she wouldn't be doing anything that would harm the camp leadership or the guards. She would be working on something that she called the silent resistance. When Felcia asked about the other side of the resistance, Klaudia had been vague and a bit dismissive, urging her to focus on what was asked of her now. By the time the camp siren sounded, indicating for the women to head to their blocks in preparation for lights out, Klaudia had almost convinced her to accept. But, instead of doing so, she'd told Klaudia she needed some time to think about it.

Now, alone in her bunk, she oscillated between hope and terror. If what Klaudia proposed worked, she could save women from Birkenau. Women like herself could work in the relatively safe surroundings of Rajsko. With a little luck, and if she did her job, it would bolster their research capabilities, no doubt delighting Dr. Caesar and strengthening Felcia's position.

If it all went well, Klaudia's plan was brilliant. Her mind went back to the words of her professor in Kraków on the eve of her arrest.

"When the time comes, we need those young minds, the future generations, ready to rebuild Poland. And that's why we do what we do, Felcia."

Felcia balled her fists in the dark. Her meeting with Klaudia might've been by chance, but the more she thought about it, the more she decided it was meant to be.

Chapter Sixteen

Sabina took a breath of fresh air, enjoying the scent of the pine trees bordering the road. It felt liberating to leave the city and the stuffy archiving room behind. She had been delighted when Mr. Piotrowski summoned her to his office and handed her a closed envelope.

"Take it to Rajsko, and make sure nobody but commander Caesar opens it." Her boss's voice had been a little strained, and he appeared slightly nervous. The message was loud and clear, and she clutched the envelope tightly as she kept a steady pace on the side of the road.

It was a good half hour's walk to the camp, and she was pleased to be outside. Summer had well and truly arrived, and the temperature was comfortable, the trees providing welcome slivers of shade from the sun high in the sky. There was a faint sound of an engine approaching behind her, and Sabina stepped to the side of the road. A Kübelwagen passed by, its occupants paying her little attention. When it turned the corner, her surroundings went quiet again.

News about the failed ambush had shaken her, but not nearly as much as the realization that the Gestapo were looking for her father. When she walked back home after work the previous evening, the square had already cleared. She had glanced up at the windows of the houses above the shops and wondered if any of the men were hiding in town.

Much to her relief, her father had been waiting alongside her mother at the dinner table when she came home. Once again, he was shifty and couldn't hold her gaze.

He headed upstairs and to bed before she could get a moment alone with him. Predictably, he had been gone when Sabina came down this morning—called to the mines on urgent business, apparently. It only further convinced Sabina he was avoiding her. The thought that he was protecting her by not telling her crossed her mind, and even though it was a comforting one, she didn't want to be shielded. Rajsko was no secret; she deserved to know the truth of what father was involved in.

The camp came into view in the distance. Sabina passed the sign marking the Rajsko town limits and grimaced. There was little left of the town she'd grown up in.

Two guards stood next to the entrance to the camp. They had spotted her well before she reached them, and they looked on with amused expressions, joking with each other. Sabina showed them the envelope, and their smiles vanished at the mention of Dr. Caesar.

"Just head straight into the main building," one of the guards said, pointing at her old school building. "Dr. Caesar is in the largest office in the back. You can't miss him."

She followed the camp's main thoroughfare, a gravel road running between the school building and the greenhouses. A couple of women emerged from a greenhouse carrying buckets. She eyed them and saw them move toward what appeared to be a well.

Stepping into the hallway of the old school, she was struck by how odd it felt to walk here alone. Her steps echoed down the halls, and all she heard were muffled voices and the clanging of glass behind the closed doors of former classrooms. The principal's office, now occupied by the Nazi commander, had a closed door, although she could see light shining through the frosted glass. The window to the office next to the commander's, that of the friendly SS officer, was dark. Sabina felt an odd sense of relief at his absence.

She walked on and was surprised to find an open door ahead on the right. Sabina cautiously walked toward it, but not before checking that she was the only person in the hallway. The memory of the guard catching her a few days ago still terrified her.

Sabina walked in and shook her head. Instead of neatly lined up tables and chairs, two large workbenches dominated the center of the room. Smaller tables filled with various sizes of glass containers lined the walls. Humid, floral air with the faint scent of fertilizer entered her nostrils, and she took a few steps into the laboratory, approaching the nearest table. Small tubes curled around glass partitions, and a small machine was humming on the floor next to her. She bent her knees a little to study the large green leaves behind the glass. When she looked closely, she could see small yellow flowers pushing their way from the bulbs at the ends of the ugly stalks.

"Hey, who are you?" A voice made Sabina turn. To her surprise and relief she was greeted by a woman in her mid-thirties looking at her with dark, curious eyes, wearing a lab coat. "You shouldn't be in here!" Sabina was surprised the woman addressed her in Polish.

"I'm sorry, the door was open, and I just sort of stumbled inside." Sabina held up the palms of her hands. Looking at the scientist, she noticed the stripes of the Auschwitz-Birkenau prisoner uniform underneath her lab coat. *A prisoner wearing a lab coat, working in a laboratory?* "I didn't mean to cause any trouble. I'll be on my way." Sabina made toward the door, but the woman held up a hand, her eyes inspecting her.

"You're from the outside?" Sabina nodded, and the woman looked confused. "But you're Polish, aren't you? What's your business inside the camp?"

Despite her white coat, there was no doubt she was a prisoner. A simple blue kerchief was wrapped around her head, where her dark hair was unevenly cut. A few wavy strands of hair hinted at what would normally be a full head of curls. As if sensing Sabina's doubts, the woman unbuttoned the top of her coat, exposing the red triangle sewn onto her uniform.

"This marks me as a political prisoner. Do you want to know what I did to end up in here?" The woman's voice was clear, her eyes boring into Sabina. She wasn't sure how to respond, but found herself nodding, mesmerized by the woman across from her. "I taught underground classes in my hometown." The woman held her gaze a while longer, then started securing the buttons of her coat.

Sabina didn't know how to respond. She'd never spoken to a prisoner of the camp before. And this woman looked relatively healthy, normal even, in her lab coat. How did this prisoner end up working in a lab?

"Can you tell me anything about what's going on outside?" The woman leaned on one of the tables. She looked at Sabina inquisitively, then shook her head. "No, first tell me why you're in the camp."

Sabina held up the envelope. "I'm supposed to deliver this to the commander. But when I saw your open door, I couldn't help myself."

"I can imagine." A smile crept onto the woman's face. "So you're a messenger?"

"I suppose you could call me that." Sabina hesitated for a second. "I work in the registry in town, and when they need something delivered to the camp, they send me."

"Hmm." The woman looked thoughtful. "I suppose we might see you around here more often, then?"

"I guess so." Sabina couldn't help but smile. She found it exhilarating to talk to an actual prisoner. "What's your name?" The words came out before she had a chance to consider them.

"Felcia." The woman held out her hand. "And yours?"

She gripped the woman's hand; it was bonier than she'd expected. "Sabina."

"It's very nice to meet you, Sabina. Now, I think you better deliver that envelope before anyone catches you in here. It wouldn't be good for either of us."

Sabina nodded and took a step toward the door, stopping and listening for any sounds in the hallway. When there were none, she stepped outside.

"Sabina?"

"Yes?" She turned to see Felcia standing near the door opening.

"Are you still in school?"

With a smile, Sabina nodded.

"Good." Felcia looked especially pleased before closing the door.

With a burst of energy from her unexpected meeting, Sabina

quickly walked to the camp commander's closed door. Standing outside, she wasn't sure how to continue. Should she wait until it opened? Or could she knock? Taking a deep breath, she knocked on the door. There was a pause before the scraping of a chair, then soft footsteps approaching on the other side. The door swung open, revealing a tall man wearing an SS officer's uniform. Four flower emblems and double lines decorated his collar straps. He looked at her in surprise, and the first thing she noticed were the soft eyes.

"Yes? What do you need?" He spoke quickly, but despite the shortness of his sentence, the tone wasn't unfriendly.

Sabina swallowed hard, taking a moment to find her words. "I ... I have a message from the municipal registry, sir." She held out the envelope, barely able to control her trembling hands.

He made her hold the envelope a fraction longer than necessary before taking it. "Ah, perfect. I was waiting for this. I thought you would be here sooner." He turned around and tore the envelope open as he walked to his ornate desk. "Come in, this should only take a moment. If all is well, you can take the signed documents back to your boss. That should expedite things. Lord knows we could have things move a bit quicker around here." He sat at his desk, eyes fixed on the document, and waved Sabina over.

She moved to the seat opposite him, taking in the room. Like in the office next door, Dr. Caesar had made few changes to the original furnishings. Sabina felt like she was back in the headmaster's office—the nerves were the same as she sat opposite Dr. Caesar.

The SS officer's eyes quickly scanned the papers in front of him. She fidgeted and placed her hands in her lap, remaining silent while Dr. Caesar's pen raced across the papers with a soft sound. As her mind started to drift, he spoke up.

"Would you like some cake?" He pointed at a small table to the side of his desk. "I received it this morning, and it's too much for me to finish on my own. Please, have some."

Sabina couldn't remember the last time she had cake. She wanted to stand up and take a piece, but also felt like she didn't deserve the treat, considering the circumstances. She didn't move, and Dr. Caesar looked up in surprise.

"You don't want any?" He stood and moved to the table, cutting a slice before handing her a small plate. As she accepted it, the thin layer of frosting made her mouth water. *When did I last have real sugar?* She picked up the fork, cut a small piece. The sugary delight overwhelmed her senses. To her embarrassment, she let out a small moan of delight. Mortified, she put down the fork.

"It's quite all right, no need to apologize. I was also very impressed." Dr. Caesar sat down again and smiled. "Please, enjoy. It will be our secret."

Sabina reluctantly picked up the fork again and gobbled the rest of the cake. Across the desk, Dr. Caesar signed the last sheet of paper before placing the document in a new envelope.

"Right, that's all done and ready for Mr. Piotrowski." Sabina was impressed by his proper pronunciation of her boss's name as he slid the envelope across the desk. "Now, before you leave, do you mind if I ask you something?"

Sabina stood up and was reaching to collect the envelope and froze at the request. As an SS officer, he didn't need to ask permission to ask her something. She gave him a puzzled look, but managed to mutter her acceptance as she took the envelope.

"If you're working at the municipal registry, you must be from around here?"

"I am, sir."

"Do you know what we're doing in this camp?"

Sabina felt as if Dr. Caesar was luring her into a trap, but she couldn't think of a better response than the truth. "From what I can tell, you're growing crops for the other camps."

"Sure, that we do." The man across from her looked a little disappointed at her answer. "But it's more than that. We're carrying out important research."

"In the school?" Sabina couldn't contain her curiosity, and she immediately regretted her words as Dr. Caesar frowned.

"The school? Ah, you mean this building. Well, this is the laboratory now. How did you know it was a school before?" His voice was neutral, his face sincere.

"This used to be my school, sir. Rajsko was my home." Sabina didn't know why she felt so comfortable sharing her background with this Nazi officer. Something about him seemed different. *Be careful. You can't trust him.*

"Interesting. Why, yes, of course there were people here before we moved in." He spoke the words with casual detachment, as if merely stating facts. For the first time, Sabina felt her temper flare a little. *This was my home.* She bit her lip before responding.

"My home is no longer here, sir. It was about two kilometers down the road. There are fields there now."

A trace of compassion appeared on Dr. Caesar's face. "I'm sorry about that." He looked thoughtful for a moment. "But your family was assigned a new place in the city, and you understand this is necessary for the war effort, right?"

Sabina nodded, repressing the fury she felt building inside. Dr. Caesar stood and pointed at the envelope in her right hand.

"Better get going. I'd like your boss to process these instructions by the end of the day. It's all in there, but make sure to tell him."

"I will, sir." Sabina turned around and headed toward the door. Then she turned back. "Oh, and sir?"

"Hmm?"

"Thank you for the cake."

Sabina stepped out of the building and followed the gravel path toward the main road.

"Hey!" A familiar voice sounded behind her. "Didn't think I'd see you around here so soon again." Sabina turned to look into the smiling face of SS officer Sternhell, who caught up with her. "How are you, Sabina?"

"I can't complain, getting sent on an errand with this weather. Beats sitting in an office."

"I had the same thought. I decided a quick inspection of the camp was in order this morning." He pulled a face. "Unfortunately, it means I'll have to process all the paperwork in the afternoon now."

They neared the main road and Sabina was keen to get back to the registry. "Dr. Caesar asked me to get this to my boss as quickly as possible, so I'm going to have to run." She moved away from the SS officer, but to her surprise, he took a step closer.

"Sabina, I was thinking it might be nice to meet outside work sometime. Perhaps a drink this weekend if it suits you."

Sabina felt a tremor shoot down her spine, but forced a smile. She'd heard of SS men harassing local girls for dates. Some took them up on it, but most begged off. Sternhell's smiling, expectant face stared back at her as she shook her head.

"I'm not sure I can do that this weekend. But it sounds nice."

To his credit, he handled the rejection better than expected, retaining the smile, but the disappointment was clear in his eyes. "That's all right. I figured I should at least ask. If you change your mind, I'll be in the main tavern on the square this Saturday afternoon. Bring a friend, if it makes you feel more comfortable."

Sabina was grateful for his manners, nodding as she turned toward the city. "I'll consider it."

The SS officer doffed his cap before turning and heading back toward the school building. As Sabina walked down the road, her head was spinning from the meetings in the past hour.

Chapter Seventeen

Felcia stepped inside the warm, humid greenhouse. The sea of green and yellow that greeted her provided a calm in the madness of the camp. Crouching to inspect one of the larger flowers on the ground, she listened closely. It appeared she was alone, which was preferred on a normal day. This morning, it was essential as she checked on a few more plants, her ears strained for the sound of the door.

When the door opened, she casually turned her head to check who entered. Klaudia gave her a nervous smile as she carefully closed the door.

"It's okay, we're alone," Felcia said when she noticed the other woman's eyes shifting between the plants. "The others are in the labs. We can speak freely."

"I've never been in here before." Klaudia seemed a little nervous as she looked around the greenhouse. "So these are the magic plants I keep hearing about? I thought they'd be bigger."

Felcia let out a laugh. "Well, as long as you have enough of them, they should provide a nice supply of rubber. That's the idea, anyway. That's my job."

"Is it working?"

"The results of the first experiments have been encouraging. These plants really are providing a higher yield of rubber than I expected."

"You seem surprised."

Felcia frowned while she ran her hand over one of the smaller specimens. "I had my doubts when Dr. Caesar provided the brief for our experiments. Well, mostly about the expectations, really. But so far, when these little plants are provided with sufficient water and light, they thrive."

"Sounds like that would be good in summer, but what about our winters?" Klaudia looked up through the glass panels of the greenhouse, to where the sun was struggling to break through the clouds.

"We'll need a lot of greenhouses," Felcia said with more confidence than she felt. Having spoken to the women in the next-door lab, relying on the weak winter sun warming the greenhouses wouldn't yield a sufficient amount of rubber for the Nazis' plans. They would need to come up with another solution.

"Have you considered my proposal?"

She looked up to find Klaudia's expectant eyes on her. Felcia rose and signaled for the other woman to follow her down the main path in the greenhouse. "Let's make sure whoever bothers to look inside thinks we're inspecting the plants." Her eyes went to the glass walls of the greenhouse, which still allowed vigilant guards to peek inside, despite the condensation. "I did think about what you asked." She stopped and crouched near a particularly large dandelion. Klaudia followed her lead.

"And, how do you feel about it?"

"I like the idea in general." Felcia dug her fingers into the soil, glad to feel it sufficiently irrigated.

"But?"

"I'm a little worried about how it is all set up. You mentioned a prisoner resistance in Birkenau?"

"You're worried about getting caught."

"Of course. Wouldn't you be?" Felcia corrected herself. "Aren't you? If we're talking about this, you must be a part of it."

Klaudia smiled and knelt down, lowering her voice conspiratorially. "I'm just the messenger. I don't know much more than what I've told you so far. I only know one other person, a woman who comes in from

Birkenau to work in my kommando every day. She tells me only what I need to know, and then relays my message back to her own contact in the main camp. This is how the resistance is set up, Felcia. If someone is caught, they only know a little bit about what's going on." She paused for a moment, her face serious. "I'm not saying it's without risk, but all you'd do is share your knowledge with the young women in the camp."

Felcia pondered Klaudia's words for a moment. "How would it work, if I agreed to teach them? You said these women would be transferred from Birkenau and placed in Rajsko. How do you make this work?"

Her skepticism must've shown, for Klaudia held up her hands. "I told you, I don't know anything about the next steps. I was told to contact you and see if you'd be interested." A faint smile. "Can I tell them you are?"

"If I am, what happens next?"

"Someone will contact you to fill you in on the details. That person will be able to provide you with the answers you seek." Klaudia's face was serious. "But realize that if you decide you want to help, you can't back out. When you're in, you stay in."

Goosebumps formed on Felcia's arms. She looked around the greenhouse, suddenly abundantly aware of her privileged position as a scientist in the camp. When the wind was blowing in their direction, the smoke from the ever-billowing chimneys down the road darkened the sky above their heads, and they could taste the ash drifting through the fields. Her mind went back to her old life in Kraków, where she could also have stayed out of the limelight; hiding and praying the Nazis wouldn't come for her. Instead, her journey doing what she felt—no, she knew!—was right had brought her to Rajsko. And now her old life reached out to her, giving her another chance to do the right thing. Determination burned inside her belly, and she turned back to Klaudia. With a fierceness in her voice she didn't know she possessed, she said, "If I save only one other woman by doing this, I will. Tell them I'm in."

When Felcia returned to the laboratory she found it hard to concentrate on her work. Her mind kept drifting back to her conversation with Klaudia. As soon as she'd stepped outside the greenhouse and saw Klaudia walk back toward the fields, she started second-guessing herself. Even if it was the right thing, joining the underground resistance in a concentration camp was especially dangerous.

For a second, panic gripped her throat.

"Are you all right?" Bianka's clear voice brought Felcia back to the laboratory. "You've hardly said a word since you returned. Something wrong with the plants?"

"I'm fine, Bianka, thanks. The plants are growing well. I think we might be able to extract the first bits of rubber ahead of schedule." She let out a deep sigh of relief as she tended to the plants in the terrarium.

"Dr. Caesar will be pleased about that. I spoke to some of the other women, and they said they weren't making much progress." Bianka nodded toward the glass panel splitting the classroom, to where two women worked in an identical setup. "They said they weren't having any luck with the slightly lower temperatures."

"Really? The difference is quite minimal. Five degrees, no?"

"They showed me their plants. They're not even showing signs of blooming yet. It's pretty bleak." Bianka sighed. "Literally. They worry about their positions if they fail to yield any rubber."

Felcia glanced at the women, deep in animated discussion. It wasn't their fault the plants weren't doing as well in lower temperatures. "I'm sure Dr. Caesar will appreciate their efforts. At least it will give us more data about the optimal conditions for growth."

"Let's hope you're right."

Felcia caught a movement behind the frosted glass of the door before sounds rang out from the hallway. Doors farther down the hallway opened, with guards barking orders. Before she could say or do anything, their door flew open as well. A tall guard she didn't recognize stepped inside.

"Out to the roll call square, now!"

Felcia eyed the clock above the door. It was only one in the afternoon. Roll call wasn't supposed to start for hours. Her throat constricted. Something was wrong. Had they caught Klaudia on the way back from the greenhouse? *Surely not!*

"What are you waiting for?" The guard moved a few steps closer, into Felcia's space. "Outside, now!"

Overwhelmed, Felcia's eyes went to the open glass container holding a piece of dandelion she'd been analyzing. "Can I close that? I was working on an experiment."

The guard raised his hand and slapped her hard. A searing pain spread across her cheek an instant later. She suppressed a yelp of pain, but Bianka's gasp of horror was clearly audible from the other side of the lab.

"You'll do as you're told, you insolent piece of shit! Don't think your fancy coat means you're anything but the *Untermensch* Pole you are!" The guard's words pelted her like hail, and Felcia dropped her head as she hurried toward the door.

"Stop!" the guard yelled, and Felcia turned around, flinching. *The beating's not over yet.* He glowered at her, but instead of striking her again, he pointed at her coat. "You'll leave that here. At roll call, you're a prisoner like everyone else."

Felcia quickly took off her coat and hung it on the nail next to the door. Bianka did the same, and Felcia noticed her shaking hands. Their eyes met for a moment, fear spreading through their bones.

As they entered the hallway, the usual silence was replaced by a cacophony of guards barking orders while dozens of feet hurried toward the exit. Panic hung in the air, as every single one of them knew what roll call at this hour meant.

Outside, the scene was similar. Women were herded into the open space between their sleeping barracks where roll call was carried out twice a day. Felcia passed through the small gate as she entered the only area surrounded by a fence in Rajsko.

The roll call square was crowded as most women had already lined up. Women from the fields had been gathered first and stood at the far end. Felcia found her spot and dared a glance around the square. Fear gripped her throat at the sight of a truck parked to the side of one of the blocks. There were only a few reasons for the use of trucks in the camp, and none promised a good outcome. She vividly remembered the steady stream of trucks rolling toward the chimneys in the back of Birkenau. She calmed herself with the knowledge that one truck would never be sufficient to transport all the women lined up in the square.

Her relief was short-lived as she spotted the figure at the front of the crowd of gathering women. Maria Mandl caressed the handle of her whip while she observed the last women taking their place in the lineup. She was too far away for Felcia to make out the expression in her eyes, but she knew from experience the woman was scanning the prisoners for the slightest excuse to punish them. A crooked kerchief or a missing button on a uniform could mean facing the wrath of Birkenau's Lager-führerin. Felcia held her breath while she prayed Mandl's eye wouldn't fall on her. She kept her gaze trained on the back of the woman ahead of her. A pang of fear shot through her body. Where Mandl was, Dreschel couldn't be far away. *Please don't let her spot me.*

The last women found their places. A shrill whistle sounded and the shuffling of feet stopped, bringing silence to the roll call area. Mandl waited a few more seconds, then her voice boomed across the square.

"It has come to my attention that there have been rumors of unrest in the camp. As much as I hate coming down to Rajsko, I felt inclined to check on these reports myself." There was no indication in Mandl's voice that she was upset about standing here, her tone accusatory. A feeling of dread built in the pit of Felcia's stomach. She had heard Mandl speak in this tone many times before, and it always preceded something terrible.

"Normally, I would let my guards handle this, but when I heard food was being pilfered from the fields and greenhouses, I couldn't ignore it. You've been trusted to provide the food for the prisoners in Birkenau, and you reward this trust by stealing it for yourself." The fake indignation in Mandl's voice was impossible to miss, and it made Felcia sick. "That's why you'll stand at attention while we search your blocks for contraband. I expect all of you to stand still with your hands by the sides of your body. Don't even think about moving, or you'll regret it."

Felcia, and the hundreds of women around her, snapped to atten-tion and took the position Mandl demanded. She hoped the days working on her feet in the laboratory had sufficiently prepared her for the torture ahead.

Groups of guards entered the blocks. As three hundred women stood silent, the sounds inside the buildings reverberated around the roll call area. The first guards came back outside, dumping all sorts of containers onto the sandy ground. Soon, the ground in front of every block was littered with the only worldly possessions of the female prisoners of Rajsko. Bars of soap, worn toothbrushes, and plenty of canned food was dumped like garbage.

"Hands above your heads!" Mandl's voice boomed, and three hundred pairs of hands moved skyward.

While most of the guards returned into the blocks, Mandl called for a few to remain outside. A woman two spots to Felcia's left was struggling to keep her hands in place, her arms shaking. Felcia closed her eyes for a second, bile rising in the back of her throat. At the same time, she clenched her jaw, summoning strength to keep her hands in the air.

An ear-piercing shriek broke the silence a few seconds later. The woman was on the ground, clutching her stomach while Mandl stood kicking at all parts of her body indiscriminately. The woman let out a few more screams of agony, but when Mandl brought down her boot on her head, a sickening crunch could be heard, silencing the woman's cries. Her body twitched a few more times, then she remained motionless.

Before the women in the square could recover from the shock of witnessing the murder, another prisoner was beaten to the ground. Felcia quickly averted her gaze when she recognized the guard dishing out the beating. It was Margot Dreschel, using a crude cudgel to beat the helpless woman on the ground to a pulp. She lasted longer than the previous victim, her cries of pain continuing for more than a minute until she was forever silenced.

Felcia's hands were shaking, and she wasn't sure if it was from exhaustion or fear. Both, most likely. She was certain Dreschel would soon spot her, and it would be over. There wouldn't be an opportunity to join the camp resistance.

She didn't fully register the cries around her as she withdrew into herself. It was just a matter of time before the blows would force her to the ground as well, never to get up.

The sound of Mandl's voice registered somewhere in the distance, and it forced her to snap back into full consciousness.

"We've finished our search, for now." Mandl stood triumphantly next to one of the piles of the women's items. "All of these items were obtained and kept illegally in your barracks. Clearly, the rumors and my misgivings about how this camp is run were accurate."

Felcia felt as if she were floating outside herself. The roll call area was littered with bodies. Some were still breathing shakily, but most of these women lay with their eyes open, staring vacantly into nothingness. There had to be at least two dozen women on the ground. She wondered how she had avoided the purge, and how time had passed so quickly. She frantically searched for Dreschel, whom she found standing on the other side of the square, next to the truck—overseeing the loading of the prisoners' belongings.

"You will all return to your bunks now, and stay there for the rest of the day. There will be no rations tonight, and possibly until I determine what we do with you."

For the first time, a collective groan went through the group. Being denied a meal, no matter how meager, meant another step closer to death. The possibility of multiple days without food was unthinkable, especially for the women working the fields. Maria Mandl smiled as she observed the impact of her heinous announcement.

"Inside, now! Before I decide on a worse punishment!" She cracked her whip, prompting the women to turn and move toward their blocks. As they did, they passed the piles containing their belongings. There were mutters of disbelief as they regarded the only items that allowed them the semblance of comfort, dumped on the ground like garbage.

Inside, Felcia breathed a sigh of relief before letting out a gasp. Mattresses and bedding had been ransacked, their blankets scattered on the ground. She rushed to her own bunk, where she was dismayed—but not surprised—to find her toothbrush snapped in half, the brush head crushed and covered in dirt. Blood rushed to her head as she failed to find a way to channel her anger at the display of so much injustice. She wanted to scream, but it would only draw attention. Instead, she crashed onto her bunk and buried her face in her hands. Tears welled up in her eyes, and she clawed her nails into her cheeks. She lay like this, breathing hard, until her anger faded. Then she sat up and looked at the scene around her.

Women sat crying on their bunks; others stared into space. Some found comfort in each other's arms. All had one thing in common; the events of the past few hours had utterly drained them. They were defeated.

Felcia clawed her hands into fists. In her mind she returned to the serenity of the greenhouse, where she agreed to join the camp resistance. Her life could be over in the blink of an eye. But she wouldn't go silently. And while she was breathing, she would fight back, in whatever way she could. Suddenly, she was impatient for the resistance to reach out. She was ready.

CHAPTER EIGHTEEN

Sabina was reading a book on the comfortable couch in the corner of the living room. Her eyes scanned the pages, but the words hardly registered. Instead, her ears were pricked to catch what was happening in the kitchen. It sounded like her mother was preparing to leave. Sure enough, her mother stepped into the living room with a large bag swung over her shoulder.

"Sabinka, I'm heading to Mrs. Baranowski's for some eggs, and then I'll go into town to see if I can find any fresh vegetables." Her mother was smiling, but her voice suggested her own doubts about the mission. It wasn't easy to find fresh produce these days. "Do you need anything? Provided I can find it, of course."

Sabina kept her tone light. "I'll be happy with whatever you can find, Mama." Then she put her book on her lap. "Would you like me to come with you?"

Her mother hesitated, then shook her head. "No, you enjoy your day off and read. You've been so busy all week, you need to relax a little as well."

"Are you sure?"

Her mother quickly opened the front door, waving her hands

dismissively. "Yes, stay. I'll be back soon." She stepped outside, not giving Sabina a chance to protest.

Not that Sabina really wanted to join her mother. She jumped to her feet and put the book on the coffee table. Watching her mother disappear down the road, she felt a tremble of excitement as she heard her father rummaging around the kitchen.

She entered to find him lying on his back underneath the sink, holding a wrench. *Good, he's not going anywhere.*

"Faucet giving you trouble again?" Sabina sat down at the kitchen table, her tone relaxed.

Her father grunted, then his head appeared from the cupboard. "That should do to keep it in place for a few more weeks. I wish I could get some new bolts, but there's no chance of that these days." With a clang, he dropped the wrench in his toolbox before wiping his forehead. He sat down across from Sabina. "How are you? I feel like I haven't seen much of you this past week."

Seriously? Sabina bit back a retort, forcing a smile instead. "You left for work before I came down for breakfast. Still busy at the mines?" She spoke sweetly, and her father smiled and shuffled closer to her.

"It's madness. Remember when I said the SS were sending more prisoners to the mines? It only got worse. And the working hours have increased. We're switching to twenty-four-hour operations next week, and they want two shifts per day." There was genuine concern in his voice, which was more shaky than normal. "They'll work those poor souls to death. But that appears to be the goal, anyway. The trucks collecting the bodies make multiple trips a day. There's even a specialized kommando to retrieve the corpses from the mines. Can you imagine? These men do nothing but carry bodies to the trucks."

Her father looked shaken, and Sabina felt sorry for him. Despite her suspicions about him not being completely open with her, she couldn't fault him for his work at the mines.

"Is there anything you can do about that? Lessen their suffering?"

"Not much, other than trying to provide enough water down there."

Sabina steeled herself, mustering up the courage to confront him.

"So, at work the other day, they were talking about what happened in town. Something about an armed robbery of a German truck." She kept her eyes on his face, scanning for a reaction. To her disappointment, he didn't flinch.

"Yes, I heard the same. The overseers at the mines were quite excited to share the gossip. From what I heard, the Nazis got a few of them, but most of the fighters got away."

"I'm glad they did." Sabina decided to play along with her father's feigned ignorance. "I can't imagine how it must feel to take on the SS like that. Must've been terrifying. Someone said the Gestapo are looking for the men that got away."

Her father shifted in his seat. "I'm sure they are. But the network is strong. Most of those boys will have left the area by now."

Sabina leaned forward, lowering her voice. "Did your contact know anything about it?"

"I didn't really discuss it with him."

Sabina could have screamed in frustration. He would not tell her. "Papa, I heard you come home late that night."

"What's that?" He tried to keep his face neutral, but his left eyebrow was twitching.

"I woke from the gunfire. At first I thought it was an escape, and I tried to get back to sleep. But when it continued, it was clear something else was going on." Sabina moved her chair closer to the table and placed her hands on it. "Then it became quiet again, and I went back to sleep. I figured I'd hear about what happened the next day. News travels quickly around these parts, wouldn't you say?"

"Hmm." Her father looked uncomfortable, his eyes shifting, avoiding her gaze.

I've got him.

"Imagine my surprise when I awoke for a second time, and someone was sneaking around the house. I was terrified, thinking it was a burglar, or perhaps someone from the gunfight looking to hide in our home. When he came up the stairs, I was paralyzed by fear, not daring to make a sound." Her father looked mortified as she continued. "But then the oddest thing happened. He stepped into your bedroom." Her father kept his eyes on the table. "For a few minutes, I thought I imagined everything, and then I went back to sleep. But the next morning, I knew it wasn't anything like that."

Sabina paused and glared across the table. *It's up to him now.* He fumbled with his hands, then took a deep breath and met her eyes. He looked back at her with an expression she didn't recognize. *Shame? Guilt? Defiance?*

"Sabinka, you are too observant. Even when you're supposed to be asleep." His eyes shone, and Sabina thought she detected a hint of pride and amusement in his voice. "I suppose the limp gave it away?"

"That, and your behavior. You looked tired, and you didn't want to talk to me or Mama before rushing out the door. It was odd enough, even before I heard what happened in town."

"I didn't want to burden you with it. I figured if I was picked up, it would be best if you and your mother knew nothing about what I'd done." A smile crept onto his face. "But I didn't take into account I'd woken you up at night."

"I probably wouldn't have heard you if the gunfire hadn't woken me earlier."

"I'm sorry, Sabinka, but all is well now. Like you said, I worried about the Gestapo coming for me at the mines the next day, but nothing happened. From what I've heard, they've stopped their search for now."

"Did they find anyone?"

He shook his head. "No, most of the younger men involved in the shootout were smuggled south. They'll stay out of sight for the next few weeks. Or months, even, I don't know."

"What was it like, Papa? Weren't you afraid they spotted you?" *I know I was.*

He leaned back in his chair. "I didn't have a gun. I was down by the river, supplying the weapons to those younger men. I was in the shadows, so I was fairly certain nobody saw me."

"What about the limp, though?"

Her father patted his leg. "When we retreated, I tripped over a loose stone. It hurt like hell, but nobody saw me. If they had, I might've been in trouble at the mines. The Gestapo did show up and questioned me."

"What did they want? That must've been terrifying."

"It was, especially when they barged into my office unannounced. I thought they were there for me, but it became clear they wanted to know about some of the overseers in the mine. Those men had nothing to do with the attack, so I didn't have to lie. They left without taking anyone, and they didn't come back."

"They didn't question your limp?"

"I only got up to salute them, Sabinka." He offered a devious smile. "I'm not an idiot."

"Does Mama know?"

The smile vanished. "No, and I'd like to keep it that way."

Sabina studied his face. He looked like her father again, his eyes meeting hers. She understood why he hadn't told her, but it still grated. Weren't they supposed to help each other, and the resistance? "I worried about you, Papa. Are you going to do this again anytime soon?"

"No." The answer came instantly, his voice firm. "When I stood waiting in the darkness, I realized this is a younger man's game. I worried about you and your mother. About what would happen to you if I was killed, or worse, if they caught me." He was silent for a moment, his eyes absent, his thoughts no doubt returning to that night. "I have no doubt they would've questioned both of you as well, if not worse. I told Marian I don't want to be involved in operations like this again."

"Marian? That's your contact?"

"Yes, that's the man you've seen around here a few times. He understood, and agreed it would be best if I keep my eyes and ears open around town."

His eyes were clear, the twinkle had returned, and she believed him.

"I worried about you, Papa."

"I'm sorry, Sabinka." His eyes went soft. "It's not your job to worry about me. I promise this was the first and last time. I'll stick to passing information along."

She nodded slowly. "About that. I was back at Rajsko the other day, and I met the commander of the camp. Mr. Piotrowski asked me to deliver some documents to him personally."

"What was that like?"

"Different. The commander wasn't what I expected."

"How so?"

"He wasn't unfriendly. Even offered me some cake while I waited.

He was nothing like the screaming guards and stone-faced soldiers passing though town."

Her father looked thoughtful. "He's a Nazi all the same, though."

"While I was there, I also spoke to one of the women working in the laboratories."

"The ones you saw earlier?"

"Yes. Turns out, all the women wearing the white lab coats are prisoners. They're cultivating plants, I think. I didn't get a chance to ask, but the entire lab was filled with the same ugly little plants."

Her father looked thoughtful. "Plants, really?"

"Much like dandelions, with the yellow flowers."

"You just walked into the lab? What about the guards?"

"That's the strange thing about the camp, Papa. Apart from at the entrance, I hardly saw any. And there's no fence. I just go from the road to the school building."

"The prisoners could just walk out?"

Sabina shook her head, remembering her run-in with the female guard. "There are guards patrolling the surroundings, and I'm sure the prisoners working the fields are watched more closely, but I spent a good few minutes talking to this female prisoner without any guards interrupting."

Her father moved his chair forward and sat up straight. "What about when you enter?"

"I report to the guards near the main road, and they let me through."

"Do they pat you down? Check your bag?"

"No. I usually just carry a folder or two, containing the documents for the administration."

"Interesting. And you're not escorted around the camp?"

"No."

"What about the prisoners working the fields? Are they free to move about?"

"I don't know—I've only seen them from a distance. There's a lot of them, though. I suspect the area is guarded quite closely."

"What about their sleeping quarters?"

Sabina shook her head. "I don't know anything about that. I've only seen the school building. There are a lot of greenhouses farther down the road, but that's all I've seen."

"Could you find out?"

Now it was Sabina's turn to sit up straighter. "Why, Papa? Is the resistance movement interested in Rajsko? Did you tell Marian about what I saw last time?"

"I haven't spoken to him about it yet." He scratched his chin. "But I think they'll be very interested in what you just told me. If there are no fences, but lots of prisoners, it could be an option."

"An option for what?" Her father was speaking in riddles again, and she didn't like it. He appeared to pick up on her confusion and reached out from the other side and gently took her hand.

"The people I'm involved with, they don't just attack German trucks. Actually, it's not so common. They're more interested in helping their people inside the camp."

"Their people?" She remembered Tosia's words. "You mean trading with the prisoners?"

"That also happens, but that's not what this is about. These are people of the resistance operating inside the camp."

Sabina's head was spinning. *A resistance inside the camp?* "How does that work?"

"As it is, it doesn't. Or not as well as it used to. I didn't know about this either, but there's a large group of people inside the camp who seek to sabotage the operations. There's been talk of an uprising for a while now, but in order for that to happen, they'll need to prepare properly."

"And they need weapons."

"That, but first, they need to stay alive. Which is why we've been smuggling food and medicine into the camp through various means. The past few weeks, however, many of our attempts have failed—guards have become more vigilant. Apart from the loss of food and medicine, it also means the group has lost much of its communications with those outside. It's a big problem."

"And you think Rajsko might provide a solution? A new route?" Sabina's voice trembled with anticipation.

"It might be. What you're saying is very promising, but we'd need to know more about the logistics of the camp. Things like how the prisoners are housed, how much freedom they really have, and if there are any connections with the main camps. Do you know anything about that?"

"Not really." In her mind she envisioned approaching the camp from the main road. The laboratory was easy to access, as were the greenhouses. She concentrated on what else she remembered. The fields in the distance, a gravel road running straight through the camp. She pictured the guards, the school building and the women working inside. *I could ask Felcia.* She imagined the scientist would be well informed. Would she be willing to share her information? *Of course she would. She's in there for teaching illegal classes.* She looked at her father and opened her mouth to share her plan, then another idea struck her. One that didn't involve her waiting for another assignment to Rajsko.

"What is it? You seem rather pleased." Her father looked at her curiously.

"I think I can get you more information on the camp from a very reliable source." She eyed the clock. It was almost two. "And I can do it today."

Sabina picked up her pace as she entered the square. She passed the pierogi store and was pleased to see a queue had formed at the counter. Joanna placed a large plate of dumplings on one of the tables near the window. She looked up and waved at Sabina, who smiled.

"So, when we meet this officer and his friends, what do you want me to say? My German isn't great." Elena sounded skeptical as they crossed the square. "And why are we meeting them again?"

Sabina smiled, forcing herself to appear more confident than she felt. "This officer from the camp invited me to come along some time. I put him off, but it might actually be useful to have a friend at the camp. I've been sent there more frequently, and by the looks of it, I'll be there a few times a week. It would be awkward if I declined."

"Doesn't have anything to do with you maybe liking him?" Elena was teasing, and Sabina ignored her. "What does he look like, anyway? Handsome fella?"

"It's not like that." She considered sharing the real reason but bit her lip. She didn't want her friend worrying. Maybe it would even be nice in the tavern. Sabina couldn't remember the last time she went. "It might be fun, you know? And if you're not comfortable, let me know, and we'll find an excuse to leave."

"So this is purely work-related then," Elena said, but it was clear she wasn't convinced.

They reached the tavern and Sabina stopped and turned before opening the door. "Your German really isn't that bad. And these men will be happy to chat with a woman, even if her German isn't perfect. Just try to relax." When Elena nodded, Sabina said a quiet prayer and opened the door.

Only half of the tables were occupied. Nobody looked up as Sabina and Elena found a spot in the corner. The smell of old wood, cigarette smoke, and stale beer brought back memories of summer evenings when her parents would take her to town, and they would end up here at some point. It would be hard to make it from one side of the room to the other back then, as half of the town would be crowding around the bar.

"What will it be, girls?" The familiar figure of Mr. Dominik appeared next to their table. Sabina looked up fondly at the elderly man. Mr. Dominik had run the tavern for as long as Sabina could remember. His age and vitality was part of local legend, with some people suggesting he was close to a hundred years old.

"Can we just have two glasses of water, please?" Sabina said, and Elena pulled a face. "We may try something a little stronger later."

"Of course, dear. Coming right up. You both doing well?" Mr. Dominik stood with his shoulders back; his words came quickly, and his eyes shone brightly.

"As well as one can be, Mr. Dominik," Elena answered, a genuine smile on her face. "Yourself?"

He made a dismissive motion with his hands and rolled his eyes theatrically. "Could do with a bit more business, but what can I do about it?" With that, he walked off toward the bar.

"He's such a kind soul," Elena said, her eyes on Mr. Dominik. "Do you think his business is struggling?"

"I don't think he's doing too poorly, considering the war." She remembered the afternoon her father went into the same tavern, and it appeared to be pretty crowded. "There's still people in here on a Saturday afternoon. That's more than most places on the square can say."

"Joanna's doing well still."

Sabina couldn't help but smile. "That's because nobody does pierogi like her. Essentials, Elena, essentials."

Mr. Dominik returned with two tall glasses of water. Sabina thanked him and took a large gulp while she looked around the room. *What am I doing here? Am I really meeting a Nazi officer for drinks?* It was an odd crowd in the tavern—six men a good few years older than her father sat playing cards at a table near the bar. The three tables on the opposite side of the room were populated by elderly couples who sat quietly nursing their small glasses of vodka. Sabina envied their seemingly stoic exterior. They appeared content to sit in silence, sipping their drinks and enjoying their partners' company. She hoped she would be that comfortable in silence when she was older.

"Did you agree on a time or anything?" Elena's voice sounded especially loud, cutting through Sabina's musings on silence.

"End of the afternoon." She eyed the clock above the bar, which indicated it was almost half past four.

As if on cue, the door to the tavern opened, and four men wearing SS officer's uniforms made a loud entrance. Elena flinched momentarily, but she quickly recovered when Sabina gave her a little kick under the table. Sabina recognized officer Sternhell and her heart beat faster. *This is it. Stay calm. He asked you to come here.*

Sternhell glanced across the small room and spotted her. His face lit up as he made his way over to their table. "You came!" There was surprise in his voice. "Do you mind if we join you?" He sat down and squeezed next to her on the bench before Sabina could answer. The other men also sat, and quick introductions were made. Mr. Dominik appeared and gave Sabina an almost imperceptible questioning look while taking their order.

"We'll have six beers," Sternhell said, before looking at Elena and Sabina. "Right? You'll join us for a few drinks?"

Elena appeared delighted at the prospect and Sabina relaxed a little. The Germans drinking might make her job a little easier. When she suggested she could meet with the German officer, her father had been skeptical, a little worried even. Sabina had convinced him by saying she wouldn't push too much. Besides, didn't all men love talking about their jobs? And these SS officers were so proud of what they were doing, she argued, it couldn't be too hard to get them to share some details. In the end, her father had agreed, but he insisted she not go alone. She looked at Elena animatedly talking across from her, the Germans hanging on her every word, and was relieved her friend had agreed to come along.

Mr. Dominik returned and placed six foaming beers on the table. They raised their glasses and one of the men said something Sabina didn't quite catch, but they clinked glasses soon after. She took a sip and enjoyed the bitter taste. It had been a long time since she'd had a beer. It soothed her nerves.

"When I left the camp just now, I hoped you'd show up, but I have to be honest." Sternhell's voice was a bit softer as he turned from the main conversation to Sabina. "I didn't for a second expect to find you sitting here." He raised his glass. "*Prost.* It's good to see you outside the camp, Sabina."

She clinked his glass. "You too, Hauptsturmführer."

The smile on his face widened, and he abruptly put his glass down. "Please, call me Paskal. You can reserve those formalities for the camp."

"Very well, Paskal." *He's actually quite handsome when he smiles.* Sabina caught herself feeling embarrassed about looking at him this way. *You're here to do a job.* She took another sip, her eyes darting across the room. She caught a few of the other patrons looking at her disapprovingly. It stung, but she decided not to pay them any attention. *They do not know why I'm here.* She turned back to Paskal, his friendly face giving her confidence. "Can I ask you something?"

He looked pleased as he leaned back onto the backrest of the small bench. "Please."

"Well, you know quite a bit about me. Where I live, what I do, all of that." Sabina hesitated for a moment, and she took a quick sip before clearing her throat. "What's your story? How did you end up here?"

"My story is much like most of the men in the SS. I joined the Hitler Youth when I turned fourteen. That's now ten years ago." He sighed and emptied his glass before continuing. "My father is a party member, and it was a given that I would join. When I finished high school, he suggested I move into the SS officer training program. Again, I had little choice." His voice was oddly flat and devoid of the emotion Sabina remembered when he spoke of what they were going to do at Rajsko. Or when he'd entered the tavern and spotted her earlier, even.

"Did you not like your training?"

"No, it was fine. I learned a lot of useful skills, and I rose up the ranks pretty quickly." He signaled for more beers. "My father was very proud, and I felt like I was living up to his expectations. Soon after finishing my training, I was stationed at some smaller camps near Berlin."

"You're from Berlin, then?"

A smile returned to his face. "Yes. Best city in the world." He waited for Mr. Dominik to set down the new drinks before raising his glass and taking a large swig. Sabina was still nursing her first beer, taking small sips.

"I've only seen photos, but it does look impressive," she said, and Paskal nodded and took another large swig of his beer.

Sabina glanced at Elena, who was keeping pace with the men and on her second beer—enraptured by their attention.

"And how did you end up getting sent to Rajsko?" Sabina's tone was casual.

"I was sent to Birkenau first, but I only ended up spending a couple of months there before getting transferred down the road. Thank God." His face turned serious. "It's a dirty place, each block even more disgusting than the last. And the smell." He scrunched up his nose. "It's hard to breathe with all that smoke."

Sabina had to control herself not to say what she was thinking. "None of that in Rajsko."

"No, Rajsko is too important. You've seen it—there's important work carried out there." He placed his empty glass on the table and tried —unsuccessfully—to catch Mr. Dominik's attention. "If what we do at

Rajsko works, it will be a triumph for the entire Reich." He stared in the direction of the bar again.

"Hey! More beers!" one of Paskal's colleagues called across the room. "Hurry up, will you? We're thirsty!" The chastening looks of the other patrons were more explicit now, and Sabina felt her cheeks burning. Despite that, she pushed on.

"What's that exactly? I understand the fields are important, since you have so many people working there every day." *And also the reason I had to move.*

"The fields are just for food. It's the research that's really making the difference." Paskal leaned closer to her. "You've seen the laboratories in the main building, haven't you?"

"I saw some women in white lab coats walking around, yes." *Tread carefully.*

"They're experimenting to see if we can grow our own rubber."

Sabina's mind went back to her meeting with Felcia. *So that's what the ugly plants are for.* Even though the research was interesting, it didn't necessarily help her father and the organization. She needed to steer the conversation back to the people working the fields.

"There's something I don't understand about the camp," Sabina said, and Paskal looked at her with interest. "Where are all the fences? It's so different from the other camps in the area."

"Ah." He smiled while cradling his beer. "We don't need a fence around the fields. The overseers make sure nobody makes a run for it."

"What about the women working in the laboratories and greenhouses?"

"They wouldn't dream of running away. They are treated almost as well as we are. Their dwellings are comfortable, they are given good food and warm showers. We need them healthy to do their job. They're scientists. The only time they're locked up is at night."

"What about the people in the fields?" Sabina held her breath, hoping she was subtle enough to keep Paskal from becoming suspicious.

"What about them? They're farmhands from Birkenau."

"So they go back and forth between the camps every day?"

He took another sip and nodded nonchalantly. "They're disposable."

"You seem awfully interested in the workings of the camp." A voice across the table cut Sabina's next question short. One of the other Germans was eyeing her suspiciously.

"It's fine, Hanno! She's just curious about what's happening at Rajsko. It's impressive, isn't it?" Paskal's tone was dismissive but light. "Let's just enjoy the evening. It's not often we have two beautiful women join us."

"No, I'd like to know where her interest comes from." Hanno wasn't letting it go, and the table went quiet. All eyes were on Sabina now. Panic gripped her throat and she looked at Elena, who had a confused look on her face. Sabina returned her attention to Hanno. She could almost feel his eyes piercing her soul. With a sigh, she nodded and placed her hands—palms up—on the table.

"You're right, I am very interested in the camp." A victorious smile started to form on Hanno's face, but Sabina continued undeterred. "I visit the camp a few times a week, and I notice things. I don't know if Paskal told you, but where the fields are now my house used to be. I grew up in the building you call the laboratory. It was my school. Our school." She paused and looked to Elena. "But that's not why I asked Paskal about the fields or the purpose. I asked because I see all the crops, the food coming from Rajsko. I ask because I'm hungry, and I'm wondering if any of the food might come our way, to the hungry people in town."

Paskal sat up and moved a little closer to her. "You know, next time you're at the camp, I'll make sure there's some food waiting for you. And your family. We have plenty." He looked to the other men. "Right, boys? I think we can manage that?" The Germans all nodded, including Hanno, whose piercing eyes had softened, the suspicion fading. Paskal then raised his glass. "Prost! To Sabina and Elena!"

The conversation returned to the table, and Sabina was relieved to join the other group's earlier discussion of pierogi, with Elena insisting they try Joanna's sometime. As she listened, her mind returned to what Paskal had told her. She would love to talk to Felcia about the research, but it was the revelation of the relative prisoner freedom within Rajsko, as well as the daily stream of prisoners coming in from Birkenau that really excited her. Her father would be pleased.

CHAPTER NINETEEN

Bianka peered at the large flower underneath the glass dome. "I can't quite believe it's growing so quickly. Did you say it just spurted up like this overnight?"

"I was as surprised as you when I walked in this morning. I didn't make any big changes, and the other plants didn't respond in the same way."

"The soil is slightly more moist." Bianka pointed at the moisture sensor. "Did you check the plants in the greenhouse yet? It's been quite hot these past few days."

"I was planning to go in the afternoon, but you're right. It might be best to head over now." Felcia grabbed her small bag of tools and headed for the door. "I'll be back in a bit."

She hurried toward the greenhouse, suddenly anxious to confirm whether the one plant in her laboratory was an anomaly, or that she'd stumbled onto something. Their research had shown the plants flourished in warmer temperatures, but they hadn't experimented with humidity and moisture levels too much yet. She crossed the short distance between the laboratory building and the greenhouse quickly and opened the door. Stepping into the humid air, she headed to her plants, only a short way down the main path. As she made her way over, she automatically scanned the rest of the greenhouse. She was alone.

Approaching the plants, she saw they were growing as expected. A pang of disappointment hit as she realized the bigger plant back in the lab was indeed an anomaly. She crouched down on her knees and opened her bag of instruments. *Might as well take some readings while I'm here.*

"Excuse me."

Felcia almost jumped out of her skin. She had been so focused that she hadn't noticed the unfamiliar woman hovering over her until the last moment. "What are you doing sneaking up on me like this?" She got to her feet and found the woman a head taller than her.

"Sorry about that. I didn't mean to scare you." The woman's voice and words were soothing, and she eyed Felcia confidently. "You're Felcia, aren't you?"

"It appears everybody knows who I am," Felcia said with a little irritation, then caught herself. "Wait. Who are you?"

The woman glanced around, then smiled. "I believe you spoke to Klaudia about joining us. I'm Olga."

"You're Klaudia's contact?"

"One of her contacts, yes. She told me about your time together in Kraków."

Felcia considered adding they hadn't been that close in Kraków, but she decided to hear what Olga had to say before volunteering any information.

"I'm told you were quite the prodigy at the university. On the fast track to a glorious career. A professorship even?" Despite the flattering words, the woman's voice remained even. "That's something a lot of women can only dream about."

"I'm afraid Klaudia overstated my importance at Jagiellonian. I was just teaching some classes, which all ended when the Nazis invaded."

"Modesty won't get you very far in these surroundings." Olga tutted as she started walking along the path. The woman's energy was so strong that Felcia found herself drawn to follow. "Those Nazis didn't stop you from teaching in Kraków, did they? You simply joined the underground movement."

"It was just a few afternoons a week." Felcia questioned how well Klaudia had relayed the information. Olga's words made her out to be some brave resistance fighter, leading the underground schooling network. It reminded her of someone else. The professor.

"Wouldn't you like to teach again? Make a real difference, besides helping the Germans with their rubber plantation plans?" It was the first time Olga's neutral tone cracked a little to reveal scorn.

This time, Felcia had her answer ready. She'd had plenty of time to think since her last meeting with Klaudia. "I'd love to. But I don't quite know how I would go about it. We have no covert locations for classes. Or books."

Olga stopped abruptly and turned to her. "Really? You're going to let those small details distract you from the real mission here? This isn't about a classroom or books. This is about transferring your knowledge to smart women." She held out her arms and took a loud breath of air. "We're in a greenhouse filled with plants. Your fully equipped laboratory is just across the road. Don't tell me you don't have anything to teach these women. You have everything available to train Poland's next botanists or biologists!"

"But where would I teach them?" Felcia felt her palms warm. Yet, she couldn't ignore the practicalities. "It's one thing to teach in an apartment, but this is very different. Where would we go in the camp?"

"The guards don't come into your block in the evenings, do they? And even if they did, I doubt they would care about a few women sitting around talking."

Olga appeared to have an answer to anything, and Felcia found her pragmatic approach infectious. "Klaudia said the women would be transferred from Birkenau. How does that work?"

"Let us worry about that, Felcia. You focus on educating them once they're here. We'll make sure they're assigned to your block. You were in Birkenau yourself, weren't you?" The woman didn't wait for a response. "Then you know your survival depends on two things. Pure luck, and whether you're lucky enough to have a useful skill. That's it. This camp, Rajsko, has different rules. You produce results with your research, and you get to live a pretty comfortable life, wouldn't you agree?"

"I suppose so, yes."

"No. There's no comparison to Birkenau. This is as good as it gets." Olga's tone was sharp. "I'm sorry, but you don't get to feel sorry for yourself. I know it's no summer camp, but just the fact that we're standing here talking to each other without a guard interrupting proves my point."

Felcia felt her cheeks burn. "You're right. I'm sorry. What happens next? I educate these women, then what? How does this help the resistance?"

For the first time, a smile appeared on Olga's face. "There's one thing you need to know about the camp underground. Things generally move much slower than we'd like. But look, you get these girls ready for the labs. Have them start out as assistants. I hear you have a good rapport with Dr. Caesar? We'll help move them from Birkenau to Rajsko. Don't ask me how. I don't know. All I know is that it's possible." She gave Felcia an intense look, then continued. "We'll get more women in different positions in the camp."

Felcia's mind boggled at the size of the operation. From Olga's words, she realized this wasn't just about teaching classes. This was about somehow taking over Rajsko with women aligned to the resistance cause. "What's the big plan?"

Another smile. "All in good time, Felcia. For now, I just need to know one thing from you. Are you ready to teach these women, and set the operation in motion?"

CHAPTER TWENTY

Sabina clutched the small bag tightly as she reported to the two guards at the main road. It contained only a flask of water, a book, and a notepad, but she felt her skin tingle as they eyed her. When she proffered the large brown envelope addressed to Dr. Caesar, the guards held up their hands and waved her inside. She smiled after she passed and walked toward the school building. They hadn't bothered searching her bag, sufficiently impressed by the message she carried for Rajsko's commanding officer.

The hallway in her old school was deserted, and she quickly made for Dr. Caesar's office. Passing Felcia's door, she was disappointed to see it closed, with no light streaming through the frosted window. *I hope she's all right.*

The door to Dr. Caesar's office was closed as well, as was Paskal's. She stood in the hallway, uncertain about what to do next. Then the door to the commander's office opened, revealing a young man in what appeared to be a more junior SS uniform. He looked at her in surprise.

"What are you doing here?" His tone was sharp, but not unfriendly. "Can I help you?"

"I have some papers for Dr. Caesar." She held out the envelope. "They're from the municipal registry. I think he's expecting me."

"The commander isn't in right now. He should be back shortly." He waved to a pair of chairs opposite the office door. "Why don't you wait for him here?"

Sabina took a seat while the SS man locked the door. He turned to her while placing the key in his pocket. "It shouldn't be long, but if you need to use the bathroom, it's right over there."

"Thank you." Sabina smiled while she watched him disappear down the hallway. She crossed her legs and placed her hands on her skirt while she listened to the murmurs from behind closed doors. She couldn't make out the words, but it comforted her to know she wasn't on her own. In truth, she didn't mind waiting for Dr. Caesar. The archiving room in Oświęcim was quite hectic, and Tosia and she were almost literally buried in work. Any excuse to get away from the pile of files was welcome, and she was pleased her trips to Rajsko were getting more frequent.

Her father had been very pleased—and impressed—when she returned from the tavern. It had taken some persuasion to get Elena to leave, but when she got home, her father was waiting. He'd naturally been intrigued about the rubber experiments, recognizing the value for the German war effort and the possibilities for resistance sabotage. Sabina promised she'd see if she could find out more, but they had then focused on the security measures for the camp. Paskal had given her enough details to reveal the potential of using Rajsko as an entry point for the resistance. They agreed Sabina would investigate the situation in the camp in more detail. Her eyes went to the bag on the floor beneath her. She had cleared the first hurdle.

One of the areas of greatest interest to the resistance was where the prisoners slept. Paskal had mentioned they were only locked up at night. She had to find out what that meant. Despite the lack of fences around the camp, it wouldn't be easy to smuggle goods in or out of the camp in broad daylight. Sabina's eyes roamed the hallway as she considered how to find out more about the prisoners' movements. Her attention was drawn to a small window next to the commander's office. She looked up and down the hallway, and when certain she was alone, stood and moved toward the window. It faced the camp thoroughfare. To her right was the main road heading to Oświęcim. Directly opposite was an open field with the little dandelion-like plants. There was movement to the left, where the door to one of the greenhouses opened. Two women dressed in white lab coats emerged, carrying buckets. They looked unhurried while they crossed the road toward what appeared to be a nearby well, filling their buckets while calmly conversing. Though Sabina couldn't make out their words, it was clear they were discussing something important; one of the women talked animatedly, the other nodding and adding her own suggestions. When their buckets were filled they disappeared back inside the greenhouse.

Sabina stepped away from the window and sat on her chair again. The exchange hadn't taken more than a minute or two, but what surprised her was the confidence with which the women moved about —there hadn't been a guard in sight.

Voices sounded in the distance, and it didn't take long for footsteps to echo through the hallway. Dr. Caesar approached with the young man she'd met earlier in tow. The commander appeared surprised to see her as he waited for his assistant to open the door.

"I didn't think you'd be here so soon. I spoke to your boss only a few hours ago." The younger man opened the door and Dr. Caesar entered, gesturing for Sabina to follow. "Let's get these signed so you can be on your way. I'm sure you're busy."

Sabina handed him the envelope as he sunk into the large chair behind his desk. "I didn't have to wait that long, sir."

"Have a seat. This shouldn't take long." He waved her to the chair opposite him while his eyes scanned the pages. "Although I fear I don't have a piece of cake to offer this time."

Sabina smiled but said nothing. She looked out the large window behind the commander. It offered a good view of the fields, as well as the main road running through the camp. She noticed a couple of women making their way toward them, both carrying crates filled with the dandelion plants she'd seen everywhere.

It took only a few minutes before the commander handed the papers back to her. "That should do."

"Thank you." She took the papers. The women outside were close enough for Sabina to make out the small, bright yellow flowers in the crates. Dr. Caesar caught her look, turned and clapped his hands.

"You must be wondering why they're carrying flowers around." It was an invitation for her to express her interest, and she nodded. That was enough for Dr. Caesar. "They are scientists, mostly Polish and Russian. Their job is to analyze the potential of those little flowers."

"Potential to do what?" There was a tremor in Sabina's voice, but she knew it was the only logical response to his cryptic description, as well as necessary to confirm what Paskal had told her.

Dr. Caesar didn't immediately answer, but gave her a smile. "To change the dependency of the Reich on the eastern countries for our supplies." It was sufficiently vague for anyone with no knowledge to be none the wiser, but after what Paskal had told her, Sabina knew enough. Best not to push any further.

"And is the research going well?"

"As well as one can expect in these conditions." He pointed to the greenhouses. "The initial results are promising, but we're running out of space to test and grow our plants. I'm looking to expand the greenhouses a little farther away. I'm just waiting for approval." When Sabina didn't say anything, Dr. Caesar appeared to catch himself. "Well, I think it might be time for you to return to town, don't you think?"

"Yes, sir. Good luck with the research," Sabina managed as she hurried out of the office, keen to get away before Dr. Caesar realized how much he'd shared with her.

"Close the door, please."

Sabina stood in the hallway and took a deep breath. Had Dr. Caesar realized how much information he'd shared with her? He appeared genuinely proud and enthusiastic about his research. Perhaps he'd forgotten who he was talking to. Or, more likely, he didn't consider Sabina a threat. Either way, she had garnered more valuable information.

She moved toward the exit, Dr. Caesar's words still floating through her mind. As Sabina tried making sense of everything, she didn't notice the person turning the corner.

"Oops, watch where you're going," a familiar female voice said, and Sabina stopped just in time to avoid bumping into the woman. "Hey, Sabina, right?"

Sabina was pleased to see the attractive young woman wearing the lab coat. "Yes. Hi, Felcia. I looked for you earlier." Sabina's eyes sparkled.

"That's nice. Can't say too many people come to visit me here." Felcia's voice had a playful tone, and her bright eyes studied Sabina with interest. She pointed at the large envelope in Sabina's hands. "Delivering important paperwork again?"

"Dr. Caesar already signed them. I'm on my way back into town." Sabina made a move to continue to the door, then stopped. *I should ask her.*

Felcia seemed to sense her hesitation. "Something on your mind?"

"Dr. Caesar told me about the research you're working on here." Sabina looked around to make sure there was no one else nearby. "He seemed very confident. Are you really able to produce rubber from those little plants?"

"Yes. Do you want to see them?"

Sabina nodded, and they quickly crossed the hallway and stepped into Felcia's laboratory. Pointing at the stalks, Felcia explained how the unassuming plants could make the difference in the war. "If the Nazis can scale up their production of these plants, they can produce all the rubber they need."

"And you're making good progress?"

"Yes, we're finishing up the first tests, and the plants are growing really well in the greenhouses."

"Dr. Caesar did mention expanding the greenhouses just now."

Felcia appeared surprised. "Well, look at that. He hasn't bothered telling us yet. It seems he's taken a liking to you." Sabina moved between a few of the glass domes, then Felcia cleared her throat. "Remember how I asked you about what was going on outside the camp?"

"Sure." Sabina turned her attention back to Felcia, whose face had taken on a serious expression.

"We never really got round to that."

"What would you like to know?"

"Well, even though we're mostly isolated from the outside, we still hear the occasional rumor. It's usually about how the war is going, and the guards talk with each other as well. But I was wondering if there's anything you may have picked up about things happening in the area around the camp?"

There was something in Felcia's voice that made Sabina stop. It was as if she was asking the question to something she already knew the answer to. "There are always things happening around the camp. Anything specific?"

Felcia smiled, slyly. "You're a smart young woman, Sabina. I want to know about any resistance activities. With all the rumors going around, I don't know what to believe. Every story is more fantastical than the last."

Sabina eyed the red triangle on Felcia's shirt, remembering the reason she was in the camp. Of course, she could've lied about it, but Sabina decided the botanist had been honest with her. She had corroborated both Paskal's and Dr. Caesar's information about the research, and there was no reason for her to deceive Sabina. She was her only connection to the outside. Sabina lowered her voice.

"There have been acts of sabotage." She detailed the assault on the German transport, omitting her father's involvement. Felcia's eyes lit up when she told her most of the men managed to get away.

"That was a bold attack. Does that happen often?"

"This was the first I heard of." She thought of her father, and added, "But it does feel like the resistance around the camp is growing. People are sick of seeing death on their doorstep. Every morning the columns of prisoners are marched past our homes, on their way to the factories and mines. In the evening, they carry the dead with them." The image formed in Sabina's mind, and she was quiet for a moment. "Not to mention what happens inside the camps."

Felcia nodded. "I was in Birkenau before they transferred me here. Trust me, I've seen it." A deep sadness cast a shadow over her face, her eyes glassy and distant. Sabina regretted her words, realizing she had unwittingly conjured up painful memories. Then Felcia's gaze returned to focus with fierce defiance. "If they were given the chance, the prisoners would fight back."

"Do you mean the stories of the growing camp resistance?" Sabina held her breath.

"How do you mean?"

"I've heard of people smuggling goods into the camp. Rumors of prisoners preparing an uprising?" Sabina paused for a moment. "To fight back?"

Felcia shuffled awkwardly on her feet, fumbling with her hands. "There's always people talking about escaping or rising up. Other than a few unsuccessful escapes, I've seen nothing of it." Felcia's eyes darted around the room, avoiding Sabina's gaze. *There's something she's not telling me.*

There were women's voices in the hallway, and a few seconds later another woman, dressed identically to Felcia, stepped into the room. She looked surprised to see Sabina, and turned her head to Felcia, who quickly spoke up.

"This is Sabina. She's a messenger from town. I was showing her some of the flowers. She was just leaving."

Sabina forced a smile and moved toward the door. Even without the interruption, she realized she had taken a big risk by stepping inside the laboratory.

"It was nice to see you," she forced herself to say casually. "Good luck with the research."

"Take care. I hope I'll see you next time you're here." The warmth had returned to Felcia's voice.

The hallway was deserted, and Sabina quickly stepped out of the building. The fresh air caressed her face, and she noticed her palms were a little clammy. Felcia surely knew more about the camp underground's activities than she was willing to share. Sabina reached the main road and turned in the direction of town. Something told her there was more to come from Felcia.

That evening, when her mother had retired to bed, Sabina and her father sat at the kitchen table. He listened without interrupting as Sabina reported on everything that she'd seen and heard at the camp.

"The prisoners working in the main camp moved about freely. I saw them going between the greenhouses and school building."

"And nobody checked your bag?" her father asked, Sabina shook her head. "That's great. I was hoping they wouldn't, but that really opens up possibilities."

"How so?" Sabina had a sense of foreboding. "Do you want me to carry goods into the camp?"

Her father fervently shook his head. "No, I don't want to involve you in anything like that."

"But they know me at the camp. One of the most senior officers likes me," she replied, sternly. "If not me, then who?"

"I don't know yet. But if anything happened to you, I would never forgive myself. Besides, you're too valuable already. You have a free pass into the camp. Even if we start smuggling things into Rajsko and people get caught, nobody will suspect you. Your alibi is perfect, and you've been a messenger for how long now? A month?"

"Almost two." She had to admit her father had a point. She also wasn't sure if she had the guts to smuggle incriminating goods into the camp. "What would you smuggle in?"

"Medication and food, mostly." His words were unconvincing, and Sabina raised an eyebrow.

"Mostly?"

"There's talk of weapons, too. But I know little about that. Either way, you wouldn't be involved."

Sabina slowly nodded her head. It all made sense. Her father's earlier mention of the need to contact and help the people of the camp underground. It was confirmed: the resistance was real.

"Papa. How important is Rajsko for the plans of the resistance?"

He shook his head. "I don't know. I haven't shared what you told me the other night yet. I wanted to wait until you confirmed what you heard. It sounds like you did."

"And what happens now?"

"Now I need to speak to my contact and see what he thinks."

She sat up. "And what do you think?"

"It doesn't really matter. I only provide them with information."

"Not to them, maybe. But I'd like to know." She kept her gaze on him until he met her eyes.

"I think you're really onto something here, Sabinka. But there are still so many unknowns. The most important one being how we would get the goods from Rajsko to Birkenau. And we'd need people inside the camp. It won't be easy."

"But it's a start, no?"

He faced her with a look of affection. "It most certainly is. I'm proud of you. Let me talk to Marian, and then we'll know more."

CHAPTER TWENTY-ONE

Felcia's legs were aching when she neared her block. She'd spent most of the day on her feet, going between the laboratory and the greenhouses. September had come, and the days were getting shorter. For Felcia and the rest of the scientists, it meant their first round of experiments were coming to a close. The freezing Polish winter would make for much harsher conditions, even in the greenhouses. While her experiments were going well, the Germans could decide they didn't need the same number of scientists in winter. Even if it meant they might not be able to find the same smart women to replace them in spring.

She shook the thought as she entered her living quarters. Not all experiments had produced the same results, but she was certain Dr. Caesar understood the need to test in suboptimal conditions. There would be plenty of time to do that in the next few months.

It was comfortably warm in the barracks, with most of the other women already inside, having made their way back to their bunks after collecting their evening rations.

The door opened again, and Felcia felt a jolt of energy as three fresh faces entered. The women were a few years younger than her, and they looked about uncertainly. The other women in the block ignored them. Felcia got up and approached them, her earlier weariness fading with every step. It was replaced by a bubbly excitement she hadn't experienced for months.

The three women turned to her, their faces lined with nervous anticipation. Felcia knew what was going through their heads. It hadn't been long since she entered Rajsko for the first time herself. The contrast with Birkenau was overwhelming. She greeted them with a warm smile, her arms spread out in front.

"Welcome. I'm Felcia. Please, come with me. It's much nicer to chat sitting down." She nodded to her bunk in the back of the room. The women followed hesitantly, but once they reached her bunk, the wrinkles on their foreheads had loosened somewhat. She placed two stools opposite her bunk and sat down, patting on the space next to her. The three women sat down, looking around the room.

"Did you arrive from Birkenau just now?"

The women looked to each other uncertainly. After a short silence, the woman sitting next to Felcia opened her mouth. "This morning. Our names were called during roll call." Her voice was surprisingly soft, contrasting with her somewhat rough exterior. She wore a ragged dress that was at least two sizes too small for her large frame. Even when sitting down, Felcia estimated the woman was at least a head taller than her. "At first, we thought it was a selection, but when it was just the three of us, we knew something else was going on."

"They took you to Rajsko right away?"

"No. They made us wait while the other women marched off to their work details. After they had all left, we were told to collect our things in the block. That was odd, because if they were going to kill us, they would just march us off to the back of the camp." The woman's voice was growing in strength. Felcia glanced at the two women across from her and was pleased to see them leaning forward, their shoulders no longer as tense. "Then a guard took us to a different group waiting near the gate. That's when we walked to this new camp. We worked the fields for the entire day, and when they called for everyone to return to Birkenau, our names were called again. That's when they told us we'd be staying here."

A quick smile escaped Felcia's lips. Klaudia and the camp underground had really come through. She wondered how far their influence stretched. They were, after all, only prisoners. Nevertheless, these women were now sitting with her. It was impressive.

"Let's make sure you remain, because I'm sure you've already seen the conditions are much better here," Felcia said, pleased to see the women's faces turn to her in anticipation. "Let's start with your names, shall we?" The women on the stools introduced themselves as Izolda and Paula, the latter anxious to speak.

"We're from Mława, near Warsaw. We grew up together, and we lived in the ghetto together when our parents were deported from the city. When the ghetto was cleared, we hung onto each other." She sighed, the hurt in her eyes at the painful memory obvious. "Somehow, we were assigned to the same block on arrival in Birkenau."

"It's hard to believe in coincidences, but I'm starting to think someone might be looking out for us," Izolda added, her eyes flashing upward for a moment. "Only a few of the people on our train are still alive. Most didn't make it past selection on the ramp."

"When did you arrive in Birkenau?" Felcia asked.

The women looked at each other, and Paula answered, "It's hard to keep track of time, but it must've been about two, maybe three months ago."

"And you?" Felcia looked to the woman on the bed next to her.

"I'm Renata, and I grew up in Łódź. When the Germans invaded, my family and I were placed in the ghetto." She paused, casting her eyes downward. "I got out, but I was caught, and ended up here. That's now more than six months ago." Her voice wavered, and even though Felcia was curious to know how she had escaped the ghetto, she decided there would be plenty of time to ask later. It was more important to help them settle. She looked at the women and realized none of them had mentioned why they were here. *They don't know, or they're not sure if they can tell me.*

"Back home, before the war, what did you do? Did you go to school? Work?"

The three women looked surprised, then Paula answered, "I was in my last year of studying agronomy."

Next to her, Izolda nodded. "Me too. Biochemistry."

They turned to Renata, who smiled ruefully. "I was preparing to

173

start my major in geology. But the university got shut down before I got a chance."

Felcia struggled to contain her excitement. She hadn't known what to expect, but the women's backgrounds impressed her. She leaned forward and spoke in a hushed voice. "Renata, you said you were surprised when you were selected at roll call. Did no one reach out to you before that?"

The young woman shook her head, and Felcia looked at the friends across from them.

"No, we also thought we were doomed. We'd seen it happen many times before. Scores of women taken from roll call, never to be seen again," Izolda said, before she cocked her head. "But I have a feeling you can tell us more about what happened. This is no coincidence."

Three pairs of eyes focused on Felcia, and she felt the back of her neck burning up. Instead of answering right away, she reached underneath the thin mattress of her bed, and pulled out three sheets of paper, as well as a pencil for each of the women. She had smuggled these from the laboratory over the past few days, and the contraband had felt like lead in her dress every single time. Her nights had been restless as the paper and pencils kept her on pins and needles. Now, the surprised looks on the women's faces made it all worth it. She placed the writing gear next to her on the bed.

"No, this was no coincidence." She explained Rajsko's purpose, and her role in the camp. The young women listened breathlessly, Paula looking around the room a few times. "Every single woman in this room has a scientific background, although we only have a few biologists and botanists like myself. But you pick up things rather quickly in these surroundings."

"Now it all makes sense. We were transferred because of our backgrounds." Izolda looked relieved.

Felcia held up a hand. "Yes, but not by the people running the camp. Not by the SS."

Izolda's eyes narrowed, and the other two women looked similarly taken aback. "Then, how? I don't understand."

"I don't know the details, but there's a prisoner movement inside the camp. They somehow got you moved to Rajsko." The women didn't respond, shock clear from their faces. Felcia pushed on. "But now that you're here, I promised to teach you everything you need to know to become useful."

"Useful?" Renata frowned.

Felcia decided not to tell them about her worries about the upcoming winter. "This research is very important to the Nazis. And from the early results, I expect they'll need more women assisting soon. When that happens, you'll be ready."

Renata still looked unconvinced. "But how do we make sure they know we're *useful*?"

Felcia opened her mouth to answer, but Paula beat her to it. "It doesn't matter. Have you looked around today? Look at the women surrounding us. Look at the beds, the clothes they're wearing. Do you remember where we woke up this morning? The stench, the dirty barracks? I thought I wasn't going to make it past noon when they called out my name." Izolda put a hand on her arm, and Paula lowered her voice. "Whatever happens next, I'll take my chances with Felcia. What's the alternative? Go back to Birkenau?" She raised her chin defiantly and looked as if she wanted to say more. Before she had a chance, Izolda interrupted, addressing Felcia.

"Paula's right; Birkenau is hell. If what you're saying is true, I'm sure we're in a much better place here than down the road."

Felcia nodded, then turned to Renata. The tall woman looked slightly embarrassed. "I'm sorry. I suppose I'm a little overwhelmed. I also feared everything was over this morning, and now you're telling us there might be a way to survive." Her attention was drawn to a couple of women talking in whispers a few beds over. "In these comfortable surroundings, even. It all seems a bit surreal."

"I understand. I felt the same when I first arrived here." Felcia felt for the woman, and she was determined to put her mind at ease as best she could. "My journey was much the same. I taught illegal classes in Kraków, and someone ratted me out. I was in Birkenau a few days later. There were plenty of times when I didn't think I'd survive to see the next day. Then, one morning, I was reassigned to Rajsko. But, unlike you, I didn't have the support of the camp underground. You are perhaps even more lucky."

"You mentioned you were going to make us useful. How?" Izolda's eyes were trained on her, intelligence and curiosity shining through. *Perfect.*

"To be honest, I don't know what your tasks will be in the next few weeks. The fact that you've been assigned to this block is promising, but I doubt you'll be invited to work in the laboratories or greenhouses anytime soon. The few newcomers we've had are usually assigned to more strenuous work."

"Like what we did today, working the fields?" Izolda's eyes were focused like spotlights on her. Felcia was impressed with the young woman's composure.

"I doubt you'll be sent back to the fields. That doesn't make sense. Fieldwork is done by the women coming in from Birkenau every day. I think it's more likely you'll be required to help maintain the camp. Collect water for the greenhouses, the laboratories, clean the blocks and bathrooms."

"But we'll be sleeping in this block." Paula eyed some of the unclaimed beds farther down the room. "I'll clean toilets all day if it means I get to stay here." Izolda and Renata nodded their agreement.

"We'll find out what your tasks are tomorrow morning. In the meantime, I'll start teaching you everything you need to know." Felcia glanced around the room quickly. None of the others paid them any attention, and there was no sign of any guards or block elders. She handed each of them a single sheet of paper and a pencil. "I'd like to get an idea of your basic knowledge. I've prepared a few questions and equations for you to work out. Why don't you spend fifteen minutes working on those, and then we'll go through them together."

The three women turned their attention to the assignments, and Felcia was pleased to see them scribbling away quickly. The equations were straightforward, and even though it had been a while since the women's brains had been engaged in this manner, Felcia was confident they would all pass this first test. The sight triggered memories of her underground teaching days in Kraków. It was hard to remember the faces of her former students, but she remembered their names. Julian. Kasia. She hoped they had somehow escaped her fate. A stab of pain went through her heart as she considered the lost potential across the country. So many bright young minds had been deprived of education for over five years now. She muttered a silent prayer and hoped the underground schools were still operating.

Voices hissing from the front of the room alerted her senses, and Felcia looked up. Cold terror gripped her heart. Two guards stomped into the room, batons in hand, their attention on a group of women sitting in a circle.

"What are you doing here? What's that?" The guard pointed at a kettle placed on the single stove in the room. "You know you're not supposed to be cooking anything in here."

"It's only tea, ma'am, I'm sorry."

A loud smacking sound was followed by a shriek of pain. Despite the dangers of taking her eyes off the guards, Felcia reached forward and snatched the papers from Izolda and Paula. Renata turned to her wide-eyed and offered her piece of paper as well. Felcia managed to stuff the papers underneath her covers just as footsteps approached, the wooden floor creaking.

"And what's this? Are you also having a nice tea party?" The same voice was next to Felcia's ear. "And who are you? I've never seen you in here before." The guard's eyes narrowed with suspicion. The silence in the room was deafening, and Felcia could feel the eyes of the other women locked on her. *I need to do something.* Before she could say anything, the guard's beady eyes shifted to her. "You I recognize. Who are these girls, and what are they doing gathered around your bed? What are you up to?"

Felcia racked her brain for a plausible explanation, then decided sticking as close to the truth as possible was her best chance. "They were assigned to our block today after coming in from Birkenau. I was about to show them to some free beds."

"That's your job now, is it?" The guard stepped between Felcia and the women sitting on stools opposite her. She stood so close that Felcia could smell the rain on the woman's uniform. "Are you also going to tell them how to speak when spoken to? Or are they mutes?" She didn't wait for an answer, but flicked her wrist and said, "Make sure they're at roll call tomorrow, so we can get them assigned properly. I'll make sure they're put to good use." A grin appeared on the guard's face before she started turning away.

"I will, ma'am, of course. I'm sorry." Felcia felt the words tumble out of her mouth part relief, part terror.

"I'll hold you responsible for it, now—" The guard's words stopped abruptly, her attention drawn by something to Felcia's side. "What's that?"

Felcia didn't have to look. The guard crouched down and held the sheets of paper in her hands before waving them in Felcia's face. "Papers? In the block?" Her eyes scanned the words and numbers in confusion. She clearly had no idea what she was looking at. That only made it worse. Her face contorted in a fit of rage. "You've been lying to me! I don't know what this is, but something's going on here!"

The blow that followed was vicious, blinding Felcia momentarily. A strong ringing blocked out all sound, bright little specks in front of her eyes clouded her vision. Before she could recover, she was struck in the side. A burning pain spread through her stomach, and she fell from her bed, landing awkwardly on the floor. She braced herself for more, but when the blinding pain subsided somewhat, she found the guard looking down at her with contempt.

"You're coming with me. Dr. Caesar will be very interested in hearing about this in the morning."

All Felcia could register was being dragged out of the block while the other women looked on in horror. As the cold night air hit her face, her world went black.

Felcia opened her eyes and blinked to adjust to the dimly-lit surroundings. A sliver of light made its way into her cell through a thin space between the door and the floor. She tried to raise herself to her feet. Her legs protested, and it took her two attempts to get up. Her temples thudded with a dull pain, and her torso hurt in more places than she imagined possible.

She didn't remember arriving in the small cell, and since it had no outside windows, she had no idea how long she'd been there. Her throat felt like sandpaper, and she licked her lips. She looked around but wasn't surprised to find no source of water. Felcia considered the possibility of calling out for only a fraction of a second. It wouldn't do her any good.

The air felt damp, and she rubbed her arms. It was quiet, and all she heard was her own breathing. Straining her ears, she tried to make out anything happening outside her cell, but all remained silent. Would the three young women be sent back to Birkenau? If that happened, she had failed the underground miserably. The terrible thought that she might be back in Birkenau struck her. *What have I done?*

A door opened in the distance. Someone approached in what she assumed was the hallway. From the footsteps, the person outside wasn't in a hurry. Keys jangled on the other side of the door a few seconds later, then the lock clicked, and the door swung open, the bright light from the hallway streaming in.

A tall male guard loomed in the doorway. "Come with me." He spoke evenly, without malice, and beckoned her as one would call a dog. Felcia followed him, her eyes further adjusting to the brightness. The hallway was surprisingly short, only two doors on either side before they reached a larger door. The guard opened it and Felcia was surprised to find herself outside in bright sunlight. The surroundings were immediately familiar, even if the building she came from wasn't. She stood to the side of the Rajsko camp.

"Come on, let's not keep *Herr Doctor Kommandant* waiting." The guard spoke more gruffly now, and Felcia hurried to keep up with him. They reached the main thoroughfare, gravel crunching underneath her feet, and soon mounted the steps of the building she worked in every day. It was quiet, with none of the women at their posts yet. They made straight for the commander's office, and Felcia felt her throat tighten.

The door was open and Dr. Caesar sat at a large desk. Felcia had never been in his office before, but she was surprised by its spartan furnishings. She would've expected Herr Doctor Kommandant to demand more comfort.

Dr. Caesar was reading a paper and only looked up when the guard announced their arrival. He made a note on the paper before placing it next to him on the desk and dismissed the guard. He stood and approached Felcia, who hadn't moved from the door. Fear roiled in her stomach, and her breath caught as he bent forward and looked at her with concern. "You look terrible. I suppose you didn't have a very good night."

Felcia stood rooted to the spot, not sure how to respond. Finally, she managed. "No, sir."

He leaned closer and inspected her face. She could feel his breath on her throbbing cheek. "The guards were a little rough with you?"

"It's nothing." She spoke through gritted teeth. In reality, pain radiated through her head with every word she spoke.

"Why don't you have a seat, Felcia. I think we need to talk about what happened." The doctor moved behind his desk, and Felcia was surprised at his calm. It wasn't at all what she had expected. It terrified her. "Would you like some water?" Dr. Caesar poured her a glass without waiting for her response and set it on the desk before her. With shaking hands, she brought the glass to her lips, careful not to drink too quickly. The cold water soothed her aching throat, and she breathed a little easier. Until she looked up to face Dr. Caesar.

He reached for a small bundle of papers on his desk. "I'm told these are yours? They were on your bed." Felcia nodded. There was no sense denying it. "Even though I can't make out all the words, I can make sense of the formulas." He looked at her sternly. "Care to explain?"

She set the glass down and swallowed hard. The evidence in Dr. Caesar's hands combined with her getting caught red-handed made it impossible to spin this into anything other than what it was. "I was sharing some of my knowledge with some of the girls in the block."

"Teaching them, you mean."

Felcia felt herself shrinking in her chair. "Yes, sir. I was teaching them."

"What were you teaching them?"

She recalled the basic formulas she'd placed on the sheets. They gave no indication that she was training them in anything related to the doctor's research. "They had questions about these formulas, sir."

He gave her an odd look. "Felcia, this will end much better for you if you speak the truth. Why were you teaching them? I don't believe for a minute these women were interested in advanced formulas."

Despite his stern expression, Felcia sensed there was something else behind the commander's questions. He seemed genuinely interested. "I thought they might be able to assist in the experiments later."

"So you wanted to train them?"

She hesitated, rubbing her painful cheek. A bump had formed. "Yes."

"That's not your job. That's mine."

"I'm sorry, Herr Doctor. I made a terrible mistake."

He stood and looked out the window, his back to her. The first prisoners marching in from Birkenau could be seen in the distance—perhaps she'd be marching back with them later.

"The results of your research are some of the most encouraging." He turned back to her, a small smile on his face. "Do you believe we can make it work?"

"Obtain rubber from the plants? I don't see why not, Dr. Caesar."

"I appreciate your optimism. I also think we're on the brink of something big. And I don't think it was a terrible mistake of yours."

"I'm sorry?"

"With the number of scientists in Rajsko today, we'll never be able to produce the amount of rubber required to keep the vehicles of the Reich running smoothly." Felcia was at a loss for words as Dr. Caesar sat back down. "What were your plans?"

"I wasn't sure yet." *Is this a trap?* Dr. Caesar looked calm and interested, his hands resting on the desk. Felcia decided there was nothing to lose. He didn't look threatening. "I met some of the new women in the camp and learned they had scientific backgrounds as well. They missed their old life, and we got to talking. Last night, we worked on some formulas." It wasn't a complete lie.

"Formulas related to the experiments."

"I figured if they understood what we're doing, they might assist when we need more women in the laboratories."

Dr. Caesar looked at her curiously, drumming his fingers on his desk. After a few seconds, a smile appeared on his face. "It's not a bad idea, Felcia. But I know you're not doing this just for the experiments. You believe if these women work in the laboratories, they are safe from Birkenau. Like yourself."

An uncomfortable feeling formed in her stomach, the room

suddenly a little more cramped. Despite her anxiety, she managed a weak "Yes."

"And did they get it?"

"I'm sorry?"

"The women, did they understand the formulas?"

"We were interrupted before I could verify, but they seemed bright, sir."

Another smile, then he tapped the small pile of papers. "They had finished almost all your assignments. How much time did they have for this?"

Felcia proudly answered, "Less than fifteen minutes, Dr. Caesar."

That impressed the doctor. "They made very few mistakes. What are their backgrounds?" He stroked his chin as she explained. "Your thinking was solid, but you had no right to do this in my camp. But I agree women like these would be very valuable when we ramp up the experiments."

Felcia shifted in her chair, still unsure where Dr. Caesar was going.

"Unfortunately, despite your good intentions, I can't let this go unpunished." His voice turned steely, and Felcia's heart dropped. "I've decided you'll spend the next week in Auschwitz's or Birkenau's penal block."

She tried to keep her composure, but her eyes were burning, her hands shaking. If life as a regular prisoner was almost impossible to survive, a stay in the penal blocks was many times worse. Prisoners were often deprived of food and water, tortured, and many never returned. A week was a death sentence. The realization made the blood drain from her cheeks.

"I'll be sure to inform the guards you're not to be hurt, and fed at least once a day. I can't guarantee they won't put you in a solitary cell, but you will not be hurt. You have my promise."

The words registered, but Felcia wasn't convinced Dr. Caesar's influence reached to the depths of the penal blocks in the larger camps. She nodded her head shakily.

"There's one thing I'd like you to think about while you're in there." Dr. Caesar's words sounded oddly far away. "Consider how you'll teach the women when you've returned."

Her senses rushed back. "When I've returned? Teach the women?"

"When you return, I'll sanction an hour of classes for prisoners who show exceptional promise. Those intelligent women you ran into. We'll find them, and get them trained to help in the experiments."

Felcia could hardly believe her ears, and it must've shown, for Dr. Caesar gave her a wry smile. "We'll discuss this when you're back. The guard waiting outside will deliver you to the penal block right away. You need to take your punishment."

Felcia stepped out of the office and followed the guard, terrified of what awaited her, but cautiously optimistic about what would happen once she returned to Rajsko. Would she really be allowed to teach a class, or was Dr. Caesar playing a sick, cruel game with her?

CHAPTER TWENTY-TWO

The car eased down the road at a slow pace. There were no other cars on the road, but the driver was in no rush. He'd exchanged small talk with the guard in the passenger seat, but they had gone quiet a few minutes ago. It suited Felcia just fine as she stared out the window. When she left Dr. Caesar's office fifteen minutes ago, the reality of her situation hadn't fully dawned on her yet. When they pulled out of Rajsko, turning left on the main road, passing the prisoners working the fields, the consequences of her covert class hit her like a sledgehammer to the chest. She was on her way to Birkenau's penal block—where Maria Mandl and her henchwomen ruled. Despite Dr. Caesar's assurances, the guards in Birkenau lived by their own rules.

The trees lining the road thinned, and the sky darkened. They were getting closer. If she were to roll down her window, she would smell the deceivingly sweet odor of fire and ash. Anywhere else in the world, it would be a comforting smell, triggering memories of warm evenings by the hearth. Here, it only served as a constant reminder of the purpose of the Auschwitz-Birkenau camp. Death.

The car slowed down as they approached a crossing. Felcia remembered it from her journey to Rajsko a few months ago, and she knew they were only a few minutes from the Birkenau gatehouse. She closed her eyes, trying to enjoy the final moments of peace. There would be precious little of that in the next seven days.

She was surprised to feel the car turn in the opposite direction. Opening her eyes, she turned around to see the road to Birkenau disappear behind them. *Where are we going?* She sat straighter and kept her gaze on the road ahead, the driver still content to go at a slow pace. The amount of traffic around them picked up, a mix of flatbed trucks and Kübelwagens jostling for room on the narrow road. They had to move to the side of the road and wait as three large trucks only partially covered by tarps on the sides came from the other direction. Felcia spotted two stern-faced SS troopers in the back, both casually holding their rifles while they peered out.

The trucks passed, and the driver pulled back onto the road. It took only a few minutes before a four-meter-high barbed wire fence loomed. A few meters within, an identical fence, creating a no-man's-land. Signs bearing skulls and bones, lightning bolts, and text in numerous languages served as deathly warnings. Beyond the second fence stood a collection of identical red-brick buildings, lined up in a perfectly symmetrical grid. Felcia felt her skin crawl. She didn't need to be told where she was. This was the main camp, also known as Auschwitz-I.

The car rolled to a stop and the driver spoke with the guard at the gate. The man peered into the back, acknowledging Felcia without emotion. He nodded at another guard, who pulled up the barrier, allowing them to slowly roll into the camp. Felcia's mind was racing as she peered out the window. To her left stood a building partly obscured by a high wall, but its chimney left no doubt to its function. Oddly, though, there was no smoke. They turned right onto what seemed to be the camp's main thoroughfare, passing the barracks she'd seen from the other side of the fence. The camp was deserted but for a few prisoners sorting a massive pile of potatoes in front of a building that appeared to be the camp kitchen. The other prisoners were surely at work. One of them looked up as the car passed, and Felcia saw the resignation in the man's eyes as he picked up a potato and started peeling.

They left the kitchen block behind, making two more turns before the fence reappeared, signaling the camp perimeter. The driver pulled in front of the very last building on their left and shut down the engine.

Even before Felcia could see where they were, the guard in the passenger seat turned around with a toothy, wicked smile. "Time to get out. We've arrived at your dwelling for the next week. I hope you enjoyed the ride." She sounded gleeful as she opened the door and stepped out. Felcia peered outside. The building looked identical to the others they had passed, with one big difference. A three-to-four-meter-high wall connected it to the block some twenty meters to the left. The windows on the ground floor were shuttered, not allowing any light in.

The door opened. "Get out. Let's get you checked in." When Felcia didn't move quickly enough, the guard roughly grabbed her arm and pulled her out of the car. She barely managed to stay on her feet as the woman's iron grip cut into her wrist, dragging her toward the building. The driver lit a cigarette, observing them without emotion as he leaned against the side of his vehicle. Felcia recovered sufficiently to keep up with the guard, and they mounted the six steps leading to the main door. Then she saw the block number to the right of the door, and almost choked. *Block 11.*

The guard sensed her hesitation and turned around. "Took you long enough. But now you know, right?" She jerked Felcia forward, through the door and into a dimly lit hallway. Felcia followed her in a daze, having been convinced she would be taken to Birkenau's penal block. Not even for a minute had she considered ending up here. *The Death Block.*

They passed by thick wooden doors on either side of the hallway. Felcia suspected prisoners were held there, but it was deathly quiet, almost as if the men and women beyond the doors hoped their silence would grant them some respite. Felcia doubted there would be any for her as they reached a stairway in the back. The guard stopped and motioned for her to proceed before her.

"Don't want you doing anything stupid like trying to push me down."

The air became colder and more damp with every step she descended into the darkness. When she reached the bottom, it was hard to see beyond a few meters directly in front of her. Light bulbs hung intermittently on the ceiling, emitting just enough light to see the cavernous hallway. Steel cell doors lined the gray-washed walls, and as

Felcia was pushed farther down the hallway, she noticed small wooden doors to the sides of her feet. Barely wide enough to fit through. She followed the wall running to the ceiling, and she noticed a tiny steel opening at the level of her mouth. The guard noticed her gaze, stopped, and chuckled.

"That's a standing cell. It's empty now, but tonight, four prisoners will return from their work detail and will sleep in there," she uttered, revealing crooked teeth. "Or try to, anyway. They can hardly move in there. Better behave yourself, or you'll end up in there yourself." She yanked on Felcia's arm and they soon reached a door in the back. The guard looked around, uncertain for a moment, until a voice appeared out of nowhere, startling Felcia.

"I'm here. You're early. I didn't expect you yet." A portly man wearing an uncharacteristically ragged SS trooper uniform appeared. He carried an enormous set of keys, jangling as he searched for the right one. Felcia was so used to seeing the clean-cut SS guards in Rajsko wearing their pressed uniforms with pride that the jailer took her by surprise. He probably didn't emerge from these caverns very often.

Producing the correct key, he placed it in the lock. When he turned it, a bone-piercing scream came from the far side of the hallway. Felcia jumped, but the man seemed unconcerned as he opened the door. No explanation was needed as another cry followed.

"In you go." The guard looked at her and gestured toward the doorway. The cell was darker than the hall, and as Felcia stepped into the room, it became clear why. The small window had been bricked up from the outside, a tiny opening at the top allowing only a slither of light to stream in.

The door slammed shut behind her, the lock clicking into place. Felcia turned around to face it in the darkness, the footsteps of the guards quickly fading. She stood silently for a moment, her pulse throbbing in her ears, and closed her eyes. *Deep breaths. Deep breaths.* Her heartbeat slowed, and she became aware of another rhythmic sound in the cell. Opening her eyes, she scanned the room, identifying two bunks bolted to the wall as her vision adjusted to the darkness. On the top bunk, she made out a shape. Taking a step closer, the shallow breathing indicated whoever was on the bunk was asleep. The thought of sleep reminded her of how tired she was. No, she was exhausted. She sat on the bottom bunk, a hard concrete slab without as much as a thin blanket. She lay down nonetheless, trying to find a somewhat tolerable position to sleep in. A long, muffled scream of agony came from the hallway. Felcia covered her ears with her hands and closed her eyes. She prayed she would escape whatever torture was carried out farther down the hall. A minute later, not even her cold, hard bunk could prevent her from falling into a fitful sleep.

Felcia woke to the sound of nearby gunfire. It was so loud she swore someone was firing the gun next to her head. For the first seconds she wasn't sure where she was. She scanned her dark surroundings, acutely aware of a sharp pain in the small of her back. The hard surface of the bunk brought her back to her senses. With an effort, she sat up, muscles everywhere in her body protesting at the effort. She winced and closed her eyes, rubbing her temples.

More gunshots, and Felcia almost fell from her bunk in shock. She looked up at the narrow slit that served as a window and heard dull thuds muffled by sand.

"Those are executions. You'll get used to the sound soon enough." The voice speaking Polish sounded from above, and Felcia jerked her head upward. She'd forgotten about the figure shrouded in darkness. "I didn't hear you come in, but I heard you snoring about half an hour ago. I figured I'd let you sleep. You probably needed it."

A command that sounded like a bark outside, followed by more gunshots and bodies hitting the sand. Felcia grimaced as she got to her feet and faced the woman. Surprisingly, she was almost old enough to be her mother. The first thing she noticed was the woman's bruised face. Black circles lined her eyes, her left eye almost completely shut. Then, her clothes. Instead of the camp uniform, the woman wore regular clothes. Awkwardly, Felcia held out her hand. "I'm Felcia. What happened to you?"

The woman swung her legs over the side of her bunk and, with an effort, shook Felcia's hand. "Anna. Don't worry, it looks worse than it is." She scanned Felcia in the dim light, then cocked her head. "You look in much better shape than most of the prisoners I've seen. Did you arrive only recently?"

Felcia avoided the question, keen to learn more about Anna before revealing anything about herself. "You're not wearing a prisoner uniform."

The women looked at each other for a few seconds, then Anna smiled. "Observant one, aren't you? I wasn't a prisoner before I was placed in this cell. I live just outside the camp, in Oświęcim."

Felcia's interest was piqued, but it was clear Anna wasn't going to tell her anything more unless she answered her question. "I'm not new. I've been in the camps for a little over four months now."

"Camps?" Anna climbed down from the bunk, stretching her legs. On her feet, she was nearly as tall as Felcia.

"I spent the first month in Birkenau, but I was fortunate enough to be relocated to Rajsko."

Anna's eyebrows shot up. "The farming camp?"

"Yes. How do you know about it?" Felcia couldn't hide the surprise in her voice. Compared to the monstrosities of Auschwitz and Birkenau, she couldn't imagine Rajsko getting much attention.

"It's hard to miss, isn't it? They flattened an entire village to make room for it. We see the prisoners from Birkenau heading there every day, working those fields that seem to stretch forever. But the thing that really gets the tongues wagging in town is the lack of fences around the perimeter. There must be forty to fifty smaller camps spread around Birkenau. Munitions factories, mines, and even the Siemens operations, they all have high fences with SS troopers guarding them feverishly. Your camp? Not quite the same." Anna spoke matter-of-factly. *There's something about her.*

"How did you end up in here?" The words came out before Felcia had a chance to stop herself.

Anna smiled and sat on the bottom bunk. "You don't mind if I sit, do you?" Felcia shook her head, and Anna continued, "Small infraction of the rules, really. I handed food to prisoners coming through the city. Well, I might also have approached a few when they worked near the camp. But the SS men were in on it, as long as we took care of them."

She looked up with a mischievous smile. "The prisoners steal plenty of goods from Kanada, the warehouses where the SS hoard all their ill-gotten loot. We made sure the guards received their share, and they let us talk to the prisoners, provide them with some much-needed food. In return, they told us"—she stopped, correcting herself—"me, what was going on in the camp."

Felcia was captivated by the woman's words. "It sounds like you had a good operation going. What happened? How did you end up in here?"

"One day, the SS showed up at my doorstep. They were looking for my daughter, Zofia. They said she was needed for questioning. When she wasn't home, they took me instead. I think someone betrayed me. There's nothing of value my Zofia could tell them. She's only fifteen years old." Anna resolutely shook her head. "No, they were there for me."

"Are there many people like you?"

"How do you mean?"

"Helping prisoners from the outside?" Felcia thought of Sabina, the young woman who'd told her about the attack on the German convoy a few weeks ago. *Maybe that hadn't been an isolated incident?* What if the resistance Klaudia spoke of inside the camp really was strengthened by those on the outside? To her delight, Anna nodded.

"There are people looking to help everywhere. In the offices, the mines, the factories. The problem is that the Nazis are getting better at finding these small groups, infiltrating, and shutting them down." Her face hardened, sadness clear in her right eye. "And when that happens, they end up on the end of a rope, or with a bullet through their head. But not before they're tortured for all they know."

"Is that what happened to you?" Felcia asked in a soft voice.

"This?" Anna smiled, running a hand over her face. "This is nothing. A small price to pay. They'll let me go soon enough." The last words didn't sound quite as convincing as she no doubt intended. A few cracks appeared in the confident exterior of her cellmate as she pointed up at the small window. "It appears they're done with their executions, for now. I'm going to try to get some sleep. I'm sure they'll come for me soon enough. I suggest you do the same. You can tell me why you're in here later."

As Anna climbed back to the top bunk, Felcia followed her advice and lay down as well. Anna hadn't mentioned the resistance or camp underground specifically, but Felcia was convinced the woman was somehow involved.

CHAPTER TWENTY-THREE

Sabina was mindlessly sorting papers. The prisoners' names registered only far enough to know where to file them. The table in front of her was littered with paper, and as she finished the last pile she stood up to cross the short distance to the cart across the room. Another clerk had parked it there an hour ago, wisely leaving the room without interrupting the women. Stacked on the cart were at least twenty large cardboard boxes containing the short files of the new arrivals. Sabina sighed; Tosia and she were running behind by a couple of days, and the full carts only seemed to increase in frequency.

"We're never going to get a break, are we?" Tosia stood from her chair and stretched her arms out in front of her, then walked to the small coatrack next to the door. "I need some fresh air. Want to take a short walk?" She already had her coat on and was halfway out the door.

Sabina caught up with her in the hallway, quickly pulling on her own coat. They climbed the short flight of stairs to the first floor, greeting familiar faces as they made it through the hallway. Sabina's legs felt a little stiff, and she was pleased Tosia had suggested the short break. Her head was a little fuzzy as well, and she looked forward to the cold September air.

The two women stepped outside and onto the small square in front of the building. The air was slightly warmer than in the morning, but it was chilly nonetheless. They passed a small fountain that was splashing cold water. Sabina looked up at the gray skies and wondered how long it would be before the first snow arrived.

"How about over there?" Tosia pointed at a wooden bench on the other side of the square, facing the municipal building. The women sat and Tosia took out a piece of chocolate. She broke it in half and handed one half to Sabina.

"Where did you get that?" Sabina held the chocolate in her hand. It was a rare treat she hadn't seen for months. "Are you sure you want to share it?"

Tosia took a bite and smiled, closing her eyes. She was silent for a good ten seconds, savoring the bitter taste. Sabina did the same, taking only a nibble. The chocolate was sweeter than she'd expected given its dark color. It had a full taste, and it reminded her of home, of Rajsko, when her father would bring home bars of chocolate every Friday.

"One of my friends traded for this a while back, and he gave me a few pieces."

"From the camp?"

"Yes. A lot of the new arrivals carry all sorts of treats. They're forced to hand over their belongings, and that's when the guards scoop up all the valuables. They hold all their ill-gotten bounty in a row of warehouses in the back of the camp. Some of the prisoners manage to smuggle a bit of food out, and use it to trade."

The small piece in Sabina's hand suddenly felt unusually heavy. A bad taste formed in her mouth and she placed the chocolate on the bench next to her.

"No sense in wasting it, Sabina." Tosia's eyes fixed on the chocolate, then on Sabina. "The trade was fair, in the end. And everybody needs to find a way to survive. Inside and outside the camp." Tosia sounded weary, her voice different than usual, as she popped the last piece of chocolate in her mouth. She gestured toward Sabina's piece. "Just eat it, please. Plenty of people have suffered for it. No sense wasting it."

Sabina didn't touch the chocolate. "What's wrong, Tosia? Something you want to share?"

Tosia scanned the square silently, her eyes a little glassy. She seemed in a trance, and Sabina was about to repeat her question when Tosia turned to her. "I got this piece of chocolate almost a month ago. I was saving it, because I was afraid it would be the final piece of chocolate for a long time." Sabina nodded, not sure how to respond. "But this morning, before I left for work, one of my friends showed up at my house. He told me the Gestapo had come for a number of my friends. They showed up in the middle of the night and hauled them off."

"Tosia, that's terrible. I'm so sorry." With the passing of time, the imminent threat of her father being lifted from his bed in the middle of the night had eased, but she still stiffened every time a car or truck passed their house.

"Nobody knows where they were taken." She pointed at the empty chocolate wrapper. "Kamil gave me this. Now, he's locked up and no doubt about to be tortured for all he knows." Her face had turned ashen, her bottom lip quivering. Sabina had never seen her normally stoic colleague—and friend—like this. Her heart ached as she reached for her hand. It was cold to the touch.

Sabina struggled to find the right words. Tosia was upset, and she had little doubt it was indeed the Gestapo that had picked up her friends. Who else goes around lifting people from their beds in the middle of the night? "Are these the friends that worked in the camp?"

Tosia's grip on Sabina's hand tightened. "All but one of them were picked up. They helped with some of the electrical work in the camp."

"Do you know if they were involved with anything else? Other than trading with prisoners?"

"They also traded with guards." Tosia's voice was returning to normal, and a look of realization appeared on her face. "Do you think the guards reported them?"

Sabina considered it for a moment, then dismissed the notion. "It would be illegal for the guards to trade, wouldn't it?" Tosia slowly nodded. "No, it must've been something else." Her father's words about the camp underground echoed through her head. What if Tosia's friends were somehow involved? He did say the guards had stopped accepting bribes. Were Tosia's friends part of the network that had smuggled in all sorts of goods, including medicine and weapons?

"Did your friends ever smuggle anything other than food into the camp?"

"We never really spoke about this in detail. They just told me most of the prisoners were desperate for food. What are you suggesting, Sabina?" Her tone had returned to normal, her eyes sharp.

"Do you think it's possible they were part of a resistance network around the camp? That they maybe smuggled in medicine and weapons as well as food?"

Tosia's mouth opened a little, the pupils in her eyes widening. She turned her head and looked away for a moment, then returned her attention to Sabina. "They never spoke about anything like that. They went into the camp and did all kinds of repairs, and they liked to trade with the prisoners, but they never spoke about anything that sounded like they were part of a resistance."

"A good resistance fighter never would." Sabina studied her friend. Tosia looked shaken, her right foot tapping nervously on the cobble-stones below. She decided to give Tosia some time to let the realization sink in. It hadn't been long ago when she'd found out the same about her father.

After a few minutes, Tosia cleared her throat and sat a little straighter. "If they were involved in anything like that, I didn't know about it. But you're right. It's quite possible they were somehow involved." She gave Sabina a curious look. "You considered that possibility rather quickly. Do you know more about this?"

Sabina faked a nervous smile. "No more than you, I'm afraid. It's just that after the failed ambush in town last month I've started eyeing the people in town differently. Anyone could be part of the resistance, right?"

"I suppose you're right. It could be anyone." Tosia's casual tone didn't mask the serious undertone. "Even you."

Sabina's neck burned up, but she kept her face neutral. "I'm not sure I'd have the stomach for it."

"Me neither." Tosia flashed a wide smile that was filled with relief. Sabina felt the same, and was keen to steer the conversation away from herself.

"Have you ever helped your friends with anything?"

Tosia looked thoughtful for a moment, then shook her head. "No, nothing I can remember."

"Never shared any information from work? Provided them with food to smuggle in?"

She kept shaking her head. "No, they never asked for anything, nor did I offer."

More relief flooded Sabina's chest. If Tosia was speaking the truth, there would be no reason for the Gestapo to come snooping around Tosia, or her place of work. She couldn't think of anything more frightening than for them to barge into the archiving room and start asking questions. Even though the Gestapo weren't active in Rajsko, it wouldn't do Sabina any good to have the all-seeing eye of the Nazis' intelligence organization trained on her place of work.

"We should probably head back." Tosia stood from the bench and inhaled deeply. "Thank you for listening. Do you think my friends are involved in illegal activities?"

Sabina got to her feet as well, and they slowly walked back toward the municipal building. Glancing at Tosia's anxious face, she decided her friend was worried enough as it was. "It doesn't sound like they're doing much more than smuggling in food. That's not enough to label them resistance fighters. With a bit of luck, they'll be released."

A spark of hope flashed in Tosia's eyes as she nodded. "I hope you're right."

As they entered the warm and stuffy hallway of their place of work, Sabina echoed her friend's feelings.

A few hours later, Sabina stepped outside into the cold evening air. It had been two days since she'd spoken to Felcia. The more Sabina thought about it, the more she was convinced Felcia could help secure more information about the camp.

Sabina crossed the main square, and she was so lost in her thoughts that she failed to notice the man appear from the shadows. She let out a shriek as she noticed the figure standing only a few paces away from her. Her shock was quickly replaced by relief when she recognized him.

"Papa! You startled me! What are you doing here?"

"Apologies, Sabinka." He gestured impatiently. "Come, follow me."

She did as she was told and was surprised to find herself entering Joanna's shop an instant later. It was empty but for a man in the back. Sabina instantly recognized him—the man her father had let into their house. Joanna moved from behind the counter and toward the door, smiling at Sabina as she turned the lock. Her father crossed the room and sat opposite the man, pushing the chair next to him out for Sabina.

Sabina turned to see Joanna disappear into the kitchen. She sat and studied the man more closely. He had dark eyes, a scruffy beard, and the strongest arms she'd ever seen. That alone was quite a feat, considering her father's size. He held out a large hand.

"Sabina, it's an honor to finally meet you properly. I'm Marian." His voice was deep but soothing. He spoke eloquently, which didn't match his rough exterior. Sabina shook his hand, noticing the firm but gentle grip. She felt at ease instantly, and it was easy to understand why her father trusted him. *Enough to have him meet me, even.* Marian didn't wait for a response as he continued. "In the interest of time, I'll keep this short." His eyes went to the door, and despite his confident tone and demeanor, Sabina understood the underlying message. *He doesn't want to have to explain why we are huddled together in a closed pierogi shop either.* "Your father has told me much about what you've done these past weeks, but would you mind if I asked you some more questions?"

"You want to know about Rajsko."

"I'd like to know as much as possible about the camp. No doubt your father has told you about the recent challenges we're facing communicating with our contacts inside?"

Sabina looked to her father, who nodded. Tosia's troubled face flashed through her mind, and she clenched her jaw. "You've lost your connections into Birkenau."

"Exactly." A sad smile crept onto his face. He produced a sheet of paper and a pencil. "Can you draw an outline of the camp while you take me through as you approach it from the road? Tell me about the guards, the buildings, the lack of fences. Can you really come and go as you please?"

"More or less." Sabina took the pencil and sketched the buildings while telling Marian everything she could remember, focusing on the school turned laboratory, the greenhouses, and finally, the prisoner's quarters in the back. "I've only seen them from a distance. There was never a reason for me to venture so far into the camp."

"And this is the only area with fences? You just walk up to the main building and greenhouses?"

"Almost, yes. There are always guards near the main road, but once you've passed them, security isn't very tight. Not from what I've seen, anyway." She caught herself, shivering as she remembered her run-in with the female guard. "But the main building is right next to the road. I'm sure there are regular patrols, though."

"You've seen them? The patrols?" Marian leaned forward. Sabina moved uneasily in her chair and recounted the encounter. Marian nodded. "Patrols are to be expected, especially when there are no fences. Interesting." He sat back, scratching the side of his nose, his eyes suddenly distant. Sabina glanced at her father, who gave her a reassuring look.

Joanna appeared with a tray of glasses, a pitcher of water and a plate of pierogi. The smell made Sabina's mouth water, and she looked up gratefully.

"This is serious work. Better make sure you eat and drink enough," Joanna said with a smile as she set the tray down.

"Thank you, Joanna," Marian said distantly.

"It's the least I can do." Joanna disappeared back into the kitchen, and Sabina eyed the steaming pierogi.

"Go on, don't let them go cold," he said, popping one into his mouth. Relieved, Sabina followed his example. She suddenly realized she was quite hungry, and she devoured another before Marian's eyes focused back on her.

"The people working in the school, the scientists. You said they move freely between the laboratories and the greenhouses? No guard escorts?"

"From what I've seen, yes."

"And nobody escorts you either. Between the main road and the laboratory." He spoke more to himself than Sabina as he turned away in thought. Sabina took a sip of water. Marian turned back, this time giving her father a questioning look. "If she can get into the camp this easily, there's a chance there."

"Absolutely not." Her father's voice was firm, and Sabina turned to him in surprise. "We discussed this, Marian. I don't want her smuggling anything into the camp."

Despite Marian's size, he immediately conceded, raising his hands. "Of course, I was just thinking out loud."

Sabina felt frustration bubble up inside her. *They're speaking of me like I'm not here.* "What would I take into the camp?" She looked at Marian, ignoring her father's burning stare.

"Sabina. I won't have it. It's too danger—" her father started, but Sabina cut him off with a confidence she didn't know she possessed.

"Papa, I can decide for myself. I want to hear Marian's plans."

Marian's eyes went between them, then settled on her father. "Can I tell her? We can decide on her role later." His calm voice appeared to soothe her father, as he reluctantly waved his hand for Marian to carry on.

"I think the area around the main building, where the laboratories are, is key. If we can get anywhere near it, we have a chance of getting supplies to the prisoners. But I agree with your father. It's too dangerous for you to smuggle anything in. The risk of a nosy, bored guard checking your bag is too big. Besides, you are too valuable to lose. You've already made connections in the camp. From what you told me, you have the ear of the commander, and one of the senior officers seems to have taken a fancy to you."

Sabina felt herself blushing. "I think you may be overselling it."

"Nonsense. Even without your father's protestations, we can't risk losing an asset as valuable as you." He looked at her with admiration as the words sunk in.

"What would you have me do?"

"It sounds like the best way to smuggle goods into the camp is through the main building. There should be sufficient freedom of movement for the women working there to collect the goods. The challenge is storing the goods once they've obtained them." He pointed at the map, his finger going between the main building and the enclosed prisoner barracks. "We need to find a way to get them into the prisoners' barracks somehow."

Sabina felt her breath catch in her throat. She imagined the distance between the main building and the prisoners' dwellings. Marian hadn't told her what kind of goods would be smuggled in, but there would still be significant risk in concealing and carrying the goods from one side of the camp to the other.

"I don't know anything about the situation at the gate." She pointed at the entry point of the enclosed prisoners' area.

Marian smiled. "Can you find out? And while you do, I'll need you to find out about another crucial piece of intelligence. Without it, the plan is dead in the water."

Sabina felt her heart thumping inside her chest, a feeling of excitement bubbling up in her throat. She didn't want to let Marian down. "What do you need to know?"

"Find out about the evening patrols."

CHAPTER TWENTY-FOUR

S abina heard Mr. Pach's voice at the front of the room, but his words didn't register. She stared vacantly at her teacher as he moved between his desk and the small blackboard, explaining complicated equations she didn't have the energy to focus on right now. All she could think about was getting out of class and to work. It had been three days since she last visited Rajsko, and she was certain Mr. Piotrowski would have plenty of documents to send to Dr. Caesar today.

Meeting Marian had further fanned the flames of her desire to help the resistance. Prior to the meeting, Sabina had feared Marian would treat her like a child, but it had been the complete opposite. It had even felt like he had taken her side when her father objected to her smuggling goods into the camp.

"Sabina, am I boring you?" Mr. Pach's voice cut through her thoughts. She looked up to find him standing in front of her. Startled, she shook her head.

"No, of course not, Mr. Pach. I drifted away for a bit, sorry."

"Perhaps it's best if we take a quick break, so that everybody can come back feeling refreshed and energized. We've got plenty of equations to go through." His voice was friendly, but he looked at Sabina reproachfully. The other students got up, and Sabina was relieved to step out into the narrow alley. The fresh air felt good on her face.

"You really were somewhere else." Elena appeared next to her, a wide smile on her face. "What were you thinking about? Wait. I think I know."

Sabina rolled her eyes and walked away from Elena. "Well, tell me what I was thinking about."

"I don't know, maybe a dashing young German officer who seems quite taken with you?"

Sabina stopped in her tracks, turning around. "What? Are you joking?" Her tone was far more aggressive than she intended, and she immediately held up her hands to a shocked Elena. "I'm sorry. I mean, no, I wasn't thinking about him at all. He's just a source."

The expression on Elena's face went from shock to curiosity as she raised an eyebrow. "A source of what? You seemed pretty cozy with him in the tavern."

Shit. Sabina looked around and was relieved to find no one else there. Elena hadn't moved, the questioning look still in her eyes. *She's not going to let this go so easily.* "Come, let's find a quiet place." She motioned for Elena to follow, and they stepped into the wider street. A little way down was a small park, and Sabina sat down on one of the benches. The park was deserted. *Perfect.*

"When I told you it would be useful to make friends with Paskal because I have to go to the camp often, I wasn't lying."

"You said it would be awkward to keep rejecting his advances."

Sabina smiled. "I did. And it would be. But Elena, that's not the only reason I was keen to meet with him."

"So you do like him?"

"Not like that." Slight frustration rose up, but Sabina took a breath and calmed herself. *She doesn't know what I've been doing. Be patient.* She looked at Elena, who seemed a little confused, and she felt a surge of affection for her best friend. If she couldn't trust Elena, then who? She took another deep breath. "Paskal is a source. My trips to Rajsko, they're not just to deliver papers from work. I'm informing the underground about what's going on in the camp."

Elena's mouth remained slightly open as she stared at Sabina. It took a few seconds before she mumbled, "You're doing what? The resistance?"

"It's nothing big. I tell them about the camp's setup. The number of guards, what happens in the buildings."

"Sabina, that's ... I'm shocked. But I'm also very proud of you. Now it all makes sense." Elena's eyes were twinkling, her cheeks flushed. "I didn't quite understand why you wanted to meet that officer and his friends. Don't get me wrong, it was fun, but it was odd."

"I'm sorry I didn't tell you. I couldn't. I wanted you to be yourself among them." Sabina felt as if a weight was lifted from her shoulders— not having realized how much energy it had cost to keep this secret from her best friend.

"So, what's the plan? Why are they so interested in Rajsko?"

"Remember when we were caught sneaking around, when they were still building it?"

"How could I forget?"

"Well, they never put up any fences around the main buildings. The resistance is hoping they might be able to smuggle goods into the camp."

"What kind of goods? Food?"

"More like medication for the prisoners." Sabina decided not to mention the possibility of weapons. "And messages to their contacts inside the camp."

"Do you think it's possible?" Elena looked serious. "I mean, if anyone knows, you would, right? How many times have you been?"

"I haven't kept count. But yes, I think it's possible. The challenge is distributing the goods to the other camps. Birkenau, especially."

Elena softly whistled between her teeth. "Sounds exciting. Can I help?"

"Help?" Sabina was taken aback by the question. She hadn't consid-ered the possibility at all. "I'm not sure what you could do, really. So far it's only talk, and I need more information before they can do anything."

Elena's face dropped ever so slightly before she looked up at a bird circling in the sky directly above them. Sabina kept her eyes on the bird as well, which seemed content to simply float. Despite everything going on around them, there was still the beauty in nature to observe.

"I know I might not always seem like the bravest or most adventurous person." Elena's voice was slightly higher pitched than normal, the nerves filtering through. "I would never have thought of spying for the resistance like you. But when we went to the tavern that night, I was surprised at how easy it was to talk to those Germans. Somehow, they weren't that scary anymore."

"I know. Paskal is quite friendly. He seems genuinely excited about the plant experiments in Rajsko." Sabina didn't mention her suspicions that he didn't approve of what was happening in the camps down the road.

"I suppose what I'm saying, Sabcia, is that if you need me to come along to extract more information from Paskal's colleagues, I'd be honored to help. Especially now you've confided in me." A lump formed in Sabina's throat. She slipped her arm around her friend's shoulders and pulled her in for a hug.

"I'm glad I told you. And yes, if you can help in any way, I'll let you know. It might just happen sooner rather than later."

"I'll be ready." They broke their embrace and Elena stood. "We better get back to class, or Mr. Pach won't let us back in."

Sabina walked to the front of the archiving room. She'd just finished the first few boxes of files, and her spirit dropped when the door opened, revealing a clerk pushing yet another full cart. He mumbled an apology before disappearing back into the hallway. Sabina closed her eyes for a moment. She was alone this afternoon as Tosia had called in sick. She hoped her friend hadn't taken the news of her friends' capture by the Gestapo too badly, although she suspected her absence had something to do with it.

With leaden feet, Sabina moved toward the cart, picking up a particularly heavy box. At that moment, the door opened again, and she was ready to lay into whichever clerk dared load even more work onto her plate.

"Ah, Sabina, I'm glad I found you. How are you getting by today? I heard Tosia is out. I hope she's back soon, for both our sakes." He spoke quickly, and Sabina waited until she was certain he'd finished.

"It's not ideal, Mr. Piotrowski, but I'll manage." She forced a smile. "What brings you down here? Are you coming to help me? You'd be very welcome."

He graced her with a smile. "It's nothing like that, I'm afraid. You're wanted in the camp."

"Rajsko? Do you need me to deliver something?" She put the box down.

Mr. Piotrowski gave her an odd look, then shook his head. "No, I received a call from the commander asking you to report immediately. Without delay, he added."

"Dr. Caesar asked for me?" Exhilaration and fear mixed to form an odd feeling in Sabina's stomach.

"It was one of his assistants, but he was quite adamant. You better leave right away."

The walk to the camp felt longer than usual, despite Sabina walking as quickly as possible. She'd considered going home to wait for her father, but she knew they would come for her if she didn't show. And when they didn't find her at home, they would take her parents—her mother would not pay the price of her activities. She had chosen this path; she would face whatever consequences awaited her.

She approached the guards at the gate and found her usual confidence faltering as she announced herself in a weak voice. One of the guards mumbled something about the brass asking for her, and waved her through. *At least they're not escorting me in. That has to count for something.* Then she remembered not even the prisoners were escorted here, and the thought did little to soothe her.

A familiar figure stood in front of her old school building—Paskal. Confusion washed over Sabina as she forced herself to keep walking toward him at a constant pace, furiously trying to suppress the twitches in her body. Had he heard of her summons, and was he here to make sure she made it to Dr. Caesar?

"Sabina! So glad you made it here so quickly!" His voice was cheerful, further throwing Sabina off. "Come, I need to show you something." He gave her a quick hug, then took her hand and pulled her into the school building.

Sabina wasn't sure how to respond, and she only managed, "I need to see Dr. Caesar. He called for me."

"Nonsense, he didn't call for you." Paskal was beaming. "I did! But I couldn't very well tell your boss you needed to come see me, now could I? Come!" He stood impatiently in the doorway. Sabina followed, her worries fading somewhat. Paskal seemed genuinely happy to see her. Despite this, she still worried it might be a trap. *I need to keep my wits about me.*

Paskal waited for her and they crossed the hallway together. "You're going to love it." He bounced on his feet as they strode along. They passed Felcia's laboratory. The door was open, but the lights were off. Sabina thought that was odd, at this hour. Perhaps she was in the greenhouses? She hoped the scientist would be back when she left. If Paskal gave her an opportunity to talk to her, that was. Judging from his behavior, that seemed unlikely.

He pushed open the door to his office and went straight for his desk. "Have a seat, wherever." He waved at a couple of chairs opposite him, then opened the top drawer of his desk and produced a small package. He held it out to her. "Here, this is for you." His voice sounded a little raspy, as if he was nervous.

Sabina took the gift. Paskal had wrapped it in brown paper, probably taken from the mail room. As she carefully unwrapped it, a piece of cheese became unstuck and fell on the carpet at her feet.

"It's probably better if you open it on the desk." Paskal's voice had returned to normal, although his nerves still showed as he hovered uncertainly over the desk, his eyes going between Sabina's hands and face.

She did as suggested, and soon an assortment of cheeses and cured meats was laid out on the desk in front of her. Paskal reached inside the drawer again and produced a small bottle filled with a clear liquid.

"How do you like it? The cheese came in this week, I think it was from Holland."

Sabina ran her eyes over the food. It had been a long time since she'd seen such a delectable spread, but her stomach turned as she considered the source. Gritting her teeth, she said, "It looks amazing. Thank you. But I can't accept this."

"Of course you can! I took my allocation, and I decided to share it with you. Please, try some." He waved at the food, then walked to a small cabinet at the side of the room. He took two small glasses and placed them on the table. Reluctantly, Sabina took a bit of a small piece of cheese. The taste was overwhelming, the creaminess mixed with a salty aftertaste, a reminder of better times. Yet, she felt dirty as she swallowed the cheese, guilty for enjoying the food stolen from people who needed it more than her. If they were still alive.

"Really good, isn't it? If there's anything you'd like next time, let me know. Kanada is overflowing, and most of it is consigned back to Germany, but we usually get a chance for first pickings." He winked at her as he poured from the bottle. "This is schnapps from Germany. It was sent as a gift from Berlin for the good performance of the camp." He handed her a glass. "*Prost!*"

They clinked glasses, and while Paskal downed the drink in one go, Sabina took a modest sip. A warm glow spread in her stomach, and she relaxed.

"You were saying something about the good performance of the camp? The experiments are going well?"

"They are. Most of the plants in the greenhouses were harvested two weeks ago, just in time for Dr. Caesar's trip to Berlin. I believe he spoke to the *Reichsführer* himself. Himmler was very happy, and he sent a case of schnapps to celebrate a few days ago. Apparently, he will inspect the progress himself on his next visit." Another pour. "It's exciting—I don't care much for what happens in Birkenau. It repels me, and frankly, I think it's a waste of resources. We should be looking to strengthen the Wehrmacht." He finished his drink with a quick flick of the wrist and smacked his lips in satisfaction. "And our research does just that. It's science for a worthy cause."

Sabina took another tiny sip of her schnapps and mirrored his excitement. "That's fantastic, Paskal. I'm so happy for you. It must be stressful to have so much depending on the success of the research in your camp."

"Yes, but Dr. Caesar knows what he's doing. And he's the commander and the one responsible."

"Sure, but you make sure the camp is running smoothly, taking care of everything so he can carry out his research in optimal conditions."

Paskal inclined his head. "I'm glad you noticed. Sometimes I'm not sure Dr. Caesar appreciates everything I do." His speech was slurring.

"I'm sure he does, or perhaps you could talk to him about it sometime," Sabina said smoothly.

"How do you mean?"

"Maybe just ask him if there's anything he needs done. He'll appreciate you coming to him, don't you think? Who knows, with the initial positive results from the experiments, he might have some ideas he'd like a second opinion on. From my interactions with him, he seems like a reasonable man."

He looked thoughtful, his eyes a little unfocused. Then he sat forward, slowly nodding. "That's not a bad idea. You're right—for such a senior officer, he's quite easy to approach. I have some ideas to improve things."

"No doubt good ideas. And who doesn't want to hear those?" Sabina poured him another drink, and he grabbed the glass gratefully. She waited for him to finish his drink and decided this was the right time. "I should head back to town soon. I don't want to walk along the main road in the dusk."

"I can arrange for a car to take you back, it's no problem." His cheeks were glowing, his eyes sparkling. "I asked you to come here, so I think it's only fair I make sure you get home safe."

She held up her hands. "That's very kind, but that's not necessary. I like the walk back, as long as it's not dark. Besides, I'm sure you have more important things to do than to arrange a ride for me." She eyed the pile of papers on his desk. "Will you need to work tonight?"

"Most likely. I'm at work most evenings, although I try to finish by eight."

"I can imagine it's pretty quiet around here by then? The prisoners will be in their blocks?" She held her breath.

"Oh yes. They have roll call at six, and then we lock the gate. It's just me and Dr. Caesar here, but he likes to head back to his wife early."

"I remember when I still lived here, I always thought it was eerily quiet around the school at night. Don't you feel uncomfortable being here on your own?"

He laughed out loud. "Oh, Sabina, I'm hardly alone. The patrols pass by every half hour or so, and they usually check in on me. Some stop by for a chat, which is nice."

"Right, that makes sense." She kept her face straight, but inside she felt jubilant. Marian and her father would be delighted. Sabina suddenly felt nervous about Paskal becoming suspicious of her questions, and she stood. "I'll get going. It was nice to see you." She turned, but Paskal's voice stopped her in her tracks.

"Wait. Aren't you forgetting something?" His voice was suddenly very clear.

"Hmm?" She turned and found him looking at her with a serious expression. Her heart skipped a beat. *Have I gone too far?*

"The cheese and sausage!" He smiled, and relief flooded Sabina's senses.

"Of course." She quickly wrapped the food in the original brown paper packaging. Paskal stood and moved to her side. She held the package in her hand, and then Paskal moved closer, hugging her. The sensation of his breath on her neck made her shudder, gooseflesh forming on her arms. Sabina prayed he hadn't noticed her response as they broke their embrace. To her relief, he was still smiling.

"Thank you for coming, Sabina. It was nice to have some time alone with you."

"You can summon me anytime." She forced a smile, then turned and moved for the door. Passing through the hallway, she heard his footsteps and felt his gaze on her. She forced herself not to look back and headed for the exit. Felcia's laboratory was still dark, and Sabina hoped she'd have a chance to talk to her next time. Just before she stepped outside, she turned around to see Paskal still looking at her. There was a goofy smile on his face—Elena had been right.

Chapter Twenty-Five

F elcia lay on her bunk with her eyes closed, listening to the sounds coming from the hallway. The wails, cries, and shouts of anguish never stopped. On the first day, she had been aware of every little sound around her. The sound of footsteps in the hallway—even distant—were enough to set her into a sweating panic. She had been certain the guards would come for her next, opening the heavy cell door and hauling her out to be one of the subjects of the terrors surrounding her. Anna had tried to calm her, telling her there was no sense in worrying about something that *might* happen.

"You have no control over what happens here. The best you can do is conserve your energy," she had said.

When the cell door opened early on the second day, Felcia had been certain it would be her turn. Instead, it had been a guard supplying them with a bucket of water and two hard pieces of bread. Felcia was famished, but Anna had reminded her to ration her food. This was the first time in three days they gave her anything close to edible. Taking the older woman's advice, and remembering her time in Birkenau, she proceeded to nibble at the bread, making it last for almost the entire day. The result was that she was even more hungry, and she hardly slept the next night, hunger relentlessly tearing away at her.

Felcia estimated they were halfway through her third day, with bright sunlight streaming in from the slit that served as their tiny window to the world. A miserable world: their cell faced the execution yard, and it saw plenty of use. It was unnerving to listen to the men and women escorted to their deaths. Some came quietly, but many went kicking and screaming, begging for their lives right until the end, when a single bullet ended their suffering.

Felcia opened her eyes and rose from her bunk. She tried to ignore the pain radiating from her back and got to her feet. Anna sat up on her bunk, her back to the cold wall.

"You've been here for more than a week now."

"Almost two," the woman answered.

"How do you not go mad? There is never a moment of peace, and you know you could be next." Perfectly on cue, a cry reverberated through the hallway, then swiftly cut off. The torturers had many ways to get people to scream, but they also knew how to shut them up instantly.

"Who says I haven't already?" Felcia couldn't help but return Anna's morbid grin. "I just take things one day at a time. No, one hour at a time. Every moment of solitude I get in this cell I spend taking my mind elsewhere, away from these horrors."

"How do you do it?"

"I close my eyes, slow my breathing, and think of the place I want to escape to."

"And does it work?"

Anna chuckled. "Not always. But most of the time."

Rapid footsteps sounded in the hallway. Felcia turned to the door, an uncomfortable feeling building up in her stomach. Her throat went dry as whoever was approaching reached their door and stopped. The jangling of keys made her take a step back. The door opened and the jailer who'd locked her up appeared. His eyes focused on Felcia.

"You. Come with me." The words were clipped, his voice cold and emotionless.

Felcia glanced at Anna, who looked at her fiercely, balling her fists. She stepped into the hallway and waited for the jailer to close the door. Then he jerked his head and they walked the length of the hallway, passing the stairs she'd descended less than three days ago. The light streaming down from the ground floor appeared as a beacon. As she followed the jailer, Sabina felt her throat constrict, and she clasped her hands to stop them from shaking. Her teeth chattered, and she suddenly felt very cold.

The jailer stopped at the very last door and knocked. A muffled grunt came from within, and the man opened the door. Felcia didn't immediately follow, fear keeping her rooted to her seemingly safe spot in the hallway. The jailer grabbed her wrist and pulled her into the room with surprising force, almost making Felcia stumble over her own feet.

Inside, it was brighter than she'd expected. In the middle of the room stood a large table with four clasps, and plenty of lights trained on it. She swallowed hard, immediately recognizing it for what it was. A torture table. Her eyes went to the sides of the room, where all sorts of horrendous-looking instruments were neatly lined up or hung along the walls. Scalpels, scissors in various sizes and shapes, torches, and tools she'd never seen before in her life chilled the blood in her veins.

"I'll take it from here, Markus." A deep voice came from the far corner of the room, and Felcia jerked her head toward it. A tall, slender man wearing a white doctor's coat emerged from behind a desk. It was the only area of the room that wasn't brightly lit. The jailer hesitated, and the man repeated his order, this time a little more forcefully. "I'll call for you when I'm done. It won't be long." The jailer left and closed the door, leaving Felcia standing awkwardly in the space between the entrance and brightly-lit torture table.

"I'll need to carry out some inspections," the man said in an abnormally loud voice, almost as if he were speaking to someone with hearing problems. "Take a seat over there." He pointed at a chair next to the torture table. Felcia hesitantly did as she was told, praying the man wouldn't direct her onto the table next. In her mind, she knew there was little chance of escaping that. *Why else would they bring me here.* She bit the side of her cheek. *Dr. Caesar promised this wouldn't happen.*

"Open your mouth, please." The doctor stood in front of her, holding a wooden tongue depressor. Felcia did as she was told. The doctor peered at her, then he took the spatula out, discarding it in an empty bin next to the torture table. Her eyes went to the surgical tray and the collection of tools next to it, within reach of the doctor, or whatever he was. The man followed her gaze and shook his head.

"Those aren't for you. I'm not going to torture you. In fact, this isn't even my office."

Felcia eyed him with surprise, and even though she wanted to believe him, suspicion rose inside her. She responded only with a curt nod.

"You don't believe me. I'm not sure I would believe me if I were in your shoes. You've been down here for five days now, and haven't received much to eat. By now you're probably having trouble determining what is real and what isn't." His tone was light, but his eyes were serious.

"Five days?" She spoke without thinking.

"You lose sense of time down here. You were brought into the cellar on Wednesday. It's Monday today." He took a step closer and took out a small flashlight. "Follow the light with your eyes, please." Felcia had trouble keeping her eyes focused, the bright light dizzying. The doctor switched it off and moved back to his desk without a word. He lifted something close to her face. She couldn't make out which tool he'd selected. The object came into focus—a paper cup.

"Here, drink. It will make you feel better." In his other hand he held an apple. Felcia took the cup and inspected the clear liquid with suspicion. "Go on, if I was going to kill you, there would be quicker ways than poisoning you." He threw the apple in the air and caught it effortlessly. Felcia was too thirsty to put up more resistance and brought the cup to her lips. The water was cold and tasted fresh, unlike the tepid water she was given in her cell. She downed the cup in one go and looked up to the doctor pleadingly. He handed her the apple and took the cup. "Eat slowly. Your stomach needs time to adjust." He walked back to his desk and she could hear him refilling the cup. Ignoring his advice, she took a large bite, the juices running down her chin as she chewed furiously. She couldn't recall an apple ever tasting any sweeter. *Slow down, Felcia. Don't eat it all in one go.*

The doctor returned and sat across from her, placing the cup on the table. "That guard shouldn't be eavesdropping anymore by now." His eyes went to the door. "They tend to get bored when they hear there won't be any torture." Felcia took another bite, unsure how to respond. The doctor lowered his voice. "I was sent by Dr. Caesar. I'm here to sign for your immediate release."

Felcia almost dropped the apple. She wasn't sure she'd heard the man correctly. "My ... my release?" It was all she could manage.

"Dr. Caesar wants you to continue your research at Rajsko. He feels you've spent enough time down here. He's keen to see you carry out the agreed duties." The man looked at her compassionately. "You're not sure if you can believe me."

Felcia felt a tear roll down her cheek. "It's all a bit much, sir. I don't understand. Who are you? Why are you nice to me?"

The man smiled and handed her a tissue from beside the torture table. Felcia took it, considering how odd the placement of the box was, and wiped her face. "We're not all monsters here. Dr. Caesar and I are good friends, and he's told me all about his research at Rajsko." He looked at her and smiled. "Well, it's also partly your research. He told me your results have been especially promising."

With the conversation shifting to the research, Felcia's confidence returned somewhat. "I've been fortunate to have been assigned favorable conditions."

"I'm sure you have, but you still need to carry out your duties with skill and precision. You're Polish, aren't you?" Felcia nodded, and he continued. "Then I'm sure you have strong feelings about helping the German army." He held up a hand. "Don't answer that, it's irrelevant, and I already know what you would say. What matters to Dr. Caesar is your performance and dedication in carrying out your research. Not all the women working for Dr. Caesar have shown the same professionalism."

Felcia considered his words. It was refreshing and terrifying to hear a Nazi doctor speak so candidly. Not even Dr. Caesar had done so, and she wondered why this man had no qualms about stating these truths. Because that's what they were. But Felcia also knew Dr. Caesar was a man of science, an educated and highly intelligent scientist. If the man sitting across from her was indeed friends with Dr. Caesar, it meant he most likely was a rational scientist as well. It made sense for him to recognize Felcia for what she was: not so much an equal, but certainly someone capable of forming her own opinions and making rational choices. *He's letting me know he understands my position. But why?*

"You will be released within a few hours, and taken back to Rajsko. There, you will return to your block as if nothing has happened." He studied her face intently. "You'll tell anyone who asks that you were locked up but don't remember much of your time here. Nothing more, nothing less. Is that clear?"

"Absolutely."

"And you won't mention this conversation, nor your early release. Tomorrow, you'll return to your laboratory and continue your work as usual."

Felcia thought of Dr. Caesar's promise of teaching a class. The man had said nothing about that, and she decided not to ask. She would find out soon enough, but she felt a sparkle of hope. *If Dr. Caesar is personally invested in getting me out of here, he might yet keep his promise.*

The man stood, indicating their meeting was over. Felcia did the same, groaning as the muscles in her back spasmed painfully.

"Remember, not a word of this to anyone."

"My lips are sealed."

Felcia was back in her cell a few minutes later. As soon as the door was closed, Anna climbed down from her bunk and inspected Felcia's face, hands, and arms.

"You look unhurt. What happened?" There was surprise and relief in her voice. "Where did they take you?"

"They didn't torture me." Felcia weighed her words. She couldn't tell Anna everything. "They ran some tests."

"Did they tell you why?"

"No." She felt bad keeping what happened from Anna, but she couldn't take any risks. She'd need to keep her head for a few more hours until she would be back in Rajsko. There, she would return to work, and pray Dr. Caesar kept his promise. And even if he didn't, she would keep her head down and focus on her research. Anything to avoid a return to this place. But then something started gnawing at her in the back of her mind.

She sat on her bunk and, for the first time since arriving, felt like she could think somewhat clearly. The apple, water, and promise of getting out had revitalized her. She looked at Anna, remembering her words on the day she arrived. The woman had been open about why and how she ended up in the same cell. They had spoken since, and even if Felcia's memory about the details was fuzzy, she didn't doubt that Anna had connections to the resistance groups operating around the camp.

"I need to tell you something, Anna. I'm getting out later today."

Anna raised an eyebrow, but her eyes were friendly. "Really? Is that what they told you just now? Do you believe them?"

Felcia nodded. "I think so. And when I leave, I want to make sure my time in here wasn't for nothing."

"How so?" Anna sat next to her on the hard bunk.

"I think there's a reason we met in here."

"You're speaking in riddles, child. Tell me what you want."

Felcia smiled, appreciating the woman's candor. "You said you supplied prisoners with food, mentioned that you worked with some of the guards in getting goods in and out of the camp." Anna nodded, but kept her mouth closed, her eyes serious. "You're not the first person to tell me about these activities. We hear things in the camp."

"I don't doubt you do. There are a lot of things happening in and around the camp," Anna said with a smile. "What are you getting at?"

"You mentioned the SS was clamping down on these smuggling routes, if I may call them that? That you thought this was the reason you were arrested and placed in here?"

"Mostly that, yes. But what's it to you?"

"What if Rajsko was an option?"

"An option for what?"

"Your smuggling runs. Your connections with the camp resistance."

Anna looked at her with interest. "Rajsko is a satellite camp. And one where the prisoners seem to be doing pretty well for themselves. You told me so yourself. The people that really need our help are in Birkenau."

"I know." Felcia was surprised and encouraged by how quickly her mind was processing the information and coming up with possible solutions. "But we have plenty of prisoners coming in from Birkenau every day. Maybe they could help?" What if Felcia could hand Klaudia—and those higher up the chain—another connection into the camp?

Anna was silent. After a minute, she spoke again. "I appreciate your thinking, Felcia. And what you told me about Rajsko, this might be a real possibility. But I'm nowhere near as connected as you seem to think."

"How do you mean?" Felcia's optimism was dampened only a little. Any connection to the outside is good. Especially one already involved in the smuggling of goods.

"I'm only a small cog in a large operation. I helped just a little by handing out a bit of food, sometimes near the camp. I'm not that connected."

"When you get out, you'll be many times more connected and able to do something than me," Felcia stated bluntly. "I'll be in the camp, unable to reach out to the outside world. But I'm certain we could accomplish something if we work together. Rajsko might be the solution to your problem. Or should I say, the problem of the organizations on the outside?"

Anna looked thoughtful, then smiled. "I don't know what happened to you just now, but you're a different person. I can't promise much, but I can promise you one thing. When I get out, I will do whatever I can to get my people to look into Rajsko."

Felcia inclined her head. "That's all I ask, Anna."

"It's better you know as little as possible about these people. What you don't know, you can't pass on." She pointed at her bruised face. "If you do get out today, promise me one thing."

"Anything."

"Wait for my people to reach out. It might take a while, or it might not happen at all. But don't try to force it. Trust me, if there's any chance Rajsko makes for a good option, they'll try to make it work. Just be patient, do your work, and don't attract any attention."

"I hadn't planned on doing anything else." Felcia smiled. "Will you do the same? I hope the next time we meet each other is under better conditions."

Anna returned her smile. "I hope so too, Felcia. I believe in you."

CHAPTER TWENTY-SIX

The road running from the city center back to Sabina's house was busier than usual. Something was happening, most likely at the camp, and even though the beds of the passing trucks were empty, she had no doubt the SS were up to something. It had been a busy day at work, and she had been happy to see Tosia back. Apart from a quick chat to inquire if she had sufficiently recovered, the women had worked without speaking much. They had made good progress in catching up on the ever-growing piles of folders and files. Sabina was glad to be home and have some time to herself, as tomorrow promised to be just as busy.

She had barely stepped inside when her mother appeared from the kitchen. Her eyes were bloodshot, her cheeks flushed and Sabina was barely able to make out her words through the heavy sobs.

"Your father ... Sabina ... What are we going to do? They took him."

"What? Who took him? Where?" Sabina rushed to her mother, who collapsed in her arms. "What happened to Papa?" A sense of foreboding grew in her stomach, and she was dreading the answer.

"The Nazis. The Gestapo. They came for him at the mines." Her mother's entire body shook as Sabina wrapped her arms around her. "This morning."

Sabina stroked her mother's hair, and they stood rooted in the doorway between the kitchen and the living room. A chill went through her heart as the words registered. Her mother was mumbling incoherently, and Sabina's mind went through all the possibilities. Had they found out about her father? Had someone sold him out? Or had he done something at the mine that fixed the Gestapo's attention on him? The last possibility didn't make her feel any better. It was the Gestapo, for heaven's sake! Her mother seemed to have calmed down a little; her body was no longer shaking as violently, and her sobs subsided somewhat.

"Who told you about this? Did they come to the house?"

Her mother broke their embrace, her tearful face and broken eyes turned to her with a look of confusion. "One of the men from the mines came down to tell me about an hour ago. Said your father was just taken away without a word, and that no one would tell them anything." Fear appeared in her eyes. "Do you think they'll come to the house? Will they come for us? Why, Sabina? Your father is a good man!"

Sabina's heart ached for her mother, and she almost told her about her father's activities, but she stopped herself just in time. There was no sense in telling her now, not in this state. Her mother was in shock, and Sabina didn't know how she would respond to the news that her husband had been involved in illegal activities. *Not to mention my own contributions.* She put on a brave face and took a deep breath.

"If they came for Papa in the morning and they haven't showed up yet, I doubt they will come for us." Sabina tried to sound more confident than she felt, and her words were for a great part based on her hope that they were true. "So nobody knows where Papa was taken?"

Her mother shook her head. "What are we going to do, Sabcia?"

It had been a long time since her mother had used her childhood nickname. Sabina felt powerless—she could always count on her father to try to make things right. Now, it was up to her to think of a solution. She looked at her mother and her heart broke again. *I have to find out what happened to him. Where they took him. If not for myself, then for Mama.*

There was one place she had in mind and she eyed the clock, realizing with dismay that there would be no one there until the morning.

Sabina tried to convince herself it didn't matter; wherever her father was, they wouldn't be able to get to him anytime soon. With a heavy heart, she looked her mother in the eye.

"There's nothing I can do now, Mama. But I promise I'll ask anyone who might have the slightest idea at work tomorrow. We *will* find Papa."

Sabina arrived at work earlier than anyone else the next morning. She wasn't scheduled to come in until the afternoon, but she'd decided to skip Mr. Pach's morning classes. He would understand. For most of the morning she went from office to office, finding sympathy but precious little information. Noon came quicker than expected, and Sabina had exhausted all potential resources. Her colleagues had heard about her father's arrest, but nothing beyond that. Sabina returned to the archiving room bitterly disappointed.

Tosia had the good sense to leave her be, only once asking if she was all right, and if she wouldn't rather go home. Sabina had dismissed the notion, making it clear she preferred to be here, trying to take her mind off things. She felt a little guilty for leaving her mother on her own, but she held silent hope someone might burst into the room with tidings of her father.

The day passed quickly, but without any news. Sabina finally gave up, dreading returning home to her mother with nothing to report.

She had barely exited the building and entered the small square in front of it when she felt a presence behind her. Her heart skipped a beat and she upped her pace, hoping whoever it was simply needed to go in the same direction. To her dismay, the footsteps matched her own pace. Sabina dared a quick glance over her shoulder and was surprised to see a boy no older than twelve trying to catch up with her. She kept walking, but slowed her pace.

"You're Sabina, aren't you?" She nodded curtly but kept walking. "Marian wants to see you in the pierogi shop."

The mention of the resistance leader made her stop in her tracks. "When?"

"Now. He's waiting for you. It's important."

Sabina's heart fluttered, hardly hearing the boy's last words. Of course it was important. Maybe Marian knew more about her father.

They sat at the same table in the back. It was still early, with other customers around, so they spoke in hushed voices.

"I'm sorry about what happened to your father. I heard about it last night, and we have people asking around. We'll find out where they took him."

"Do you think they know about his connections to you?"

Marian paused, looking thoughtful. "I don't know, Sabina. Could be, but even before I met your father, he was involved in illegal activities. Sure, not quite as serious as what we do, but he was helping prisoners working in the mines long before he came into contact with us."

"So you think it might have something to do with his role at the mines?" The thought gave Sabina an odd feeling of relief. Helping an odd few prisoners survive the grueling conditions in the mines with some extra water and bread wasn't anywhere near as serious as aiding the armed resistance, surely?

Marian held up his hands. "I wish I could tell you, but it's all speculation at this point. But look, our network is extensive, and right now, every single person in the vicinity is asking around, trying to find out what happened, and why. Looking at this from my perspective, and I'm sorry if this sounds selfish, but if he was picked up because they found out about our operation somehow, that puts me and everyone else involved in grave danger." He looked at her intently for a few seconds. "Including you."

Sabina took a sip of her water while she pondered Marian's words. She felt restless, frustrated, and disappointed. On her way over to the shop, she had convinced herself Marian would have some information on her father's whereabouts. Now, despite his assurances, she struggled to put one foot in front of the other. And a new feeling had snuck up on her. Fear. Her involvement in the operation had felt safe, a little detached even. She was only a courier supplying the resistance with information. But her father had participated in an assault on the

Nazis. She wanted to be angry with him, but instead, she felt pride. He had stood up for what he believed in. *Don't I owe him to do the same?*

"Sabina, I'm sorry if this comes across a little rude, but I need to ask you something else." Marian's voice was softer than usual. "Your father is usually the one I contact to set meetings, but well, the situation is a bit different now. Did you find out anything new about Rajsko? About the patrols?"

Sabina felt a jolt of energy. She had told her father about her unexpected summons and celebratory drinks with Paskal, but that was the night before he was picked up. As she shared her intelligence with Marian, the flicker in his eyes grew with every word. When she told him about the nightly patrol schedule, he was smiling.

"You're certain he said they came around every half an hour?"

"Yes."

"This is incredible information, Sabina. It sounds like this officer really trusts you, or is very fond of you."

"I think the schnapps helped."

"Sure, but let's not underestimate your importance here." The smile was still on his face, but his eyes had turned serious. "Which is why I think you shouldn't, under any circumstance, do anything to risk losing his trust."

"What does that mean?" Sabina frowned, already certain she wouldn't like the words coming out of Marian's mouth next.

"I know we spoke about you perhaps assisting with the smuggling, but I'm now completely in agreement with you father. You won't be involved beyond your official duties with the municipal registry. No smuggling of anything from you. You're too valuable."

Sabina listened and had no objections. In fact, after what had happened to her father, she felt relieved not to be asked to smuggle anything inside. "Do you think I'm in danger?"

Marian shook his head. "It's very likely your officer in the camp isn't aware of what happened to your father. The Gestapo probably don't even know you visit the camp so regularly. Not yet, anyway." The last words made Sabina's skin crawl. Marian realized his slip of the tongue and hastily added, "As long as your father doesn't mention your trips, I don't think they will make the connection. On paper, you are just a clerk in a stuffy archiving room."

Sabina wasn't convinced, but she agreed she couldn't stop showing up in Rajsko, nor did she want to. Her father's arrest and her talk with Marian only further strengthened her conviction to be involved. "So what will you have me do, apart from my official duties?"

"You're quite a remarkable young woman, Sabina." Marian grinned. "For now, let me handle the possibility of opening a smuggling route into the camp. Your information is promising, but we need to confirm it." He paused, and Sabina had a good idea of how they would confirm this. She didn't envy whoever was sent to Rajsko in the middle of the night. "Meanwhile, there's something I need you to investigate. You'll need to be very careful, but you're the only one with enough access to the camp to make it work."

She leaned forward, a tingling sensation in her stomach. "What would you have me do?"

CHAPTER TWENTY-SEVEN

Felcia walked out of the lab and into the hallway. Her steps light as she clung onto two valuable sheets of paper. There was a tickle in her throat as nerves shot through her body, but she straightened her back and immediately felt more confident. *He'll be delighted.*

She had returned to Rajsko four nights ago. The guard hadn't shown up at her cell until well into the evening. Felcia feared her release had somehow been declined. It wasn't until she fell onto her soft bed in the Pflanzenzucht block that she truly allowed herself to believe she had survived Block 11. Most of the women were asleep by the time she entered, but a handful had acknowledged her return with hushed greetings and relieved smiles. It felt a bit like coming home, and she was glad to be back among her people.

Dr. Caesar hadn't said anything when he ran into her the next morning in the hallway, and Felcia had followed his lead. If he wanted to pretend he had nothing to do with what happened to her, that was fine with her. All that mattered was the ideas for further research, and Felcia steeled herself. The door to Dr. Caesar's office was closed and she hesitated, then found her resolve and rapped her knuckles on the door in quick succession. There was a grunt from inside, and she gently pushed open the door.

Dr. Caesar sat alone behind his desk and beckoned to her. "Felcia, come in. Please close the door. Glad you're here. I'm curious to hear your ideas."

"Pleased you asked, sir. But also a little surprised."

"Don't be. You're one of the most experienced botanists in the camp, and you know everything about the Polish winters. What do we need to do to make sure those ugly little plants continue sprouting, despite the freezing temperatures?"

"I'm afraid there's a very simple answer, based on the research we've done in the past months." She handed him the thin sheets of paper and waited as his eyes scanned them. After a few minutes, he placed them on his desk.

"More greenhouses. I suppose that makes sense. Do you think it will be enough, though?"

"Sir? Enough?"

"We can build a host of greenhouses here, but we have limited space. We know the soil quality is perfect here, but would the plants do just as well, say, in Germany? Or a few kilometers west, even?"

Felcia thought quickly, assessing the information. "I think it would work, sir. But it would be good to test. Is there any chance we could obtain soil from these different places, and perhaps analyze it?"

Dr. Caesar smiled broadly. "You see, this is why I wanted to make sure you survived your ordeal in the penal block. You actually come up with good ideas, rather than just carry out orders. Let me see what we can do, and I'll have you work on the soil analysis, if you'd like."

"Whatever you need, sir." She was rising to leave when he held up his hand.

"Just a minute, please. There's something else I wanted to ask."

"Sir?"

"I wanted to let you know you'll be starting your classes this evening. You can use your own laboratory; there should be enough space. It will also give you a chance to start with some practical examples when they're ready. How does that sound?"

Felcia struggled to find her words. "That's great. Thank you, sir. I will need to let the girls know."

"I've told the guards you're allowed to be in here between six and eight. You'll need to take your dinner here, but I doubt that will be a problem, right?"

"Absolutely, sir." Felcia pictured the scene: teaching the young women from the comfort of her laboratory. She could hardly believe it. *Dr. Caesar is really keeping his promise!*

"Right. Well, let's get back to work, shall we? Plenty of preparations required before we're ready to grow rubber this winter." He dismissed her with a quick wave, and Felcia opened the door, struggling to hide the fire in her belly. Stepping into the hallway, she closed the door softly and allowed herself a little shriek of excitement.

She jumped a little when someone softly cleared their throat behind her. She turned, surprised and relieved to find a familiar face sitting in the corner, a large envelope on her lap. "Sabina, nice to see you!"

"Felcia!" Sabina smiled and stood, then her face turned serious. She lowered her voice. "Will you be in your laboratory later? Say, in half an hour?"

"Yes." Felcia was surprised by the young woman's intense gaze. "Why?"

"I'll come find you. I have news." Sabina knocked on Dr. Caesar's door and waited for the sound of his voice before stepping inside. As she closed the door, she gave Felcia a quick wink.

Felcia was back in her lab a minute later and, as she tried to start work, found it hard to focus. If Dr. Caesar's announcement about starting her classes wasn't enough, Sabina's behavior left her rattled. She was pleased when Bianka went to check on some things in the greenhouses. A minute later, there was a knock at the door, and Sabina slipped inside.

"Sorry about that just now. I was just so pleased to see you back. I was wondering where you'd been." Sabina's voice was warm and genuine, and Felcia found it impossible not to smile.

"It's nice to see you, too. Are you allowed in here?" Felcia said, a little nervous.

"I didn't ask, but if anyone barges in, I'll say I got lost as I was looking for Dr. Caesar's office." Sabina's face turned serious as her eyes scanned Felcia's. "Are you all right? You look pale, as if you haven't slept for days."

Felcia waved a hand dismissively. "I'm okay. They don't feed us very well in here, you know that. What brings you here?"

"I have news. You asked me about any groups operating outside the camp."

"Yes." Felcia felt her heart beating faster.

"We were interrupted by your lab partner when we discussed the camp underground." The young woman's eyes bored into Felcia, betraying a matureness far beyond her years. It felt like she was looking right through her. "I think you weren't telling me everything you knew."

Felcia managed a nervous chuckle, but she knew it sounded not even a little convincing. "What do you think I know?"

"I'm not sure. It's just a hunch. When you spoke of your illegal classes before you were caught, you sounded proud and defiant. And you keep asking me about what's happening outside the camp. Maybe we can keep each other informed?"

"Informed about what's happening inside the camp? What's it to you?" Felcia's voice quivered a little, her breathing slightly quickened.

Sabina hesitated, averting her eyes. She moved along the large table in the middle of the room, stopping to study one of the samples of the Kazakh dandelions. Felcia watched her, but forced herself to keep quiet. *Something's going on. Better not push her.*

"How much do you know about the smuggling operations into the main camps?" Sabina's voice was clear, but Felcia saw the tension on her face. *This means something to her.*

"Not much. Only that the people on the outside are having trouble getting things in recently." Felcia thought of Anna, and hoped she was no longer locked up in Block 11. There was no doubt Anna would continue her activities once outside, although she'd probably be more covert about it. Felcia looked at Sabina and a thought struck. "Why? Do you know more?"

Sabina looked at her with the same piercing stare. "On my way over this morning, I thought about our talks the other times I was here. When I told you about the attack on the German trucks in town, you seemed pleased. Happy, even. And you're obviously no stranger to illegal activities. It's how you ended up in here." Sabina's eyes went to Felcia's chest, where her political prisoner triangle was visible from under her lab coat. "But it's not just that. There's something about you I can't place. An anger, or sadness?"

Felcia's heart skipped a beat, and she found herself unable to speak, avoiding Sabina's eyes.

"You lost someone, didn't you?" The young woman's voice had turned soft.

Felcia looked up to find genuine compassion in Sabina's eyes. "Haven't we all?" For the first time since arriving in Rajsko, she allowed the harrowing memory of her friend's execution to rise to the top of her consciousness. "My best and only friend was murdered in Birkenau." Her voice sounded shrill and alien, as if someone else was speaking. "I watched as they strung her up in front of my very eyes."

Sabina took a step closer. "I'm so sorry, Felcia." She took her hands, her touch soft, radiating a feeling of warmth Felcia couldn't remember experiencing in many months. Tears rolled down Felcia's cheeks and she bowed her head as she surrendered to her grief. Sabina squeezed her hands, then pulled Felcia toward her, embracing her. They stood like that for a few seconds, then Felcia returned to the reality of her situation. Having Sabina in her laboratory was dangerous. For both of them.

"Why are you really here, Sabina?" She used her shirtsleeve to wipe the tears from her face.

Sabina took a deep breath before answering. "Can I trust you, Felcia?" She phrased the question like a statement, and didn't wait for Felcia's answer. "I think I can. And I think we can help each other."

"How?"

"The resistance in and around Birkenau is real. We both know this. If you could help them, you would, right?"

"I suppose so, yes." Felcia felt a pang of guilt at not mentioning more of what she knew.

"And I want to help the resistance outside the camp." Sabina's voice caught, a trace of emotion filtering through. She recovered and quickly continued, "The smuggling routes to the main camps have mostly collapsed, and they're looking for a new way to get supplies to their connections in the camp."

"And they want to use Rajsko to do so." Felcia's heart jumped in excitement. Anna must've gotten out and shared her plan. She was amazed by the speed at which they operated, and stunned that Sabina had been part of the resistance from the start. "How long have they been talking about this? How concrete are these plans?" She struggled to contain her excitement.

"That's not really relevant." Sabina appeared surprised by her response, and Felcia realized it was perfectly possible that they had identified Rajsko independently. The thought of Anna still withering away in the cramped, cold cell produced a dull, aching feeling in the pit of her stomach. "The important thing is whether you'd be willing to help." Sabina's voice was slightly uneven, her eyes blinking as she evidently fought her nerves. "Avenge your friend's death by sabotaging the German operation from the inside."

Felcia's breath caught in her throat, her heartbeat increasing. "What would you have me do?"

"We would need the goods moved from Rajsko to the other camps. You said people came in from Birkenau every day?"

"Yes, but as I told you last time, it's close to impossible for me to talk to them, let alone have them take things back to Birkenau. They are always surrounded by guards." She didn't mention Klaudia. *Not yet.*

"What if you don't have to worry about that part? They would come to you. The people on the outside would only ask for you to be their connection into Rajsko."

Felcia looked at Sabina, the words slowly sinking in. "You're asking me to hide the goods before they're taken to Birkenau?" A tremor went through her body.

"We haven't worked out all the details yet. I know about the school building and the greenhouses, but that's as far as my knowledge about the camp goes. We need someone on the inside. Someone who has access to almost every area in the camp." She looked at Felcia solemnly, but expectantly. "We need you, Felcia. You can tell us when and where we can drop goods, and when the prisoners from Birkenau come in."

"And your people can really do this? Move goods to Birkenau?"

"Let us worry about that. If you become our contact in Rajsko, we'll take care of the Birkenau connection." Sabina sounded confident.

Felcia considered Sabina's proposal. The thought of assisting the camp underground was exhilarating. She still had her doubts about how they would get the goods to Birkenau, but if Sabina's connections came through, it could work. Marzena's face formed clearly in her mind, nodding and smiling.

"If I say yes, what would you have me do exactly?"

Sabina looked relieved. "So you're considering it?"

"I want to know exactly how this will go before I commit."

"I can't make any promises now, but I hope we can make this work. I'll be back soon." She turned toward the door, pausing to listen for any sounds on the other side.

"Sabina?" The young woman turned around with a questioning look. "Why did you pick me?"

A smile appeared on Sabina's face. "Because I like you, Felcia. And I trust you."

CHAPTER TWENTY-EIGHT

Sabina left work a few hours later. After leaving Felcia at Rajsko, she had made a quick stop at the pierogi store. Joanna assured her Marian would be there in the evening. It had been hard to focus on her duties at work. Thankfully, time had passed quickly, partly due to Tosia's constant chattering. Most of her friends had been released, and it had given Sabina hope that Marian might bring good news about her father as well.

The pierogi store came into view, and Sabina upped her pace. With a bit of luck, Marian would already be there. The door jammed a little, and Sabina put her shoulder into it. Stepping inside, she enjoyed the thick, humid air. Joanna stood behind the counter, preparing a large plate for a family near the window. She turned and smiled before nodding her head to the back of the shop. "He's already here. I'll bring you something to eat in a minute. You must be hungry."

Sabina nodded gratefully while she made for Marian's table. He was reading and didn't notice her until she sat across from him. He folded the piece of paper and slipped it inside his coat.

"You're sneaking around like a little mouse. I should be more careful." He gave a wry smile. "How are you, Sabina?"

"I've had an eventful day, but I'm sure you suspected as much."

"I was pleased to hear you were looking for me."

"And I was surprised when Joanna said you were doing the same. Would you like to go first?" Sabina tried to sound casual, but she felt the nerves tickling her throat.

"We've located your father."

Fear and relief gripped Sabina, and she struggled to ask the next question. "Is he alive?"

"As far as I know, he was this morning. He's held in a jail in Katowice."

"A Gestapo jail?"

"Yes."

Katowice was only thirty kilometers to the north, but it might as well have been the other side of the continent. Still, Sabina felt an odd sense of comfort at the knowledge that her father was alive, even though he was unlikely to be well. She dreaded coming home later, when she would have to share the news with her mother.

"Do you know how he's doing? Will they keep him there?"

Marian shook his head. "We have to assume they're questioning him. But our source could only confirm he was brought in two days ago, and hadn't left since. I'm sorry, Sabina, I don't know what happens inside the jail."

The news that he was alive was what really mattered. It could've been much worse. At least there's a chance they'll let him go.

"What happens next?"

"I don't know." Marian let out a deep sigh. "There's nothing we can do for him. We have to assume he'll talk to some extent. For his sake, I hope he admits to helping those prisoners in the mines. Give those inter-rogators something, and pray they believe that's everything he knows."

A lump formed in Sabina's throat. "And if they don't?"

"Let's not consider that possibility. It does us no good. Our contacts in Katowice will let us know if anything changes."

"What would change?" Sabina's voice was small yet her insides burned like an oven.

"In the best case, he's released. But I have to be honest—I don't think that's very likely."

"Not even if he admits to only helping prisoners at the mines?"

Marian shook his head. "That would still be severe enough to see him assigned to hard labor."

Stay positive, Sabina. He's alive.

Joanna appeared at the table and put a plate with a dozen pierogi between them. She sensed the somber mood and simply placed a fork before each of them before leaving. Neither made a move for the food.

"I'm sorry I couldn't bring you better news," Marian said after a minute. "If there's anything we can do, we will."

Sabina looked up to find Marian's face lined with compassion. "I appreciate it, Marian." She picked up her fork and reached for the pierogi; the smell made her acutely aware that her last meal had been breakfast. She had been too jittery to eat anything after meeting Felcia and then hearing Marian wanted to see her in the evening. She put the dumpling in her mouth and chewed furiously. "I have some more encouraging news. I spoke with my contact in Rajsko this morning."

"Contact?" His eyebrows shot up. "Does that mean she's agreed to help us?"

"She's open to it, but she needs some assurances." Sabina recounted her conversation with Felcia, and Marian listened without interrupting. When she finished, he clicked his tongue and leaned back in his chair, putting his hands behind his head.

"Did you know about her friend before you asked her?"

"I had a hunch."

He looked at her approvingly. "That was smart. You showed good judgment. Still, it's a big leap to go from teaching illegal classes in Kraków to assisting the resistance in a concentration camp. How did you know she would be open to it?"

Sabina hesitated and crossed her legs. "I didn't. But I figured the worst that could happen was her saying no."

"What if she had reported you to a guard?"

"It was a risk I had to take." Sabina pushed the thought of Felcia betraying her to the back of her mind. "But I was fairly certain she wouldn't. You should've seen the fire in her eyes when I mentioned avenging her friend's death."

Marian gave her a hard look, then reached for a cold pierogi himself. He ate slowly; Sabina could practically see the gears in his head turn. He wiped his mouth, then returned his dark eyes to her. "And you trust this woman, yes?"

"I do." Sabina held his gaze and answered without hesitation. "She'll come through."

"Very well. I'll set the plan in motion."

"What do you want me to tell my contact?"

"Tell her we're checking the logistics, and that we'll reach out to her with more details soon. Make sure she tells no one, not even those inside the camp she trusts. The less people know about this, the better."

It took two agonizing days for Sabina to be asked to deliver a set of documents to the camp. After the meeting with Marian she had been anxious to deliver the news to Felcia. It was a frosty morning, and she set a quick pace, reaching Rajsko within half an hour. The guards recognized her, and they let her pass with only a cursory glance.

The temperature inside the building was comfortable, and the hallway quiet. She spotted movement behind the frosted glass of Felcia's door and decided to catch up with the scientist first. *She might not be here later, and it will only take a minute.* Clutching the folder containing the papers for Dr. Caesar, she crossed the short distance from the main entrance to Felcia's door. As she rapped her knuckles softly, she felt a presence behind her. Her stomach dropped even before she heard a familiar voice.

"What do you think you're doing?"

Sabina turned around to find the bucktoothed guard who'd questioned her before standing there. Her eyes burned with suspicion, her right hand hovering over the baton on her belt. *Shit.* She opened her mouth, but no sound came out. Her mind blanked, the palms of her hands instantly clammy.

The guard stared back. "Lost our words, have we?" Her eyes shot to the folder in Sabina's right hand. "What's that? Is that for the scientists?"

Before Sabina could answer, the door opened, and Felcia appeared. Her eyes grew large as they went between Sabina and the guard.

"Were you expecting something?" The guard spoke in a deceivingly mild tone. "I'm sorry for interrupting whatever is going on here."

Felcia barely managed to conceal her horror at the situation and remained quiet, but Sabina found her voice. "I'm sorry, I was looking for Dr. Caesar's office."

"Were you, now?" The guard's voice oozed suspicion. "Seems odd to knock on the door of what is clearly labeled a laboratory, don't you think? You can read German, can't you?" She stepped forward and tapped on the small sign on the door. Sabina's confidence sank as she realized her mistake. A smirk appeared on the guard's face as she turned to Felcia. "I knew you were up to something, and now I've caught you red-handed. I'm sure Lagerführerin Mandl will be very interested."

"What's going on here?" a voice boomed from the other end of the hallway, and the three women turned their heads as one. Sabina could have almost cried with relief as Paskal strode from his office. It took him less than ten seconds to reach them. He looked at the guard with annoyance. "What are you doing here, Dreschel? Are you interrupting Dr. Caesar's research?"

The woman shifted uncomfortably on her feet, no longer appearing as confident, and it took her a few seconds to answer him. "No sir, I caught this woman trying to sneak into the laboratory." She motioned at Sabina. "I was only making a round through the building. I wouldn't have gone into the laboratory myself, or interrupted anything. Sir." The last word was spoken in clipped tones, bordering on insolence.

Paskal either missed it, or pretended to do so, as he turned to Sabina. "Is that true?" His tone was no less harsh, but Sabina saw the softness in his eyes. She shook her head.

"I think it's a big misunderstanding. I was looking for Dr. Caesar's office. I'm sorry, I wasn't paying attention."

He kept his gaze fixed on her for a few seconds; she felt her throat constrict. Would Paskal take the guard's side? She was aware where Dr. Caesar's office was. He broke their gaze and turned to the guard, who looked almost as confident as before Paskal appeared.

"Aufseherin Dreschel, this woman is a civilian tasked with bringing us important documentation. If I ever find you harassing her, or any of the other messengers, again, I will have you demoted. It was an honest mistake." Dreschel's eyes went wide at the reprimand, her expression turning sour. "Is that clear?"

"Yes, sir." Dreschel's voice was barely a whisper, but Sabina spotted the murderous look in her eyes as she chanced a quick glance. It chilled her to the bone.

Paskal turned his attention to Sabina. "And you will come with me. Dr. Caesar is away on official business, so I will sign your papers." He waved at Felcia dismissively. "Back to work."

He turned without another word, taking two steps toward his office. Sabina stood stunned, as did the other two women. He stopped and turned, annoyance clear on his face. "Well? Are you coming? I don't have all day." And then to the guard, his voice cold and harsh: "Dreschel, get moving. I don't want to see you in here again today."

The guard jumped at his words, but not before she gave Felcia another death stare. Sabina hurried to follow Paskal, who was already halfway down the hallway. As she heard Felcia's door close and Dreschel's footsteps fade, she realized she had just made an enemy in the camp. A knot formed in her stomach. Paskal had made it clear Sabina was not to be harmed, but he'd said nothing about Felcia. Would the guard take out her fury on her friend?

CHAPTER TWENTY-NINE

Felcia held the door for her three students. Renata and Paula crossed into the hallway and moved toward the main exit, but Izolda paused when she stepped out of the laboratory. Felcia closed the door and turned toward the young woman.

"Something you wanted to ask?"

Izolda nodded and turned to the other women waiting at the door. "Why don't you go ahead. I'll catch up with you in a bit." Paula gave her a look but followed Renata outside without another word. Izolda returned her attention to Felcia. "I just wanted to say we really appreciate what you're doing for us. I can only imagine where I'd be if you didn't bring us to Rajsko."

"I don't decide who gets picked." Felcia fidgeted with her hands.

Izolda shook her head. "I know, but still. You took the risk to teach us, and look where it got you. I know you don't want to tell us what happened after they took you away, but it can't have been good. We worried you wouldn't come back." She paused, concern in her eyes. "And when you did, you looked a shade of the woman you were. Whatever happened to you, it was partly our fault."

"Nonsense." Felcia surprised herself with her sharp tone. "I knew what I got into when I agreed. And so did you. I was just relieved to see none of you follow me."

"We got off lightly." She smiled sadly as her eyes went to the closed door of the laboratory. "Although it would be easier to be in the same block as you, so we could talk outside the classroom as well."

"I think Dr. Caesar wanted to make sure there were no more incidents like before. It only takes one ill-informed guard to haul us off to the penal block." Felcia forced a smile. "At least there can be none of that when we're in here, right?"

"I suppose so. I'm just happy we get this time with you. Do you think we'll be assigned to the labs anytime soon?"

"I honestly don't know. If it were up to me, I'd have you assisting us already, but I'll have to wait for Dr. Caesar to decide. Your progress has been very encouraging." Izolda's face dropped ever so slightly, and Felcia hastily added, "As soon as he gives me an opportunity, I'll try to get you off housekeeping duties."

Izolda caught herself, for she quickly shook her head. "I don't mean to sound ungrateful. I don't mind our current work. I'm just keen to put the lessons into practice."

"No need to apologize. It's perfectly understandable." Felcia took a few steps toward the exit. "Come, let's get to our blocks. It's close to curfew. Don't want to get into trouble at the gate."

The walk to the fenced-off area where they slept was short, and the women each went their way. When Felcia opened the door to her block, she recognized some of the women who worked in the camp's kitchen. It was quite common for them to take the day's scraps and leftovers and prepare them on the small stove in their block. Although technically illegal, none of the guards appeared too bothered by it. Felcia suspected the women in the kitchen had made arrangements.

Felcia walked on, nodding at a few of the women looking up from their reading. She reached her soft bunkbed and lay down, closing her eyes. Her spine tingled as she recalled the look in Dreschel's eyes. No one had ever looked at her with such hatred. The SS officer's intervention had been even more odd. Felcia had never seen any of the senior SS men concern themselves with prisoner management. Sure, Dr. Caesar looked after the women carrying out his research, but she'd never seen him dress down a guard the way the young officer had that morning. The more Felcia thought about it, the more she was convinced something was going on between Sabina and the officer. It had only brought more questions about the woman that was now her sole connection to the outside world. And the resistance. If she was involved with the SS officer, could she be trusted? Or was she playing him to her own advantage?

The door opened with a crash, and Felcia didn't need to open her eyes to know something was wrong. No prisoner would open the door in this manner. The sound of boots on the wooden floor grew louder. She opened her eyes to see three women in guard uniforms enter. Margot Dreschel was among them. *She's come for me.* Felcia didn't move a muscle as she remained in her bed and slowed her breathing, trying to make herself invisible. Her eyes fixed on the scene in the front of the room, and she waited for the inevitable calling of her number.

Dreschel's eyes went to the women huddled around the stove. An ugly smile formed on her face as she took a few steps toward them. "Did you take that pot from the kitchen? I'm quite certain you're not supposed to be cooking in here." The women shrank back as she approached and looked into the cauldron. Dreschel tilted her head, inspecting the pot's contents. "Potatoes, cabbage, and what's that, carrots?"

One of the women nodded and answered in a weak voice, "We asked if we could take some of the old vegetables."

Dreschel's head shot to the woman, and Felcia could feel the hate radiating from her, even from her relatively safe spot in the back. "Did you really? I'm not sure who approved this." Then the tone of her voice softened. "But I might be wrong. Why don't we ask the Lagerführerin about this?"

She turned to the door, which opened with perfect timing. A collective gasp of terror went through the room as the most powerful woman in Auschwitz-Birkenau entered. Maria Mandl walked with purpose, the silence amplifying the soft creak of freshly polished leather boots as she turned on her heel. The whip she normally held at the ready was neatly coiled up on her belt.

Felcia could hardly believe the Lagerführerin had taken the time to inspect her block. Something had to be very wrong.

Mandl casually glanced into the room, and Felcia swore her gaze lingered slightly on her before she turned her attention to Dreschel. "What's going on here, Margot?"

"This one says they have permission to cook in their block. Even admitted to taking the vegetables from the camp kitchen." Dreschel's voice had returned to her regular poisonous, snakelike tone as she pointed at the unfortunate woman who had spoken earlier.

Mandl approached the women around the cauldron. They sat with their heads bowed, avoiding Mandl's gaze. Felcia was too far away to see the look in the Lagerführerin's eyes, but she could feel the fury radiate all the way to her bed. Mandl took the large wooden ladle and stirred the cauldron's contents. Quietness brooded like the calm before the storm.

Without warning, Mandl raised the ladle and lashed out at the nearest woman. The blow struck her on the side of the head, and she let out a surprised yelp. She reached for the painful spot, but Mandl had already delivered a second blow, this time connecting squarely with the woman's nose. Blood gushed out as she howled in pain. She tried to protect her face, but two guards, including Dreschel, pinned her arms behind her back. They roughly pulled her to her feet, and Mandl dropped the ladle, landing a punch in the woman's face. Then another, and another. Felcia looked away, but she couldn't block out the woman's screams as Mandl unleashed her uninhibited fury. Screams withered to soft moans as the sickening, dull sounds of Mandl's fists connecting with her face continued. Within a minute, Mandl had reduced the woman's face to a bloody mess. Felcia looked up to see the woman's eyes glassing over, and she hoped she would soon lose consciousness. Mandl wouldn't stop until she did, or worse.

But the Lagerführerin had other plans. Panting, she reached for the cauldron. With an effort, she turned it over, sending the thick, boiling stew onto the floor. Almost in the same movement, she grabbed the barely conscious woman and threw her in the steaming liquid. Felcia let out a gasp as the woman's body twisted in pain. She tried to get up, but Mandl placed her boot on the back of her head, pushing her face into the scorching liquid. The woman's screams were drowned out, but her entire body convulsed. Felcia's stomach roiled and she fought the urge to throw up.

After what felt like an eternity, the woman stopped struggling, and Mandl lifted her boot. The two other guards dragged her body from the stew. Incredibly, the woman was still alive, a soft moan escaping her lips. Mandl looked on in satisfaction as the guards pulled the woman out of the block, wiping her forehead with a handkerchief. Then she turned to the rest of the women and spoke in a clear voice.

"You're all conspirators. That woman's punishment was a warning to you all. Now, everybody to the front. You'll clean up this mess right away."

The women rose from their beds as one, and Felcia stumbled to her feet, keeping her head down as she made her way forward. Dreschel and Mandl stood talking to the side while the prisoners hurried to grab cleaning rags from the room next door. Felcia grabbed a mop and bucket, filling it with water.

When she returned to the main room, she was dismayed to see Dreschel standing near another woman who was swabbing the floor, berating her for doing it wrong. The mop and bucket suddenly felt ten times heavier as she approached the mess on the floor. With a feeling of impending doom, she started cleaning, keeping her ears trained on Dreschel, droning at the other woman only a few meters away. When she stopped talking, Felcia kept her face focused on the ground and gripped the handle of her mop a little tighter. It didn't matter.

"Well, well. Look who we have here." Dreschel stood less than a meter behind her, and Felcia couldn't ignore her. She turned and saw the woman observing her with glee. "I suppose you were also involved in this little project, weren't you?" Dreschel took another step closer, and Felcia could feel the woman's warm breath on her neck, making the little hairs stand up.

"I wasn't, ma'am. I don't have access to the kitchen." Nothing she said would make a difference. She took another large swipe at the stew on the floor before she dunked the mop into the bucket of water.

"Don't be smart with me." Dreschel's voice hissed in her ear. The next words chilled the blood running through Felcia's veins. "A shame your officer friend isn't here to save you now, don't you think?"

Before Felcia could respond, a sharp blow to the back of her head had her seeing stars. She dropped the mop and felt herself spinning on her legs. Another blow to her left temple had her ears ringing and the room spinning also. Her knees gave out, and an instant later the floor came rushing up at her. After that, her world went dark.

CHAPTER THIRTY

A few kilometers north, Sabina hurried across town. There was just over an hour left before curfew, and she was excited to meet with Marian before going home. Another teenage boy had knocked on her door in the archiving room that afternoon, asking her to meet Marian at Joanna's later. She didn't have to ask the boy what it was about.

It had been an eventful day. Dreschel was different from the other, mostly male, guards. They were happy to have a short chat before letting her through and then leave her alone. Whenever she saw them patrolling the grounds, they looked somewhat relaxed, only occasionally stopping prisoners to ask them what they were doing. Dreschel, from what Sabina had seen of her, stalked the camp grounds, a hunter searching for prey. Sabina shivered at what could've happened if Paskal hadn't been there to intervene. *I need to be more careful.*

Felcia was on her mind as she turned onto the main square. Sabina worried about her friend. *Friend?* She allowed herself a smile, but her thoughts quickly turned darker. Felcia didn't have the luxury of leaving the camp, and Sabina could vividly picture the look Dreschel had given both of them after she had been admonished by Paskal. Sabina hoped Felcia had been able to avoid the woman, for Sabina had no doubt Dreschel would look to enact revenge.

Marian sat at their usual table, and the thought of telling him about Dreschel and Felcia crossed her mind, but only for a minute. As she took her place opposite him, she decided not to worry him needlessly. She would take care of any problems in Rajsko.

"We don't have a lot of time, so I'll make this brief," Marian started without preamble, then appeared to catch himself. "Good to see you, Sabina. Thanks for coming."

"Of course. Did you talk to your connections?"

"I did." He looked uneasy, drumming his fingers on the table. "They are a little apprehensive."

"How so?" Sabina couldn't hide her disappointment.

"They're not sure we, or the women in Rajsko, can deliver. They think it sounds too good to be true, and they're hesitant to commit."

Sabina's disappointment gave way to frustration. "What does that mean? Aren't these people supposed to be part of the underground? They understand the risks and dangers, don't they?" She felt her cheeks flush.

"They understand." Marian looked back at her calmly, his eyes soft. "But these people are on the inside, and a single mistake means death."

"Even when the plan comes from you?"

"They have every right to be cautious. No one knows the situation inside the fences as well as them." He placed his hands on the table. "Look, Sabina. I want this to work just as much as you, but we only know the situation in and around Rajsko. We don't know how to get the goods into Birkenau, or how to distribute them to the right people. They do. We need them on our side."

"Did your people inspect Rajsko at night?"

"They did, and they confirmed what you told me. The patrols pass by twice an hour. Apart from that, most of the camp is shrouded in darkness, except for the fenced-off prisoner area. That's brightly lit throughout the night."

"So, where are you in all of this? How can we convince your contacts in Birkenau that we can deliver the goods?"

"The only way we can placate them is by showing them."

"Show them ... how?"

"We need to get the goods into Birkenau. Without their help."

Sabina sat up. "Take away any doubt about our side of the operation."

"Exactly. Let's start with getting into Rajsko one more time." He leaned forward, taking out the piece of paper with the crude map Sabina had drawn earlier, pointing at her old school. "I think it makes the most sense to cross the road and drop the packages near this building. It would be the fastest way in and out, don't you agree?"

Sabina thought for a second, then nodded. "It's also where Felcia passes by a number of times a day. None of the guards would consider it odd for her to walk by the side of the building. She might even be able to retrieve the packages on her way to work, or after visiting the greenhouses." She pointed at the lines that represented the greenhouses on the other side of the road running through the camp. "I think it would work."

Marian studied the map silently for a minute, then looked up. "Okay, let's assume we've smuggled one or two packages into the camp. How will we get them to Birkenau?"

Sabina considered her response. It was the part of their plan she had assumed would be covered by Marian's connections. She'd even told Felcia as much. Felcia had mentioned the workers in the fields. She racked her brain to remember Felcia's exact words. It was near impossible to contact them. *Near impossible.* Sabina made a decision. "I think my contact might be able to help with that."

"Really?" Marian looked at her in surprise. "How?"

"I'm not completely sure yet. Maybe the prisoners coming in from Birkenau. I think that's our only option."

"You don't sound confident."

Sabina let out a deep sigh. "My contact said it was near impossible. But it sounds like we have to try."

Marian looked at her, his eyes full of respect. "We only need to show them it's possible this one time. Trust me, once they see that the route through Rajsko works, they will find more ways to collect the goods. They're just being extra cautious."

"I understand." And she really did. Sabina recalled the terror she felt when Dreschel caught her knocking on Felcia's door. And she wasn't even a prisoner. She could hardly imagine what it was like for prisoners looking to smuggle goods into Birkenau. It was incomparable with Rajsko. "I will check with my contact the next time I'm sent to the camp."

Marian looked pleased. "We've got everything ready to go on our side. Once you confirm there's a route into Birkenau, we can send the first supplies."

CHAPTER THIRTY-ONE

Felcia stood in the cold, the rain mercilessly beating down on her. She shivered but gritted her teeth, keeping her eyes locked ahead. A guard passed on her right, counting under his breath. His comfortable raincoat made her painfully aware of her own soaked prisoner uniform, chilling her broken body.

It had been two days since Dreschel beat her into unconsciousness. When she came to, she found herself in her own bed. The woman in the bed next to her was still awake, and she looked relieved when Felcia asked how long it had been. When she tried to sit up, a searing pain radiated from her lower back to her head, instantly making her regret her effort. She had spent the rest of the night uncomfortably trying to find an acceptable position. In the end, she settled for lying on her side. Thankfully, the other women of the block came by to bring her water and soft pieces of bread. How they had arranged those, she didn't ask. Instead, she gratefully accepted their care and chewed on the bread. Come morning, she felt slightly better, and when the block elder came by, she told her to rest up another day. Felcia had initially protested but, when she was unable to rise from her bed, accepted she had no choice. When the other women left for work, they assured her they would inform Dr. Caesar she would only be absent for the day.

A piercing whistle from the front brought her back to the present. Roll call was over, and the neat lines broke as a few hundred women went their own way. Felcia scanned the crowd once more and was relieved there was no sign of Mandl or Dreschel. She paused for a moment, closing her eyes as she collected enough strength to make it to the laboratory. *Once I'm inside, I'll be fine. I can work.*

"Need some help?" Bianka showed up alongside, offering her arm. Felcia gratefully took it. "Are you sure you can work today?"

"I have to." She remembered Dr. Caesar's words about everybody being useful. There was no way she would risk being on the wrong side of that calculation. "There's too much to do. I'll make it work."

It took twice as long as normal to reach the main building, and Felcia couldn't hide her relief when they had climbed the steps to the main entrance. Her relief was short lived as a deep voice sounded behind them. "I heard you weren't doing so well, but I didn't expect you to be limping into work." Dr. Caesar caught up with them and observed her, his face a mix of shock and concern. "What happened, Felcia?"

Felcia forced a weak smile. "I'm all right, Dr. Caesar." No doubt he was aware of what had happened in their block. "I'm happy to be back at work. I have much to do today."

His gaze lingered on her for a few seconds longer, and Felcia feared he would push for a clearer answer. Instead, he nodded slowly. "Very well. Just be careful. Stay out of trouble, Felcia." He turned and moved gracefully down the hallway. The meaning of his words weren't lost on Felcia. *He knows.*

The rest of the morning passed quickly, with Felcia falling into a familiar rhythm of work. It felt good. At her desk, analyzing the latest batch of samples from the greenhouses, her fears subsided somewhat. The results were better than expected, especially with the many gray, rainy days they'd experienced in the past weeks. *Maybe I can get the girls working in the laboratory sooner rather than later.*

The door opened and Felcia looked up to find Bianka returning. She had been going back and forth between the greenhouses all morning, also bringing in Felcia's samples. Felcia gave her a smile, but Bianka's face was surprisingly serious. Felcia put down her pen. "What's wrong?"

"There's someone outside asking about you."

Felcia's heart skipped a beat. "Who?"

"That girl that comes around the camp every so often."

Sabina. Felcia felt a flutter of excitement, then a pang of fear. The last time she saw Sabina ended up with her being beaten into unconsciousness.

"What did she want?"

"Asked if there was a place to speak with you safely. I told her she could come into the lab if you were okay with it, but she seemed hesitant."

"Where is she now?" Felcia stood, a wave of pain shooting through her back. She closed her eyes and waited for it to pass.

"Are you all right? I can tell her to leave, if you want." There was concern in Bianka's voice as she rushed to Felcia's side, putting an arm around her shoulder.

"No, no. I'm fine. Where is she?"

"I told her to wait by the entrance."

That wouldn't do. Felcia couldn't very well be seen walking alongside Sabina, nor could she risk bringing her into the laboratory again. She turned to Bianka. "Can you take her to the greenhouse? I'll meet her there."

Bianka gave her an odd look but didn't question her as she nodded. "Will you manage on your own?"

"I'll have to. I'll be there in a few minutes. Make sure no one sees you."

She found Sabina and Bianka crouching on their knees in the back of the greenhouse. Despite her nerves, Felcia couldn't help but smile. It was a smart move; anyone casually glancing through the large windows would assume Sabina was any other prisoner inspecting or tilling the flower beds.

Sabina seemed shocked as Felcia approached, and she made a move to rise. Felcia shook her head and crouched down herself. Bianka looked at her inquiringly, and she nodded.

"Just let me know if you need anything; I'll be right outside," Bianka said as she rose and headed for the exit. Felcia waited until the door closed behind her before turning to Sabina. "I didn't expect you back this quickly."

"What happened to you? It was that guard, wasn't it?" Sabina looked horrified as her eyes shot across Felcia's face. Her concern was genuine. "I'm so sorry, Felcia. This is all my fault. I should never have knocked on your door like that." Tears welled up in the girl's eyes, and Felcia felt her own eyes burning.

"No, it wasn't your fault. I was in the wrong place at the wrong time. Let's not talk about it further."

Sabina didn't look convinced, her eyes narrowing. "Felcia, I promise I'll be more careful moving forward."

"It's okay. There's just one thing I need to know."

"The SS officer."

Felcia was only slightly surprised. "What was that all about?"

Sabina averted her eyes and shifted her weight from one knee to the other. Felcia waited patiently, then the girl focused her clear blue eyes on her again. "I met Paskal on one of my first trips to Rajsko, when Dr. Caesar was away. He took a liking to me, and I've been using him for information. We got lucky when he appeared when he did the other day." She spoke unflinchingly, not blinking once while keeping her eyes on Felcia's. "I understand how it may have looked, but there's no other angle. I'm fully committed to the resistance."

A silence fell, and Felcia studied Sabina. She desperately wanted to believe her, but a small voice warned her to be cautious. *She might be playing me.* Before she could say anything, Sabina looked up again, her eyes now teary.

"They have my father, Felcia. The Gestapo took him, and they're keeping him in a prison." Sabina's words were raw with emotion, and Felcia felt her heart break. "I'm continuing his work. He started all of this. I don't know if he'll ever make it out alive." Her voice broke and she went silent.

"Sabina, I'm so sorry." Felcia reached for her hand, which felt cold despite their surroundings. Sabina had allowed her to take it, and when she squeezed it softly, the young woman responded in kind. Felcia felt her pain. They sat for a minute longer, then Felcia broke the silence. "I believe you."

Sabina looked up, her eyes a little red, but with relief etched on her face. "I would never betray you. We're fighting for Poland."

Felcia's heart burst and she squeezed Sabina's hand a bit harder. "We don't have much time. I'm sure this wasn't the only reason you came here."

"I have news. The people on the outside are ready to start moving goods into Rajsko. They are confident."

"That's great. "When?"

Sabina raised her hand. "That's not all. The Birkenau underground won't cooperate."

"What? Why not?"

"They have their doubts about our ability to pull this off."

"What does that mean?" Felcia felt indignation rising. "They don't trust us?"

"That's the feeling I'm getting. They want us to prove we're able to get goods into Birkenau before they'll commit." Sabina's face was set in hard lines. "Felcia, I need your help even more than before. We only need to do this once, prove to them that it's possible."

"Let's start at the beginning. How will you get the goods into Rajsko?"

As Sabina explained her plan, Felcia imagined the scene. "As long as you're not smuggling large packages inside, it should work. But I don't think you should drop them near the main building. I understand it's convenient for whoever is bringing them in, but it's too exposed. There are always guards near the main road, and they might become suspicious if they see movement around the main building. It would be better to use the well next to the greenhouses."

"We can do that. It's not much farther, and it will be dark enough, right?"

"Yes, as long as you stay off the main road running through the camp."

"Now, getting the goods to Birkenau." Sabina paused, looking nervous. "I can only think of one option. Is there any way you can get in touch with the prisoners coming in to work the fields every day?"

Felcia looked at her, not immediately responding. Sabina's thinking made a lot of sense. She nodded slowly. "There might be a way, but I can't guarantee it'll work. I'll need to call in a favor, and I'm not sure I have enough credit to do so."

"I can't ask for more," Sabina said. "But I can promise you one thing."

"What's that?"

"If you can clear the path to Birkenau, and we end up doing this—" She paused, her voice thick with emotion, her face set in deep lines of determination. "I will be the one bringing the first package into Rajsko."

Felcia's heart was thumping as she stood near the doorway of the block. Scores of women passed by, some giving her curious looks. Rajsko was a small camp, but most prisoners kept to themselves, only permitting themselves a handful of friends, even in their own block. To these women, Felcia was a stranger.

Her heart leaped when she saw a familiar figure approach. Her throat was dry as she took a deep breath. Everything depended on the next few minutes going well. She was still reeling from Sabina's revelation that she would make the first smuggling run.

"Klaudia, could I have a minute of your time, maybe?"

The woman nodded and motioned to the side of the narrow corridor. "What are you doing here, Felcia?" She spoke with a soft voice, but her tone was hurried.

"I'll keep it short. Have you started smuggling food to the other camps yet?"

The woman's eyes widened before she looked around, making sure nobody was eavesdropping. "Are you mad? Why are you bringing that up here?" Her tone sharpened, her eyes narrowing.

"I'm sorry. I have no other option, and this can't wait." Felcia kept her tone civil, but she found irritation bubbling up inside. *I'm not doing this for myself.* "Have you?"

"You shouldn't pry into business that doesn't concern you." Klaudia's tone was dismissive, and Felcia had to control the urge to snap at her. She took a step closer and lowered her voice.

"I've made contact with a group on the outside. They want to smuggle supplies in for the underground in Birkenau." Klaudia's aggressive stance faded quickly, her shoulders dropping. "They want to bring them in through Rajsko."

"My contact in Birkenau hasn't mentioned any of this." Klaudia's raised an eyebrow. "They would've consulted me if something was happening. Are you sure?"

"That's because the Birkenau leadership doesn't believe it's possible." Felcia brought Klaudia up to speed in quick and hushed tones, keeping her eyes on her surroundings. "So, I'll ask you again, could you help us get the first package to Birkenau?"

"We could." Klaudia looked undecided. "But what if this is a trap? Are you absolutely certain you can trust these people?"

"I trust my contact. That's enough for me," Felcia answered without delay, her voice steadier than ever.

"I'm not sure. I have to agree with the leadership. It sounds risky."

Felcia's frustration nearly got the better of her, but she controlled herself. "Imagine if we make it work, though. It would reignite the underground. And consider how it would make you look to the leadership, delivering the Rajsko connection." Klaudia's eyes lit up at the last words, and Felcia pushed on. "You won't even have to make the collection. I'll do it. That way, if this is a trap, I'll be the one that's caught. All you have to do is tell me who to hand it to for delivery to Birkenau." Felcia's heart was beating in her ears as Klaudia mulled over her response. After what felt like an eternity, the other woman started nodding.

"That's fair. Let me know when you've got the package. I'll get it to Birkenau."

CHAPTER THIRTY-TWO

The icy night air gnawed at Sabina's cheeks. The frozen, mossy ground beneath her feet crunched softly, and she was grateful for the cover of the tall trees surrounding her. Sabina knew this path like the back of her hand, lit by the occasional sliver of moonlight filtering through the clouds overhead. The darkness brought welcome cover, and she grasped the small bag tighter. The night was quiet but for the odd owl hooting overhead.

The woods thinned, and Sabina slowed at the sight of nearby camp lights. There would be less cover as she neared the road, and there was no need to rush.

Sabina reached the bottom of the ridge and hid behind a bush. The last time she was here with Elena the guards had caught them. Things were very different now. Now, there would be no explanation for what she was doing stalking around in the darkness. Not even Paskal would be able to help her.

She peered across the road, only a few meters away. The camp was darker than she'd expected, and it looked very different from daytime. Only the area where the prisoners were fenced in was brightly lit, making the school building a dark silhouette. Across the gravel path cutting through the camp, the light bounced off the glass structures of the greenhouses before it was absorbed in the darkness of the surrounding fields.

Sabina pricked her ears while she searched for movement. The spot where the guards greeted her in the daytime was abandoned. It almost seemed too easy, as if one could simply walk into the camp. Sabina knew better as her eyes adjusted to the odd lighting just across the road and near the school building. It was easy to make out the area around the school building, and she could see the well to the east, a few meters farther into the camp. Felcia had been right; it was shrouded in darkness, and the narrow space between the school building and the well made a perfect hiding place. *Now for the small matter of getting there.*

She rubbed her hands, then brought them to her lips and softly blew. In the silence of the night, she considered her approach. Once the guards passed, she would have to move quickly. Get to the well, drop the package, and make her way out again. She estimated she would be in and out within minutes. Still, as she sat on her own, her nerves were frayed, her heart beating fast. Worse, her mind wouldn't stop conjuring images of guards springing from the darkness, flashlights exploding into life as they ambushed her. *No, no, no. Don't think like that, Sabina.* She started silently counting in her head in an effort to banish her worries.

Sabina had reached a hundred and fifty-two when she heard soft voices across the road. It would've been easy to miss them if it wasn't for the small, flickering orange glow dancing in the darkness next to the school building. She listened intently, her eyes focused on the cigarette. Although it was impossible to make out the figures, she could see movement in front of the building. A few seconds later, two men stepped into the light streaming down the gravel road. They walked with the slow, relaxed gait of men who expected no trouble. And why would they? The prisoners were locked up inside their blocks a few hundred meters away. They stopped and spoke in undecipherable tones until the taller motioned toward the greenhouses. They walked on, then turned off the road and disappeared into the darkness between the glass buildings. The silence of the night returned.

Sabina closed her eyes and took a deep breath. This was it. Clasping the small bag containing her illegal goods tighter, she exhaled deeply. *Now.*

She emerged from behind the bush, completely exposed. The soft ground gave way to the solid asphalt of the road as she dashed toward the school building. Sabina pushed herself harder, speeding up as she almost felt the faint light from the back of the camp on her face. The safety of the school building was only a few meters away, and her legs burned as she prayed there were no guards looming in the shadows. The distance felt longer than usual, the sound of her quick breathing blocking out all other sensations.

The lights dimmed, and she found herself against the wall of the school building. Breathing hard, she took a moment to recover, listening intently for any indication she'd been spotted. All remained quiet, apart from her heart pounding in her ears. Sabina allowed herself a minute to catch her breath, then moved along the walls, passing the main entrance. The door was closed, and not even a flicker of light came from any of the windows. She reached the side of the building within seconds, pausing briefly. The well was only a few meters down the road, but for Sabina to reach it, she would have to move along the side of the building, close to the gravel road, and into the faint light. *Keep moving.* Sabina steeled herself, then turned the corner and, without another thought, sprinted toward the well. Her body tensed, any minute expecting a shout—or worse—to ring out from the darkness.

She reached the shelter between the school building and well sooner than expected. Felcia had been right: there was plenty of unkempt vegetation here. Sabina positioned the package against the side of the well, beneath the dense undergrowth. For good measure, she scooped a couple of generous handfuls of leaves atop it. Satisfied with her handiwork, she rose to leave when she heard not-so-distant voices. Sabina froze, her eyes shifting between the prisoner barracks, the greenhouses, and the road in between. She saw nothing, but the voices were there, and increasing in volume. *They're approaching, but from where?* She strained her eyes and ears, but the darkness beyond the nearby buildings made it impossible to tell. Sabina shrank back into the hiding space between the well and the school building.

"I must've dropped it in front of the laboratories. Just let me check."

"Hurry. I don't want anyone to catch us making our way back."

Sabina recognized the voices. The two figures emerging from between the greenhouses were the same guards on patrol she'd spotted from across the road. They walked with a clear sense of urgency.

"It's fine," the first voice said with slight irritation. "If anyone sees us, which I sincerely doubt, we'll just say we heard something."

"Sure, that'll be convincing. Nothing ever happens around here. This has to be the most useless patrol in the area. Those prisoners aren't going anywhere." The second guard matched his colleague for irritation. "My feet are frozen. I need to get my boots fixed."

They passed Sabina's hiding place, not slowing their pace. She held her breath, not daring to move a muscle until they turned the corner. The men's voices trailed off, and she considered her next move. She didn't doubt they would return the way they came, resuming their patrol after finding whatever they'd lost. If they paid somewhat more attention, it would be impossible for them not to spot her. *I need to move.* Her hands were shaking as she looked around, her ears focused on the voices beyond the corner. They still sounded far enough away for her to find a new spot. She looked down the road heading farther into the camp. The guards had come from the greenhouses on the other side. Perhaps she could circle around the school building in the opposite direction? Her stomach turned at having to step into the brighter lights, but she had no choice. *Or maybe I can lie down, and they won't look my way?*

The voices became louder again, sounding more relaxed. *They're coming back.* Sabina looked down the road one more time. *I can't stay here.* Without hesitation, she got up and sprinted for the other corner of the school building, completely exposed by the bright lights, her shadow chasing her along the wall. The voices of the guards faded as time slowed down. Sabina focused on the ground in front of her, making sure she wouldn't trip on any loose roots. She remembered playing tag here, and it wouldn't be the first time she tripped around the school building. This time, the consequences would be fatal.

She turned the corner of the building and didn't stop running. The thought of another patrol possibly making its way from the other side played in her mind, but she pushed it aside. *I need to keep moving.* After a few meters, she returned to the cover of darkness as she moved into the dark gap between the school and an adjacent building. Sabina ran on despite the relief of the darkness. She didn't stop until she made it to the far side of the school and turned the corner. Leaning against the side of the building, Sabina sank to her knees, making herself small. The voices of the guards on the other side of the building filtered through. They were too far away for her to make out their words, but their tone was casual, relaxed. Sabina let out a deep sigh of relief. Her shirt clung to her back, her hands were shaking, and she felt sweat dripping down her forehead. Despite her discomfort, she couldn't help but smile as she looked into the dark woods ahead of her. She'd delivered the package. It was up to Felcia now.

CHAPTER THIRTY-THREE

The path to the greenhouse had never been longer. With each step, Felcia's feet felt more laden with lead. She kept her gaze on the ground to avoid her eyes constantly shifting and scanning the area around her. *You're allowed to be here. The greenhouse is an extension of your work area.*

She had arrived at the greenhouse and was reaching for the door handle when a voice behind her made her freeze.

"What are you doing out here?"

Felcia turned around to find a female guard approaching from the main thoroughfare. The unfamiliar woman eyed her suspiciously, and Felcia spotted the woman's hand moving to the baton on her belt. Felcia turned from the greenhouse, swallowed, and kept her face neutral as she answered.

"I work on Dr. Caesar's research in the lab." She nodded to the laboratory building opposite the road.

"Is that so?" The guard stood less than a meter from Felcia, and she was surprised by the woman's age. She couldn't be much older than twenty. Despite her youthful appearance, her face was lined in steel, jaw clenched, eyes narrowed. "If you work in there, what are you doing out here? On your own."

Felcia was taken aback, and she didn't immediately answer. She'd never been asked to explain her trips to the greenhouses before. *Had something changed?* The back of her neck burned up. The guard cocked her head, her hand tapping on the hilt of the baton, jolting Felcia into a response. "I need to check on some of the plants in here. In the greenhouses."

The guard looked her up and down, and Felcia felt a trickle of sweat on her back. The small package underneath her lab coat suddenly felt as if it was on fire.

"You know, I might be new, but I have a sixth sense about when someone's a bit off." She took out a small notebook and pencil. "Name and number?"

Felcia looked at the woman in stunned silence. This was the first time she'd been written up. She couldn't remember any of the other guards ever doing this. As she informed the young woman of her details, she wondered if she'd have preferred a scolding or a beating at this point. Felcia shivered at the thought of her name catching the attention of a few more senior guards. *Don't worry about that for now!* There were more pressing concerns; the package grew heavier every passing second.

"I'll look into your story, and if you're lying, I'll be back." The guard put the notebook away and smiled crookedly. "Well, are you going to keep standing around here, or are you going in?"

Felcia stood confused for a few more seconds, then snapped back to the present. "I'm sorry, yes. I assure you I'm not lying. If you'd just check with Dr. Caesar, I'm sure he'll—"

"You don't tell me what to do!" The young woman's face twisted into a scowl, her voice snarling as she took a step toward Felcia. Her face was so close to Felcia's that she felt the guard's spittle landing on her cheeks. "I don't care if you're lying or speaking the truth. I'll find out, and if there's anything, even the slightest hint of a lie in what you told me, you'll regret it."

Felcia blinked hard, trying not to betray the fear that made her stomach roil. "Of course," she managed.

"Now get inside!" The woman gave her a push that had Felcia stagger back and into the door of the greenhouse. To Felcia's horror, she felt the package move underneath her coat. She caught herself with one hand, using the other to make sure the package didn't slip out. Relief filled her when she felt the package was still securely fastened.

"Are you deaf? Get inside before I change my mind." The guard fingered the hilt of her baton, and Felcia quickly opened the door and stepped inside. The warmth of the greenhouse embraced her. Her skin tingled and she realized her teeth were chattering. She took a step from the door, fearful the guard would follow her inside, but then she heard footsteps receding. A moment later she spotted the guard through the glass windows on the side of the greenhouse. She walked along the road running parallel to the building, not once glancing through the windows. Felcia kept her eyes on the guard as she disappeared from sight. Her heartbeat returned to normal, and strength returned to her wobbly legs.

"Felcia?" The familiar voice startling her belonged to Klaudia, appearing from nowhere. "Are you all right? You look a little pale."

Felcia shook her head, clearing the fog from her brain. "I'm fine. Sorry for making you wait." She felt immense relief at seeing the woman as she reached inside her coat. "I've got it."

"Not wasting any time." Klaudia smiled and accepted the package. It was no larger than a packet of cigarettes, but to Felcia a massive load was lifted. "What's in here?" Klaudia gently shook the package, a rattling sound coming from within. "Pills?"

"Should be medication. I didn't look inside. I just took it as it was." Felcia remembered her journey to collect the package from the well that morning. Even though it wasn't out of the ordinary for her to make an early trip to collect water for her plants, she now worried about everything that could've gone wrong. What if she'd run into the peculiar, nosy guard while she was scouring the dirt? Or if they'd found it before she had a chance to collect it, and they were waiting for her? She tried to push the thought from her mind. All that mattered was that she'd delivered the valuable goods to Klaudia.

Klaudia casually pocketed the package. "I have to say I'm impressed and surprised, Felcia. I didn't think you would come through."

Felcia was about to protest but then changed her mind, and simply nodded. If she were honest, she was equally surprised. She'd almost not gone through with it that morning. But then she remembered her promise to Sabina. *This will make a difference.*

"I'll get it to Birkenau, and I'm sure they'll get back to you. I'm sure they'll be equally impressed, and then things can move quickly." Klaudia took a few steps toward the door, then turned back. "I'll be in touch soon, Felcia." Klaudia patted the pocket containing the medication. "This is more valuable than you realize, and the leadership will be thankful. Just make sure you're ready for what's next. I suspect they'll want to ramp up the operation soon. Do you think your contacts on the outside can handle it?"

Felcia thought of Sabina, remembering the young woman's infectious optimism and drive in getting this far. She would be delighted by the developments. She looked at Klaudia and smiled. "I have no doubt."

PART III

Oświęcim, Poland
October 1943

CHAPTER THIRTY-FOUR

Sabina entered the pierogi shop and was pleased to see quite a number of tables occupied. Joanna was busy in the kitchen, and she turned around briefly enough to acknowledge her. The air in the room was more humid, steam coming from numerous pots in the kitchen. Sabina smiled and walked farther in, where she spotted Elena sitting on her own in the back corner. She appeared a little gloomy, but as soon as she spotted Sabina, her face lit up.

"There you are! I was worried you wouldn't show. Mr. Pach isn't very pleased with you at the moment."

Sabina pulled a chair out, its legs scraping on the floor, and sat down. "I'll be back in class tomorrow. It's been a hectic few days." She let out a sigh as she took off her jacket and hung it over her chair, then focused her gaze on her friend. "I'm glad to see you. How are things in class?"

"You know, the same as usual. We're preparing for the math test next week. David has been way too enthusiastic about it." She rolled her eyes. "You should see how he's constantly barraging Mr. Pach about the assignments. It's exhausting."

Sabina grinned. "I'll make sure to bring him down a few pegs tomorrow. Can't have him dominating the classes too much." She turned and looked for Joanna, who carried a large tray of pierogi to a table in the front. Her mouth watered. "Have you ordered anything yet? I'm starving."

Elena shook her head and pushed the small, handwritten menu toward her. "Why don't you choose? I'm not that hungry, anyway." Then she leaned forward and, before Sabina could look at the menu, lowered her voice and spoke conspiratorially. "What have you been up to that's important enough to skip class? Work? Or something else?"

"Both." Sabina studied the meager menu, but the option of half a dozen spinach-and-onion pierogi was tempting enough. It had been a long day in the archiving room, and lunch had consisted of a dry sandwich with a very thin slice of cheese. Her stomach grumbled, and she placed the menu back on the table. Elena was looking at her in anticipation, and Sabina continued. "Work's been pretty crazy. Tosia and I can't keep up with everything coming our way."

"What about your trips to Rajsko? The German officer?" Elena did nothing to hide her curiosity, a smile dancing on her face. "Making any progress there?"

Sabina paused for a moment. After placing their order, Sabina made a decision. Elena was there when they entertained the German officers, and she knew what Sabina was up to. "You can't tell a soul about what I'm about to tell you, okay?"

The smile disappeared from her friend's face and made way for a serious expression. "Of course. Your secrets are safe with me, you know that."

Sabina nodded and moved her chair forward, her body pushing against the table as she placed her hands flat on it and leaned forward. "We've started taking goods into Rajsko."

If Elena was surprised, she didn't show it. A small smile crept onto her face. "I knew it. I thought something big was up when you didn't show up for class two days in a row. How did they do it?"

"What do you mean?"

"When we approached the camp in the daytime, they were onto us in minutes. It can't have been easy for the people in the resistance to get into the camp at night. It must be swarming with guards."

"Actually, it wasn't that difficult in the dark. There aren't too many guards."

Elena opened her mouth to speak, then stopped, her eyes wide. She put her hand to her mouth and spoke softly, the words slightly muffled but audible enough: "You made the smuggling run."

Sabina nodded, feeling slightly uncomfortable from the awe appearing in her best friend's eyes. "I had to." She thought of her father and Felcia. "It wouldn't have been possible if I hadn't made the first run."

"For your father." Elena read her mind, and Sabina cast her eyes downward in an attempt to hide the tears welling up. Elena reached across the table and took Sabina's hands in hers. They were soft and warm. "I'm so proud of you, Sabcia. I can't imagine what it was like. Do you want to talk about it?"

"I'm not sure. It was terrifying and exhilarating at the same time." She looked at Elena, whose eyes were fixed on hers with a curious twinkle. A soft squeeze of her hands. Sabina was back in the camp, hiding behind the well as the patrol passed. Elena listened without interruption, her mouth slightly agape when Sabina detailed her dash across the other side of the school building.

"They could've easily heard you. Or seen you."

"If I hadn't taken the chance, they would have definitely seen me by the well. I was lucky they were preoccupied the first time they passed me." Sabina felt her heart beating a little faster, her breath a bit shorter.

"The most important thing is that you made it out." Elena looked thoughtful. "Do you know if they collected the package inside the camp?"

"I haven't heard anything. Mr. Piotrowski hasn't sent me back yet, and my contact in the resistance hasn't reached out either. It's been two nights, and to be honest, I'm getting a bit nervous. What if they caught her?"

"You can't think that way. You did what you said you would. It's up to your people in the camp now. I'm sure they'll be careful. They have everything to lose."

Sabina nodded. "That's what's been gnawing at me ever since I returned. What if they decided it was too dangerous? Or if they decided they didn't trust me in the end?"

"Then that's their loss." Elena's voice was unusually harsh. "If they can't see the dedication with which you've picked up your father's duties, then they're blind." She went quiet as Joanna showed up with a full plate of dumplings.

"Dig in, girls. I added a few extra for you, on the house. You look like you haven't eaten a proper meal in days, Sabina." She gave her a look that was mockingly reproachful, winking as she added, "And I'm sure you've been rather busy. Working hard, taking care of everything in the municipality. You look after yourself."

"Don't worry about me." Sabina took a fork and reached for a dumpling. "I've got Elena looking out for me." She popped the dumpling into her mouth and chewed. It was tender, the sharp flavor of onion overwhelming.

"I'll leave you to it. Let me know if you need anything else." Joanna smiled and disappeared back toward the kitchen, leaving them alone in the back room. They ate in silence, Sabina devouring four pierogis while Elena nibbled on one, looking contemplative.

"What's on your mind?" Sabina put her fork down and leaned her head on her hands.

"I was thinking of your connections in the camp. From what you told me, I can't imagine they decided to abandon the operation. Not at this point. They have too much to gain." She took another small bite, then shook her head. "I think you should be patient. It might take them a bit longer to get the goods to Birkenau. It sounds to me like that's the riskiest part of your smuggling operation."

"They would have to cross at least two checkpoints. Out of Rajsko and into Birkenau."

"Exactly. And didn't you say Rajsko was their only option?"

Sabina shook her head. "I'm not sure. They don't tell me about all their options, but from what I understand, Rajsko appears to be the best option."

"Whatever happens next, I'm sure you'll hear about it soon enough." Elena spoke with finality, and Sabina felt heartened by her friend's confidence. *Maybe I'm too nervous, or too close to see clearly.*

Sabina was about to agree with her friend, and change the subject, when Elena continued. "Let's assume the news is good, and the goods made it to Birkenau. What's next?"

"I can't imagine anything other than ramping up the operation. Hopefully with the blessing and support of the underground in Birkenau." Sabina remembered Marian's conviction when he said they would need the underground leadership involved for this to really make a difference. She prayed they had done enough to convince them. At the same time, she felt a flutter of frustration. If this wasn't enough, what would be?

"Do you think I could play a part?"

Sabina wasn't sure she'd heard her friend properly. "I'm sorry?"

"You can't make all the runs into Rajsko. You'll need more people. Can I help?"

"You want to smuggle goods into the camp?" Sabina heard the surprise in her voice and quickly added, "Are you sure?"

Elena shrugged, but she looked determined: eyes shining, jaw clenched. "I've been thinking about it ever since you told me why we'd gone to the tavern that evening." She paused, and Sabina nodded.

"You mentioned you wanted to help when I spoke about the smuggling run the last time."

"Yes. But I never thought you would be the one taking the goods into the camp. I thought they would be, I don't know"—Elena searched for the right words—"resistance fighters doing that. But then I realized you're one of them. You are a resistance fighter."

Sabina's throat constricted with pride. They had been best friends for as long as she could remember; still, she worried about involving her. "Are you sure? I could ask if there are other tasks you could help with. You don't have to go into Rajsko from the start."

Elena looked back as if stung by a wasp. "Because it's dangerous? Come on, Sabcia. I know that place almost as well as you. I also grew up there. I went to the same school. I know every blade of grass."

"I know." Sabina didn't want to tell her friend their school was very different now. It was clear Elena's mind was made up. Besides, she'd have to run it by Marian first. They would worry about the details later, if—and it was a big if—he would be open to it. She nodded slowly, smiling as she looked at Elena's frowning face. "I'll raise it with my contact next time I see him." Elena's face lit up, but Sabina held up a hand. "But only if we're absolutely certain everything's properly in place."

Sabina got home an hour later, well before curfew. Her mother sat waiting at the kitchen table, a stew cooking on a low fire behind her. Instantly, Sabina knew something was up, and she hurried to the table.

"What's wrong, Mama? Did something happen?"

"Someone came by for you this afternoon." She spoke in a soft voice almost devoid of emotion. "A young man. Said he had urgent business with you."

Sabina frowned. "What did he look like?"

"The last time a stranger came by the house looking for your father, he disappeared a few weeks later." Her mother looked at her with sad eyes. "This feels awfully similar."

"Mother." It was all Sabina could stammer as she looked at the broken woman across the table. Her throat went dry, her eyes burning as she fought tears. At the same time, her mind was racing as she went through the possible men calling at her home. "Did he say what he needed me for, other than urgent business?"

Her mother shook her head. "He didn't want to say. I asked him a few times, but he said he really needed to see you. Said he would be at your usual meeting spot tomorrow around lunchtime."

"What did he look like?" She held her breath in anticipation.

"Not too tall, a bit scrawny even. Scruffy hair. Maybe a bit younger than you." She eyed Sabina curiously. "You know, you can tell me if you're romantically involved with someone. You don't need to stalk around in the shadows with him."

Realizing who it was, Sabina let out a nervous laugh at her mother's suggestion, surprising herself. "It's nothing like that, Mama! With everything going on at work, I hardly have time for school, let alone men."

Her mother appeared to relax for the first time as she held up her hands. "It's none of my business, but I wouldn't mind, that's all I'm saying. Although I'm not sure this one would be quite your type. Seemed a bit nervous."

It was the first time Marian had sent his messenger to her home. Whatever he wanted to talk about had to be important.

"You haven't eaten yet, have you, Mama? It smells delicious."

Sabina stood and walked to the stove, grabbing two large bowls from the sink.

"I was waiting for you," her mother answered in a weak voice.

With every ladle of stew she scooped, Sabina's guilt grew. She swallowed hard, turned back to the table, and placed the bowls in front of them. As she took the first sip she decided to wait on news from her father. Then, she vowed to tell her mother the truth.

Marian's dark eyes were deep pools of sympathy as he looked back at her from the other side of the table. His hands were folded on his lap.

"He's in the camp?" Sabina's voice was tight with fear. "Since when?"

"They transferred him two nights ago. My contact in the penal block recognized his name and told one of the men working on the outside." He looked troubled as he shifted in his seat. "I'm sorry, Sabina. I know this isn't the news you were hoping for."

His words sounded like they were coming from a distance. The pounding in her head made her feel numb, and the noise of the pierogi shop disappeared into a blur. Marian's news was awful. After a minute, she blinked hard and turned her attention to Marian, who looked calm and composed, a man in control. It gave her some hope.

"Is there anything we can do for him?" Her voice was small as she hung between hope and fear.

"I've asked some of my contacts inside to see if they can reach out to him, maybe provide him with some extra supplies. It's the best we can do for now. The penal colony is tough, Sabina."

"It's a death sentence, isn't it?" Sabina spoke the words flatly in an attempt to diminish their meaning.

"Your father is a strong man, physically and mentally. If anyone can

survive this, it's him. I promise we'll do whatever we can to help him."
Despite his best efforts, Marian sounded unconvincing. After a pause,
he spoke again, his tone slightly more upbeat. "I do have some good
news, something that might help your father as well."

Sabina looked up, her head heavy. "What is it?" She was aware she
sounded only moderately interested, but didn't care. Her father was
being worked to death in Birkenau.

"The same people who told me about your father also brought news
of your goods making it to the underground leadership. Your connection came through." Marian was careful to remain composed, but when
Sabina looked up, his eyes sparkled with excitement. "They're distributing the medication to the hospitals in Birkenau and Auschwitz as we
speak."

Despite the significance of their achievement, Sabina couldn't
muster up more than a thin, weak smile. "Did we convince the leadership now?" Her voice was still devoid of emotion.

Marian leaned forward. "Sabina. You should be proud. Without
you, we would never have accomplished this. If your father knew, he
would be so proud. In fact, I'll do everything in my power to make sure
he hears about this. Penal colony be damned. We'll find a way to share
the news."

Sabina tapped her foot against a table leg. She heard the words, but
they didn't register. *It doesn't matter. If Papa dies, it's a hollow victory.*

Chapter Thirty-Five

Felcia stood outside the school building, facing the gravel road running through the camp. Opposite it, she could see several women working in the greenhouses.

It was a surprise to see a lone figure make her way down the road. Felcia's eyes widened when she recognized Klaudia. She looked around and was relieved to see no nearby guards when the other woman reached her.

"Felcia, I'm glad you're out here. I came up with a ruse to gain entry into the lab, but this makes things a bit easier. Especially if someone were to catch us. I'm just asking for directions, I suppose."

"Did you come all the way from the fields?" Felcia looked to a group of men and women working a plow in a nearby field. "What sense does it make to have them working there now, anyway?"

"Damned if I know. But let's skip the niceties. You could've told me you had connections in the underground leadership, instead of playing coy." She sounded annoyed.

"I'm sorry, what?" Felcia's surprise was genuine, and she struggled for a better response. "I don't have any connections with them."

Klaudia raised an eyebrow. "You're saying you didn't know who the medication you had me smuggle into Birkenau was meant for? I find that hard to believe."

Felcia's ears burned hot, and her neck prickled. "I know only the woman that smuggled the goods into the camp. I know she works with an organization on the outside, but she's not shared anything about the people in Birkenau. I assumed you knew. You're my only connection to Birkenau."

Klaudia crossed her arms and frowned, forcing Felcia to meet her piercing eyes. As she did, Felcia felt indignant, and she held the other woman's gaze defiantly. They stood there for a few seconds, until Klaudia broke their stare. "Very well. I still think it's interesting how my contact knew all about what to expect, even before I handed over the package. It seems you and I aren't the only connection to the leadership."

"That sounds like a good development." Felcia weighed her words carefully, suddenly apprehensive. *What's her agenda?*

"I'm sorry." Klaudia appeared to sense Felcia's misgivings, and she held up the palms of her hands. "I fear I may have jumped to conclusions. I was surprised, that's all. Perhaps you should ask your contact about what she knows about the Birkenau leadership."

"I will." Felcia had no intention of doing so. She trusted Sabina, and the less she knew, the better. "Was this all you wanted to discuss? I should get back to work." She made a move toward the door, but Klaudia stopped her.

"How are your classes going? The girls doing well?" Her voice was a little too sweet, like she was trying to make up for her earlier slipup.

"They're doing well. Smart, pick things up really quickly." Felcia was keen to end the conversation and took another step.

"Great. Well, just so you know. Because of the success of the first smuggling run, I've been told activities will be ramped up soon."

Felcia stopped in her tracks. "What does that mean?"

"More packages coming in, more transfers to Birkenau. They really haven't told you, have they? It appears I really misjudged your connections."

Felcia's chest felt tight. She resented Klaudia's condescending tone, even if she was partly right. Had Sabina kept Felcia in the dark on purpose? And was Rajsko not their only way in? Had Sabina overstated the importance of their activities? Felcia looked at Klaudia and felt foolish. Was she the only person unaware of all the moving parts?

"I'm sure your contact will update you soon enough," Klaudia said. This time, her voice was neutral, almost empathetic. "Don't feel bad. I didn't know about your role either, did I? The only way for the resistance to work is for everyone but the top to know as little as possible." She smiled ruefully. "And we're nowhere near the top."

Felcia nodded: Klaudia made a good point. "Why did you ask about the classes?"

"Ah yes, I almost forgot. The leadership got nervous about having one person collecting the packages. When things ramp up, it might become suspicious to see you moving about all the time. They were adamant that for this to work, we need to be more creative about where the packages are dropped, and by whom they're collected."

Realization dawned on Felcia. "You want the girls from my class to collect the packages?"

Klaudia smiled. "That's the idea. It's the perfect cover. You have them collect the goods and keep them in your lab until we're ready to pick them up."

A shiver ran down Felcia's spine, but she managed to maintain her composure, her face emotionless. "And you'll continue smuggling the goods into Birkenau?"

"At times, yes. But from what I've heard, they're keen to kick the operation into a higher gear."

"Which means?" Felcia had an uncomfortable feeling she knew the answer.

"They're going to send their own people in to collect more valuable goods." She accentuated the last words. "You'll find out soon enough. I'm sure your contact from the outside will tell you all about it." Klaudia looked around and turned on her heel, suddenly seeming restless. "I should get back to the fields, before someone spots us talking."

Felcia watched Klaudia walk away. Her eyes went to the dark sky in the distance. Would this first modest victory be the spark that ignited the uprising? Klaudia's words brought hope, and Felcia clung onto them.

In her mind, she struggled to make out the memory of Marzena's face. A tear rolled down her cheek, and she balled her hands into fists. It may have been too late for her friend, but she felt Marzena's strength in everything she did. When the uprising happened, it wouldn't just be Felcia's victory. It would also be Marzena's.

CHAPTER THIRTY-SIX

Sabina woke up feeling as if she'd put her head down just a few minutes ago. The little clock on her bedside table indicated it was a bit past seven. She sighed, closing her eyes again. *Just a few more minutes.* She could hear her mother clanging pots and pans in the kitchen, and she reluctantly opened her eyes and swung her legs out of bed. Still groggy, she got dressed and went downstairs.

The smell spreading from the kitchen made her mouth water and her stomach rumble, reminding her she'd hardly eaten anything before going to bed. In her efforts to avoid her mother, she'd raced up the stairs when she returned home, hastily informing her mother she wasn't hungry.

Entering the kitchen, she couldn't help but smile. Her mother was busy working a large pan of scrambled eggs. *Lord knows how she got hold of those.* Sabina sat down, and her mother turned around.

"There you are! I was about to wake you. You'll be late for school."

"It's only half past seven, Mama. I've got plenty of time to make it."

Her mother took the pan from the stove and placed it in the middle of the table. "Well, you're not going anywhere until you've finished these. You didn't eat anything last night. You're not taking proper care of yourself." Before Sabina could protest, her mother scooped a few generous steaming spoonfuls onto her plate. She wagged her finger. "I don't want to hear a word from you until you've finished there."

Sabina took a large bite. Her father's disappearance had taken a toll on her mother. She was a tough woman, and she tried to hide her worries from Sabina. But her mother's gaunt face, the dark circles around her eyes, and the slightly hunched back were impossible to ignore. It was the strain of not knowing. It was time to tell her.

Sabina waited for her mother to finish cleaning up. When she joined her at the table, Sabina put down her fork. "Mama, there's something I need to tell you." She took a deep breath as her mother tilted her head ever so slightly. "It's about Papa."

Her mother's eyebrow twitched, but the rest of her face remained perfectly still. "Have you heard something at work?" Her voice was tremored.

"Not at work, Mama." Sabina's hands were shaking, and she stood and moved to sit next to her mother. She took her hand, which was unusually cold. Their fingers intertwined, Sabina faced her mother. "There is no easy way to say this. They've taken Papa to the camp. He's in Birkenau." Fear appeared in her mother's eyes, her upper lip trembling. Sabina tightened her grip, but felt a slight resistance.

"Are you sure? How do you know?" her mother stuttered, trying to suppress her emotions. "And when?"

"Last night. And yes, my source is trustworthy. He's heard from people inside the camp."

Her mother let go of her hand and turned her face away. Sabina understood—she remembered her own shock when Marian told her. They sat in silence for a few minutes, hardly moving.

Her mother turned back, looking surprisingly composed. "You're sure about this?" Sabina nodded. "How? Who told you?"

"You need to know something about Papa." This was the part Sabina dreaded most. It didn't feel right for her to reveal this. But with her father's situation so dire, her mother needed to know. "Papa was—" She hastily corrected herself: "Papa is part of an underground movement." She paused but was surprised to see her mother nodding. Sabina gasped as the realization dawned. "You knew."

"Of course." Her mother gave her a sad smile. "Your father and I never had any secrets. We tell each other everything." Then she gave Sabina a sharp look. "Or at least, that's what I thought. It appears he didn't share the whole story about his involvement. Or should I say, your involvement?"

Sabina felt her cheeks redden; the pieces of the puzzle had fallen into place for both women. "I'm sorry, Mama. I didn't want to burden you with this. I didn't know you knew about Papa."

Her mother moved forward and opened her arms. Sabina gratefully accepted the embrace, experiencing a feeling of security she realized she'd missed dearly. Her mother gently stroked her hair and spoke softly. "It's all right. You were right not to tell me. And I don't want to know exactly what you're doing now, although I have my suspicions."

They held each other silently. Reluctantly, Sabina broke the embrace and faced her mother. Her mother's eyes were damp, just like her own, and they both wiped their faces.

"Sabcia, whatever it is you're doing, please be careful. I can't lose you as well." Her mother's voice was fragile and hoarse. "We need to pray for your father's release, but please promise me you won't do anything that gets you both locked up. I'm not sure I could manage that."

"I'm very careful, Mama." She felt guilty the moment her words left her lips, and she averted her eyes. She wasn't careful at all. With an effort, she turned back to her mother. "I won't be caught, Mama. I promise you that."

Hope flashed in her mother's eyes. "I know. Whatever it is you're doing, I'm sure you're careful."

"We can talk about all of this later." Sabina stood, suddenly anxious to get some fresh air, some space.

"Of course. I'm glad there are no more secrets between us." Her mother's voice had returned to normal, and Sabina gave her a quick peck on the cheek before she hurried outside.

The gravel crunched under Sabina's feet as she casually scanned her surroundings. A wind howled through the camp, and the guards at the main road had retreated into their small guardhouse. Sabina looked up to see dark, threatening snow clouds looming overhead. Nearing the greenhouses, she checked the road once more before quickly making for the door and entering.

The warm air embraced her like a comfortable blanket, and she exhaled deeply as she looked around. The greenhouse appeared empty, until she spotted movement from the corner of her eye. Felcia gestured from behind a rather voluminous plant.

"Sabina, come. It's better to talk over here." The scientist spoke softly, but her voice traveled quickly through the enclosed space. Sabina crossed the distance in a few quick steps, and to her surprise, Felcia reached for a quick hug. "I'm so glad to see you. When Bianka told me you were here, I felt so relieved."

"I could say the same about you." She quickly recalled her nocturnal escapade smuggling the medication into the camp.

"You really had to run from a patrol?" Felcia looked at her in awe. "That must've been terribly frightening."

"I didn't really think about it. It seemed like the only thing I could do. I worried more about the guards finding the package before you had a chance to."

Felcia nodded. "Me too. I nearly didn't go through with it the next morning."

"I'm glad you did. I heard the leadership in Birkenau were very pleased. And a little surprised." Sabina smiled triumphantly, expecting Felcia to do the same. When the scientist gave her only a curt nod, she frowned. "You heard differently?"

"Was this a test of my loyalty?" Felcia looked to the floor.

"A test? What do you mean?"

"To see if I could get the package to Birkenau? My contact said the leadership is connected to your group on the outside."

"They are. I told you that, didn't I?" Sabina was confused, furiously trying to remember if she'd kept anything from Felcia. "The whole reason we're going through Rajsko is because they lost their previous connections."

Felcia looked thoughtful, a fire still burning in her eyes. "I find it odd that they seemed completely aware of what was coming their way, and seemed to expect it would all go to plan. From what you told me, they seemed skeptical at best."

"They were!" Frustration filtered through Sabina's voice. "They didn't think a bunch of women could pull it off. We showed them, didn't we?"

Felcia eyed her for a few moments. "How much did you really know, Sabina?"

"I've never kept anything from you. Why do you think I made the delivery myself?"

"How much do you know about the people outside?"

Sabina thought of Marian and her father, feeling a pang of grief. She bit her lip, then responded. "Only what I need to know. I couldn't tell you how many are involved, but the people I do know, I trust with my life." Her eyes burned as she spoke the last words, and she quickly turned her face away.

"Hey, what's wrong?" Felcia moved toward her. "Sabina? Are you all right?"

Sabina's chest heaved as she tried to control her ragged breathing. At the touch of Felcia's hand on her arm the flow of tears was uncontrollable. Felcia embraced her and the world turned into a blur. Sabina closed her eyes, a memory of her father appearing—a smiling face, as clear as if he were standing right in front of her, telling her everything would be all right. "But it won't be," she whispered softly. "It's not all right."

In the distance, she heard Felcia's voice, but she couldn't make out the words. She opened her eyes again, the comfort and safety of her father's smile vanishing, and making way for the bright light of the greenhouse. She took a step back. The fabric of Felcia's coat was wet at the shoulder, and Sabina felt embarrassed. "I'm sorry about that," she said in a croaking voice.

Felcia gave her a sympathetic look. "Don't worry about it. Are you feeling better?"

"It's my father, Felcia. The Gestapo took him. They're keeping him in Birkenau."

Horror appeared on Felcia's face. "I'm so sorry, Sabina. I don't know what to say."

"He's in the penal colony. He's the reason I'm doing this. My father wanted to help the people inside the camp, but now he's ended up in there himself." Sabina felt her strength slowly returning, despite the weight of her words.

"I'm sorry I doubted you," Felcia said, her voice softer than usual. "I had no idea."

Sabina straightened her back. "You couldn't know. I'm not the one on the inside. You've got enough on your mind without having to worry about me." She felt self-conscious. "I'm sorry for burdening you with this."

"Friends should share these kinds of things." Felcia's voice was strong. "No matter the circumstances."

Sabina felt a surge of affection. "Thank you. I think you're the only person that really understands."

"I'm sure of it," Felcia said with a sincere note in her voice. Before Sabina had a chance to ask a question, she continued, "We don't have much time. I wanted to let you know that my contact said the leadership will ask to have the smuggling operations scaled up. Did you hear anything about this?"

Sabina shook her head. "Not at all, but it makes sense. Did they say what that meant?"

"No, she was quite noncommittal. Said you would know more."

"I haven't heard anything yet, but I can only assume it means we'll be bringing more packages into the camp."

"And different goods, maybe?" Felcia looked at her curiously. "I know I may be clutching at straws, but the talk of a possible prisoner uprising keeps growing. They'll need weapons, won't they?"

"I haven't heard anything about weapons. Not yet, anyway." Sabina considered the idea. It would be an enormous operation. Impossible, surely? Even if they could smuggle in weapons through Rajsko, it would take months, if not years, before they had enough weapons inside the camp to consider attacking the supremely well-armed SS guards. Yet, it also brought hope. There might be possibilities for her father to break out. She immediately dismissed the thought; her father didn't have time to wait for an uprising. Sabina turned back to Felcia.

"I'll check with my contact to see what's going on. For now, I'm just happy to see you safe and well."

"You too." Felcia's smile was warm and genuine as the women hugged. The scientist moved to the door and stepped outside. Thirty seconds later, she hurried back inside. "The coast is clear. Go!"

Outside, Sabina decided to pay a short visit to the school building. Dr. Caesar had already signed her papers, but she wanted to see if Paskal was in. It had been a while since they'd last spoken, and she knew his friendship—even if he thought it was more than that—was important to cultivate.

The door to his office was open, and she knocked softly. He looked up from a pile of paperwork with annoyance at first, which transformed into a smile at the sight of the visitor.

"Sabina! Come in, come in!" He stood and waved her inside, motioning to the comfortable chairs in the corner of the office. "What a delightful surprise! Can I get you something to drink? I obtained some really good wine this weekend." He moved toward a small cabinet, but Sabina shook her head with a smile.

"I still have work to do when I get back. Maybe next time."

He looked disappointed, but only for a moment as he sat across from her. "What brings you here?"

"Just wanted to see how you're doing, really." Sabina was surprised at how easy the words came to her. "I needed Dr. Caesar to sign some papers, and thought I'd see you."

His face lit up. "I'm glad to hear that. I actually wanted to ask you about something."

"Okay." Sabina sat up, intrigued. "What is it?"

He fumbled with his hands, eyes darting across the room for a moment before settling back on her. "I was wondering if you'd like to go out to dinner with me."

"Are you asking me on a date? You know this is frowned upon." Her tone was mock serious. There were butterflies in her stomach. When she approached his office, it was with the intention to gain even more of his trust. This was perfect.

He looked uncomfortable as he moved in his chair. "Oh, right, well, yes. I suppose we don't have to. You could even come to the camp in the evening, and then no one will have to see you. Would that work, perhaps?" He crossed his legs awkwardly.

Sabina couldn't help but laugh out loud. Paskal looked mortified, and she quickly said, "I would love to go out to dinner with you. Why don't you pick the place, and I'll meet you there." With another smile, she stood. "But for now, I'll have to get back to work."

He remained seated for another second, staring at her. Then he seemed to understand, and a wide smile spread across his face. "You were joking, yes?"

"Yes, Paskal. I was joking." She threw her head back. "When would you like to go?"

"This Sunday? I'll send a car for you."

"Can't wait."

Marian let out a low whistle when Sabina finished telling him about her findings in the camp. Having left work, she now sat with him at their usual table at Joanna's.

"So it's true? They are planning an uprising?" Sabina asked.

"They're always planning an uprising." He spoke somewhat dismissively. "But nothing has come of it so far. There have been a few escapes, sure, but those were planned exceptionally well, and always involved only one or two people actually escaping."

"Do you think it's possible, with our new route?"

"There's always a possibility. But the route to Rajsko alone wouldn't be enough." He shook his head. "Not even nearly enough. What they need is strong outside support."

"Us?"

"Our cell wouldn't be enough. We'd need the support from much larger Home Army cells. And up until now, they've been unconvinced it's a good idea. No, let me rephrase that. They've categorically ruled out storming the camp. The chance of failure is too high."

Sabina shrank into her seat. "So you're saying we won't be arming the people in the camp?"

He smiled. "I didn't say that. I don't think it's a bad idea to arm them, at the very least prepare them to strike back. You can't start the preparations soon enough."

"So you're with the camp leadership on this?"

"I'll do what I can, yes. Even if it means I'm going against the Home Army position. I don't answer to them. But first, we need to send more medication into the camp. And the camp underground has some material they need smuggled out."

Sabina sat up. "Really? Do you know what it is?"

"Could be anything. Maps of the inside, prisoners lists, I don't know. Whatever it is, if they deem it important enough to take the risk of smuggling it between the camps, it must be valuable."

"When do you want the medication taken into the camp?"

"Soon. I'll let you know. But Sabina, you won't be involved."

"What do you mean?"

"We can't risk you getting caught. It would end our entire operation in Rajsko. Without your connections, we would be going in blindly."

Sabina listened to him and felt oddly relieved. Marian was right. It was exciting to think back to the night she'd gone into the camp, but if she was completely honest, she wasn't keen on repeating it.

"You can still let your contact know when to expect shipments, but that's where your involvement in the smuggling ends. You're going back to information gathering. Understood?"

She nodded her acceptance, and Marian looked keen to end the conversation, rising from his chair. She cleared her throat. "There's one more thing I wanted to discuss with you."

He sank back into his chair. "Sure, what is it?"

"I want you to do more to help my father. More than just promising to see what you can do." She clasped her shaking hands under the table.

"I'm not sure what it is you're asking, Sabina. It's not easy to reach people in the penal colony."

She looked up. "You said that a few days ago. And nothing's

changed. He's still in the most dangerous, deadly area of the camp." Her voice trembled.

"You want me to get him transferred from the penal block?" His expression didn't change, nor did the tone of his voice.

"Yes. We both know it's a matter of time before some guard decides he isn't working hard enough and beats him to death. I need your assurance that you'll try to get him out of there, Marian." She thought of her mother's words that morning, the ache in her heart at her mother's worried face. With a cracking voice, she spoke the next words: "If you don't, I'll walk away from the Rajsko route."

She forced herself to hold his gaze. The big man glared at her at first, then turned his head away, staring out the window behind Sabina. *Have I gone too far?* Marian looked thoughtful and distant, ignoring Sabina. Unsure what to do with herself, she focused on the flowery wallpaper while her mind raced, conjuring up all sorts of thoughts. She didn't dare look at Marian, who brooded across from her, seemingly content not to speak. *I overstated my importance. He's furious.* She opened her mouth, then quickly closed it. An odd feeling of calm came over her. She had done enough for the cause, never asking for anything in return. As had her father. *I'm not being unreasonable.* There was movement across the table, and Marian cleared his throat.

"I understand, Sabina." His voice was firm, but there was no trace of anger. Sabina met his eyes and saw the initial anger had faded. There was respect in his eyes. "You and your father have gone beyond what many others in the organization have. You, especially. You risk your life almost daily going into that camp. There might be something I can do for your father, but it's by no means certain to work."

CHAPTER THIRTY-SEVEN

Felcia knocked on the closed door and waited for the muffled response before pushing it open. Dr. Caesar sat behind his desk and looked up briefly.

"Felcia, take a seat, please. This won't take long."

She shuffled warily to one of the seats, and her unease must've shown, for Dr. Caesar glanced up and said, "Don't worry, you've done nothing wrong. I just need your opinion on a few things."

It was never good to be singled out. Not even by Dr. Caesar, whom she trusted more than any other German in the camp. Even after she questioned whether he'd forgotten about her in the depths of Block 11, he had kept his promise. She eyed the commander, and she was once again struck by how unlike the other higher-ranking officers she'd seen strutting around the camp he was. He wore the same military-style uniform, but his entire conduct was that of a scientist. He observed rather than intervened. Where others snarled at and beat prisoners, he stopped by to inquire about the progress of the experiments.

"Right, Felcia." He leaned back in his chair. "I wanted to get your thoughts on the cultivation process in the greenhouses. I went by a few times this week and noticed there's not much going on in there. More worryingly, I see very few of our scientists making their way between the labs and the greenhouses. What's that all about?"

Felcia had noticed the same, and while she worried about the plants' slow growth, it wasn't unexpected. "I think the only way we can offset the disappointing results is by increasing the temperature in the greenhouses. We've had precious little sun." Perhaps focusing on the plants would steer attention away from the women not spending enough time in the greenhouses. She knew why. They all felt it was a waste of time. With little to no direct sunlight, the plants wouldn't grow.

Dr. Caesar nodded slowly. "You think heat will help? I was thinking it was the lack of sunlight."

"It is," she quickly responded, immediately hoping she hadn't spoken before her turn. Dr. Caesar tilted his head, waving his hand for her to continue. "But I fear we won't see much of the sun. Begging your pardon for my perhaps somewhat pessimistic outlook, but I've experienced enough Polish winters."

That brought a smile from the German officer. "And how do you think increasing the temperature will help?"

She shifted in her seat. "Well, to be honest, it's a gamble. I'm not certain it will. Sunlight would be ideal, but from what I observed in earlier experiments, the plants in warmer, more humid environments did better."

He took off his glasses and started polishing them, leaving Felcia waiting. She wondered if her honesty had been a mistake, and if this wasn't what the doctor had wanted to hear. When he finished cleaning both lenses, he replaced them and grunted in satisfaction.

"Much better. Now, where were we. Ah, yes. I think it's worth a try. Let's up the temperatures in two of the greenhouses and see what happens in the next few days, shall we?"

"Yes, sir. Although ..." She stopped herself, suddenly unsure if she should continue.

He looked at her impatiently. "Although what? Speak your mind."

"A few days may be too short to see results, sir."

"Okay, a week then!" He waved his hand dismissively. "Just make sure you keep an eye on it, yes? And while you're at it, get those other women in line, will you?" He turned around and looked out the window. "The only people I see are working the fields. Not a soul has gone between the lab and greenhouses in the past hour."

"Of course, sir." Felcia moved to get up from her chair when he turned back.

"One more thing, Felcia. The classes. How are they progressing?"

"Quite ... Very well, sir."

"How many women are you teaching now? Three?"

"Five. We had two new arrivals last week with backgrounds in pedology."

He looked impressed. "Remarkable. You wonder how many smart people are hidden from us in the other camp."

Or never even make it past the ramp. She bit her tongue. Instead, she simply nodded. "They've already provided a number of very interesting insights."

"Would you consider any of your students ready to assist in the lab work?" He looked outside again. "I feel we could use some fresh blood." He muttered something under his breath Felcia couldn't understand. She thought of Izolda, Paula, and Renata. They had been ready to assist in the lab from the moment they arrived, but Felcia had been waiting for the right moment to suggest it.

"The initial three would be great additions, Dr. Caesar." She spoke without hesitation.

"Excellent. I suggest you have one of them assist you and your partner, and have the others assist in the lab next to yours. That way, you can keep a good eye on them. I expect you'll find time to get them up to speed, and continue tutoring them?"

"Certainly, sir." The additional tasks would stretch her time even more, as did the classes, but it was worth it. To have the three women included in the lab setup meant they were moved another step farther from the gas chambers. As long as she could make sure Dr. Caesar recognized their value, they would be safe. There was no doubt they would make for excellent assistants.

"Good." He grabbed a piece of paper. "Their names and numbers?" After Felcia provided the information, he looked up again. "Are they currently in the same block as you?"

"They are not, sir. They're with the women working the fields. They're in Stubendienst."

He scribbled some more. "I'll have them moved to your block, so you can keep an eye on them. We'll find some other women to take their places in the Stubendienst, starting tomorrow."

Felcia smiled. "That's great, sir. I'm sure they'll be keen to get started."

"Yeah, yeah. Make sure they realize their privileged position, will you?" He looked out the window again, and Felcia understood the message.

"Of course, sir."

A flick of the hand indicated their meeting was over, and Felcia stepped into the hallway and resisted the urge to let out a jubilant shriek. Having her three protégés move to the lab was one thing, having them stay in the same block was unexpectedly good news. It would make collecting and keeping the packages smuggled into the camp so much easier to manage.

CHAPTER THIRTY-EIGHT

S abina sat propped up under a blanket in her father's favorite reading spot in the living room. She held a book, but the words danced on the pages, and she found it almost impossible to focus. It was Friday evening, and she was exhausted, but restless. Her mother was clanging pots and pans in the kitchen, and Sabina shook her head.

She placed the book on the coffee table and stood, stretching her stiff legs. Sabina had spent most of her day on her feet at work as she went between the archiving room and a number of the clerks' offices. It had been nice to escape the basement, even if it meant carrying thick files up and down the stairs. It was a good distraction from the endless thoughts causing havoc in her brain.

Marian hadn't shared what he had in mind for her father. Nor was he willing to give her any indication about when he would know more from his contacts inside the camp. And even when he did speak with them, there was no guarantee they would be willing to cooperate, he'd warned. Despite that, Sabina couldn't help but feel hopeful. The wait, however, proved excruciatingly long. It had been three nights since they'd met, and there'd been no news.

She picked up her mug and drained the last of her tea. As she moved to the kitchen and passed by the large window facing their front yard, she thought she detected a flash of movement in the darkness. Sabina froze in place, trying to make out anything in the darkness of the yard. After five seconds, she was certain there was nothing there. *I must be imagining things.*

When she entered the kitchen, she found her mother on her knees underneath the sink.

"I fixed this faucet the other day, but it just keeps leaking. I don't know what I'm doing wrong." The frustration in her voice made way for sadness when she spoke the next words. "I wish your father was here to help. He'd know what to do."

Sabina crouched next to her mother and hugged her tightly. They had been sitting together on the kitchen floor for a few seconds when there was a faint knocking at the back door. Sabina wasn't sure she'd heard correctly at first, but feeling her mother's body tense confirmed someone was indeed there. *Are they coming for us?* She dismissed the thought almost immediately. If the Gestapo or SS were coming for them, they wouldn't knock on their door. Not like that. They would knock it down. Sabina looked at her mother. *What should we do?*

Her mother read her thoughts, shaking her head. Sabina wondered who would dare defy the curfew and traverse the darkness.

"Sabina?" The voice behind the door was familiar, but she couldn't immediately place it. The call was repeated, now more forcefully and slightly louder.

"Who is it?" her mother whispered, still clutching Sabina's shoulder. Both women eyed the door.

Sabina shook her head, hoping the person would leave. To her horror, she saw the door handle move. Her mother's grip tightened. Sabina craned her neck, eyeing the large chopping knife on the counter. *Can I make it in time?* Her gaze turned to the door; it slowly opened. Sabina finally found enough courage to rise and take an awkward step in the direction of the knife.

The door opened farther, and a muddy boot appeared. Sabina crossed the short distance and grabbed the knife. As she turned around, clutching her weapon, the intruder stepped inside, revealing his face. Sabina almost dropped the knife in relief. It was Marian, raising his hands apologetically.

"I'm sorry for sneaking up on you like this. I really didn't want to, but I couldn't wait at the front door." Sabina had never seen him this mortified, and she let out a nervous laugh, more out of relief than anything. "And I'm afraid what I have to say couldn't wait."

Sabina placed a mug of tea in front of Marian and sat across from him. Her mother had retired to the living room. Even if she knew that Sabina was involved in the resistance efforts, they agreed she would know as little as possible about the actual activities.

"I've found a way to get your father out of the camp." Marian lifted the mug and blew on the tea.

Sabina's heart fluttered, and she was momentarily at a loss for words. She recovered enough of her composure to ask, "How?"

"A group of prisoners has discovered an opportunity to smuggle a small number of people out. It's risky, and we'll need to move very quickly, but there's a very good chance they could get your father out."

Marian's words came at her through a haze. When he said he would look into the possibilities, she hadn't thought he would propose an escape. A transfer within the camp to get him out of the penal colony at best, but that had been the maximum she had dared hope for. "I'm sorry, I'm a little overwhelmed. Just a few days ago you said it would be difficult to move him, and now we're talking about an escape? What changed?"

He grinned. "Things can change quickly within the camp. Mostly for the worse, but now it looks like we may have a caught a fortunate break. We should seize it. Quickly."

Sabina nodded. "How do we make this happen?" Why had Marian come to her home directly? Something was different. "You need my help for this to work, don't you?"

"I do. My people on the inside are willing to include your father in this, but only if we give them something in return."

"What do they need?" Sabina's head was spinning, her hands were shaking. *Anything. Just tell me what it takes to save my father.* "How will they do it?"

Marian shook his head. "I can't tell you that, not yet anyway. But I believe this chance won't come along often." He paused for a moment. "Normally, I wouldn't ask this of you. But they insist on carrying out the escape in the next few days. Maybe even this weekend. They were a bit vague on the specifics."

This weekend. Papa could be out within a few days. The thought made Sabina choke up, and she struggled to retain her composure. She took a quick sip of the scorching tea in front of her. "What do they want in return?"

"Two things." Marian's answer came instantly, as if he were waiting for her to ask. "Life in the camp is dangerous, and people only trust those they know very well. If they approach him out of the blue, in the penal colony at that, they're afraid he might not come with them. They need you to persuade him."

Sabina felt her blood run cold. "How would I do that? Do they want me to go into Birkenau?"

"No, nothing like that. They want you to smuggle in a message to him through Rajsko, and make sure it reaches him in the penal colony. And it needs to be done as soon as possible. They might make their move as early as tomorrow evening."

Tomorrow was Saturday. The municipality was closed, and there would be no paperwork for anyone to sign. Her neck burned in frustration. "I'd need to bring it in tomorrow to stand a chance of it reaching him in time." She spoke more to herself than Marian. "There's no good reason why I would show up at the camp."

"Can you think of a reason why you need to stop by? Maybe an urgent message for the commander, an unusual request that needed to be passed along? The camps don't exactly keep office hours, do they?"

Sabina initially shook her head, then a thought flashed in her mind. She looked up and smiled. "There might be a way." It was risky, but if it meant she could get her father out, it was worth it. "What's the second thing?"

Marian frowned. "I considered rejecting this request out of hand when they asked, but I felt you should be the one deciding."

"Tell me." Sabina felt her stomach clenching involuntarily.

"They want you to take a special package into the camp. Something more valuable than the medication we've supplied so far." His frown deepened. "I think you know what I'm talking about."

She nodded. "When?"

"It's the payment for your father's spot in this escape." He paused and gave her a serious look. "They need it paid up front."

Sabina exhaled deeply. Her heart was beating in her chest, and she had trouble keeping her shaking hands under control. This was her chance—very likely her only chance—at getting her father out. She thought of her mother sitting in the room next door, no doubt racked with nerves, and perhaps a bit of hope. Sabina swallowed hard and met Marian's gaze. There could only be one answer.

Sabina's breath rose in small clouds in front of her as the camp loomed up ahead. It was still early, and morning dew still hung on the fields. She slowed her pace, hoping her breathing would ease, and she eyed the two guards from a distance. *Come on Sabina, you can do this. Just act normal. They like you.*

The first to notice her was the taller guard, Mattias, who offered a kindly smile when she approached. He nudged the other guard, who she recognized as Johannes. The opposite of Mattias; sparing with his words, but normally quick to let Sabina through. She smiled back at Mattias, feeling her confidence grow.

"Sabina, quite unusual to see you here on a Saturday." The smile remained on his face, but the surprise was evident in his eyes. "What brings you here?"

She stopped, reminding herself her cover story was perfectly plausible. Hoping she sounded more confident than she felt, she started talking. "My boss rushed in just before I left work last night. He forgot about some papers." She patted the small bag slung over her shoulder. "But by then it was almost dark, and I had to hurry home. I promised him I'd bring them over as soon as I could today. Did no one tell you I would be coming?"

Johannes responded. "No, it's quite unusual for us to have visitors during the weekend."

"It's unusual to have visitors at any time, Johannes," Mattias said, shaking his head at his colleague, but winking at her. "But you can come and go as you please, Sabina." He paused, the smile vanishing just for a moment. "Well, almost as you please. I wouldn't advise approaching the camp after dark." From the nervous chuckle, Mattias appeared to find himself rather funny, and Sabina humored him by laughing along, helping her settle her nerves. She took a step toward the gravel road of the camp.

"I'll just report to the administration then, if that's all right with you?"

Mattias nodded, but Johannes held up his hand. "Can I just take a look inside your bag?"

Sabina hesitated, the smile slipping from her face momentarily. Her bag was almost never checked, but she recovered quickly enough. "Yes, of course. As you wish." She slipped the bag off her shoulder almost casually and handed it to Johannes. Mattias mumbled something about it being unnecessary, but Johannes opened it and took out the manila folder. He appeared to consider opening it, then decided not to as his eyes went back to the inside of the bag. Sabina held her breath as his hand disappeared inside and he looked up, frowning. He took out a small pocket knife.

"What's this?"

Sabina felt herself sweat, but before she could answer, a voice traveled from a distance.

"What's happening here?"

She was both shocked and relieved to see Paskal hurrying in their direction from the school building. It took him less than ten seconds to cross the distance. He glared at Johannes, who was still holding her bag. "Are you emptying a lady's purse?" His voice was full of contempt. Sabina heard Mattias mutter something that resembled "I told you so." And she barely stifled a smile. Johannes seemed to go between two thoughts, but when he met Paskal's glare, he quickly handed back Sabina's bag.

"Come," Paskal said, taking Sabina's arm. He turned his head to Johannes as they walked away. "We'll discuss this later."

Sabina hoped Paskal didn't feel her thumping heart as she allowed him to escort her inside the school building and into his office. After he closed the door, he gave her a curious look. "What are you really doing here?" His eyes went to her bag. "I saw a folder in there, but I don't believe we're expecting anything today, are we?"

She shook her head. The ruse she used on the guards wouldn't work on Paskal. Instead, she gave him a coy look, bending her knee as she shifted her weight. "It's slightly embarrassing. I came to see you."

"Well, that's a good enough reason for me." He beamed while he took a step closer. Sabina took a step back, grinning. There was flash of disappointment on his face.

"A bit forward, don't you think? We haven't had our first proper date yet," she said mockingly, surprised by how natural flirting came to her. It worked, for his smile widened. Pushing on, she said, "But I forgot what we had agreed on tomorrow. Where are we going, and what time?"

He looked a little puzzled. "I would send a car for you at seven."

"Oh yes, of course." She faked ignorance and shook her head. "I'm sorry, I've been a bit busy these past days, and forgot. Have you booked anything?"

"I have, but it's a surprise. It's not in town, anyway. I remembered you said you didn't feel completely comfortable being seen with me."

"Oh, I was just teasing." The lie came easy. "Now I'm even more curious."

"You'll find out soon enough." It Paskal's voice that was teasing now. "But that was all you came for?"

She nodded before half turning in the direction of the open door. About a dozen women in prisoner uniform arrived and made their way to the various laboratories.

"I know you get on well with that scientist," Paskal said, startling her as she turned her focus back to him. "It's okay if you want to go and say hello. I'll make sure none of those venomous guards bother you." He looked serious, and Sabina wasn't sure what to make of it. As if reading her mind, he nodded toward the hallway. "Go on. I'll see you tomorrow evening."

"I'm looking forward to it," Sabina said, surprised the words felt genuine. "Seven, right?"

"Seven." He smiled and followed her into the hallway. She felt a little insecure as he stood in the doorway. She passed by Felcia's open door, and she hesitated. *Was this a trap?*

"Go on, have a chat, but don't be too long." Paskal leaned against the doorframe and motioned for her to go inside. At that moment, Felcia appeared, giving her a curious look. Sabina considered why she was really here and knew she had no choice but to see Felcia. If she didn't, the possibility of her father escaping was dead in the water. She took a deep breath and turned into Felcia's laboratory.

Closing the door, she let out a sigh on noticing Felcia was alone. She opened her jacket and reached inside. Felcia's eyes widened when she produced the distinctive looking package. Sabina held it out and spoke quickly: "Do you trust me?"

The curious look hadn't left Felcia's face, but her eyes showed concern. "Of course I do, Sabina. What is it?" Her eyes went between the package in Sabina's hand and her eyes. Her own hands still hung beside her body.

A pulse of affection went through Sabina. A lump formed inside her suddenly dry throat. "I need your help. And we don't have much time."

CHAPTER THIRTY-NINE

I t started when Felcia and Izolda were clearing their instruments in the lab for the day. There were shouts outside, and Felcia initially didn't pay them any mind. It wasn't unusual for guards to raise their voices when the work details returned. That changed when a harsh voice sounded in the hallway.

"Outside, all of you Polish swine, now! Don't make me ask you twice!" The words were followed by loud clanging noises as guards smashed their batons against the steel doorposts. Izolda jumped up and looked at Felcia with frightened eyes. "Hurry, hurry!" The voice was louder, and Felcia jerked her head toward the door.

"Keep your head down," she said as she moved toward the door. Izolda didn't need to be told twice, and they entered the crowded hallway. Renata and Paula came from the next-door laboratory, their faces etched in fear.

Outside, the chaos was even greater. Women streamed in from all directions, harried on by guards who appeared more hurried and zealous than usual. Most had their batons out, using them to drive the frightened prisoners down the gravel road. Felcia joined the stream and tried to stay out of the guards' reach. Despite her best efforts, she was struck twice when the passage narrowed at the gate to their living quarters. The

301

dull pain radiating from her shoulders instantly vanished when she saw who was waiting for them at the head of the roll call area. Her blood ran cold and she kept her head down as she found her place in the lineup. She didn't know how long she'd been standing there, listening to the shuffling of feet around her, when a familiar voice instantly silenced the murmurs of more than three hundred women.

"It's interesting to think of the human psyche, isn't it?" Maria Mandl's voice effortlessly carried across the yard. "Whenever you're in a bad place, you wonder how much worse it can get, and the only thing you want is for things to get better." Felcia kept her gaze fixed on her feet but couldn't help but frown. *What?* "It's easy to see when you're in a bad place. But it's much harder to accept when it's the other way around. When you're doing well, you just want more of it. You take, take, and take even more." She spat the last words, and Felcia's skin crawled. She risked a peek up at the woman who wielded the power of life and death over every single woman standing here. She flinched when she saw the murderous look on Mandl's face. To her dismay, Margot Dreschel stood next to the Lagerführerin; Felcia instinctively lowered her head.

"And that's what you've been doing here. Greed has been festering in Rajsko. Warm beds, good food, and your comfortable laboratories aren't enough to keep you satisfied." Mandl did nothing to hide her contempt. Felcia bit on the inside of her cheek and swallowed her anger. "I suppose I shouldn't have been surprised when I heard you're keeping valuables in Rajsko. Gold taken from the stores in Kanada, even."

Felcia couldn't help but look up. Mandl's claim was so fantastical it defied all logic. Who would think to steal gold and store it in Rajsko? They had no use for it. Then her stomach turned, fear gripping her heart. She was smuggling goods into the camp. It wasn't so far-fetched to think she was the only one involved in these activities. *Could it even be the same smuggling ring?* She thought of Sabina; was she in contact with more women in the camp? Felcia dismissed the possibility; it was hard enough to coordinate the operations between the two of them. It was impossible. *But if we're able to do it, there might be more women doing the same.* She glanced at the faces surrounding her—all intelligent, resourceful women.

At a flick of the wrist from Mandl, a host of female guards stepped into the crowd. Felcia didn't recognize any of them; Mandl must've brought them from Birkenau. Without warning, they started tearing at the clothing of seemingly random prisoners. The simple uniforms gave way easily, and some of the women shrieked as they were stripped to their underwear. Mandl looked on at first, then decided to join in, homing in on a couple of women standing near the front. She descended on them like a hawk, bringing the first woman to her knees with a fist to the face. Another woman yelped involuntarily, and she was dispatched with a sharp kick to the groin. When both women lay squirming on the ground, Mandl ripped at their clothes. All the while, Mandl was silent.

Howls of pain and embarrassment filled the air as the guards continued their carnage. Felcia bowed her head, unsuccessfully trying to block out the sounds while praying she would remain invisible. *Please, don't let Dreschel see me.*

Felcia didn't know how long it was before the sounds of suffering were reduced to sobs and moans, and Mandl raised her voice again. "It appears you're all smart enough not to hide anything in your clothes." She sounded only mildly disappointed. Felcia dared to look up and was sickened by the scene around her. Half-naked bodies littered the ground of the *Appelplatz*. Some lay with their arms wrapped around their bodies, shivering as they tried to retain some of their dignity while fighting the bitter cold. Others lay motionless, the bruises on their bodies clearly visible. Some had pools of blood forming around their heads.

"I suppose we'll just need to keep looking." Mandl nodded at Dreschel, who stepped forward and yelled a number of commands. The guards sprang into action, making a show of kicking in the doors of the blocks that served as the women's living quarters. Meanwhile, a few snowflakes slowly drifted from above. Felcia cursed inwardly but was surprised when Mandl spoke next.

"Well, look at that. We can't have you poor women lying on the ground without clothes, can we?" She looked up at the sky, then at no one in particular as she faced the crowd. "Why don't you take some of the clothes over there." She pointed at a large heap next to one of the buildings Felcia hadn't spotted before. *What is this madness?*

When some of the women cautiously got up and risked approaching the pile, Felcia waited for Mandl's imminent next move of cruelty. The women sifted through the pile, first one prisoner than another pulling a dress over her head. Mandl looked on. When one of the women passed Felcia, the wicked Lagerführerin trick came to bear. The clothes were torn and filthy, the pungent smell impossible to miss at it penetrated Felcia's nostrils. Felcia closed her eyes and said a silent prayer.

The first guards came out carrying everything ranging from bed sheets and canned food to toothpaste. They dropped it all in front of the blocks, then started smashing everything to bits. Felcia looked on in horror, remembering the last time this happened. The guards continued for what felt like an eternity, and Felcia was certain every bit of comfort had been destroyed. Not a single piece of gold had shimmered anywhere.

But Mandl wasn't finished yet.

"Go see about the laboratories. They must've gotten more creative with their hiding places."

A dozen guards stalked off down the road, and Felcia's heart filled with dread. *The package.* If they searched the area around the laboratory, there would be no way to explain its contents. It would all be over. *I won't let that happen.*

Finally, the stomping of boots returned. Felcia's skin crawled as she saw the figures march past her from the corner of her eye. She didn't dare turn her head, and she dropped her gaze to the ground. The guards reached the front, and as she heard Mandl grunt approvingly, she closed her eyes in resignation. *They've found it.* She rolled on her heels, readying herself to move forward.

"Well, it appears my hunch was correct." Mandl's sounded triumphant. "And to keep this right under the nose of the camp commander. I'm sure he'll be pleased to hear we found this once he returns."

Felcia forced herself to look up and gasped. The object Mandl held in her hands wasn't at all what she'd expected. Her breathing slowed as relief washed over her. Instead of the package Sabina had handed her for temporary safekeeping, the Lagerführerin held up a large glass jar filled with pills. Felcia's eyes shot between Mandl and the jar, and she controlled herself just enough not to snort in derision when it hit her. None of the senior women standing alongside Mandl seemed the least bit surprised—this was all premeditated. Why would anyone working in the laboratory be careless enough to have such a large jar lying around?

As her eyes left the jar, she felt an intense stare, and she made the mistake of meeting it. Margot Dreschel had her eyes focused on her.

"We'll deal with the women responsible for this accordingly. For now, you are all to return to your blocks," Mandl said sinisterly. "And enjoy your night."

As the women around her slowly started shuffling away, Dreschel raised a hand, her finger pointing menacingly at Felcia. She shook it once, then slashed it across her throat twice before nodding her head and casually looking away, as if nothing had happened.

Felcia was still in shock the next morning, but she'd forced herself out of bed.

The initial relief she'd felt when the guards hadn't returned with her package had made way for doubts when she returned to her block. What if they had found it, but simply decided to wait and see who would come to collect it? Was that why Dreschel had made the gesture? Did she already know? Felcia's brain had come up with all sorts of doom scenarios, and she'd considered leaving the package where it was.

But that wouldn't solve any of her problems. Someone was bound to find it at some point, and the consequences would be dire. Every single person working in the laboratories would be executed. And what about Sabina? She couldn't let her friend down.

Felcia steeled her nerves on the way to work that morning. She entered her laboratory as usual, greeting Bianka, and got Izolda started. After about an hour she decided the time was right.

Felcia announced the need to check on something in the greenhouse, eliciting no more than a grunt from Bianka. Izolda didn't seem to notice, too caught up in her work. Felcia crossed the hallway and stepped outside into the crisp morning air. The soft crunch of the frozen ground at her feet felt delicious. The previous evening's snow hadn't persisted, and she was grateful not to leave any marks. Along the gravel road toward the greenhouses, she scanned the surroundings. When she was certain she was alone, she moved in the opposite direction, toward the well next to the laboratory building. She crouched down in flash, and felt her heart skip a beat as she searched for the package. An instant later, she felt something hard, and she grasped it, quickly stuffing it into her lab coat. Moments later, she was back on the gravel road as if nothing had happened. Felcia waited for the inevitable shout, but all remained quiet. She paused in the middle of the road, considering whether to return to the lab or go to the greenhouse. She chose the former.

Bianka and Izolda looked up for only a moment when she returned. The package felt heavy underneath her coat, and she considered where to store it. Sabina had said they would come to collect it today. She noticed the next-door laboratory was empty and turned to Bianka.

"Hey, what's going on next door? Where are Dorota and Lena?" As soon as she asked, she knew. Bianka gave her a sad look, and Felcia shook her head. "I'm sorry. I should've known."

The contraband had been discovered in the next-door laboratory, and both women had been picked up after roll call. Felcia had no doubt they were in Block 11 of Auschwitz, and she prayed their deaths would be swift.

She took a deep breath and stepped into the room. It felt colder than usual, or was she imagining things? The laboratory was identical to her own, and she opened a large cupboard in the back. It was almost empty, and she reached for the package and placed it inside. It would have to do for now.

Felcia returned to her own lab, and now Bianka gave her a curious look.

"What were you doing in there?"

Felcia held up a hygrometer. "I misplaced mine."

Bianka shrugged, appearing satisfied with the explanation. Felcia returned to her own post and let out a deep breath. Now she waited.

Felcia was cleaning one of the large glass containers in the corner when she heard something in her lab. Peeking from behind a large plant she saw a handsome man holding a toolbox standing in the doorway. He eyed the dandelions placed on the desks with interest.

"Close the door, please!" Felcia said, startling him. He did as she asked. "Who are you? And how did you get in here?"

"The door was open, and I was told this is the laboratory? I'm here to carry out repairs. I'm Joel, I was sent by Bruno."

Felcia felt a flutter of excitement, and was pleased that Izolda and Bianka had left for the greenhouses a few minutes ago. "If Bruno sent you, I'm glad you're here. I'm Felcia, and I run this laboratory." She held out her hand. "I hope the guards didn't give you too much trouble?"

Joel's eyes scanned the laboratory, a confused look on his face. Felcia smiled. "I know, this is an odd place, isn't it? We're growing crops and doing research while people down the road are, well ..." Her smile faded as her voice trailed off. "I don't need to tell you."

"What are these flowers I see here and in the greenhouses?" He pointed at one of the plants on her desk.

"Experimental flowers brought in by the Germans. They're called Kazakh dandelions, and we're trying to optimize their growth." Another confused look from Joel. "Rubber. The Germans need it for the war. They hope this is a cheap and quick way to grow it."

"And is it?" He looked doubtful.

She shook her head. "It seems to be working, judging from our experiments. But I doubt we have the space to grow enough plants for the quantities they need."

"What about the crops in the other greenhouses?"

"For the SS and their families. I know they don't care about feeding us in the camp, but they certainly don't want their guards starving. Most of the greenhouses on the other side of the camp are filled with crops and flowers for German consumption."

"Flowers?"

"We've managed to create some of the best flower species in Europe here. Although it's not surprising when you have some of the best botanists in the world in one place." Felcia turned around and moved to Bianka's desk, picking up a hygrometer. "But you're not here to listen to me talk about what's happening in Rajsko. This hygrometer is acting up a bit. Can you take a look?"

"Sure." Joel looked relieved to get to work, and Felcia indicated at Bianka's free desk. She sat at her own desk and studied him from the corners of her eyes as he opened the device and picked out some tools. Felcia liked his calm demeanor, and wanted to ask him about the underground's activities in Birkenau. *Too soon.*

"I think I've got it," Joel interrupted her thoughts as he held up the hygrometer. "Care to test it?"

"Sure."

They entered the next-door greenhouse, where Felcia stuck the hygrometer into the soil and added water to the ground. After a few seconds, the dial moved. She turned to Joel. "I think you've fixed it. It's responding as expected." As they walked back to the lab, she looked around to make sure they were alone, and lowered her voice. "Now, let's get you what you came here for. It's in the drawer in my laboratory. Make sure you hide it in your toolbox as soon as I take it out."

She reached into the cupboard and took out the package. It was heavier than she remembered as she handed it to Joel. He took it and quickly moved back to his toolbox, burying it under the tools. He was only just in time as a guard walked in. The man appeared surprised at first, then hostile.

"What are you doing in here? You're not supposed to be here." He reached for the pistol on his hip and pointed it at Joel. "Put your hands up."

Felcia quickly stepped in. "He was here to fix some tools. My hygrometer was broken." She lifted the tool, drawing no more than a confused look from the guard. *He probably doesn't know what it is.*

"Interesting," the guard said, indicating he considered it everything but. He pointed at the toolbox. "You need such a large toolbox to fix a hygro— that?"

"I also fix other things, sir," Joel said in a deferential tone. "I always have the same toolbox with me."

"Open it."

Felcia's heart was in her throat as she watched Joel slowly open the top of the toolbox—inside was nothing but screws and bolts. The guard gave an annoyed grunt. "The bottom part."

Joel did as he was told. The paper wrapping of the package was in plain sight. The guard glanced, and to Felcia's relief, he appeared to miss it from his angle, for he nodded and flicked his wrist. "Okay, all appears in order." Then he turned to her. "Was there anything else he needed to do, Felcia?"

"No, sir. He was just leaving."

At that, Joel closed the toolbox, looking at her with a nervous grin. Then, he made for the door ever so calmly, leaving Felcia alone with the guard.

"Make sure you let us know when you're expecting visitors next time, okay?" he said, looking a bit awkward before he left. As he closed the door, Felcia felt as if she could breathe again. She hoped Joel made it back to Birkenau with the pistol. Sabina's father's life depended on it.

CHAPTER FORTY

S abina looked across the table. Paskal was wearing a smart green jacket, which accentuated his eyes. The waiter appeared and Paskal suggested Sabina order first. Paskal took the bottle of wine in the middle of the table and refilled Sabina's glass, even though she'd only taken one or two sips. He then did the same for his own empty glass. They clinked glasses, and Sabina smiled at him as she put it down. He looked at her curiously.

"Is there something on my face?" He sounded a little nervous, and Sabina shook her head, the smile still on her face.

"No, nothing like that. I was just thinking this is the first time I've seen you without your uniform."

"Ah, yes. Well, I know most of my colleagues prefer wearing their uniform everywhere, but I didn't think it was appropriate for a date." He took another sip of wine. "I thought you might like to see a different me."

Sabina tilted her head a little. "I do like it. It feels almost normal." She immediately regretted her choice of words, but Paskal didn't seem to notice.

"I know what you mean. This is the first time since arriving in

Poland that I'm out on a date." He caught himself and looked a little sheepish. "This is a date, right?"

Sabina nodded and smiled. "Sure. But I'm not certain you're being completely honest with me. You've been here for a while now."

He shook his head vigorously. "No, really. I've been so busy that apart from a few drinks with the other officers in Birkenau I haven't had a chance to go out." He looked around the small restaurant approvingly. "How do you like it? One of the guards told me this place was nice."

"It is." When the car stopped in front of Sabina's house an hour ago, she had been surprised to find Paskal waiting inside. For some reason, she thought she'd meet him at the restaurant. The car ride had been a little awkward, but then they passed Rajsko to head farther south, and when they entered the large city of Bielsko-Biała some twenty minutes later, she started to look forward to the evening. It had been a long time since she'd been in a larger city, and the restaurant was indeed very nice. "When you said we wouldn't stay in Oświęcim, I didn't think we'd go all the way out here."

He waved his hand. "I thought you might like to get away from your usual surroundings for a bit. I know I do. It's nice to imagine no one knows anything about us around here, don't you think?" He picked up his glass and took a large gulp. "But tell me a bit more about yourself, Sabina. Maybe about your life before the war?" He leaned forward, his eyes sparkling with interest.

"My life before the war!" Sabina said, aware of her surprise filtering through. "I can hardly remember. It's odd to think about it, really."

"I'm sorry, did I touch on a painful memory?" Paskal looked abashed. "I really didn't mean to."

"No, no. It's nothing like that. I suppose I'm a little thrown by your question." She paused while the waiter placed small plates and a basket of bread in front of them. "I spent my whole life in Rajsko. I played hide-and-seek where the camp is now, and your office used to be a secretary's office. Dr. Caesar has the headmaster's office." She smiled, and spotted a sadness in Paskal's eyes.

"And then we came and moved everyone out of their homes. I'm sorry that happened to you and your family." He focused his eyes on the bread, but he didn't reach for it. "Do you have any brothers or sisters?"

"I'm an only child. You?"

"I have a sister, Kristina. She lives in Berlin, close to my parents. Works as a teacher." He took a piece of bread and buttered it, his gaze distant as he popped it into his mouth. Sabina did the same, and they ate in silence for a moment. "It's funny how things turn out sometimes. Kristina always wanted to be a teacher, and my parents were happy for her to pursue that career." His voice was a little strained, sounding wistful.

"And you?"

He looked up, a fire in his eyes. "It was a little different for me. When Hitler was elected, I was only twelve years old." He scoffed. "Can you imagine? My father was a strong supporter. He'd joined the party a few years before, and that meant he had a good position when Hitler was sworn in as chancellor. Naturally, I joined the *Hitlerjugend*, the Hitler Youth, the day I turned fourteen. From then, my future was planned for by my father."

Sabina was surprised by the regret in Paskal's voice. "What did you want to become?"

"Not this." Paskal took a large gulp of wine and immediately refilled his glass, emptying the bottle. He looked around, but there were no waiters in sight. "I didn't dream of being an SS officer in a Polish camp." He seemed to catch himself and offered a smile. "I'm sorry, I don't want to complain. This will sound a little cliché, but I was always fascinated by planes growing up."

"So you wanted to become a pilot? Why not join the *Luftwaffe*?"

He shook his head. "That wasn't my father's plan. Besides, I never dreamed of flying a fighter or a bomber. I wanted to see the world, take people on their holidays, business trips, or whatever purpose they had. Joining the air force was never on my mind." He managed to get the attention of a waiter and pointed at the empty wine bottle. "My father insisted I join the SS; he has friends in high places. Well, he was right. Now I'm one of the youngest second-in-commands of one of Himmler's most important camps. I suppose if I had a doctor's title, I might be vying with Dr. Caesar for command of Rajsko."

"Your father must be proud?" Sabina asked, taking a small sip of her wine.

"I don't know. I haven't heard from him in months. He's too busy working his way up the party ladder." Paskal sounded frustrated.

"But you're doing a really good job, aren't you?"

He looked at her and smiled, the gloom lifting from him for a moment. "You know what? I'm glad I was assigned to Rajsko. I wouldn't have met you if I hadn't."

There was genuine warmth in his words—he surprised her with his candor, showing a very different side to himself. She reminded herself he was still an important source as well. "A while ago, you mentioned the camp would be expanded. How is that going?"

"Ah, yes. Still very much a work in progress. Lots of paperwork from Berlin. But I'm hopeful we'll have everything set up before summer. Dr. Caesar is anxious to ramp up the research."

"It sounds like you're not just doing a good job, but would it be too much to say you're even enjoying it a little bit?" Sabina said with a smile, hoping she didn't speak out of turn. She wanted to steer the conversation back into the positive. She liked Paskal better that way.

"Let's just say I'm glad I get to work in Rajsko, and not the camps down the road." His mouth twisted in distaste, and he didn't miss Sabina's raised eyebrow. "We both know what's happening in Birkenau. It's horrible." He was silent for a moment, and Sabina sensed it was better to remain quiet. "The people back home, in the cities, they have no idea what's going on here. And it's not just Birkenau. There are hundreds of camps scattered around Europe. I'm loyal to Germany, Sabina, but I don't agree with what's happening down the road from Rajsko."

Sabina nodded. "I understand."

"I'm not sure you do." His voice was suddenly sharp. "Along with Dr. Caesar, I try to do good. The women working in Rajsko live in good conditions. There is relatively little abuse, at least when we can help it. I know we can't control everything, and guards will be guards, but I'm trying to focus on the good we're doing."

"I know," Sabina said softly. "I've seen it." She remembered Paskal stepping in with Dreschel.

"I want you to know that I want no part of what's happening in Birkenau. If they ever move me back there, I will refuse." He sounded determined, although Sabina questioned how much of a say he'd have in where he was stationed. "I'll resign."

She reached across the table and took his hand, surprising both Paskal and herself. "You're a good man, Paskal. I know you're trying your hardest to have the women in Rajsko work in the best possible conditions." She weighed her words carefully, and she was relieved to see him nodding, a faint smile returning to his face. Sabina raised her glass and waited for him to do the same. When their eyes met, she smiled. "Let's try to enjoy the rest of the evening. I'm glad I'm here with you."

His careful smile grew as their glasses clinked.

Sabina awoke the next morning to voices downstairs. She eyed the clock on her nightstand and rose with a shock. It was almost eight; she was supposed to be in class in half an hour. She jumped from her bed when there was a knock at her door, her mother's face appearing a second later.

"There's someone here for you, Sabina."

"Who is it?" Sabina asked while she pulled a warm sweater over her head.

"The same man from a few nights ago."

Sabina looked at her mother dumbfounded, then pulled on a skirt and rushed downstairs and into the kitchen. Marian sat at the kitchen table, chewing on a piece of bread.

"Marian. Good morning." Sabina felt flutters in her stomach. "Something wrong?"

He shook his head. "No. I have news from the camp. The escape is on."

"With my father?" She held her breath.

"Yes. The gun came through. Whatever your contact did, it worked."

"When is it happening?"

"This afternoon. Care to join me at the rendezvous point?"

Without hesitation, Sabina sat down next to Marian. School could wait.

The darkening square was deceptively quiet. Sabina peeked through the curtains of the apartment above the pierogi store. Apart from a few people going between the stores on the other side, there was no indication anything out of the ordinary was about to take place.

"So, tell me again, how long will it take until they make it here?" Sabina turned to Marian, who stood leaning against the doorpost on the other side of the room, looking oddly calm as he shrugged his shoulders.

"I don't know exactly. Despite the meticulous organization inside the camp, things can change all the time. But don't worry. Once the truck pulls into town, we'll know about it. Everything's in place." He moved across the room and stood next to Sabina, opening the curtains a little further, pointing to the spot where the road leading onto the square narrowed. "The truck will have to go through there. You see those men standing in the alley, with the cart? They'll block the passage when the truck approaches."

"And then my father can escape?"

"He's hidden in a crate in the back. We'll have him out of there in no time, and then onto the trail." Marian spoke confidently, not a trace of doubt in his voice. It soothed Sabina as she thought of her father. Surely the truck had cleared the camp by now, slowly making its way to them? She could hardly believe it was really happening. The only regret she felt was at not having told her mother about the escape. Marian had warned her against sharing the news; it was better to tell her mother once her father was safe and well. There would be plenty of opportunities to see him in the future.

The sound of the approaching truck was like thunder in the quiet night. Sabina felt her heart thumping as she peered through the curtain, opening it just wide enough to see the area directly in front of them. The men adjusted their grip on the cart's handles and lifted it from the ground. Their taut expressions revealed their determination, mixed with a hint of trepidation. Sabina admired their courage as they stood tall against uncertainty. The man standing at the front of the cart rapidly signaled with his hand, and the cart shot forward, out of the alley and into the street.

The squeaking of brakes and hissing of the protesting engine were unmistakable as a large truck—its bed covered by a canopy—rolled to a stop almost directly below Sabina's position. The driver honked the horn impatiently, but the men around the cart ignored him. Instead, they rummaged through the cart as if searching for something. At the same time, four men appeared from the shadows behind the truck. Sabina sucked in a breath in anticipation, her stomach tightening.

The men approached the tarp from the back, and when they were about a meter away, it swung open from the inside. The men froze. Sabina's eyes went wide, her mind struggling to process what her eyes witnessed. Time slowed down as the outlines of figures appeared from the darkness in the back of the truck. Had her father and the others escaped? The thought lasted only for the briefest of moments. Three of the figures jumped out of the back, and an instant later, bright orange-yellow flashes of light illuminated the area. The deafening sound of gunfire echoed through the air as she ducked for cover. Screams of pain and the thumping of bodies hitting the ground below mingled with angry shouts in German and the sound of people fleeing for their lives. And just as quickly as it had started, another round of gunfire erupted. Sabina felt her heart racing as she realized that this was no longer just an escape attempt—it was a fight for survival against SS soldiers who showed no mercy.

Sabina lay on the floor of the apartment, hands covering her ears. The gunfire stopped abruptly, followed by the sound of one of the SS men calmly relaying orders to the others. Still in a daze, Sabina turned to look at Marian, only a few meters away on the floor. His face was pale as a sheet, his earlier confidence vanished. As the reality of their situation sank in, Sabina could only think of one thing. *What happened to Papa?*

CHAPTER FORTY-ONE

Felcia jolted awake, her heart racing. The beds nearby were empty, and some of the other women were already awake and moving around. Her eyes were dry and crusty as she rubbed them, trying to clear her vision. As she sat up, she felt dizzy and queasy, with dark spots clouding her sight. Her shirt clung uncomfortably to her sweaty chest. She stood, using the wall for support, and closed her eyes to steady herself. After a few deep breaths, she started to feel more stable.

She changed into her work uniform and stepped out to the roll call area. It was as busy as usual, and she was relieved to find a free toilet. Felcia sat down with a sigh, half listening to the chatter of the women around her.

"They hung the bodies of the men outside the camp gates. The women working the fields said it was a horrific sight, but the guards made everybody look at them as they swung in the wind. One of them said they were all missing their fingernails, and that they had burn marks all over their naked bodies."

Felcia's ears perked up as a tall prisoner spoke to a group of six hanging on her every word.

"I'm sure they were taken to Block 11 before they were killed. Oh, those poor men. And such a brave effort." The woman's words were compassionate, but Felcia thought she detected a bit of satisfaction in the attention she received.

"What was their plan?" another woman asked.

The tall woman shook her head. "They worked in one of the garages. Their plan was to hide in one of the trucks as it made deliveries outside the camp. Or between some of the other camps, I'm not sure."

There were murmurs of appreciation. "What went wrong?"

"What always happens. The SS got wind of the plan. Someone probably ratted them out. It wouldn't surprise me if that person finds himself in Block 11 sometime soon as well. Can't trust a rat."

Felcia's blood curdled. "When was this?" Her voice sounded distant, as if someone else was speaking.

"The day before yesterday."

She dropped her head. It was too much of a coincidence. It had to be Sabina's father's escape they were discussing. People spoke of escapes all the time, but very few actually happened. Even fewer succeeded. Her heart ached for her friend, but as she rose from the plank that served as a toilet seat, she felt woozy—her own concerns should be considered first. Dr. Caesar's words echoed in her mind as she washed her hands and splashed cold water on her face. Rajsko only had space for women that were useful. And in her current state, Felcia didn't belong to that group.

"Felcia, you need to get to bed. You're barely able to stand up, let alone do any useful work." Izolda stood next to her, a deep frown marking her face. "We'll cover for you, don't worry. If you continue, it'll only get worse. Bianka?"

The other woman appeared beside Izolda as if in a haze. Her words were garbled as a blinding pain shot through Felcia's head. She didn't have the energy to argue with them. Reluctantly she allowed Izolda to escort her back to their block, where the younger woman helped her out of her clothes and into her soft bed. The blankets felt cool to the touch, and she drifted away as her head hit her pillow.

Felcia had barely shut her eyes when she heard a voice calling her name from afar.

"Felcia, wake up. Inspection." The words were spoken in a gentle tone at first, then more urgently, a hand shaking her shoulder. "Felcia. Wake up!"

She opened her eyes to see the worried faces of Izolda and Bianka hovering over her. She blinked hard as the sound of footsteps shuffling around her registered. Women passed by in a hurry. Then, a familiar voice.

"Felcia? Why are you in bed?"

Izolda's face dropped at the appearance of Dr. Caesar. His face was stern, but immediately softened when their eyes met. "You look awful." He placed a hand on her forehead, concern evident in his eyes. "You're burning up!"

"I'm all right, Dr. Caesar." Feeling weak but determined, Felcia responded to Dr. Caesar's concern with a quiet assurance and attempted to sit up. However, as soon as she moved, the room began to spin uncontrollably and she had to lie back down on her pillow. She squeezed her eyes shut, struggling to keep down the all-too-familiar feeling of nausea rising in her throat.

"It's pretty clear you're not." The tone of the doctor's voice left no room for discussion as he turned to Izolda and Bianka. "I'm guessing she didn't go to bed willingly? Did you have anything to do with this?"

The women looked terrified, and Felcia found enough strength to mutter, "They forced me to go to bed, Dr. Caesar. If it wasn't for them, I think I would've collapsed in the lab."

He nodded, keeping his attention on the other women. "Very well. It's a good thing your friends have more sense than you. Come, help me get her to the car outside."

Fear gripped Felcia. "Where are you taking me?"

"Why, the infirmary, of course." Dr. Caesar's answer was curt, and she was lifted from her bed.

Felcia hardly remembered getting in the car as she drifted in and out of consciousness. She was vaguely aware of the voices, but found it impossible to make out their words.

The slamming of car doors woke her, and she stared into the bright lights outside. Her door was opened, and she was helped out of the car. The surroundings looked oddly familiar, but she didn't immediately place where she was.

"Can you walk?" The guard's voice was more gentle than she expected. Or it could just be her state that had her imagining things. She nodded and took a cautious step forward, feeling the man's grip on her arm tighten, saving her from an awkward and potentially painful slip.

They stepped out of the bright glare of the lights, and Felcia's heart dropped at the sight of the building in front of her—Block 11. *What am I doing here?* Panic gripped her, and she took a step back. "Something's ... something must be wrong. Dr. Caesar said ..."

To her horror, the guard pulled her along. "We're in the right place. Come, please follow me. Dr. Caesar is aware of where you are. He said to take good care of you."

Felcia struggled, and the guard decided he wasn't going to fight her, lifting her from her feet. He carried her up the small flight of steps and into the building. Hot tears ran down her cheeks as they entered a brightly lit hallway. *Why am I back here?* It was her last thought before the door closed behind her.

CHAPTER FORTY-TWO

The bedroom was almost completely dark, the curtains tightly drawn, only a bit of daylight filtering through from underneath. Sabina lay in bed, no longer tired, but too lethargic to consider getting up. Her mother had come in twice that morning, offering her something to eat. The plate of scrambled eggs and toast stood untouched on her bedside table. She wasn't hungry, not even a little bit.

Memories of her father flooded back, and with it, the grief. She had cried silently, hoping her mother didn't hear. *I'll have to tell her eventually.*

It had been four days since that dreadful afternoon in the town square. Sabina had returned home in a daze, struggling to believe what she'd witnessed. The SS soldiers hadn't lingered after confirming the resistance fighters were all dead. One of them had still been alive, and Sabina had overheard the Germans' indifferent conversation about what to do with him. In the end, they had disposed of him with a single bullet to the head. Marian had pulled Sabina from the window, but she'd still heard the shot. It would haunt her forever.

Marian had half-heartedly suggested it was possible he had somehow not been around the truck when the Germans found out, but it was of little consolation to Sabina. She could feel it in her bones; her father was dead.

A knock at the door pulled her from her thoughts. She looked up in annoyance.

"Hey, Sabcia. Can I come in, please? Your mom told me you wanted to be alone, but, well ... I worry about you." She spoke softly, and Sabina found it impossible to send her best friend away, and sat up, patting a spot on the bed next to her. Elena sat down and put her arms around Sabina. "Here, I brought a little something," she said, placing a small box of cookies between them.

Sabina took one, and as she ate, found she was quite hungry. Taking another one, she managed a weak smile. "I'm glad you're here. I've missed you." Her voice sounded like a croak.

"And I missed you. I know you said you didn't want to speak to anyone, but I really needed to tell you something." Elena sounded confident, a little hopeful even. "Marian sent me."

Sabina raised an eyebrow. She had little interest in hearing from Marian. She'd come to feel a little resentful of the man, blaming him for her father's death, even though she knew that wasn't fair. She shook her head. "I don't want to hear from him. I'm not ready yet."

"I understand." Elena nodded, her eyes filled with compassion. "But this is different. Marian believes your father is still alive."

Sabina sighed in exasperation. "He said the same right after I heard those men get shot."

"He says men inside the camp have seen your father alive."

"What?" Sabina almost choked on a cookie, her eyes wide. A jolt of hope shot through her body. Her father, alive? It sounded too good to be true. "How?"

Elena held up her hands. "I don't know all the details. You should speak with him. He's anxious to see you."

"When?" Sabina suddenly felt restless.

"This afternoon. He'll be waiting for you at Joanna's."

As soon as Sabina caught a glimpse of Marian sitting at their usual table, she was grateful for his presence. It wasn't his fault that somebody had betrayed them. She took a seat and he greeted her with a hesitant smile.

"How are you, Sabina? I take it Elena told you the good news?"

"Is it really true? Is my father still alive?" Sabina spoke quickly. "Are you sure?"

"Yes. He was last spotted yesterday afternoon. The prisoners of the penal block were confined to their bunks after the escape, but they were sent back to work yesterday afternoon. Your father was among them."

Sabina's heart surged. "I can't believe it. I was certain he was dead."

"I feared for him as well." Marian paused and looked uncomfortable before continuing. "But it doesn't mean he's safe."

"How so?"

"I've been thinking about the escape. It's pretty clear someone told the Germans about the plan. The problem is, we don't know how much this person knew."

"But my father wasn't picked up. They might not know he was part of it?"

"Not yet, no. But it worries me that they kept the prisoners inside the penal block for a couple of days. They must suspect people were involved. None of the other prisoners were locked up like them."

"Maybe they're just cautious? These men have the most to gain from an escape, don't they?"

"Maybe." Marian looked unconvinced. "There is nothing like an escape, even a foiled one, to get the camp administration nervous. It makes them look bad in Berlin, and you can be sure Himmler, if not Hitler, hears about this. The SS will be interrogating anyone they suspect had even a tiny bit to do with this. It only takes one mention of your father for him to be picked up for interrogation, or worse."

"And my father dies." It wasn't difficult to put the pieces together. Sabina's initial hope ebbed away. "So what can we do?"

"Not an awful lot, I'm afraid." Marian's voice was flat, disappointment clear on his face. "I'm sorry, Sabina. Security will be extra tight, and my contacts in Birkenau are keeping their heads down."

"What about the uprising?" Sabina's desperation to do something —anything—grew.

Marian shook his head. "From what I've heard, that's not happening anytime soon. They still need many more weapons, and the different factions in the camp haven't agreed on how it would take place. It could be months, still."

Sabina felt powerless. Even if her father somehow managed to stay out of the hands of the interrogators, his chances of survival were still depressingly slim. Despite her efforts in the last week, she realized they had made no progress in getting him out of the camp. If anything, it felt like the situation had worsened.

The next day, Sabina's mother insisted she return to work. When she walked into the archiving room, the return to normalcy felt soothing. Her father's plight was still on her mind, but nothing good would come from sitting at home.

It didn't take long before a summons came from her boss. Her absence meant the paperwork for Rajsko had piled up. No one had informed him Sabina wasn't available, and he appeared nervous at the reaction from the camp.

It meant Sabina found herself approaching the camp as the sun reached its highest point in the sky. It had been almost a week, and she was keen to see Felcia. And, she had to admit, she hoped to run into Paskal as well. Considering everything that had happened in the past days, their dinner felt an eternity away. After hearing him speak so candidly against the regime he worked for, she found it difficult to see him as the enemy.

The guards let her pass without incident, and she entered the school building. The door to Felcia's lab was open, and as there was no one else in the hallway, she quickly poked her head through the door opening. To her disappointment, only Bianka, and a younger woman she didn't recognize, looked back at her in surprise. Sabina felt awkward, but managed a smile.

"Is Felcia not in? At the greenhouses, maybe?"

Bianka shook her head. "She's been taken away."

"What? Where?" Sabina felt her stomach drop. *Not Felcia, too?*

"She wasn't feeling well, and Dr. Caesar had her moved to the infirmary." Bianka shifted on her feet. "But we figured she would've been back by now. It seemed like a common flu. We're a bit worried something happened to her."

"What do you mean, 'something happened to her'?"

The other woman spoke up. "I'm not sure we should be talking to her about Felcia. Can we trust her?"

Sabina stared daggers at the stranger and opened her mouth, but stopped when she noticed Bianka looking thoughtful.

"You know what, you may be right, Izolda," Bianka said, nodding at the woman before turning to Sabina with a look of mistrust. "I'm not sure I feel comfortable telling you more about Felcia. We'll let her decide for herself, assuming she returns to Rajsko safe and sound."

Sabina was stunned into silence. *She can't be serious.* She blinked, but Bianka's stare hardened. She nodded meekly and exited the room, Bianka closing the door behind her. Were they blaming her? *Who do they think they are?* Anger welled up in her stomach, and she eyed the door as she considered storming back inside.

"Sabina?"

She turned to find Paskal standing a few meters away. His eyes sparkled, and she felt her anger dissipate when she looked at him. "I was wondering when I would see you again. Is everything all right?" He moved closer, but stopped short of hugging her. Sabina longed for his touch, for some comfort, but she understood it wouldn't be appropriate here.

"I was a little under the weather, but I think I'm okay now." She forced a smile. "I enjoyed dinner."

"Me too." He gave her a sheepish grin. "I may have talked a bit too much, sorry. I tend to keep going on when given the chance."

"No, it was nice. I'd love to do it again." Sabina caught herself. "I'm sorry, that was perhaps a bit too forward."

He shook his head. "Not at all, I was hoping you felt that way. Especially since I hadn't heard from you since." A twinkle appeared in his eyes. "There's something I want to show you outside. Do you have a minute?"

Sabina looked at the papers in her hands. They could wait. "Sure, lead the way."

Paskal led her down the gravel road and past the greenhouses, to a large clearing. "Remember when you asked me about the expansions? Dr. Caesar informed me this morning we received permission to build more greenhouses here. Berlin is encouraged by our results, and they want to make sure we have enough capacity to continue the research." He was beaming, and Sabina couldn't help but smile.

"That's great, Paskal. I'm happy for you."

He continued, his enthusiasm filtering through as he pointed at the uncultivated fields at the horizon. "And we've also been promised more workers from Birkenau. Those should be full of crops come summer."

The mention of Birkenau made Sabina flinch, her father's situation returning to the forefront of her thoughts. She looked away, but Paskal had noticed.

"Are you okay, Sabina? Was it something I said?" He put his hand on her shoulder, and she felt tears welling up in her eyes. *Come on, Sabina, get ahold of yourself.* The chastening thoughts did nothing to contain the tears rolling down her cheeks.

"I'm sorry. I don't want to burden you with my worries."

His hand went to her chin, and he gently lifted her face. "Please tell me what's wrong. Can I help?"

"It's my father."

"What's wrong? Did something happen to him? Is he unwell?" Paskal said in a soft but firm tone.

She looked Paskal in the eyes and considered telling him the truth.

"He's not well. I'm worried about him."

The lines on his forehead deepened. "Is there something I can do? Do you need some extra food?" Then he shook his head, looking as if he said something dumb. "You need medication, surely. I can get the best medicine from our warehouse in Kanada. But I won't be able to get it to you before tomorrow." He looked worried. "But I have some very strong American medicine in my office. It should make your father feel a bit better until tomorrow. Would that work?"

Sabina's heart swelled, and she nodded. "That would help a lot, Paskal. Thank you."

CHAPTER FORTY-THREE

F elcia stirred as sunlight streamed through the window, illuminating her face. She tried to turn away, but it was too bright and disorienting. Squinting, she slowly opened her eyes. The room was filled with rows of beds, most of them occupied by men and women in various levels of awareness. Some slept soundly, while others engaged in quiet conversation with their neighbors. A handful were engrossed in reading books.

Was this a dream? She remembered Block 11 very differently. The headache had disappeared, and when she placed her hand on her forehead, she was relieved to find it normal to the touch.

"Hey, you're awake." A clear voice addressed her in German, and she turned to find an attractive woman wearing a nurses uniform on the other side of her bed. "I was wondering when you'd come to. You were mumbling in your sleep quite a bit this past night."

Felcia looked up, and her confusion must've shown, for the woman shook her head and put up a hand apologetically. "I'm sorry. You speak German, right?"

It was then that Felcia detected that the nurse spoke with a slight accent. She couldn't place it, but she wasn't a native speaker. "I do," Felcia answered. "Where am I?"

"Do you mind?" The nurse produced a stethoscope and leaned forward, placing the instrument on Felcia's chest. As she did, her nurses uniform shifted to reveal the striped prisoner uniform underneath. Felcia let out a soft gasp. The nurse was just like her.

"I know, it's a bit cold. I'm sorry," the nurse said, misunderstanding the cause of Felcia's surprise. "Deep breaths, please." Felcia did as she was told, and after a couple of breaths, the nurse appeared satisfied, putting the stethoscope away. "Sounds much better than when you came in," she said in a cheerful voice.

"I'm sorry, could you tell me where I am? Is this the hospital?" Felcia sat up in her bed.

"You're in Auschwitz-I. They brought you in five nights ago. You were burning up. We're pretty sure it was malaria. You're lucky they brought you here, and not to Birkenau." Her face was serious. "I'm not sure you'd still be around."

"So this isn't Block 11?" Felcia asked cautiously.

The nurse shook her head. "Oh no, that's next door. You're safe here." A shadow crossed her face, but it was quickly replaced with a comforting smile, almost as if she wasn't telling Felcia the entire story. "It was an unusual situation though, when you came in. It's not often we're given such clear instructions on how to treat a patient."

"How so?"

"Well, the guard told us Dr. Caesar wanted to receive regular updates on your progress. When you were diagnosed with malaria, he even had some medication brought in especially for you." She scribbled something on a notepad. "As I said, highly unusual. I'm mighty relieved you appear to be doing better. You are feeling better, aren't you?"

"I feel like I've slept for days."

"That's because you have. You needed it."

"Your German is really good. Where are you from?"

The nurse smiled. "I'm from the Netherlands. We're taught German in school, so when they invaded my country, it was easy to pick up. I could say the same about you, though. From your file I saw you're Polish."

"I'm a botanist. A lot of the books I used for my studies were in German." On impulse, she held out her hand. "I'm Felcia."

"Agnes. I'm glad you pulled through, Felcia. I worried about you when you came in."

"I'm quite sure I have you and your colleagues to thank for that."

Agnes leaned a little closer. "Dr. Caesar's medication helped a lot. I wish that was more common. We never have enough medication in the hospital, although things have gotten somewhat better recently." She looked around to make sure no one was listening. "We've been receiving packages with medication from the outside for a few weeks. It's nowhere near enough, but at least we can help the sickest patients a bit better."

Felcia's heart swelled, but Agnes' words also triggered a different emotion: worry. If she had been in the hospital for five nights, who was taking care of the deliveries? Sabina must be worried. Agnes' words only made the need for their work even more important. "When do you think I might be able to return to Rajsko? I'm feeling pretty good."

Agnes smiled. "Dr. Caesar has been asking about your return for the past two days. It seems he's pretty keen on having you back. As far as I can tell, you could return as soon as tomorrow." When she saw Felcia's look of disappointment, she frowned, but her eyes were twinkling. "Or … would you prefer it to be sooner?"

A few hours later, Felcia returned to the laboratory. Bianka was facing away from her, but when she turned and saw Felcia, she flinched in shock, as if she had just seen a ghost.

"Felcia!" She dropped her pencil and hurried across the room. "I can't believe you're back. We were so worried!" Bianka threw her arms around Felcia and squeezed her hard, tears pouring down her face. Felcia was stunned at the reception; she'd never seen her like this.

When they broke their embrace, Felcia looked around the lab. "Where's Izolda?"

"She's in the greenhouse. I'm sure she'll be just as relieved to see you. Where were you? We didn't hear anything; we feared the worst."

"It turns out I had malaria, and they took me to the hospital in the main camp." Bianka listened without interrupting, and when Felcia finished, Izolda came in. The young woman stopped in the doorway, her mouth opening wide, and responded much like Bianka had.

"Are you sure you're better?" Izolda asked after Felcia had updated the younger woman as well. She was heartened by how much the women cared about her.

"As well as can be. I had five nights of sleep. I can't wait to get started again," Felcia said, slipping on her lab coat. "But even more importantly, the nurse mentioned that they were very thankful for the shipments of medication coming in. I don't think she knew they were coming through Rajsko, or I would've expected her to be more curious."

"About that," Bianka said, exchanging a look with Izolda, her eyes shifting between Felcia and a cupboard in the back of the room. "While you were away, we received two more packages."

Felcia's eyes went wide. "How did you know they were coming in? Did Sabina tell you?" It heartened her to think the women continued the smuggling route, even without her. Bianka chewed her lip, looking uncomfortable. Izolda avoided meeting her eyes. "What's wrong?"

"Well, Sabina did come in asking about you, but ... well," Bianka said, shifting her weight from one leg to the other. "We were worried about you. We thought something had happened, that Dr. Caesar had sent you to the gas chambers. And, well, the girl seems unusually close to Dr. Caesar's second-in-command."

Felcia felt as if she'd been slapped. "What did you do?"

"Not much," Bianka said quickly. "We said we didn't know where you were."

Felcia felt aghast. Had their connection been broken because her lab partners didn't trust Sabina? It was ridiculous; Sabina was the reason the smuggling route worked. Surely, Bianka and Izolda could see that? She shook her head, considering how she could reach Sabina now that she was back. *I'll need to look out for her myself.* Controlling her exasperation, she looked at Bianka. "If Sabina didn't tell you about the packages coming in, how did you know?"

"We didn't." Izolda spoke for the first time. "But we weren't sure who was bringing in these packages, and we assumed it couldn't just depend on Sabina." She held a look of defiance. "We figured if something had happened to you and the packages still came in, we would at least collect them like you told us to, and figure out how to get them to Birkenau later."

"We couldn't just leave them outside, could we?" Bianka appeared to have recovered some of her confidence as well.

Felcia looked at the women and felt her earlier irritation fade away. "So you continued checking the collection points, even when you didn't trust Sabina?"

The women nodded. "We trust you. That's all that mattered," Bianka said.

"I'm proud of you," she said, and she meant it. "But you really shouldn't question Sabina's commitment. You don't know half the things she's gone through to make this work." *And still is.* Izolda and Bianka looked half-abashed, and Felcia was quick to soften her tone. "It's okay. You did what you thought was right. The most important thing is that you retrieved the packages. Are they still here?"

"They're in the cupboard." Bianka pointed to the back of the room.

Felcia realized her absence had paused the entire operation. It was all very well and good to have more women collecting the packages, but she was still the one handing them to Klaudia or Joel. The system was too dependent on her. That oversight would need to be fixed. *Now.* She turned to Bianka and Izolda, who eyed her keenly.

"How would you like to be more involved?"

Chapter Forty-Four

S abina looked at the boxes on Paskal's desk in amazement. The brand names didn't mean anything to her, but there was medication from all over the world on the SS officer's desk.

"This should help your father through the next few days, at the very least," Paskal said, pushing the small boxes across his desk. "How is he doing? Did the American medication help?" He looked concerned, and Sabina hated lying to him.

"Yes, he was doing much better this morning." She opened her bag and scooped the packages inside. "I can't thank you enough."

"It's fine. We have so much coming in from the transports that I'm not sure those in charge in Birkenau know what to do with it." He spoke casually. Sabina could think of a few uses for the medication.

"What happens to it?" She knew better than to ask if they could use it in the prisoner hospitals. She thought of Felcia and hoped her friend was doing better. The door to the laboratory was closed just now, and after her assistants' earlier reception she wasn't keen to knock on a closed door again.

He shrugged. "Most of it is taken to the front, I believe. Those boys need everything they can get." He pointed at a box Sabina was holding.

"That's British, and it's supposed to be some wonder painkiller. Have your father try it."

"Thanks again, Paskal. I really appreciate it." She wasn't lying; the people in Birkenau would make good use of it. "I should head back to the registry. It was mayhem when I left."

"Do you need a ride? I'm heading in the same direction." He grabbed his keys from his desk.

Sabina shook her head. "I still need to see Dr. Caesar. It might take a while." It was only half a lie; she needed to hide the medication outside. Felcia's colleagues might not trust her, but that wouldn't stop her smuggling route. Elena had made her first few runs, reporting back that the packages she left behind had disappeared the next evening. She'd also returned with a number of charts and messages from Birkenau, detailing the camp's operations. Even without Felcia, the smuggling ring continued.

"All right, we're still on for tomorrow?" Paskal's voice interrupted her thoughts. "I understand if you don't feel like it, with everything going on with your father."

Sabina shook her head and smiled. "No, I look forward to it. Are you picking me up?"

"I'll be there at six." He looked relieved as they stepped out of his office and he locked the door. Sabina's spirits lifted as she saw Felcia emerge from her office across the hallway. The Polish scientist's face lit up with a large grin as she made her way down the hall and out of sight. Sabina couldn't hide her own sense of relief as she let out a deep sigh. Paskal looked up. "Are you sure you're okay to go tomorrow? We can go another time."

Sabina turned back to Paskal and shook her head resolutely. "No, six it is. It'll be good to get out of the house. Besides, he's asleep for most of the time anyway, and my mother is there as well." She was surprised and a little ashamed at the ease with which the lies tumbled from her mouth.

"Great." Paskal looked down the hallway. It was empty, and he moved quickly to give Sabina a peck on the cheek. It had become their customary way of saying farewell, at least when they were alone. This was the first time he'd done so in a public place. Sabina smiled and moved to the other door. "I should get these signed by Dr. Caesar," she said, patting a thick folder.

She watched Paskal leave. His uniform marked him as the enemy, but his actions showed a very different man. He'd been very clear about his rejection of Nazi doctrine, his horror clear at what was happening in Birkenau. And now he was giving her medication that was meant for the Nazi soldiers. Sabina was surprised by the recent shame she'd felt at lying to him. That was new, and it made her uncomfortable. She steeled herself. *You need to get your priorities straight.* If Paskal knew who she really was, and what she did, would he still like her? As she knocked on Dr. Caesar's door, she suspected she knew the answer.

Sabina was back in the hallway less than five minutes later. Dr. Caesar had been curt, signing the paperwork in a rush, without any of his usual chitchat, and it had given Sabina time to consider how she would approach Felcia.

Moving toward her friend's laboratory door, she decided she wasn't going to let the other women stop her from seeing Felcia. The medicine in her bag was reason enough to seek her out. She gritted her teeth as she kept her eyes on the door.

"Sabina." The voice sounded distant, but when Sabina turned she found Felcia closing the main door, her cheeks rosy from the cold. "I'm so glad you're here." She crossed the distance to Sabina and opened her arms. Sabina hugged her friend tight, a wave of emotions going through her.

"I was so worried about you. The women working in your lab said you were taken to the infirmary, but they seemed unsure of what was going on exactly." Sabina released her friend. Felcia smiled and gestured toward the door of her lab.

"I'm fine now. Come inside, I'll tell you what happened."

They stepped inside, and Sabina was disheartened to see Felcia's lab partners in the next room, focused on something. They would surely be here soon.

"I worried about you as well," Felcia offered, her voice strained. "I heard about the failed escape. Your father?" Her words trailed off.

"He's still in Birkenau. I don't know how, but somehow he hadn't made it to the rendezvous point for the escape."

Felcia's eyes glimmered with relief. "That's wonderful news! I feared the worst."

"So did I. But he's not safe there. Marian is convinced someone on the inside told the Germans about the plan. It's only a matter of time until they find out my father was part of it." Sabina's voice was heavy.

"Maybe they won't." Felcia took her hand. "As long as your father is alive, there's hope."

Sabina wasn't convinced by her friend's words, and she was keen to change the subject. "What happened to you?"

"Malaria, apparently." Felcia's tone was casual, but the relief on her face was palpable. "Spent a few nights in the hospital in Auschwitz, and then I was returned here."

Sabina raised an eyebrow, but before she could talk the door opened, and the two other women walked in. Sabina braced herself for another awkward encounter. To her surprise, Bianka stepped forward with a smile.

"We owe you an apology, Sabina. We worried about Felcia when she was away for longer than we'd expected. We were seeing ghosts around every corner."

"And you were one of them. We're sorry." The other woman held out her hand, looking abashed. "Let's try this again. I'm Izolda. Felcia told us about everything you've done in the past months. I feel terrible for doubting you." Sabina took her hand, overwhelmed by the change of attitude, and not immediately speaking.

"It was Bianka and Izolda who picked up the packages coming in while I was away," Felcia said, a hint of pride in her voice. "And they'll be more involved moving forward. I've connected them to the people taking the goods into Birkenau."

Sabina remembered the medication in her bag. "Well, then I suppose I should hand this to you."

Izolda's and Bianka's eyes widened as Sabina placed the boxes on the table in the middle of the room, but it was Felcia who spoke next.

"Place it in the cupboard in the back. We don't want anyone walking into the lab finding all of this out in the open." She looked at Sabina in surprise and awe. "Where did you get this? And why did you smuggle it into the camp in broad daylight?"

"I didn't. I got it from Paskal."

Felcia looked dumbstruck, opening her mouth before quickly closing it and waving a hand. "I'm not going to ask. We'll get this to Birkenau as soon as possible. Thank you, Sabina."

"I'm just glad you're okay. I'll let Marian know everything is normal again in here." She watched Izolda stashing the boxes of medication in the cupboard in the back of the room and smiled in appreciation. "But it seems I was wrong to worry in the first place."

As they settled into their seats at the quaint restaurant, Paskal's buoyant mood was palpable. The chatter of other diners filled the small space, and Sabina couldn't help but notice a few men in SS uniforms scattered among them. Paskal acknowledged them with a curt nod. Sabina was grateful he had again chosen to dress down for the occasion. It made her feel less out of place, wondering if Paskal intentionally chose his outfits to blend in with the surroundings. The inviting smell of roasted meat wafted through the air, mingling with the sounds of clinking glasses and soft laughter. Despite the presence of Nazi officers, the atmosphere felt warm and inviting. Normal, even.

"There's something exciting I wanted to share with you." Paskal raised his glass, his eyes dancing on the other side of the table. His enthusiasm was infectious, and Sabina raised her glass as well, a genuine smile appearing on her face. "The expansions were approved by Berlin this morning. We'll be allowed to start construction soon." They clinked glasses, and as Paskal took a large gulp, Sabina took a more measured sip.

"That's great news, Paskal! Congratulations." She was genuinely happy for him.

"Dr. Caesar gave me full control over the project. I've already started planning everything. There's so much that needs to be done. We'll start with the greenhouses, hopefully next week."

Sabina made a show of nodding as he went into the details of the construction of the new buildings. Inside she was thinking about her father instead. When she met with Marian the evening prior, she'd updated him about Felcia's expanded team. With the operation secured, Sabina had inquired about her father. Marian made it clear communication with Birkenau was difficult; security had only ramped up more, and a number of his usual contacts hadn't shown up for their jobs outside the camp recently. He worried about them, and it was clear there was little to no chance of any escape attempts in the near future. Marian had offered to smuggle in additional food and medication, but they both knew that was only a stopgap solution. Her father needed to be moved from the penal colony.

"I'm sorry. I'm being inconsiderate."

Sabina looked up to find Paskal eyeing her with a frown.

"I'm harping on about my project without asking about your father. Has his situation improved? Have the pills helped?" He scratched his neck, an uncomfortable look on his face.

Sabina felt a surge of affection for the German, immediately followed by guilt. There was no denying he cared for her, and she was starting to believe she might feel the same way. "He's doing a bit better, yes."

"I'm glad." He appeared to relax a little, the frown softening. "I know you worry about him a lot, and I'm happy I could help in some way." He lifted his glass to his lips and took a sip.

Sabina looked at him, and as his words registered, a thought struck. She dismissed it almost immediately, but as Paskal put his glass down and smiled, she found herself entertaining the thought again. It was risky, but if she did nothing, her father would soon perish in the penal colony. Marian had never explicitly said so, but his words had always implied the dangers. After their last meeting, she knew Marian couldn't help her. She looked across the table. *Might Paskal?* She took a large swig of her wine and took a deep breath, drawing a curious look from Paskal.

"You said construction on the greenhouses will start in a week?"

"If we can get the materials in time. I'm hopeful they'll be able to send them with an incoming transport soon. Why?"

"Do you have any say in who gets to work on the expansions?"

He shrugged. "It will most likely be a new work detail from Birkenau."

"I see." Sabina had to contain the hope rising in the back of her throat. "And would you be involved in picking the men?"

"That would normally be done by the administration in Birkenau. Why do you ask?"

Sabina looked at him and made a decision. "I haven't been completely honest with you about my father." Across the table, Paskal clenched his jaw, his expression hardening ever so subtly. Nerves shot through Sabina's body, but she knew there was no way back. "He's not sick, or at least not that I'm aware of. He could be, but that's not why I'm concerned about him. He's in the penal block in Birkenau."

It felt as if the air had been sucked from the space between them. Paskal looked back at her with a look she couldn't place. *I've gone too far.* He looked away, but not before she thought she detected a hint of disappointment in his eyes. Her heart dropped and she felt her hands shaking as she waited for his response. After studying the room around them for what felt like an eternity, Paskal turned his gaze back to Sabina.

"How did he end up there?" His voice was calm, but not as warm as usual. "What did he do?"

"He's a foreman in the mines, and he handed extra rations to the prisoners working there." Sabina thought she did an adequate job at controlling her shaking voice. "They found out, and they took him to Birkenau."

"How do you know he's in the *Strafkompanie*? Sounds like an overly harsh punishment."

"Someone at work has connections in the camp." She chuckled nervously. "Well, a lot of people have connections. We have prisoners coming in to carry out all sorts of tasks. They talk."

Paskal appeared to accept her explanation, nodding slowly. "How long has he been in the camp?"

Sabina wasn't certain, but she thought she detected a hint of the usual warmth in his voice. "A couple of weeks."

"Two weeks in the SK?" He sounded shocked. "And he's still alive? Your father is a strong man, I'll give him that."

"I'm not sure he will survive much longer if nothing changes." Sabina looked at Paskal, his expression seemingly back to normal. *It's now or never.* "Can you help?" Her voice was small, betraying every bit of her anxiety.

"You're asking me to place your father in my construction crew."

Sabina nodded, aware—but not caring—that there was desperation in her eyes. Her father's hope of survival rested on Paskal's next words.

His eyes never left hers, his gaze thoughtful yet gentle. Sabina's throat went dry as she tried to read what was going on inside his head. He took another sip of his wine before putting the glass down agonizingly slowly.

"You took quite a risk telling me the truth." His voice was level, and Sabina sucked in a sharp breath. "But I understand." A flicker of something in his eyes—regret, disappointment?—before he continued. "I can't imagine what it was like for you to ask me this."

Sabina moved forward and reached for his hands. He allowed Sabina to slip her fingers into his, emboldening her. "My father has always been there for me when I needed him." She cleared the lump forming in the back of her throat. "And now I feel I might be able to help him when he needs it most. With you." She squeezed his hand and was encouraged to feel him do the same.

"I'll see what I can do, Sabina. It won't be easy to get him released from the penal colony, and I may need to call in some favors." His face softened, a confident smile appearing. "But I'll do everything within my power to get your father out of there. Anything for you."

CHAPTER FORTY-FIVE

Felcia's morning crawled by. She knew from the moment she awoke it would be a tough day. She felt drained, and when Izolda and Bianka announced they were going to take care of some work in the greenhouses, she'd felt instant relief at having the lab to herself for a bit. It wasn't the first time since her return from the infirmary that she felt tired, and she was almost certain it was an aftereffect of her malaria infection. The first few days her stamina had increased, but now she was exhausted at the end of every day.

She leaned against the large table in the middle of the room and was trying to focus on her work when there were shouts outside. A door slammed, then she jumped up as a number of gunshots followed each other in rapid succession. The sound of boots crunching the gravel confirmed something was happening nearby. More shots, then a pained cry in the distance. Felcia squeezed her eyes shut, trying to make the sounds disappear. Voices shouted commands in German before more gunshots rang out in the distance. Felcia prayed that whoever had made a run for it managed to reach the woods. Anyone trying to escape Rajsko would have to plow through the heavy fields between the camp and the relative freedom of the trees. Even then, the odds were firmly stacked against them, as the SS would release their hounds. Felcia hadn't heard of a single successful escape since she arrived, but it hadn't stopped the number of people trying from increasing.

The excitement outside faded as quickly as it appeared, and silence soon returned. Felcia exhaled slowly and returned to her work. After a few minutes, there was a cautious knock on her door. Seconds later, the familiar face of Joel the handyman appeared around the corner. He looked shaken, his voice trembling.

"Well, that was all a bit too exciting for my liking." He put his toolbox down and closed the door. "Do you have a lot of those escapes going on here?"

"This was the third attempt this week—people are getting desperate. I suppose they didn't make it?"

"Not from what I could see. I rushed inside when the shooting started." His voice sounded less strained, his chest no longer heaving. "I'll tell you, that was the best timing possible, though."

"How so?" Felcia felt her fatigue fading as she smiled at the handsome handyman.

"One of the guards at the main road was a little too thorough. Nearly found what I was carrying, patting me down before the shooting caught his attention." Joel reached into his pants and produced a small linen satchel. He held it out to Felcia. "I brought the payment. I trust you'll be able to get it to them?"

Felcia hesitantly took the small bag, sensing its size wasn't indicative of the value of its contents. "Can I open it?"

"Go ahead, just be careful not to drop anything."

Felcia peered inside the small bag and gasped. Small stones glittered in the bright laboratory light. "I think our contacts in the Home Army will be very pleased with these."

"Can you imagine what they would've done if they'd caught me with that?"

Felcia opened a drawer, nodding as she placed the satchel inside. Joel looked at her curiously. "Do you think we can trust them?"

"Our contacts on the outside? We have no other choice. They've come through every time so far. I was a little surprised when the Home Army changed their tune about sending weapons, but if my contact is confident, that's enough for me."

Joel looked relieved. "When do you think they'll arrive?"

"Hard to tell. Let's just be patient. Nothing we can do to change anything anyway."

This drew a dry chuckle from the handyman, and he moved toward the door. "I better pretend to carry out some repairs in the greenhouses to make sure the guards don't become suspicious. Take care, Felcia."

"See you around, Joel." Felcia watched the door close and found herself trembling. She would need to carry the satchel containing a small fortune to their hiding place. Its contents were valuable enough to see her end up dangling on the end of a rope.

Felcia waited until the workday had ended before making her move, just before roll call. Bianka and Izolda had left a few minutes earlier, and Felcia had placated them with the excuse of finishing up one last thing. In reality, she was mustering up her courage to step outside.

She took a deep breath and opened the drawer. The satchel seemed to stare back at her, and she snatched it, quickly stuffing it inside her pocket. There was a small bulge, but it would have to do, she decided. She grabbed a bucket and headed out of her laboratory.

It was dark when she stepped into the cold of the late afternoon. A few other prisoners hurried by on the gravel road, anxious to get to roll call. Felcia waited until they were out of sight, then quickly moved to the well on the side of the building. She lowered the bucket, then scanned her surroundings. There was no one nearby. *Now.* She crouched down, pretending to grab the rope to pull the bucket back up, but removed a loose brick in the well instead. Stuffing the satchel in and replacing the brick took less than a few seconds, and she rose, pulling on the rope as if nothing had happened.

Felcia sighed in relief when she undid the rope from the bucket and slowly walked back to the main building, forcing herself not to run. She neared the steps leading into the building. *Almost there.*

"What are you doing stalking around outside at this hour?"

The familiar voice caused a chill to rip through Felcia's body, and she nearly dropped the bucket. Instead, she gripped the handle hard, her knuckles cracking. She turned, her eyes confirming what she already knew. In the dim light stood Margot Dreschel, gently tapping her baton in the palm of her left hand.

"A bit late to be carrying water around in the dark, don't you think? Bit dangerous too, considering what happened this afternoon." The woman slowly took a few steps closer.

Felcia tried to control her shaking hands, unsure if she should put the bucket down. "I need to water my plants for the night." She couldn't help her anxiety filtering through in her voice. "I thought I could make it just before roll call."

Dreschel grunted something Felcia didn't catch. She stood only a meter away. Felcia stayed rigidly still, not sure if the guard expected a response, and decided to remain quiet. It proved to be the wrong decision. Dreschel's right hand flashed upward, and before Felcia could respond, the hand holding the bucket exploded in pain. She could do nothing but drop it, water instantly drenching her simple shoes. Felcia reached for her burning hand, but this only resulted in another blow as Dreschel expertly lashed out at the small of her back, causing Felcia to drop to her knees as pain radiated up and down her body. The chill seeped through her drenched clothes as her knees dug into the cold ground.

"You've been getting away from me for too long, you piece of filth," Dreschel hissed, standing over her. "Sucking up to Dr. Caesar, making friends with the other SS officers. But you won't escape me forever." Felcia's world was spinning and she felt nauseous, feared she would pass out. *If that happens, I'm dead.* "But it won't be much longer. Change is coming to Rajsko, and you won't be able to escape your fate any longer."

The way the guard spoke had Felcia convinced she would receive the killing blow any time now, and she braced herself in anticipation.

"The Lagerführerin has decided Rajsko needs a bit of trimming." Dreschel let out a bloodcurdling chuckle. "I don't need to tell you what that means, do I? Rest assured I'll make sure you won't escape this time."

Dreschel straightened herself and took a step away. Felcia closed her eyes, certain the woman would administer another beating. When nothing happened, she opened her eyes to find Dreschel observing her with an amused expression.

"Don't worry. It will all be over soon." She grinned savagely. "I'll make sure you don't escape the selection. You're mine, scientist." Then she turned on her heel and casually strolled back toward the gravel road, whistling a horribly off-key tune.

Chapter Forty-Six

Despite the dark clouds looming overhead, Sabina walked down the road with a sense of optimism. It had been weeks since she'd felt this way, but the dinner with Paskal had turned out better than expected. It had been difficult to focus at work the next day while she waited for Mr. Piotrowski to summon her. He hadn't, and when she came home she'd struggled to keep the news from her mother.

Now, halfway down the road to the camp, she clasped her gloved hand around the document folder a little tighter. She was keen to see if Paskal had any news, although she knew it was probably a little too early. *It's only been two nights, Sabina. Calm down.* Yet her stomach fluttered, and she knew it was only partly at the prospect of good news about her father.

The camp came into sight, and she realized how odd it was that so much of her life revolved around the people inside. The guards waved her through without any fuss, and her pace increased as she approached the school building.

Stepping inside, she was pleased to see the lights in Felcia's laboratory were on. She'd have to check in on her friend later. Elena had asked if she could pass a message to Izolda—Elena had well and truly embraced her new role.

Sabina moved down the hallway to Paskal's open door. Her heart skipped a beat as she approached. He was sitting behind his desk, wearing a freshly-pressed uniform, which made Sabina stop for a moment.

"Sabina!" He looked up before she could speak, the smile lighting up his entire face as he hurried toward her. He closed the door and put his arms around her, giving her a soft kiss on the cheek. She enjoyed his touch, but she couldn't suppress a slight shudder as the lightning-bolt-shaped SS's on his shoulder straps almost brushed her face. Paskal didn't notice as he took her hand and guided her to the pair of chairs facing his desk. "I'm so glad you're here. I have some great news."

Sabina sat and tried to appear composed, but her heart was pounding in her chest. Controlling her voice, she said, "About my father? About the expansions?"

"Indeed, about both," Paskal said as he sat next to her. He'd recently made it a habit not to sit on the other side of the desk when she was there. "I made some rounds in the administration in Birkenau yesterday. The building materials for the new greenhouses won't arrive until next week, but that doesn't mean we can't get started on the road."

Sabina sat forward, urging him on, feelings of hope and anxiety making her throat go dry. "And? What did they say?"

"Initially, they wanted me to wait, but I brought Himmler's letter to Dr. Caesar. That made them change their tone pretty quickly. The first group will start work tomorrow." He smiled, and Sabina didn't dare ask the words on the tip of her tongue. "Including your father."

Sabina felt weak with relief as she let out a deep sigh. Tears welled up in her eyes, and it was impossible to stop a few from escaping down her cheek. Paskal handed her a tissue, which she gratefully accepted. He took her hands and spoke in a gentle voice. "It was a bit of a struggle, as one of the men questioned me about taking someone from the Strafkompanie."

"How did you manage it?"

Paskal grinned. "I told him if he didn't like it, he could take it up with Himmler."

"I don't know how to thank you," Sabina said, and she really didn't. "Will my father be moved to Rajsko?"

"No, he'll have to return to Birkenau every day. But he won't be in the penal colony anymore. He should be moved today, so he'll be able to report to his new work detail tomorrow morning."

Sabina nodded. It made sense; Rajsko only had female prisoners, after all. Getting her father from the penal colony was a big achievement. Her face was glowing, and she looked up at Paskal. "Will I be able to see him?"

"I think we should be able to get you some time with him tomorrow. I'll come up with an excuse to pull him from the group. But don't tell anyone about this arrangement. It needs to remain our secret."

"Of course." Sabina hardly heard his words as she struggled to process the thought of embracing her father tomorrow. *Should I tell Mama?* Tomorrow couldn't come quickly enough.

Sabina had only marginally recovered from the shocking good news when she crossed the short distance to Felcia's laboratory. She took a deep breath and composed herself before knocking on the door. Paskal had signed the papers, including instructions for Sabina to return the next day. She had lost count of the number of times she'd thanked him. Her heart was bursting as Felcia opened the door, but any thoughts of sharing her good news vanished when she saw the troubled look on her friend's face.

"Come in, quickly." Felcia's voice was strained, her eyes darting to check the hallway behind Sabina. She quickly closed the door, the atmosphere in the laboratory unusually tense.

"What's wrong?" Sabina glanced at the worried faces of Izolda and Bianka on the other side of the room before focusing her attention back on Felcia. "You look like you saw a ghost."

"It's Dreschel, Sabina. She cornered me yesterday evening. Told me there's a large selection coming, and that she'll make sure I'm a part of it." Her voice was shaky, her face pale as snow, and Sabina felt as if a boulder had formed in her stomach.

"What? No, that can't be right. Dreschel has no authority over you, does she?" Sabina cursed herself for adding the last two words. "She doesn't. You fall under Dr. Caesar."

"Dreschel doesn't, but Mandl can do whatever she pleases."

"Have you spoken with Dr. Caesar?"

"That's the thing. He was called away to Berlin last night." Felcia's eyes were wide with fear. "I'm certain Mandl and Dreschel have planned it this way. Without Dr. Caesar, there is no one to stop them. Mandl outranks everyone."

"She can't just call a selection, can she? You're too valuable."

"Mandl can do whatever she wants. She'll come up with an excuse." It was Bianka who spoke up this time. "She's done it many times before."

"Dreschel must've known Dr. Caesar was going away. She wouldn't have been so cocky otherwise," Felcia said grimly. "I don't know what to do, Sabina."

"Did she say when?"

Felcia shook her head. "Only that it would be soon."

Sabina's head was spinning. Was her friend about to be sent to the gas chambers? It was beyond unfair; her joy at Paskal's news about her father was pushed to the back of her mind as she racked her brain to think of a way to save Felcia. "Can you hide?" She asked more out of hope than anything else, not surprised when Felcia shook her head.

"There's nowhere to go. If they find me missing, they'll search the camp for as long as it takes to find me." She looked to Izolda and Bianka. "And if it takes too long, they'll probably take it out on them. I can't do that, Sabina, I really can't."

Heavy footsteps sounded in the hallway, and all four women froze in place. The unmistakable sound of boots stomping by outside made Sabina's heart skip a beat. Any moment now, the door would be jerked open, the SS guards ready to take the scientists away. And what about her? She'd have no excuse for being in here. Suddenly, Sabina realized Dreschel—or whoever it was—would see her presence as an excuse to take her as well. She closed her eyes and prayed for them to leave. A few seconds later, the footsteps receded, and the hallway returned to its previous quiet. The air returned to the room as Sabina exhaled deeply.

Felcia looked up to see three pairs of frightened eyes looking back at her. Sabina's connections would do them no good. There was only one person that could do something. She took a step closer to Felcia and clasped her friend tightly around the shoulders, forcing herself to sound more confident than she felt.

"I will do everything possible to keep you from Dreschel's clutches."

"What are you going to do?" Felcia's voice was small, that of a frightened child.

Sabina clenched her jaw in an effort not to lose her composure. "I'm going to see if I can get you moved somehow. Where she can't find you."

Felcia nodded weakly. "I trust you, Sabina, but I'm not counting on anything. Dreschel is close to Mandl, and she rules every single women's camp in the area."

"I know," Sabina said, turning to the door to hide the tears of frustration burning in the backs of her eyes. "But I'm going to try anyway."

Marian shook his head across the table. "You know it's impossible to break someone out of a camp without anyone noticing. Even Rajsko."

Sabina bit her lip to hide her disappointment and rising anger. *It's not his fault.* "There has to be something we can do."

"Your officer can't help?" Marian's face was neutral, but Sabina thought she detected a trace of suspicion in his words. She decided to ignore it.

"He wasn't in his office when I left. I won't be able to speak to him until the morning. It might be too late by then."

The big man clasped his hands on the table and sighed deeply. "I wish there was something we could do, but the logistics just don't work. By now Felcia is in the gated area of the camp, and you know as well as I that there is no way to break in there without being seen, let alone to get someone out."

Sabina decided there was no use arguing with Marian. He was right, even if it was impossible to accept. She tried to console herself with the thought that it was entirely possible Dreschel had only tried to rile Felcia up, or that nothing would happen tonight, but Sabina couldn't shake the thought of her friend being marched out of Rajsko in the darkness of the night.

"Look, I know this is hard, and you don't want to hear it, but there's nothing you can do until the morning. The best thing you can do is pray for your friend and seek out your officer tomorrow. He might be willing to help, but I wouldn't count on it."

Sabina nodded. Marian was right about having to wait until the morning, but he was wrong about Paskal. He would help. She was certain of it.

CHAPTER FORTY-SEVEN

As the sun slowly rose in the sky, it created a long shadow that stretched across the gravel road. With her feet shifting restlessly, she stood near the steps of the school building, alternately clenching her right hand into a fist and releasing it. She kept her gaze fixed on the main road ahead. The column of men slowly approaching was larger than she'd expected. Wearing identical clothes, their heads shaved, and their faces turned toward the ground, it was impossible to make out any individuals. Despite that, Sabina still scanned the group for signs of her father's confident gait. As she peered, she realized none of the men resembled her father. Her breath caught in her throat when she realized he might not have made it through the night. She felt a presence next to her and turned to see Paskal.

"They'll be here in a few minutes." He spoke with an oddly authoritative voice and only a hint of his usual warmth. "I'll pick your father out of the line before they get started on the roadwork."

Sabina nodded, and Paskal moved on to instruct a group of nearby guards she didn't recognize. They listened, one or two stealing curious glances at her, no doubt wondering what she was doing standing outside the main building. Sabina ignored them and returned her focus to the group of prisoners now shuffling down the gravel road.

As they lined up on the opposite side, a number looked up curiously. They were of all ages, but every single one looked at least ten years older than he was. Sabina couldn't make her father out in the first row of faces, and worry started gnawing at her again.

Then, a stout man came into view, reminding Sabina of her father. *That can't be Papa.* The man walked hunched forward, taking careful yet determined steps, the effort evidently painful, yet pride winning out to keep him going. Sabina narrowed her eyes, and when the man took his place in line, he glanced up long enough for Sabina to recognize her Papa. His eyes showed the briefest glimpse of hope, and she knew, despite his sorry state, that he was aware of his surroundings. *Look up, Papa. Look at me. I'm right here.*

Her heart pounded. His muscular arms seemed to have disappeared, but Sabina was most concerned about his posture. It was obvious he was struggling to stay upright, one hand constantly going to the small of his back as he winced in pain. Sabina's heart broke, and she wanted nothing more than to rush to him and support him. Instead, she stayed in place. Watching. Waiting.

It took another minute before her father looked up again. This time, his gaze went to the school building. His eyes passed by Sabina for the briefest moment. Then they returned to meet hers. A look of disbelief flashed on his gaunt face as he blinked hard. Time appeared to stop as Sabina silently mouthed, "Papa," her chest tightening from relief at finally seeing her father alive. His eyes filled with love, a flash of energy crossing his face momentarily.

Then the harsh barking of commands filled the air as the guards sprang into action. Sabina watched as they went up and down the column of prisoners. To the side, Paskal looked on in approval. She lifted an eyebrow as she noticed something odd about him, but couldn't place what it was.

Inside the building, Felcia was trying—and failing—to focus on her work. She was exhausted after her second restless night. Try as she did, sleep had been impossible to catch as her tired brain kept her awake with visions of Dreschel bursting into the barracks to drag her away. Visions of her time in Birkenau vividly returned; the starvation in the Death Block, the indifference with which women were herded toward the gas chambers and crematoria. Nor had she forgotten about her time in Auschwitz, where the wails of the tortured souls in the basement of Block 11 had suddenly returned to the forefront of her mind.

She hadn't heard back from Sabina yet, and even though it worried her, she trusted her friend was doing whatever she could. Still, her anxiety only grew with every passing minute. Bianka and Izolda had tried to comfort her, to little avail. What if Dreschel had found out Felcia had been involved in getting Izolda transferred and assigned as her assistant in Rajsko somehow? Felcia closed her eyes and forced herself to abandon that line of thinking. *You're getting too paranoid.*

The thought had barely left her mind when the door flew open, slamming against the wall with a loud crash. Felcia didn't even need to look up to know who it was.

"Out, all of you. Now!" The grating voice of Margot Dreschel filled and instantly sucked all the air from the small room. "Line up outside the building!" *This is it.* Felcia put down her pen and notepad and tried to exit the laboratory without acknowledging Dreschel, but the guard's eyes burned onto her face. She had no choice but to look up. Dreschel's eyes were dark pools of black with fire burning in their centers. Dreschel was rubbing her hands together as she took a step into the doorway, barring Felcia's passage.

"It won't be long now. I've been waiting for this moment, and I've got a spot reserved for you in Birkenau." Dreschel spoke menacingly, the fire in her eyes growing with every word. "Don't think you'll get away with stepping into the gas chambers." She moved out of the way with a grin. "Line up with the rest. I'll come find you."

Felcia did as she was told, her heart a ball of ice. Her head was spinning, nausea rising in the back of her throat. She searched frantically for a way out, finding none. The entire hallway swarmed with female guards pulling women from the laboratories. *They can't take all of us, surely? Who is going to continue the research? If only Dr. Caesar was here.* Then a terrifying thought struck. What if Dr. Caesar was aware of this? The thought further chilled her as she stepped outside in a daze.

The scene was surreal. On the opposite side of the road stood a group of haggard-looking men, surrounded by guards screaming at them. She recognized the SS officer Sabina had built some sort of relationship with on the far side looking on. *Paskal, wasn't it?* Following the stream of women coming from the building, she almost missed someone calling her name. She turned and saw Sabina standing next to the building, looking on in horror. *What is she doing here?* Felcia's mind went rampant. Had they found out about Sabina's connections as well? And who were those men? She almost bumped into the woman in front of her as the line stopped, and she pivoted to stand facing the men on the other side of the gravel road. She turned her head to Sabina, who was studying the men intently. Felcia tried to follow her friend's gaze but was unable to see who she was focusing on.

For a moment, nothing of note happened while the last of the scientists came from the main building. Then, Paskal started moving about the lines of men. He moved slowly, as if inspecting them. He addressed a few of them, but Felcia couldn't make out the words. Some answers brought his approval, while she could see him click his fingers twice, and the men were hauled from the lineup and placed aside. Felcia had a sinking feeling these men would follow them to Birkenau later.

Felcia carefully cast her eyes on Sabina. Her friend appeared to feel her gaze, and turned to her. Felcia gave her a questioning look, and Sabina gave her a pained, confused expression. *She doesn't know what's happening either.* Felcia wished she could ask what she was doing here. She looked to the door of the main building and was relieved to see it vacant. But it couldn't be much longer before Dreschel would appear.

Something was happening with the men, for Paskal was leaning forward, his face close to the ear of one of the prisoners. It was difficult to process, but it appeared as if he was whispering something in the man's ear. He was by far the oldest of the group, and Felcia imagined the man would soon make his way to the discarded pile as well. There was something familiar about his face. She glanced at Sabina again and noticed her friend paying very close attention to the proceedings.

A loud, animallike roar made Felcia jerk her head back to the group. The man Paskal had whispered to appeared to have grown in stature, growling at the German officer. He roared, and Paskal looked at him in amused fascination. Then the man did the unthinkable: he pulled back his arm and threw a clumsy punch at Paskal. The blow was easily dodged, but the gravity of the action was felt by all present. Men let out surprised gasps of horror and respect alike. The loudest shriek came from Felcia's left, where Sabina stood with her hands clasped in front of her mouth, barely concealing a look of pure horror. The prisoner's eyes shot to Sabina, instantly filled with regret. Paskal turned and followed his look, a savage grin twisting his face.

It was then that Felcia understood what was happening. This wasn't just any prisoner. It was Sabina's father!

Things happened very quickly. Paskal held up a hand to the guards approaching with batons raised. Disappointment lined their faces as the officer spoke. "I'll take care of this piece of shit myself!" In one smooth movement, he turned and landed a punch into Sabina's father's face. The sound of his fist connecting was oddly dull, but there was no doubt it had found its mark as the prisoner's legs gave out and he crashed to the cold ground.

The square went silent as Paskal stood over the broken man on the ground. The guards took a few cautious steps forward, but yet again Paskal stopped them.

"As I said, I'll take care of him myself," he said, his voice deep and authoritative as he knelt next to Sabina's father. Felcia risked a glance at her friend, who looked distraught. Despite her own predicament, Felcia's heart burned for her friend.

Paskal lifted Sabina's father from the ground. Felcia was surprised to see the man back on his feet. A proud man, despite knowing what was in store for him. He didn't go down without a fight. Paskal gave him a nudge toward the main road. When Sabina's father didn't respond quickly enough, Paskal grabbed him by the elbow, dragging him along.

Nobody on either side of the road spoke while the two men walked out of the camp and crossed the road. There, Paskal pushed Sabina's father up the small hill before disappearing into the woods. When they did, the guards appeared to remember what they were doing, and they started screaming at the remaining men to start finding their tools, pointing at a truck stationed near the road. Chaos returned to the area, but Felcia only had eyes for her friend near the main building.

Sabina stood slumped, her face ashen and focused on the small opening in the tree line where her father and Paskal had disappeared minutes ago.

Her thoughts were interrupted by two loud bangs from the woods. Everybody in the camp paused for a moment as the horror of what had happened sunk in. Even the guards appeared surprised, but they quickly recovered, harrying the prisoners back into action with the butts of their rifles and batons.

Even from a distance, Felcia could see her friend shaking uncontrollably. She tried to get her attention, but Sabina was apathetic, oblivious to her surroundings. Felcia wanted to comfort her, put her arms around her, but right at that moment, Dreschel stepped out of the building, surprised at the activity outside. Felcia expected she would be moved along soon, forever taken from her friend. Not being able to help her or say farewell seemed an unbelievably cruel way for this friendship to end.

To Felcia's surprise, Dreschel spoke to one of the nearby guards, then stalked down the gravel road. Perhaps they weren't going anywhere just yet? Felcia held on to the sliver of hope that she might still get a chance to say farewell to Sabina. Maybe a very quick hug.

Felcia spotted movement from the corner of her eye, and Paskal strolled back into the camp. Nothing in his manner suggested he had just executed a man in cold blood, and Felcia felt her skin crawl. Sabina trusted this man, and he had turned around and murdered her father. Felcia avoided another glance at her friend, fearing it would drive her over the edge herself. Instead, she kept her eyes on Paskal, shooting daggers at him, hoping he would look up to see her hate. She was beyond caring about what would happen next; Dreschel or Paskal, it would all be the same. *I'm dead either way.*

The Nazi officer had no interest in her as he spoke with a guard holding a clipboard. He pointed at the clipboard, and the guard struck through something running the width of the page. With a mere pointing of his finger, Paskal had casually confirmed the death of Sabina's father. There would be no questions asked as to what he did; there had been plenty of witnesses. Nazi witnesses. What the prisoners saw or thought didn't matter. Fury built up inside her, but she felt powerless.

Paskal nodded to the guard and moved away. To Felcia's surprise, he walked to her group, his eyes scanning the women. She thought his eyes lingered on hers, and she did her best to give him her best scowl, but he seemed oblivious.

"Right, I'm going to need one of you to come with me and help bury that body." Paskal's voice sounded detached, as if he were recruiting volunteers to help clean up a spilled carton of milk. "No sense in dragging the body all the way back to the camp." He glanced at the group of women for only a few seconds before his eyes shot to Felcia. "You. You look strong enough." She felt as if struck by lightning. This was no coincidence. *Oh God. What's happening?* "Grab a shovel from the truck and follow me."

Felcia reluctantly took a few steps forward. She glanced at Sabina, but her friend kept her eyes fixed firmly on the ground. Felcia frowned. *That was odd.* Before she could come up with an explanation, she heard Paskal's voice again.

"Come to think of it, this is a two-person job. It will take forever otherwise. You, come with us as well."

Felcia couldn't believe it. Paskal was no longer facing the group of women. Instead, Sabina scuffled in their direction.

"Come on, hurry up. I don't have all day." Paskal's voice was icy and scornful. Felcia found it hard to imagine how Sabina had considered him a friend. He was the prototypical SS demon.

Felcia slowed her pace to allow Sabina to catch up with her. When they reached the truck and reached for shovels, she risked a glance at her friend. Sabina's eyes were swollen, wet from tears—those of a heart-broken soul. Felcia shook her head, only whispering a barely audible "Sorry."

Seeing her friend like this, Felcia could no longer contain her own emotions, tears flowing from her eyes, not caring if anyone saw. She glanced over her shoulder and saw Paskal talking to one of the nearby guards.

"I'm so sorry, Sabina. I can't imagine how you feel," she whispered in hurried tones.

Her friend shook her head in resignation. "No, I'm sorry, I—"

"What are you doing standing around there! Come, come!" Paskal took a few steps and pulled on both women's shirtsleeves. "Time to get to work!"

The walk through the woods was done in silence. Every step from the camp was one closer to death. Oddly enough, Felcia had made her peace with that. There was a small part of her that took satisfaction in escaping Dreschel's clutches in the end, even if it meant she would die at another Nazi's hand. It didn't matter. She had survived far beyond the average.

Sabina hadn't said a word. I'm proud to be her friend. We'll face death with our heads held high.

Felcia was surprised at how long they spent walking through the trees. On impulse, she reached for Sabina's hand. It felt cold and clammy, but her friend grasped hers weakly, their fingers locking. It felt oddly comforting as she focused on the man walking ahead of them. Could they make a run for it? Perhaps overpower him? Then her eyes went to the pistol strapped to his hip, and she knew either option would likely result in death. Yet, she felt she had to try. *But how can I let Sabina know?*

While Felcia pondered running, they entered a small clearing. On the far side lay a heap of leaves, and Felcia didn't immediately recognize what it was. Then she saw the shape of a man's body in an Auschwitz prisoner uniform, and she realized she was looking at Sabina's father's corpse. Instinctively, she squeezed her friend's hand a bit tighter.

Paskal turned around, an odd smile on his face. "Well, here we are. Away from the camp, finally." His voice sounded different from before, and Felcia frowned. Maybe she was imagining things. Sabina gently let go of her hand and turned to her.

"I'm sorry about all of this, Felcia." Her face had regained some color, and the gaze from her eyes was no longer one of sorrow and mourning. Before Felcia could respond, she heard movement in the bushes to the side of the clearing. Felcia blinked hard. *It can't be.* Her jaw dropped involuntarily, and she turned to Sabina, her mouth not responding to the commands her brain was sending.

From the bushes appeared the older man she'd seen earlier. The one she was certain was marched to his death only half an hour earlier. Sabina's father.

Sabina sprinted the short distance to embrace him. Paskal remained where he was, a few paces from Felcia, observing the reunion of father and daughter.

"Papa!" Tears streamed from Sabina's face, but these tears were of unbridled joy. She held his face in her hands, kissing his cheeks. Her father was clearly trying to keep his emotions under control, but failing as he answered her in a frail, broken voice.

"I can't believe you pulled this off, my dear, dearest Sabinka." The corners of his mouth twitched, his legs shaking from the struggle of staying upright. "When he told me he was going to murder you first, and then me, I lost it." He pointed at Paskal, his hand shaking.

Paskal nodded, a trace of embarrassment on his face. "I'm sorry about that, Mr. Krupka. But Sabina thought that would draw the most extreme, genuine reaction from you." He then focused his attention on Sabina. "I already apologized for punching him. But I couldn't let that go in front of the others. I held back at the very last moment, I promise."

Sabina smiled through her tears. "I know, Paskal. You took quite a risk yourself."

Felcia stepped forward. "Can you please tell me what's going on here? You schemed all of this together?"

Paskal and Sabina turned to her, appearing almost surprised she was still there. It was Paskal who spoke first. "I'm sorry, but we couldn't warn you about this."

"Whose body is that?" Felcia pointed at the heap of leaves.

"There's no body. Just a heap of leaves with a prisoner uniform. In case any of the guards insisted on joining me." Paskal's words trailed off, the meaning not lost on anyone in the clearing. Felcia looked at him in disbelief. She had trouble processing what she'd seen in the past hour. Was he really on their side?

Paskal pointed at the shovels. "Start digging, Felcia. We still need your grave, just in case someone does decide to check on this in the next few days."

She looked at him dumbfounded. "My grave?" There was a tremor in her voice.

"You're going to make a run for it in a bit." Sabina, holding her own shovel, stepped closer to her friend. "And when you do, Paskal has no choice but to shoot you."

The sky was turning orange by the time Sabina and Paskal walked back into Rajsko, each carrying a shovel. A chill hung in the air, and she was pleased to step into the warmth of the school building. The laboratories were dark, the hallway quiet as they walked to Paskal's office. He opened the door, placing his shovel next to it. Sabina did the same, and instead of sitting down, she followed Paskal to a filing cabinet in the corner.

He produced a key and opened it, flicking through a number of folders before finding the correct one. The faces of women she'd never seen before stared back at them until Felcia's appeared. The photo was taken at Birkenau, with Felcia looking years younger than she did today. There was even a hint of defiance in her eyes.

Paskal looked at her with a smile. "Ready?"

"Absolutely."

He handed her a pen and pointed at an empty area labeled "Additional Notes" at the bottom of the document. Sabina looked at Felcia's picture one more time, smiling at the memory of her friend, then filled in the empty space.

Deceased. Attempt to escape.

Author's Notes

The idea for this book started while I was writing Tracks to Freedom. Felcia played no more than a cameo role in Joel's grander scheming around Auschwitz-Birkenau, but the seed was planted. Rajsko intrigued me, and I wondered if there was a story there. The camp was, after all, used to smuggle all sorts of goods into the most notorious Nazi extermination camp.

As I started my research, I soon found very little information on Rajsko. A very short mention on the Auschwitz-Birkenau museum site, and one slightly more expansive section with about a dozen photos on a site detailing various Nazi camps. Equally surprising, not a single work of historical fiction covers this seemingly forgotten sub-camp. I knew I was onto something. I just needed to keep digging.

It wasn't until I started combing through survivors' testimonies that I could imagine daily life in Rajsko. As with Camp Westerbork in the Netherlands, Rajsko was very different from the standard Nazi concentration camp. Living conditions in Rajsko were far superior to those in the main camps, but the threat of death was never far away.

The Kazakh dandelion research was real, and many of the women working in the Plant Experimental Station were scientists from all over Europe. While most didn't possess the specialized knowledge or degrees for the research, they quickly adapted, realizing their survival depended on their usefulness to the Nazis' research.

I was surprised by the regular mentions of Lagerführerin Maria Mandl visiting Rajsko. As the most powerful woman in Birkenau, she seemed to have taken a genuine interest in the scientists of Rajsko. From the eyewitness accounts, it was clear she resented the women's—in her eyes—privileged position. Mandl was known to have a burning hatred for Poles, and most of the female scientists working in Rajsko were Polish or Russian. Margot Dreschel often accompanied Mandl, and I've based both women's actions on survivors' accounts. Their cruelty was horrifying, requiring very little of my imagination to put it to the page. Mandl wasn't just the most powerful woman in Auschwitz-Birkenau; she was also the most feared.

On the surface, Dr. Joachim Caesar was the opposite. He was known never to use violence against prisoners, even protecting them from SS attacks, and one prisoner described him as a guardian angel. Other sources argue he was fully aware of what was happening in the main camp and did nothing about it, only protecting those valuable enough for his purposes. The truth is likely somewhere in the middle, and his treatment of Felcia reflects this.

I based the fictional character of Paskal Sternhell on testimonies showing the different levels of commitment to the Nazi cause among the SS men in the camps. Several well-documented escapes wouldn't have been possible without help from those in power. I drew direct inspiration from SS guard Edward Lubusch's actions in the ill-fated escape of Mala Zimetbaum and Edek Galiński from the main camp. I'd like to believe there were more undocumented acts of humanity among the tens of thousands working in the camps.

Before I move on to Felcia and Sabina, I know there will be questions about some characters that will feel familiar to readers of previous books.

The prisoner in Felcia's cell in Block 11 is Zofia Zdrowak's mother. Anna Zdrowak spent a couple of months in Block 10 but was released and survived the war. Like her daughter, she was an active member of the Sosienki resistance movement outside the camp. It was fitting that she provided Felcia with more information about their activities.

The nurse tending to Felcia in the Auschwitz hospital is Dutch Agnes Markx from Tracks to Freedom.

Sabina's primary contact is the same Marian Mydlarz, who played a significant role in Zofia and Jacob's operations in Beyond the Tracks. While there is no evidence that the real Marian was directly involved in the smuggling operation, I deemed it plausible enough, considering his leading role in one of the most active resistance cells in the area. If his actions in Beyond the Tracks and this book make him seem larger than life, I make no apologies for that. Those brave souls who risked their lives in the shadow of Auschwitz-Birkenau deserve recognition.

Felcia and Sabina are both fictional characters. They allowed me to craft a story of friendship, bravery, and loyalty while experiencing Rajsko and its surroundings through their eyes. I based their smuggling operations on the actual activities of Helena Płotnicka, her daughter Wanda Płotnicka, and Władysława Kożusznik. Unfortunately, very little is known about how they smuggled the goods into Rajsko or the women themselves. What is certain is that they dropped the goods near the main building in the middle of the night. Of the three women, Helena Płotnicka was captured and died in the main camp. The fate of her daughter Wanda and Władysława Kożusznik is less clear.

And finally, Mr. Krupka and Felcia's escape. There are no documented escapes from Rajsko, but based on the camp setup, I decided it would've been possible, especially with the assistance of an SS officer like Paskal Sternhell.

If you enjoyed reading the story, a review on your favorite reading platform or store would be most welcome. If you'd like to get in touch, or find my other books, be sure to visit my website, michaelreit.com.

All my best,
Michael

About the Author

Michael Reit writes page-turning historical fiction. His books focus on lesser-known events and people in World War II Europe.

Born in the Netherlands, he now lives in beautiful Vienna, Austria, with his partner Esther and daughter Bibi.

Connect with Michael via his website:
www.michaelreit.com

Or via Facebook:

 facebook.com/MichaelReitAuthor

ALSO BY MICHAEL REIT

Beyond the Tracks Series

1. Beyond the Tracks

2. Tracks to Freedom

3. The Botanist's Tracks

Orphans of War Series

1. Orphans of War

2. They Bled Orange

3. Crossroads of Granite

Stand-alones

Warsaw Fury

Printed in the USA
CPSIA information can be obtained
at www.ICGtesting.com
LVHW041917210424
778026LV00003B/204